全国高校网络教育公共基础课教材

大学英语自主学习手册

3

专升本阶段

总主编：欣 羚
主 编：孙 颖 李 海
副主编：张露蓓 王 焰
编 者：张 睿 陈小鸥 金 艾 李 捷 孔展屏

U0105699

外语教学与研究出版社
FOREIGN LANGUAGE TEACHING AND RESEARCH PRESS
北京 BEIJING

图书在版编目(CIP)数据

大学英语自主学习手册. 3 / 欣羚总主编 . — 北京：外语教学与研究出版社，2008.6
全国高校网络教育公共基础课教材. 专升本阶段
ISBN 978 - 7 - 5600 - 7636 - 2

Ⅰ. 大… Ⅱ. 欣… Ⅲ. 英语—高等学校—自学参考资料 Ⅳ. H31

中国版本图书馆 CIP 数据核字 (2008) 第 096313 号

出 版 人：于春迟
责任编辑：吴晓玉
封面设计：牛茜茜 王 薇
版式设计：平 原
出版发行：外语教学与研究出版社
社 址：北京市西三环北路 19 号 (100089)
网 址：http://www.fltrp.com
印 刷：北京双青印刷厂
开 本：787×1092 1/16
印 张：21.5
版 次：2008 年 7 月第 1 版 2008 年 7 月第 1 次印刷
书 号：ISBN 978 - 7 - 5600 - 7636 - 2
定 价：31.90 元

前　言

　　《大学英语自主学习手册》系列为全国高校网络教育公共基础课教材《大学英语》系列的配套学习材料，供高校网络学院不同层次非英语专业学生作为教材辅助学习材料使用，也可作为教师课堂授课的参考书和练习册。

　　手册编写充分体现了网络教育中英语语言学习的特殊性，内容涵盖全国高校网络教学考试委员会制定的《全国高校网络教育大学英语(B)考试大纲》(2007年修订版)、《全国高校网络教育大学英语考试指南》所涉及的范围。

　　本系列手册注重难易度的把握，强调对所学知识的系统复习和巩固。编者根据教材及大纲要求，遵循循序渐进的原则，针对重点、难点知识设计练习；重视知识的扩张性和延展性，在反复操练中适当加深难度、拓宽广度，使语言文化知识学习和语言技能培养同步进行。

　　本系列手册将知识性、实用性和趣味性融为一体。在知识点讲解和练习安排上充分考虑成人的学习和心理特点，使整个学习过程实现以知识为线索，学有所用的理想状况。

册数安排

　　该系列手册分为一至四册，分别针对全国高校网络教育公共基础课教材《大学英语》的一至四级。每册含八个单元，每单元均针对教材中的主题和内容，做到紧扣教材，联系实际，对知识点进行整合、对比和总结，使学员的英语语言能力得到综合训练。

主要模块

　　本系列手册针对网络教育英语教学和学习的特殊性，根据教材内容划分单元，每单元内容如下：

● 单元导读

　　本部分为单元主题导入，采用中文解释方式，便于学生理解，能有效激活学生已有的相关知识背景，激发学生学习兴趣，积累文化知识。

● 课文精讲

本部分对教材课文中出现的语言点进行详解，同时介绍课文篇章结构及相关阅读、写作技巧。具体包括：

☆ **文章导读、背景知识、文章写作风格及结构**：针对课文中出现的与文化或背景知识相关的关键词或短语进行解释，导入主题，对课文进行串讲。包括用中文简要概括文章大意，用中文对篇章结构和写作风格进行分析等。

☆ **词汇点睛、短语解析**：将重点词汇和短语结合课文内容及考点，通过同根词、音近词、形近词的比较，帮助学生快速、准确地理解词汇含义并掌握其用法。

☆ **难句突破**：重点选择有丰富语言点、文化知识或句式较难的句子加以注释和讲解。采用中文分析句子结构，给出英文释义和中文翻译，对句子中出现的特殊句型、搭配进行中文讲解，并给出其他英文例句及中文翻译。此外，补充相关句型、搭配的比较和辨析。比较和辨析均用中文讲解，并给出英文例句和中文翻译。

☆ **参考译文**：每篇文章配精彩译文，均为精心之作，字斟句酌，文笔传神，帮助学生准确理解课文，领悟文章主旨。

☆ **习题全解**：对课后的全部练习，给出参考答案及部分中文译文，并附有深入浅出的解释，最大限度地方便学员自学。

● 语言拓展

本部分对教材扩展学习部分的日常用语、阅读技巧、写作技巧和语法知识四个板块进行详细讲解，并视情况作相应扩展。具体包括：

☆ **日常用语(Use of English)**：用中文对教材对应板块中的相关口语表达加以解释和适当补充，激发学习兴趣，增加学生口语练习素材。

☆ **阅读技巧(Reading Skills)**：为教材对应板块中的相关练习提供参考答案，必要时作一定讲解。

☆ **写作技巧(Writing Skills)**：为教材对应板块中的写作练习提供范文，供学生学习和参考。

☆ **语法知识(Grammar)**：为教材对应板块中的习题提供答案，并提供讲解和中文译文。

● 每课一练

本部分旨在提供与课本知识相关的补充拓展练习。具体包括：

☆ **词汇结构**：30个单选题，其中词汇和语法约各占一半。词汇题目考查本单元学习的重点词汇、短语（特别是A课文）；语法题则考查本单元所学的语法专项知识。

☆ **阅读理解**：两篇与学生水平相适应的阅读理解练习，每篇5个题目。

☆ **练习答案**：每课一练答案及详解。

Contents

Contents

1

Distance Learning

单元导读

　　远程教育是一种新兴的教育形式，它用现代化的手段，把优秀的教育资源送到教育资源欠缺的地方，为更多的人提供学习的机会、条件。学生对课程设置、课程选择和教学内容，对学习时间、地点和进度，对可供利用的教学媒体和学习资源，对教学组织形式和教学考查形式，对学习方法和学习策略等都有更多的发言权和决策权。作为一种新的学习方式的尝试，初学者在远程学习过程中遇到一些困难并不可怕。怎样制定适合自己的学习计划？如何克服学习过程中的孤独感？如何树立长久的学习信心？怎样把握远程学习的技巧？怎样提高学习效率？如何对待作业与考试？学习完本单元，相信你会有新的思考。

课文精讲

文章导读

　　现在，越来越多的人在接受网络教育。你想知道网络教育与传统教育相比有什么优点吗？你想了解在线学习的感受吗？下面这篇文章分别从学生、教师和教育家的角度谈了网络教育的特点和利弊，将有助于你加深对这一新生事物的了解。

背景知识

　　纽约州立大学最初于1816年成立于纽约波茨坦，但直到1948年其教育系统才真正趋于完善。学校位于纽约州，由64个学院组成。纽约州立大学是一所综合性公立大学，可授予学士、硕士和博士学位。此外，学校创建了全美最大的远程教育项目之一，提供4,000门课程以及60项学位和证书项目，共有70,000学生正在接受学校的远程教育。纽约州立大学是美国最大、最全面的州立大学教育系统。

文章写作风格及结构

　　本文为一篇记叙文。作者简要介绍了网络课程的特点，并且分别从学生、教师和专家学者的角度分析了远程教育的优势以及面临的一些问题。整篇文章内容清晰，写作要点简单明了，选材新颖，对读者颇有吸引力。

Parts 部分	Paragraphs 段落	Main Ideas 大意
Part I	1—4	Charles Sturek's experience of distance learning is different from traditional way of learning. 查尔斯·司徒瑞克所经历的网络课程学习不同于传统的教学模式。
Part II	5—10	The advantages of distance learning are shared by many students. 远程教育给许多学生带来便利。
Part III	11—16	The disadvantages of distance learning are warned by the experts. 一些专家学者指出远程教育还存在诸多问题。

🌑 词汇点睛

1 credit

n. approval or praise 赞许，名誉，光荣

- 例句 • She didn't really get the credit she deserves. 她实际没有得到她该得的荣誉。

  Why should he get all the credit? 为什么他受到了所有人的赞扬？

  Their brilliant success brought credit to the motherland. 他们巨大的成功给祖国带来了荣誉。

- 短语 • **to one's credit** 在某人名下，属于某人

  She's not yet 30, but already has five books to her credit.

  她还不到30岁，但已经写了五本书了。

2 recall

vt. to remember a particular fact, event, or situation from the past 回想，回忆（常用recall doing sth.）

- 例句 • I don't recall seeing him. 我不记得曾在哪里见过他。

  You should try to recall exactly what happened. 你要尽力回忆事情发生的确切情况。

- 短语 • **recall sth. to one's mind** 回忆起某件事

- 辨析 • **recall, remember, recollect, remind**

  这些动词共有的中心意思是 "to bring an image or a thought back to the mind"。

  You should always recall friends' kindness. 要多回想朋友的友善。

  I can't remember his name. 我记不起他的姓名。

  I can't recollect how the accident happened. 我记不起事故是如何发生的了。

  The film reminded him of what he had seen in China. 这部影片使他回想起在中国所看到的一切。

3 overwhelm

vt. to have such a great effect that you feel confused and do not know how to react 使不安，使不知所措

- 例句 • Emotion overwhelmed the actor when he won an award.

  这位演员得了奖，激动得不知所措。

- 扩展 • **overwhelming** *adj.* (通常作定语) 压倒一切的，势不可挡的，巨大的

  She won the election by an overwhelming majority. 她以压倒性的优势赢得了选举。

4 constraint

n. sth. that limits your freedom to do what you want 束缚，限制

- 例句 • He ignored all moral constraints in his pursuit of success.

  在追求成功的过程中他忽略了一切道德约束。

  There are no constraints on your choice of subject for the essay. 文章内容不拘，你可任选。

- 扩展 • **constrain** *vt.* 限制，约束

  Our research has been constrained by lack of funding. 缺少资金制约了我们的研究工作。

5 adjust

vt. to change slightly in order to gradually get used to a new situation 调节，调整，使适合

- 例句 • I must adjust my watch; it's slow. 表慢了，我得调调。

  He adjusted himself quickly to the heat of the country. 他很快适应了这个国家酷热的天气。

- 短语 • **get adjusted to...** 调整以适应……

- 扩展 • **adjustable** *adj.* 可调节的；可调整的

  adjustable seat-belts 可调节的座位安全带

  adjustment *n.* 调节；调整

  I've made a few minor adjustments to the seating plan. 我对座次表作了小的调整。

- 辨析 • **adjust, adapt**

  adjust表示为达到新的要求而进行的细微的变化或改变，也用来指人为了适应变化的环境而调整自己。

  adapt表示为达到新的要求而进行较大程度的改变或变化，强调进行改变的目的。

6 anyway

adv. in spite of the fact that you have just mentioned 不管怎样，无论如何（常用于口语）

- 例句 • I don't know if it was lost or stolen; anyway, it's gone.

  我不知道它是丢了还是被偷了；不管怎么说，它没了。

  My mother says I mustn't go, but I'm going anyway. 母亲说我不能去，尽管如此我还是要去。

7 embrace

vt. 1) to accept and use new ideas, opinions, etc. eagerly （欣然）接受，采纳

- 例句 • I don't know whether they'll embrace your idea. 我不知道他们会不会采纳你的意见。

  2) to put your arms around sb. and hold them in a friendly or loving way; hug 拥抱

- 例句 • *She embraced her son before leaving.* 她在离开前拥抱了儿子。

  n. 拥抱

- 例句 • He held her in a warm embrace. 他热情地拥抱她。

8 participate

vi. to take part in an activity or event 参加，参与

- 例句 • They asked high school students to participate in the anti-drug campaign.

  他们要求高中学生参加反毒品运动。

  She actively participates in local politics. 她积极参与本地政治活动。

- 短语 • **participate in** 参加……，参与……

- 扩展 • **participation** *n.* 参加，参与

Teachers often encourage class participation. 教师常鼓励学生积极参与课堂活动。

participant *n.* 参加者

All the participants in the debate had an opportunity to speak.

所有参加辩论的人都有机会发言。

- 辨析 • **attend, take part in, participate in, join**

attend 常用于以一般的身份出席会议，到课堂听讲或听音乐会等。

take part in和participate in表示主语在有关活动中担任一定的角色，其中take part in较普通。

join是指参加一个组织。

9 resource

n. 1) *sth. such as a book, film, or picture used by teachers or students to provide information* 资料

- 例句 • The local library is a valuable resource. 当地图书馆是一个宝贵的资料库。

2) *(usually pl.) sth. such as land, mineral, or natural energy* 资源

- 例句 • Our financial resources are limited. 我们的财力有限。

That country is rich in natural resources. 那个国家的自然资源很丰富。

- 扩展 • **source** *n.* 来源；出处

The news comes from a reliable source. 这条消息来源可靠。

A book is the source of knowledge. 书是知识的源泉。

10 instruction

n. 1) *(fml) teaching that you are given in a particular skill or subject* 教导

- 例句 • In this course, students receive instruction in basic engineering.

在本课程中，学生能得到基础工程学方面的指导。

His method of instruction was most agreeable. 他的训练方法很容易接受。

2) *(usually pl.) the written information that tells you how to do or use sth.* 指示

- 例句 • Please read the instructions carefully before you assemble the model plane.

请在组装模型飞机前仔细阅读说明书。

3) *(usually pl.) a statement telling someone what they must do* 命令

- 例句 • I shall await instructions. 我将等待指令。

- 扩展 • **instruct** *vt.* 教，教导；命令，指示

He instructs his pupils in mathematics. 他教学生数学。

The captain instructed the soldiers to retreat. 上尉命令战士撤退。

11 otherwise

adv. under other circumstances 否则，不然

- 例句 • We must run. Otherwise we'll be too late. 我们得跑着去，要不就太晚了。

The sailors would have otherwise fallen into the sea. 要不然这些水手早就掉进大海了。

12 fulfill

vt. if a hope, promise, wish, etc. is fulfilled, the thing that you had hoped, promised, wanted, etc. happens or is done 实现，履行

- 例句 • A nurse has many duties to fulfill in caring for the sick. 护士在照顾病人时要尽很多责任。

One should fulfill one's promise. 一个人应该履行自己的诺言。

13 performance

n. 1) how well or badly you do a particular job or activity 表现

- 例句 • His performance in the exams was not very good. 他的考试成绩不太好。

  2) an act of performing a play or a piece of music 表演

- 例句 • The theater gives two performances a day. 这家剧院每天演出两场。

- 扩展 • **perform** *vt., vi.* 做，履行，完成；演出，表演

  He performed his experiment over and over again. 他把实验做了一次又一次。

  The singer has never performed in New York before. 这位歌唱家从未在纽约演出过。

14 urge

vt. (fml) to strongly suggest that sth. should be done 催促，力劝

- 例句 • He urged me to accept the compromise. 他劝我接受妥协。

  They urged that the bill (should) be passed immediately. 他们强烈要求立即通过那项议案。

- 用法 • 某些动词后所接宾语从句中的谓语动词要求用虚拟语气，用来表示建议、命令和要求等。

  其形式为：（should）+ 动词原形。这类动词有：

  ask 要求，advise 劝告，command 命令，determine 决定，decide 决定，demand 要求，direct 命令，insist 坚持，intend 打算，order 命令，propose 提议，recommend 推荐，request 要求，require 要求，suggest 建议，urge 主张。

15 caution

n. the quality of being very careful, not taking any risks, and trying to avoid danger
谨慎，小心

- 例句 • Proceed with caution. 小心行事。

  You should exercise extreme caution when driving in fog. 在雾中开车要极为小心。

- 扩展 • **cautious** *adj.* 小心的；谨慎的；细心的

  be cautious about/of sb./sth.

  The bank is very cautious about lending money. 银行在贷款方面十分慎重。

  She was cautious of strangers. 她对陌生人很戒备。

16 significantly

adv. in an important way or to an important degree 重要地，重大地

- 例句 • Beijing's power and water consumption drops significantly. 北京的水电消耗量有了显著的下降。

  Profits have risen significantly. 利润已经大大提高了。

- 扩展 • **significant** *adj.* 有意义的；重要的，重大的，可观的

  There is no significant change in the patient's condition. 病人的状况变化不大。

  It's significant for a country to participate in the Olympics.

  参加奥林匹克运动会对一个国家意义重大。

  significance *n.* 意义；重要性

  What is the significance of this symbol? 这个符号是什么意思？

  Few people realized the significance of the discovery. 很少有人意识到这一发现的重要性。

17 exceed

vt. to be more than a number or amount, especially a fixed number 超过，超出

- 例句 • The price will not exceed $100. 价格不会超过100美元。

  He was fined for exceeding speed. 他因为超速行驶被罚款。

  Their success exceeded all expectations. 他们的成功出乎一切预料。

- 扩展 • **exceedingly** *adv.* 极端地，非常，极其

  an exceedingly difficult problem 极其困难的问题

18 considerably

adv. much, a great deal 相当（大，多）地

- 例句 • That considerably added to our difficulties. 那件事大大增加了我们的困难。

  It's considerably colder this morning. 今早冷得多。

- 扩展 • **consider** *vt.* 考虑,认为（常用consider doing sth.）

  I'm considering changing my job. 我正在考虑换换工作。

  They consider themselves to be very lucky. 他们认为自己很幸运。

- 辨析 • **considerate, considerable**

  considerate *adj.* 体谅（人）的，考虑周到的

  considerable *adj.* 相当大（或多）的,值得考虑的,相当可观的

  He is considerate of others. 他很体谅别人。

  That was very considerate of you. 你想得很周到。

  The building suffered considerable damage. 大楼受到相当严重的损坏。

  The losses are considerable. 损失很重。

19 interaction

n. 1) the activity of talking to other people and understanding them 交互活动，互动

- 例句 • There is a need for greater interaction among the different departments.

  有必要进一步加强各个部门之间的协作。

  2) a process by which two or more things have an effect on each other and work together 相互作用，相互影响

- 例句 • Price is determined through the interaction of demand and supply. 价格是通过供需之间的相互作用来决定的。

- 扩展 • **interact** *vi.* 互相作用,互相影响

  Children learn by interacting (with one another). 孩子们在相互影响中学习。

20 discipline

n. 1) the ability to control your own behavior and way of working 自制，自控

- 例句 • The children are happy at school, but they lack discipline. 孩子们在学校里很快活,但很散漫。

  2) the practice of making people obey rules and orders, or the controlled situation that results from this practice 纪律

- 例句 • Our soldiers are strict in discipline. 我们的战士纪律严明。

21　extensive

adj. large in amount, area or scope 广泛的，大量的

- 例句 • Her knowledge of the subject is extensive. 她这方面的学识很渊博。

  The fire caused extensive damage. 大火造成了巨大的损坏。

- 扩展 • **extend** *vt.* 延伸, 伸展

  The road extends for miles and miles. 这条路向远处延伸。

  Can you extend your visit a few days longer? 你能多停留几天吗?

- 辨析 • **intensive**

  intensive *adj.* 强烈的，加强的；彻底的

  intensive training 强化训练

  An intensive search failed to reveal any clues. 经过彻底搜查未发现任何线索。

22　premature

adj. happening before the natural or proper time 过早的，早熟的

- 例句 • a premature baby 一个早产婴儿

  A fire in the gallery caused the premature closing of the exhibition.

  在美术陈列室里发生的火灾迫使展览会提前结束。

- 扩展 • **mature** *adj.* 成熟的

  The peaches are not yet mature. 桃子还没有成熟。

  He's not mature enough to be given too much responsibility. 他还不成熟，不宜委以重任。

23　critical

adj. very important because what happens in the future depends on it 关键性的，至关重要的

- 例句 • This was a critical moment in his career. 这是他职业生涯中的关键时刻。

  His condition is reported as being critical. 据报道他的病情危急。

24　socialization

n. the process by which people, especially children, learn to behave in a way acceptable in society 交际，交往，社交

- 扩展 • **society** *n.* 社会

  Knowledge plays an important role in modern society. 在现代社会中，知识扮演着重要角色。

  social *adj.* 社会的

  social problems/welfare/reforms 社会问题、福利、改革

25　associate

adj. someone. who is a member, etc., of sth., but who is at a lower level and has fewer rights 副职的

- 搭配 • associate professor 副教授

  vt. to make a connection in your mind between one thing or person and another 联想（常用 associate... with...）

- 例句 • We associate the exchange of presents with Christmas. 我们由交换礼物联想到圣诞节。

  The name of Nero is associated with cruelty. 尼禄的名字使人联想到残忍。

- 扩展 • **association** *n.* 协会；联合，结交；联想

the Drama Association 戏剧协会

There has always been a close association between these two schools. 这两所学校一向有密切联系。

What associations does the sea have for you? 你从大海能联想到什么？

26 paramount

adj. more important than anything else 至高无上的，最重要的（该词无比较级和最高级）

- 例句 • This matter is of paramount importance. 此事至关重要。
- 同义词 • **foremost, greatest, primary**

27 instant

adj. happening or produced immediately 即刻的，即时的

- 例句 • The film was an instant success. 这部电影一上映就大获成功。

We must meet the instant need of the people. 我们必须满足人民的急需。

n. a very short period of time 时刻

- 例句 • Please go away this instant. 请立刻离开。
- 短语 • **on the instant** 立即，马上　　**for an instant** 有一会儿

in an instant 立即，当即
- 用法 • **the instant** 可引导时间状语从句，相当于as soon as，表示"一……就……"。

🔊 短语解析

1. to one's credit 在某人名下，属于某人

【例句】Unless good intentions are translated into action, they are useless and will never be counted to one's credit.

在良好的愿望转化为行动之前，它们毫无用处，也绝不会给谁带来任何荣誉。

2. get adjusted to ... 调整以适应……

【例句】Only after our eyes get adjusted to the dark can we see that the room is filled with piles of books.

只有在我们的眼睛适应了那里的黑暗后，我们才看见原来屋子里堆满了一捆捆的书。

It would take time for him to get adjusted to new surroundings.

他需要时间来适应新的环境。

3. engage... in ... 使加入……，使参加……

【例句】She was engaged in protecting wild birds. 她致力于保护野生鸟类的工作。

She is now engaged in writing letters. 她现在正忙着写信。

【扩展】engage oneself in = be engaged in 从事……

I engaged myself / was engaged in writing when he visited me. 他来时我正忙着写作。

4. access to 使用，接近，进入之途径或权利

【例句】Students must have access to a good library. 学生必须要有使用好图书馆的便利条件。

Only high officials had access to the president. 只有高级官员才可以接近总统。

5. rob sb. of sth. 使某人丧失某物

【例句】I was robbed of my cash and check-book. 我的现金和支票簿被抢了。

Those cats robbed me of my sleep. 那些猫吵得我无法入睡。

难句突破

1. (Para. 1) *With 11 Internet courses and three master's degrees to his credit, 28-year-old Charles Sturek recalls the panic he felt during his first week of e-class.*

【解析】1）"with + 名词/代词 + 介词短语"引导的伴随状语，表达的状态是伴随着句子谓语动词的动作而发生或存在的。如：The master was walking up and down with the ruler under his arm. 大师来回走动，尺子夹在腋下。With a textbook in her hand, Linda fell asleep. 琳达手里拿着一本教科书睡着了。

2）不同层次学位的英语表达：bachelor's degree 学士学位；master's degree 硕士学位；doctor's degree / PhD 博士学位。

【译文】28岁的查尔斯·施图雷克已经修完了11门网络课程，并拿到了3个硕士学位。回忆起第一周的网络课程学习，当时的恐慌心情，至今仍记忆犹新。

2. (Para. 3) *In a class with few set time constraints, he struggled to understand where to "be" at any given time.*

【解析】struggle to do sth.: 努力做某事，特别是有一定困难的事

【译文】由于上课几乎没有固定的时间限制，他费了好大劲才搞清楚什么时候该到哪里"上课"。

3. (Para. 4) *It took a face-to-face meeting with the professor to get adjusted to online learning.*

【解析】face-to-face: *adj.* 面对面的

构词法：把两个或两个以上的词按照一定的次序排列构成新词的方法叫做合成法，而构成的新词叫合成词，类似的合成词还有out-and-out 彻头彻尾的，person-to-person 个人对个人的。

【译文】直到与教授的一次面谈后，（他）才开始适应了网上学习。

4. (Para. 5) *It has been less than a decade since schools first embraced the Internet for distance learning.*

【解析】since通常是和完成时搭配使用。如：It has been more than ten years since we first met. 自从我们第一次见面以来已经有十多年了。I've been thinking of the problem since last week. 上星期起我就在想这个难题了。

【译文】这些学校采用互联网进行远程教学已有将近十年的时间了。

5. (Para. 6) *... according to Paul Edelson, Stony Brook's dean of the School of Professional Development.*

【解析】according to: 根据，按照，根据某人的说法、解释

Stony Brook's dean是Paul Edelson的同位语，用逗号隔开。

【译文】石溪分校职业发展学院院长保罗·艾德生指出……

6. (Para. 8) **"E-learning has many benefits over the physical classroom"** ...

【解析】over引起比较，相当于多于，超过。例如：

Most of the carpets cost over $100. 大部分的地毯价钱超过100美元。

Children over the age of 12 must have full-price ticket.

超过12岁的孩子需要买全票。

I value quality of life over money. 与金钱相比，我更注重生活的质量。

【译文】"网络教学在很多方面优于现实课堂教学。"

7. (Para. 8) **... engage students in must-participate discussions and media-rich resource materials over the net.**

【解析】1) engage... in: 使加入，使参加

2) must-participate与media-rich都是由两个词组成的合成词，其中，must-participate表示"必须参与的"，而media-rich表示"媒体资源丰富的"。

【译文】……让学生在网上参与必须完成的讨论，以及使用丰富的网上媒体资源。

8. (Para. 9) **It also gives time-constrained or remotely located part-time students access to college level instruction they might otherwise never have.**

【解析】句子的主干是it gives students access...，其中套了一个定语从句instruction (that) they might...。注意：that引导限定性定语从句时，that可以省略，而非限定性定语从句不能由that引导。如：

The letter that I received was from my father. 我收到的是我爸爸的来信。(限定性定语从句)

Tom's dog, which was now very old, became ill and died.

汤姆的那只老狗生病死了。(非限定性定语从句)

【译文】这（网络教学）也为那些时间有限或地处偏远地区的非脱产学生提供了接受大学教育的机会，要不然，他们就绝对不可能有这样的机会（接受大学教育）。

9. (Para. 11) **But even as established universities race ahead with online programs, many are urging caution.**

【解析】as 在这里作连词（conj.）。

as 的词性可为介词（prep.），副词（adv.）或连词（conj.）：

① as作为介词（prep.）的时候表示"当作，作为"。如：I'm speaking as a teacher. 我以老师的身份讲话。 She works as a waitress. 她当女招待。

② as作为副词（adv.）的时候通常以as... as的形式出现，用于副词和形容词之前以构成比较句型。如：He is as tall as his father. 他和他父亲一样高。（其中第二个as是连词）

This dress is twice as expensive as that. 这件连衣裙比那件贵一倍。

文章第二段当中的He said he was as overwhelmed as any college freshman by the time he "arrived" at his first online session. 其中第一个as就是用作副词，第二个as用作连词。

③ as作连词（conj.）的时候有以下几种意思：

a. 表示"在……期间"，相当于while。如：I watched her as she combed her hair. 她梳头的

时候我一直看着她。

    b. 表示"由于"，相当于because。如：You can go first as you are the eldest. 你可以先走，因为你最大。

    c. 表示"尽管，即使"，相当于although。如：Young as I am, I already know what career I want to follow. 虽然我还年轻，我已经知道我将来想要从事什么职业了。

    d. 表示"以……方式，像……一样"，相当于like。如：Do as I say and sit down. 照我说的，坐下。

    e. 表示"为……之事实"。如：Taiwan as we know, is an island of China. 如我们所知，台湾是中国的一个岛屿。

    f. 表示"也一样"。如：She's unusually tall, as are both her parents. 她特别高，她父母也都那么高。

【译文】然而，尽管一些老牌大学在网络教育方面走在前列，很多大学仍然提出了警告。

10. (Para.12) *Critics point out that dropout rates for e-classes are significantly higher than that for face-to-face classes, in some cases exceeding 40 percent.*

【解析】其中higher than that中的that是代词，指代dropout rates。that常用来指前面提到过的名词，如：This book is not so interesting as that I read yesterday. 这本书不如我昨天读的那本有趣。

【解析】一些批评者指出，网络课堂的退学率明显高于面对面的现实课堂，有时甚至超过40%。

11. (Para.13) *Some are concerned that rushing Internet course work to the undergraduate level could rob students of critical socialization.*

【解析】1) rob sb. of sth.: 剥夺/抢夺/抢劫某人某物

    2) concerned *adj.* 表示"担心的；烦恼的；忧虑的"，通常用 be concerned about/for sth. that... 等结构。如：

We're all concerned for her safety. 我们都为她的安全担忧。

I'm concerned that they may have got lost. 我担心他们可能迷路了。

【译文】一些人担心在本科阶段仓促地开设网络课程可能会使学生缺少必要的社交生活。

12. (Para.14) *David Pomeranz, associate president at Stony Brook, said budgetary concerns of smaller classes, legal issues of course ownership and the low level of the technology are all concerns, but the quality of teaching remains paramount.*

【解析】1) 这个句子的主干是David Pomeranz said...，其中associate president at Stony Brook是David Pomeranz的同位语。

    2) concern作名词的时候表示"考虑，忧虑，焦虑"。如：There is a growing concern that they may have been killed. 人们越来越担心他们可能已遭杀害。

【译文】石溪分校副校长大卫·波姆莱斯谈到，小班的预算考虑、课程所有权的法律问题、以及技术水平较低，都是人们关注的问题，但教学质量仍旧是人们关心的焦点。

13. (Para. 15) *It is not the kind of instant give-and-take of a live audience.*

【解析】 live: *adj.* 现场演出的

give-and-take: 互动（合成词），类似的词还有如：come-and-go 来来回回。

【译文】（基于网络的学习）并不像传统的教学那样，能给学生提供即时的面对面的教学活动。

参考译文

网上学习先行者得失未卜

28岁的查尔斯·施图雷克已经修完了11门网络课程，并拿到了3个硕士学位。回忆起第一周的网络课程学习，当时的恐慌心情，他至今仍记忆犹新。

施图雷克五月刚刚毕业于纽约州立大学石溪分校。他告诉我们，当他"进入"第一个在线学期时，他和所有大一新生一样感到手足无措。

"我把所有的课程资料都打印出来，一起装订在六环活页夹里，"施图雷克说。由于上课几乎没有固定的时间限制，他费了好大劲才搞清楚什么时候该到哪里"上课"。

直到与教授的一次面谈后他才开始适应了网上学习。总之，这是一种完全不同的模式，它与"板书+讲授"的传统教学模式几乎没有什么直接联系。

自从学校首次采用互联网进行远程教学以来，已有将近十年的时间了。现在，已经有几所大学正在筹备下一步的大跨越，纽约州立大学石溪分校就是其中之一。

石溪分校职业发展学院院长保罗·埃德尔森指出，远程学习将是教育领域下一步的大跨越。

埃德尔森教授从事在线研究生课程教学已有数年。

他提到："网络教学在很多方面优于现实课堂教学。"这些优势包括：网络教学可以更有效地让学生参与必须的网上讨论，以及敦促学生使用网上丰富的媒体资源。

此外，网络教学也为那些时间有限或地处偏远地区的非脱产学生提供了接受大学教育的机会，要不然，他们也许永远不会有这样的机会。

埃德尔森谈到："网络教学为高等教育实现了提高学生写作技巧和思维能力的梦想。"

然而，尽管一些老牌大学在网络教育方面走在前列，很多大学仍然提出了警告。

一些批评者指出，网络课堂的退学率明显高于面对面的现实课堂，有时甚至超过40%。

教授们认为在线课程要求更大量的准备工作和更多的师生互动。基于这个原因，在线课堂的学生人数通常限制在20人以内。学生们也认为在线课程会要求投入更多的时间，而且纪律更严格。另外，大量的本科课程还不成熟。一些人担心在本科阶段仓促地开设网络课程可能会使学生缺少必要的社交生活。

石溪分校副校长戴维·波梅兰兹谈到，小班的预算考虑、课程所有权的法律问题、以及技术水平较低，都是人们关注的问题，但教学质量仍旧是人们关心的焦点。

波梅兰兹目前正在研究基于因特网的网络学习，以期确定学校今后在这方面的发展。他指出："这不同于现场的、即时的、面对面的传统教学活动"。

专家们认为申请网络课程学习相当容易。

习题全解

文章大意

1. 根据课文用合适的词填空。

【答案】 1) get adjusted to   2) the Internet   3) many benefits

4) the next big thing   5) the quality of teaching

【解析】 get adjusted to 表示"使适应……"；according to the text 表示"根据课文"；problems do exist 表示"问题仍然存在"，do 强调动词 exist；taken into consideration 表示"纳入考虑范围"；paramount 表示"极为重要的"。

【译文】 虽然查尔斯·施图雷克刚开始觉得很难适应远程学习，他还是完成了学业。 他毕业于纽约州立大学，那是几所准备利用互联网进行远程教学的大学之一。从课文上我们得知远程学习与传统的课堂教学相比有很多优点，远程学习将是教育领域下一步的大跨越。然而这其中确实也存在一些问题。要发展基于网络的远程学习，应当考虑到几个问题，其中教育质量是首要的。

2. 文中讨论了基于互联网的远程学习的优点和问题，请填写优点与问题列表。

【答案】

Benefits: 1) It has a better ability to engage students in must-participate discussions and media-rich resource materials over the Net. (Para. 8)

2) It also gives time-constrained or remotely located part-time students access to college level instruction. (Para. 9)

3) It fulfills the dream for higher education of improving performance of writing and thinking skills. (Para. 10)

Problems: 1) Dropout rates for e-classes are significantly higher than for face-to-face classes. (Para. 12)

2) Online courses can require considerably more preparation work and student interaction.(Para. 13)

3) It requires lots more time and lots more discipline. (Para. 13)

【译文】

优点：1) 网络教学可以更有效地让学生参与必须的网上讨论，以及敦促学生使用网上丰富的媒体资源。

2) 此外，网络教学也为那些时间有限，或地处偏远地区的非脱产学生提供了接受大学教育的机会。

3) 网络教学为高等教育实现了提高学生写作技巧和思维能力的梦想。

问题：1) 网络课堂的退学率明显高于面对面的现实课堂。

2) 在线课程要求更大量的准备工作和更多的师生互动。

3) 在线课程会要求投入更多的时间，而且纪律更严格。

文章细节

根据文章回答问题。

【答案】

1) He felt panic. (Para. 1)

2) Because there were so many course materials, and with few set time constraints he felt it hard to understand where to be at any given time. (Paras. 2-3)

3) He met with the professor face to face. (Para. 4)

4) Online distance learning. (Para. 6)

5) He thought distance learning was the next big thing in education, because it has many benefits over the physical classroom (These include a better ability to engage students in must-participate discussions and media-rich resource materials over the net, and it also gives time-constrained or remotely located part-time students access to college level instruction). (Para. 6 & Paras. 8-10)

6) Because the dropout rates are significantly higher than for face-to-face classes; online courses require lots more time and discipline and online course work could rob students of critical socialization. (Paras. 12-13)

7) The quality of teaching. (Para. 14)

【译文】

1) [问题] 查尔斯·施图雷克在第一周网络课程结束以后感觉如何？
   [答案] 他觉得很惶恐。

2) [问题] 为什么当他进入第一个在线学习期会感觉到手足无措？
   [答案] 因为有太多的课程材料，没有固定的时间限制，他费了好大劲才搞清楚什么时候该到哪里"上课"。

3) [问题] 他是如何适应在线学习的？
   [答案] 他和教授进行了一次面谈。

4) [问题] 根据课文，纽约州立大学下一步大跨越是什么？
   [答案] 在线远程学习。

5) [问题] 保罗·埃德尔森是如何看待远程学习的？为什么他说远程学习将是教育领域下一步的大跨越？
   [答案] 他认为远程学习是教育界下一步的大跨越，因为和传统的课堂相比，远程学习有很多优点。（其中包括网络教学可以更有效地让学生参与必须的网上讨论，以及敦促学生使用网上丰富的媒体资源。网络教学也为那些时间有限，或边远地区的非脱产学生提供了接受大学教育的机会。）

6) [问题] 为什么尽管一些老牌大学在网络教育方面走在前列，他们仍然提出了警告？
   [答案] 因为网络课堂的退学率明显高于面对面的现实课堂。在线课程要求更大量的准备工作和更多的师生互动。大量的本科课程还不成熟。一些人担心在本科阶段仓促地开设网络课程可能会使学生缺少必要的社交生活。

7) [问题] 戴维·波梅兰兹认为发展基于网络的远程学习，人们关注的焦点是什么？
   [答案] 教学质量。

词汇练习

1. 请用下面所给词汇或短语的适当形式填写句子。

1) 【答案】get adjusted to
   【译文】国际旅行者的秘诀之一是预定夜间航班。这样到目的地时已是深夜，就可马上入睡，以帮助他们适应当地时间。

2) 【答案】participate

【译文】特里没法参加比赛，因为他脚伤了。

3) 【答案】exceed

　　【译文】大体而言，费用不会超过500美元。

4) 【答案】Caution

　　【译文】谨慎，即小心行事、不贸然涉险的品质，乃安全之本。

5) 【答案】at any given time

　　【译文】有人认为流浪在伦敦街头、无家可归的苏格兰年轻人随时都有一万人左右。

6) 【答案】access to

　　【译文】密码是允许进入计算机系统的一串保密字符。

7) 【答案】engage in

　　【译文】所有学生都应该参与体育活动，这确实是需要优先考虑的事。

8) 【答案】associated

　　【译文】人们通常将健康的生活同开阔的乡村和自产的食物联系起来。

9) 【答案】urged

　　【译文】他的朋友力劝他改掉坏习惯。

10) 【答案】critical

　　【译文】在信息时代，知识对商业运作非常关键。

2. 请用括号里的词构成恰当的短语，再用其适当形式填写句子。

1) 【答案】 engaged in

　　【译文】敝公司从事工艺品的进出口业务。最近几年对玻璃艺术品投入了更多关注。

2) 【答案】point out

　　【译文】许多专家指出，体育锻炼对人体的健康有直接帮助。

3) 【答案】stepped into

　　【译文】他们的研究工作进入了新阶段。

4) 【答案】struggle against

　　【译文】由于无家可归、孤立无援，我们不得不跟严寒、饥饿作斗争。

5) 【答案】According to

　　【译文】据天气预报，下周天气寒冷。

6) 【答案】rob... of

　　【译文】他们正计划从银行家那儿抢劫一枚价值连城的钻戒。

7) 【答案】associate... with

　　【译文】这首歌总让我联想起学校生活。

8) 【答案】 to her credit

　　【译文】她已成功地写过两本书。

3. 请将下面的复合词分类。

adj.+ n. 形容词 + 名词	part-time (兼职的), short-term (短期的), long-distance (远程的, 长途的), short-wave (短波)
n. + vt. -ed 名词 + 动词过去分词	time-constrained (有时限的), snow-covered (被雪覆盖的), hand-made (手工的), heart-broken (心碎的), state-run (国营的)
n. + adj. 名词 + 形容词	media-rich (多种媒体的), ice-cold (冰冷的), paper-thin (极薄的), brand-new (崭新的), duty-free (免税的)

(to be continued)

(continued)

num. + n. 数字 + 名词	28-year-old (man) [28岁的(男人)], second-hand (二手的), five-year (plan) [五年(计划)], first-class (一流的), two-hour (delay) [两小时的(延迟)]
compounds with three or more words 由三个或更多词构成的复合词	face-to-face (面对面的), chalk-and-talk (传统教学模式的), word-for-word (逐字的), wait-and-see (观望的), life-and-death (生死攸关的), give-and-take (交互，互动)

语法结构

1. 仿照例句用 otherwise 将下面每组的两个句子改写为一句。

"otherwise" 是副词，意为"如果不……的话，否则"，作连接性状语用来引出另一个句子，指如果前句的情况不发生或不出现，那么后句的情况发生。如：Put your coat on, otherwise you'll get cold. 穿上外套，否则你会感冒。We were delayed at the airport. Otherwise we would have been here by lunch time. 我们在机场耽搁了，否则我们在午饭时间前就到这儿了。

1) 【答案】Do it now, otherwise it will be too late.

【译文】现在就做，否则就太迟了。

2) 【答案】We'll go early, otherwise we may not get a seat.

【译文】我们要早点去，不然可能没有座位。

3) 【答案】Seize the chance, otherwise you will regret it.

【译文】抓住机会，否则你会后悔的。

4) 【答案】I was not there, otherwise I might have helped.

【译文】我那时不在，要不我会帮忙的。

5) 【答案】I've got one page to write, otherwise I've finished.

【译文】我还差一页就完成了。

2. 仿照例句用 It has been... since... 改写下列句子。

"It has been... since..." 这个句型当中，it 是虚义 it，用作没有具体意义的主语，在这里表示时间。主句用现在完成时"it has been + 表示时间段的词或词组"，since 引导的部分是从句，谓语用一般过去时。整个句子的意思是"自从……以来，(到现在)已经有(多长时间)了。" 如：It has been eight months since her father died. 自从她父亲死后到现在已有八个月了。

1) 【答案】It has been six years since he graduated from high school.

【译文】他高中毕业已有六年了。

2) 【答案】It has been fifteen years since I saw him last time.

【译文】从我上次见他到现在已有15年了。

3) 【答案】It has been nearly three decades since China carried out the "opening up policy".

【译文】中国实施"开放政策"已有30年了。

4) 【答案】It has been almost two years since I began to study in this university.

【译文】我在这所大学学习已有差不多两年了。

5) 【答案】It has been six years since I began to study English.

【译文】从我开始学英语到现在已有六年了。

综合练习

1. 完型填空。

1) 【答案】B

【题解】"on campus" 为固定搭配，意为"在大学校园内"。

2) 【答案】C

【题解】"too + 形容词 + 不定式 to" 为固定结构，意为"太……而不能……"。本句意为"这是不是听起来太美好而令人无法相信呢？"

3) 【答案】A

【题解】available（资源、工具等）可得到的，可利用的；achievable（目标、成就等）可完成的，可达到的；approachable（人）可亲近的，（地方）可到达的；accomplishable（目标、任务等）可完成的，可实行的。本句意为"有数以千计的在线课程能够在万维网上找到"，故用 available。

4) 【答案】A

【题解】turn to 转向，求助于；turn in 上交；turn on 打开开关；turn up 出现。

本句意为"几十年来，学生们利用远程教育来进一步实现他们的教育目标。"

5) 【答案】D

【题解】本句意为"随着信息技术和互联网的飞速发展……"，故选with。

6) 【答案】B

【题解】real 真实的，现实的；virtual 虚拟的，模拟的；true 真正的，符合事实的；actual 实在的，实际的。此处的virtual classroom指"虚拟课堂、模拟课堂"，故选 virtual。

7) 【答案】A

【题解】in... case (s)为固定搭配，指"在……的情况下"。如：in such a case 在这样的情况下；in most cases 在大多数情况下。

8) 【答案】A

【题解】access 使用或接近的权利、机会或方法，常与介词 to 连用。如：Students must have access to good books. 学生必须有机会读到好书。means（常作单数用）为达到某种目的而采用的方法、手段。如：Every means has been tried. 每种方法都尝试过了。link 联系；（链条的）环，节。如：a link in a chain of evidence 一串证据中之一环。connect（动词）连接，连结。如：The two towns are connected by a railway. 这两市镇有铁路相连。本句意为"在多数情况下，上课只需要有电脑、浏览器和能够上网就行了。"

9) 【答案】A

【题解】learn skills 学习、学会技能；give 和 make 一般不与 skill 搭配；earn 赚，挣得，博得。如：to earn $10,000 a year 一年赚一万美元；to earn one's living 谋生；He soon earned the respect of the players. 他很快赢得了球员的尊重。此处指"为工作学习新技能"，故选 A。

10) 【答案】B

【题解】此处需要一个副词来修饰动词 attend，故首先排除 regular 和 usual 这两个形容词。regularly 指"定期地、有规律地"。如：It's important to exercise regularly. 定期地锻炼很重要。usually 指"通常地"；如：He's usually early. 他通常早到。本句中指"没有时间定期上课的人"，故用 regularly。

【译文】 你想足不出户就轻松地提高职业技能吗？你想不踏入高校校园就取得大学学位吗？这是不是听起来太美好而令人无法相信呢？目前互联网上有数以千计的课程，这个数字很快还会扩大到几万。

学生们依靠远程教育的帮助来推进他们的教育目标已有几十年了。从函授课程到电话课程，远程学习不断在满足那些无法到学校上课学习的人的需求。随着信息技术和互联网的飞速发展，现在你可以在电脑上就拥有虚拟课堂了。在大多数情况下，上课只需要有电脑、浏览器和能够上网就行了。

一般而言，在线课程针对在职的成年人，即那些想获得高级学位或掌握对工作有用的新技能，但又没有时间定期上课学习的人。对那些能够自我激励，喜欢独自对着电脑工作并乐于使用技术的人来说，远程教育的效果最好。更重要的是，它是你不得不尝试的事物之一。

2. 用括号中的词汇和短语将下列句子译成英语。

1) **【答案】** It has been over a year since he began to study in this online college, but he still finds it hard to get adjusted to online learning.

2) **【答案】** Our company is mainly engaged in developing computer software and networks.

3) **【答案】** Only students of this university have access to the book resources in this library.

4) **【答案】** As online students, we are also expected to actively participate in some class discussions. 也可用 Being online students, we should also actively participate in some class discussions.

   【题解】 be expected to do sth. 意为"应该做某事"。如：You are expected to study hard. 你应该努力学习。

5) **【答案】** They urged the local government to approve their reform program soon.

   【题解】 approve sth. 指"同意、认可、通过……"。如：The minutes of the meeting were read and approved. 会议记录经宣读并通过。

文章泛读

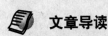

TEXT *B*

文章导读

伴随着信息技术、网络技术的发展和普及，网络教育（online education）应运而生。本文主要介绍了网络教育的发展现状，它对学生的要求，以及网络教育与传统教育的比较。总之，网络教育可能不像我们想象的那么简单，只有当你对网络教育的特点有了充分认识后，才能在网络教育和传统教育之间作出恰当的选择。

背景知识

远程教育是指将课件传送给外地的一处或多处学员的教育。依照这个定义，远程教育的历史可以追溯到19世纪30年代开始的商业函授课程。但是随着先进的信息技术，特别是互联网的出现，远程教育的特征发生了深刻的变化。现在远程教育是指通过音频、视频（直播或录像）及包括实时和非实时在内的计算机技术把培训课程传送到远处（校园外）的教育。

文章写作风格及结构

本文为一篇说明文（expository writing），作者详细介绍了网络教育这一新兴教育模式的特点，通过与传统教育的比较，侧重于阐述网络教学的优势及受众对象。整篇文章条理清晰、论点突出、语言平实，让读者对网络教育有了进一步的认识。

Parts 部分	Paragraphs 段落	Main Ideas 大意
Part I	1	With the development of technology, online education has become more and more popular in the world. 随着技术的发展，网络教育在全世界也愈发受欢迎。
Part II	2—3	The author introduces the comparison between online education and traditional schooling, and points out that time management skills are important to students. 作者对比了网络教育和传统教育之间的优劣势，并指出学生应具备合理安排时间的能力。
Part III	4	No matter which one you choose, it's up to you to make achievements. 无论你选择传统高校还是网络教育，成功与否将取决于自己的努力。

词汇点睛

1 locate

v. 1) to find the exact position of sb./sth. 定位

- 例句 • I'm trying to locate Mr. Smith. Do you know where he is? 我要找史密斯先生，你知道他在哪里吗？

  The baker located his bakery in the new shopping centre.

  面包店主在新的商业中心区开设了面包店。

  2) to be in a particular position 坐落于……（尤用于被动语态）

- 例句 • Shanghai is located/situated in the east of China.(= Shanghai lies in the east of China.)

  上海位于中国的东部。

- 短语 • **be located/situated in** = lie in 位于，坐落于

- 辨析 • **locate, situate**

  locate, situate常用被动语态；lie用主动语态。

- 扩展 • **local** *adj.* 地方性的，本地的

  Last Tuesday he received a letter from the local police. 上星期二他接到当地警察局的一封信。

location *n.* 位置，定位

Have they decided on the location of the new building yet? 这座新建筑的位置他们定下来了吗?

2 prospect

n. sth. that is possible or likely to happen in the future, or the possibility itself 希望，前途

• 例句 • There's not much prospect of Mr. Smith's being elected as Congressman.

史密斯先生被选为议员的希望不大。

The job has no prospects, i.e. it offers little possibility of promotion.

这工作毫无前途，也就是说，晋升的机会很小。

• 扩展 • **retrospect** *n.* 回顾

It was, in retrospect, the happiest day of her life. 回想起来，那是她一生最幸福的日子。

prospective *adj.*（尤作定语）预期的；未来的；可能的

prospective advantages 预期的利益

prospective bride 未来的新娘

3 outweigh

vt. to be more important or valuable than sth. else 比……重要，胜过，强过

• 例句 • The advantages of this plan largely outweigh the disadvantages. 这计划利远大于弊。

This outweighs all other considerations. 这一点是首先要考虑的。

4 annoyance

n. 1) *a feeling of slight anger* 恼怒，为难

• 例句 • To her annoyance the stranger did not go away. 让她烦恼的是，那个陌生人并没走开。

2) *sth. that makes you slightly angry* 恼怒的事情

• 例句 • One of the annoyances of working here is the difficulty of parking near the office.

在这儿工作有一件伤脑筋的事，就是在办公室附近很难停车。

• 扩展 • **annoy** *vt.* 使（某人）不悦; 惹恼

It annoys me when people forget to say thank you. 遇到有人忘记道谢的时候，我就不痛快。

annoyed *adj.* 颇为生气的

I was annoyed by his bad manners. 他的无礼使我恼怒。

annoying *adj.* 使人颇为生气或烦恼的

How annoying! I've left my wallet at home! 真讨厌，我把钱包落在家里了。

• 辨析 • **anneyed, annoying**

形容某人生气用annoyed，形容某事情令人生气烦恼用annoying。

5 accommodate

vt. 1) *to provide someone with a place to stay, live, or work* 提供住宿

• 例句 • This hotel can accommodate up to 500 guests. 这旅馆可供500位来宾住宿。

The school was not big enough to accommodate all the children.

学校不够大，不能为所有孩子提供住宿。

2) *to change or adjust sth. so that it fits or harmonizes with sth. else* 适应，迎合

• 例句 • I will accommodate my plans to yours. 我修改一下计划以便和你的计划相适应。

• 扩展 • **accommodation** *n.* 住所

Hotel accommodation is scarce. 旅馆的房间不足。

6 crucial

adj. extremely important, because everything else depends on it 极其重要的，决定性的

- 例句 • Getting this contract is crucial to the future of our company.

  签订此项合同对本公司的前途至关重要。

  The success of this experiment is crucial to the project as a whole.

  这项试验的成功对整个计划是极其重要的。

- 短语 • **be crucial to/for sth.** 对……极其重要   **at the crucial moment** 在紧要关头

7 specifically

adv. concerning or intended for one particular type of use 特别地，尤其

- 例句 • You were specifically warned not to eat fish. 已经特别叮嘱过你不要吃鱼。

  The houses are specifically designed for old people. 这些房子是专为老年人设计的。

- 扩展 • **specific** *adj.* 确切的；具体的

  specific instructions/aims 明确的指示/目标

  special *adj.* （通常作定语）特殊的；特别的

  He did it as a special favour. 他做这事算是特别照顾。

- 辨析 • **specific, special, specifically, specially**

  specific强调具体的，special强调特殊的，specifically和specially分别是它们的副词形式。

8 accustom

vt. to make yourself or another person become used to a situation or place 使适应

- 例句 • He quickly accustomed himself to the local food. 他很快使自己习惯了当地食物。

  I've been accustomed to working hard. 我已习惯于努力工作。

- 短语 • **accustom oneself to sth.** 使自己习惯于某事

  be accustomed/used to doing sth. 习惯于做……

- 扩展 • **custom** *n.* 习惯，风俗

  His custom was to get up early and have a cold bath. 他的习惯是早起，然后洗个冷水澡。

  accustomed *adj.* 习惯的

  He took his accustomed seat by the fire. 他坐在火炉旁他常坐的座位上。

9 confine

vt. to keep sb. in a place that they cannot leave 关起来，禁闭

- 例句 • After her operation, she was confined to bed for a week. 她手术后已卧床一周了。

  I hate to be confined in an office all day. 我讨厌整天被关在办公室里。

- 短语 • **confine sb./ sth. in/to sth.** 限制在某空间内

- 扩展 • **confined** *adj.* 受限制的

  It is hard to work efficiently in such a confined space. 在这样狭小的空间里工作很难提高效率。

10 hesitant

adj. being reluctant or unwilling 犹豫的，吞吞吐吐的

- 例句 • I'm rather hesitant about signing this. 我不大愿意签这个字。

  She's hesitant about making new friends. 她在结交新朋友上有疑虑。

- 短语 • **be hesitant about (doing) sth.** 犹豫做某事

- 扩展 • **hesitate** *vi.* 犹豫（做某事）

If you need any help, don't hesitate to ask. 你如果需要什么帮忙请尽管说，不要有什么顾虑。

He hesitated before he answered because he didn't know what to say.

他在回答之前犹豫了一下，因为他不知道说什么。

hesitation *n.* 犹豫

She agreed without the slightest hesitation. 她毫不犹豫地同意了。

11 contact

n. communication or meeting with a person, organization, country, etc. 交流

• 例句 • We can learn much by being brought into contact with opposing opinions.

通过接触反面意见，我们可以学到很多东西。

We made contact with the ship by radio. 我们通过无线电与那条船取得了联系。

• 短语 • **be in contact with**　与……有联系

get/come into contact with, make contact with　和……取得联系

lose (be out of) contact with　和……失去联系

vt. to write or telephone someone　联系

• 例句 • I'll contact you by phone tomorrow. 我明天跟你电话联系。

• 用法 • contact 作动词，本身已内含"与……联系"的意义，因而不要再加with。

12 enroll

vt. to officially arrange to join a school, college, class, etc., or arrange for sb. else to do this

入学，入会

• 例句 • We enrolled him as a member of the union. 我们吸收他为会员。

She has enrolled in evening classes. 她已注册上晚间课程班。

• 扩展 • **enrollment** (also **enrolment**)　*n.* 登记；注册

13 option

n. sth. that you can choose to do in a particular situation　选择

• 例句 • You must do it; you have no option. 你必须做，你没有选择。

There are three options open to us in that matter. 在这个问题上我们有三个选择。

• 短语 • **at one's option**　任意、随意

He always spends money like soil at his option. 他常常任着自己的性子挥金如土。

• 扩展 • **optional** *adj.* 可以选择的，非强制性的

optional subjects 选修课

Formal dress is optional. 是否穿礼服自便。

🔵 短语解析

1. take sth. by storm 袭取，强夺；使大吃一惊

【例句】The soldiers took the city by storm. 士兵一举攻占了那个城镇。

The play took Paris by storm. 该剧轰动了巴黎。

2. along with 与……一起

【例句】There was a bill along with the parcel. 随同包裹来的还有一张账单。

The baby's mother escaped from the fire along with two other children.

婴儿的母亲与其他两个孩子一道逃离了火灾现场。

3. look into 调查，查看

【例句】A working party has been set up to look into the problem. 已成立工作组调查该问题。

His disappearance is being looked into by the police. 警方正在调查他失踪一事。

4. rule sb./sth. out 排除，取消，认为某人或事不合适

【例句】He was ruled out as a possible candidate. 他已经没有可能成为候选人。

An ankle injury ruled him out for the big match. 脚踝受伤使他不能参加这场大赛。

5. due to sth. 由于……

【例句】This accident was due to driving at a high speed. 这场交通事故是由于高速开车而引起的。

Her illness was due to bad food. 她的病是由于吃了变质的食物造成的。

6. up to sb. 由某人决定

【例句】An Indian or a Chinese meal? It's up to you. 吃印度菜还是吃中国菜？由你决定吧。

It's up to you whether you pay or not. 你付不付款自己决定。

7. set aside 留出（专用的时间或金钱）

【例句】She sets aside a bit of money every month. 她每月都存一点儿钱。

I try to set aside a few minutes each day to do some exercises.

我每天尽量腾出一些时间锻炼一下身体。

8. be confined to sth. 局限于……

【例句】His genius was not confined to painting. 他的天才不仅仅局限于绘画。

He is confined to the house by illness. 他因病而出不了门。

9. equip sb./sth. with sth. 用……来装备……

【例句】The soldiers were equipped with the latest weapons. 士兵们配备着最新式的武器。

We equip our children with a good education. 我们给孩子们良好的教育。

10. fall behind 落后，退步

【例句】France has fallen behind in coal production. 法国在产煤方面落后了。

The major world powers are afraid of falling behind in the arms race.

世界各大强国均唯恐在军备竞赛中落后。

🔆 难句突破

1. (Para.1) *For this reason, online education has taken the world of higher education by storm.*

【解析】for this reason: 正因为如此

【译文】正因为如此，网络教育以暴风骤雨之势席卷了高等教育界。

2. (Para.1) *Whatever your family situation, current job, economic standing, or background, you can enjoy a web-based-instruction along with other hard-working students from all corners of the globe.*

【解析】由whatever引导让步状语从句，表示"无论……"。如：

Whatever you think of him, you have to admire his determination.

无论你对他的看法如何，你都不得不佩服他的决定。

Whatever happens, you know that I'll stand by you.

无论发生什么，我都站在你这一边。

She had vowed to remain true to the President whatever happens.

她发誓无论发生什么情况她都忠实于总统。

【译文】无论你的家境如何、现在的工作怎样、经济水平如何、背景怎样，你都能和全球各个角落的莘莘学子一起通过网络接受教育。

3. (Para.1) *When looking into the prospect of earning a degree—associate, bachelor, master, or doctorate, do not rule out the possibility of online education.*

【解析】looking into为现在分词作状语，when引导分词分句。现在分词作状语可以表原因、时间、结果、条件、让步、行为方式、伴随状况等。如：

Being too old, he couldn't walk that far. 因为年纪太大了，他走不了那么远。（表原因）

While reading the book, he nodded from time to time. 他读书的时候频频点头。（表伴随）

Standing on the building, you can see the whole city.

站在楼顶上你可以鸟瞰整个城市。（表条件）

【译文】要获取学位（包括专科、学士、硕士、博士学位）的话，网络教育也是一个选择。

4. (Para.2) *Traditional colleges and universities have developed distance learning programs to accommodate individuals who would not otherwise have the time or funds to earn an advanced degree.*

【解析】who引导定语从句修饰individuals。

【译文】一些传统高校开设了远程教育课程，以帮助那些没有空余时间或没有足够资金的人获得更高的学位。

5. (Para.2) *If you are under the impression that courses offered online will be a walk in the park, think again!*

【解析】1) offered online作定语修饰course。

2) that引导同位语从句。同位语从句一般置于下列名词后：belief, doubt, fact, hope, idea, message, news等。如：

The fact that his proposal makes sense should be recognized. 应当承认他的建议是有道理的。

The idea that everyone should be required to vote by law is something we don't agree with.

我们不主张由法律规定每个人都要投票。

We have heard the news that many more teachers will move into new buildings before Teachers' Day. 我们听说教师节前更多的教师会搬进新房。

【译文】要是你以为网络课程很容易的话，那你就错了。

6. (Para.3) ***Instead of being confined to a stuffy classroom filled with students, these online classes have a more personal feeling.***

【解析】 instead一般放在句尾表示代替，更换。也可以用instead of，of后面要加名词或动词的ing形式。如：

We've no coffee. Would you like tea instead? 我们没有咖啡了，改喝茶好么？

Let's drink tea instead of coffee. 我们喝茶吧，别喝咖啡了。

It will take days by car, so let's fly instead. 开车去要好几天呢，咱们还是坐飞机去吧。

Let's fly there instead of driving. 我们坐飞机去吧，别开车去。

【译文】 与沉闷而拥挤的传统教室相比，网络课堂给人更加浓厚的个性化氛围。

7. (Para.3) ***While many students would be hesitant to speak one to one with a class instructor, online programs find their students more willing to contact their professors via e-mail.***

【解析】 while表示比较。如：

I do every single bit of housework while he just does the dishes now and again. 我做遍所有的家务而他却只是时不时地洗洗盘子。

He likes football, while I prefer rugby. 他喜欢足球，而我喜欢橄榄球。

【译文】 传统课堂的很多学生都不太勇于与老师单独交流，而网络课堂的学生则很愿意通过电子邮件和老师联系。

8. (Para.3) ***Of course, not attending a class also comes with additional barriers.***

【解析】 not attending a class是动名词作主语。如：

Collecting information is very important to businessmen. 收集信息对商人来讲很重要。

It is no use sitting here waiting. 坐在这里等没有用。

【译文】 当然，不到教室上课也会带来额外的学习障碍。

9. (Para.3) ***Students that lack the proper time management skills may find themselves overwhelmed with course work at the end of the semester or falling behind in their studies.***

【解析】 1) that引导定语从句修饰students。

2) overwhelmed和falling behind都是find的宾语补足语，类似分词作宾补的情况还有如下例子：

I saw the girl getting on the bus. 我看见那个女孩儿上了车。

He had his clothes washed. 他叫别人洗了衣服。

We had the fire burning all day. 我们让火燃了一整天。

【译文】 那些不会合理安排时间的人到了期末不是被繁重的课业所累，就是学习成绩退步。

10. (Para.4) ***For busy individuals or students wishing to return to school without greatly affecting their everyday lives, an online degree program may be the best option.***

【解析】 wishing to... everyday lives 作定语修饰individual or students。

【译文】有些忙碌的人既想尽可能维持自己目前的生活状况，又想继续求学，那么，网络学位课程应该是他们最好的选择了。

参考译文

网络教育与传统教育

　　在这个技术高度发达的时代，世界变得越来越小。国内交流能够即时完成，而不像以前需要花上几周的时间。借助于环球网络，你还能够轻而易举地和世界各地志趣相投的人们联系，轻松得就像大家住在同一个小镇上。正因为如此，网络教育以暴风骤雨之势席卷了高等教育界。无需迁至另一个城市、另一个州或者另一个国家，你便可以将你所选定的高等教育机构搬至自家后院。无论你的家境如何、现在的工作怎样、经济水平如何、背景怎样，你都能和全球各个角落的莘莘学子一起通过网络接受教育。要获取学位（包括专科、学士、硕士、博士学位）的话，网络教育可以是一个选择。在很多情况下，通过网络教育获取学位远比通过传统大学学习获取学位更加轻松，且花费更少。

　　从开设伊始至今，网络学位课程得到了长足的发展。一些传统高校开设了远程教育课程，以帮助那些没有空余时间或没有足够资金的人获得更高的学位。网络教学需要学生完成与现实课堂教学相当的学习任务和作业量。要是你以为网络课程很容易的话，那你就错了。网络课程学习通常比传统大学学习难，因为学生必须自己协调工作和学习两个方面。合理安排时间的能力非常重要，因为学生不可能每天都有专门的时间留出来学习。学生们得花上一段时间才能适应这种学习方式，但无论如何，网络课堂的利还是大于弊。

　　网络学位课程和传统高等教育的主要区别在于学习地点不同。较之沉闷、拥挤的传统教室而言，网络课堂给人以更加浓厚的个性化氛围。传统课堂的很多学生都不太勇于与老师单独交流，而网络课堂的学生则很愿意通过电子邮件和老师联系。学生的大量参与增进了他们对教材的理解。当然，不到教室上课也会带来额外的学习障碍。学生必须具备合理安排时间的技能才能成功完成网络课程。那些不会合理安排时间的人到了期末不是被繁重的课业所累，就是学习成绩退步。

　　不管你决定去传统高校就读，还是报名参加网络大学课程，成功的机会是均等的。完成学业和获取学位最终都取决于你自己。有些忙碌的人既想尽可能维持自己目前的生活状况，又想继续求学，那么，网络学位课程应该是他们最好的选择了。

习题全解

1. 请在括号中分别填写代表描述网上学习和传统学习特点的序号。

【答案】Online learning (1　2　3　4　5　6　7)

　　　　Traditional schooling (3　4　7　8)

【译文】1) 使世界显得更小。(Para. 1)

　　　　2) 给人们提供一个更加平等的受教育机会。（Para. 1）

　　　　3) 提供了获得更高学位的可能性。（Para. 1）

　　　　4) 要求一定的学习任务和作业量。（Para. 2）

　　　　5) 要求较强的合理安排时间的能力。(Paras. 2 & 3)

　　　　6) 更加个性化以及涉及更多的个人参与。（Para. 3）

7) 给你成功的机会。 (Para. 4)

8) 可能会更麻烦或花费更高。 (Para. 2)

2. 请用适当的介词填空。

1) 【答案】under

【解析】under the impression of 认为；觉得

【译文】初到美国的人觉得这个国家总是处于匆忙和压力之中。

2) 【答案】to

【解析】be up to sb. 由某人决定

【译文】是否在网上修硕士学位取决于你。

3) 【答案】in

【解析】in an instant 一瞬；立刻

【译文】车祸发生在交通高峰期的一瞬。

4) 【答案】of

【解析】instead of 代替, 而不是……

【译文】他没有受过传统教育，而是自学成才的。

5) 【答案】by

【解析】take... by storm 袭取，强夺；使大吃一惊

【译文】《哈利·波特》系列在全世界掀起了一股热潮。

6) 【答案】with

【解析】along with 与……一道

【译文】布莱克先生给我们作了精彩的演讲和风趣的评论。

7) 【答案】to

【解析】be accustomed to 习惯于

【译文】一旦你适应了新的文化，你甚至会享受它。

8) 【答案】to

【解析】due to 由于……

【译文】他考试失败是因为他不知道如何在网上有效地学习。

3. 请用下面所给出词汇或短语的适当形式填写句子。

1) 【答案】earn

【译文】他打算取得尽量多的学位。

2) 【答案】fall behind

【译文】没有人可以保持原位不动；不进则退。

3) 【答案】set aside

【译文】学生被要求每天抽出半小时练习英语口语。

4) 【答案】outweighs

【译文】对我来说，完成一项任务的过程比结果本身更重要。

5) 【答案】be equipped with

【译文】求职时，最好能具备良好的英语技能。

6) 【答案】are... confined to

【译文】由于所住的街区环境不好，孩子们通常都被迫呆在家里不能出去。

7) 【答案】overwhelmed

【译文】由于受不了强烈罪恶感的折磨，凶手自杀了。

4. 将下面这段话译成汉语。

【答案】无论你是决定去传统高校就读，还是报名参加网络大学课程，其成功的机会是均等的。完成学业和获取学位最终都取决于你自己。有些忙碌的人既想尽可能维持自己目前的生活状况，又想继续求学，那么，网络学位课程应该是他们最好的选择了。

【解析】第一句话中的"whether... or..."结构表示二者任选其一，意为"无论……还是……"。chance 此处指"可能性"，既可作为可数名词，也可作为不可数名词使用。如：He has no/a poor chance of winning. 他没有可能（只有微小的可能）会赢。What are our chances of succeeding? 我们成功的可能性有多大？第二句中的 in the end 是短语，指"最后，最终"。如：He tried many ways of earning a living; in the end he became a farm labourer. 他尝试过许多谋生的方式，最后他做了农场工人。第三句中的 wishing to return to school without greatly affecting their everyday lives 是后置定语，修饰 individuals or students,而这个长定语中的 without greatly affecting their everyday lives 是伴随状语，意为"在对日常生活没有大的影响的情况下"。

文章泛读

文章导读

目前，远程教育已经成为一个热门话题。虽然远程教育炙手可热，优点多多，可是由于每个人的性格不同，学习习惯和学习风格各不相同，远程教育是否就一定适合你呢？什么样的学习者最适合远程教育呢？相信读了本文你会找到答案。

背景知识

网络学习又叫"在线学习"（Online-Learning）、"基于网络的学习"（Web-based Learning）或"数字化学习"（E-Learning),是一种在网络环境下，通过学习者对各类网络学习资源的浏览与访问，通过师生之间基于网络的互动和交流而进行的一种学习。

文章写作风格及结构

本文为一篇说明文（expository writing）。作者详细介绍了一个成功的网络学习者应具备的四个素质，并一再强调网络学习应该和个人的个性、习惯相结合。整篇文章条理清晰、论点突出、语言平实、例证丰富、内容全面、观点新颖，让读者对网络教育有了更深刻、更客观、更全面的认识。

Parts 部分	Paragraphs 段落	Main Ideas 大意
Part I	1	Distance education is not for everyone. 并非人人都适合接受网络教育。
Part II	2	Successful distance learners have four qualities. 成功的网络学习者应具备四个素质。
Part III	3	You have to think twice before applying to an online school. 结合自身的个性特点，你需要认真考虑是否适合网络学习。

词汇点睛

1　enjoyable

adj. sth. enjoyable gives you pleasure 使人愉快的，令人快乐的

• 例句 • We had an enjoyable weekend. 我们度过了一个愉快的周末。

It was much more enjoyable than I had expected. 这比我预期的要愉快得多。

• 扩展 • **enjoy** *vt.* 享受，喜爱

We enjoyed our trip to Europe. 这次到欧洲旅行，我们非常愉快。

The twin brothers always enjoy going to the concert.

这对双胞胎弟兄对于听音乐会总是兴致勃勃。

注意：跟动词时只能是动名词，不跟不定式。

enjoyment *n.* 乐趣，享乐

I get a lot of enjoyment from my job. 我从我的工作中得到许多乐趣。

2　rewarding

adj. making you feel happy and satisfied because you feel you are doing sth. useful or important （指活动）值得做的，令人满意的

• 例句 • Gardening is a very rewarding activity. 园艺是一项非常有益的活动。

Nursing can be a rewarding career. 护士是一项很有意义的职业。

• 扩展 • **reward** *n.* 报酬，奖赏 *vt.* 报答，酬谢

He was given a reward of $100,000 for his invention. 他的发明为他赢得了十万美元的奖赏。

I will reward you for your help. 我会答谢你们的帮助的。

unrewarding *adj.* 报酬低的，不值得做的

3　characteristic

n. (usually pl.) a quality or feature of sth./sb. that is typical of them and easy to recognize 特征

• 例句 • A characteristic of the camel is its ability to live for a long time without water.

骆驼的特点是不喝水也能活很长时间。

What are the characteristics that distinguish the Chinese from the Japanese?

中国人区别于日本人的特征是什么？

adj. very typical of sth. or of sb.'s character 典型的，特有的

• 例句 • He spoke with characteristic enthusiasm. 他以他特有的热情说话。

- **短语** • **be characteristic of** 有……的特色

  注意：这个短语通常要以"特点"作主语，而以具有该特点的主体作介词of的宾语。

  That behavior is characteristic of him. 他的为人就是这样。

- **辨析** • **characteristic, character**

  One may have a character, but may have many characteristics, all of which constitute one's character.

  一个人可能只有一种"性格"(character)，但可能有多种"特征，特点"(characteristic)，所有这些"特征、特点"便构成了一个人总的"特征、品质"(character)。

4 determine

  vt. to find out 确定（某事物），决定

- **例句** • She will determine how it is to be done. 她会决定如何去做这件事。

  He has not determined what he will study. 他还没有决定学什么。

- **短语** • **determine to do sth.** 决定做某事

  determine on/upon sth. 决定某事

  He determined to drink and smoke no more. 他决心不再抽烟喝酒了。

  They determined on an early start. 他们决定早些出发。

- **扩展** • **determined** *adj.* 有决心的，坚决的

  I am determined to do better than Mike. 我决心比迈克做得更好。

  determination *n.* 决心

  That girl has great determination; I am sure she will do well.

  那女孩子决心很大，我肯定她会做好的。

5 fit

  vt. if a piece of clothing fits you, it is the right size for your body 形状及大小对（某人）合适；合身

- **例句** • These shoes dont's fit me. 这双鞋我穿着不合适。

  n. the particular way in which sth. fits 适合

- **例句** • The coat was a good fit. 这件大衣很合身。

  The garment is a tight fit. 这件衣服很贴身。

  adj. suitable or good enough for sth. 适宜的，合适的

- **例句** • After the interview, the employer concluded that she was fit for the job.

  面试后老板下结论说她适合做这项工作。

  The food is not fit to eat. 这食物不适宜吃。

6 motivate

  vt. to make sb. want to achieve sth. and make them willing to work hard in order to do it 激发（某人）的兴趣，促成 (常用作被动语态)

- **例句** • Like so many people, he's motivated by greed. 像大多数人一样，他也受到贪欲的驱使。

  Examinations do not motivate a student to seek more knowledge.

  考试不能激励学生去学习更多的知识。

- **扩展** • **motivation** *n.* 动机

  The stronger the motivation, the more quickly a person will learn a foreign language.

  一个人学外语的动力越强，那么他就学得越快。

7 appreciate

vt. 1) to understand how good or useful sb./sth. is 赏识，高度评价

• 例句 • You can't fully appreciate foreign literature in translation.

看翻译作品很难欣赏到外国文学的精髓。

I think that young children often appreciate modern pictures better than anyone else.

我认为小孩对现代图画往往比任何人都更有鉴赏力。

2) to be grateful for sth. that sb. has done; to welcome sth. 感激，感谢

• 例句 • We appreciate your efforts for the development of the company.

我们感激你对公司发展所作的努力。

We greatly appreciate your timely help. 我们非常感谢你们及时的帮助。

• 扩展 • **appreciation** *n.* 感谢, 欣赏

She showed an appreciation of my help. 她感谢我的帮助。

Appreciation of works of art is bound to be dominated by a particular kind of interest.

对于艺术作品的欣赏必然受到一种特殊的兴趣爱好的支配。

8 majority

n. most of the people or things in a particular group 大多数，大半，大多 (集合名词)

• 例句 • The majority was/were in favor of the proposal. 多数人赞成这个建议。

The majority of children in our class have brown eyes; only three have blue eyes.

我们班大多数孩子是棕色眼睛，只有三个是蓝眼睛。

• 扩展 • **major**

adj. 较大的；较多的；主要的

We have encountered major problems. 我们遇到大问题了。

vi. 主修

He majors in civil engineering. 他主修土木工程。

n. 专业

Her major is English. 她的专业是英语。

minor *adj.* 较小的, 次要的, 二流的, 未成年的

The young actress was given a minor part in the new play.

这个年轻女演员只分到这出新戏中一个小角色。

minority *n.* 少数

The minority is subordinate to the majority. 少数服从多数。

9 available

adj. sth. that is available is able to be used or can easily be bought or found

可用的或可得到的

• 例句 • This was the only available room. 只剩下这个房间可用了。

I'm sorry; those overcoats are not available in your color and size.

对不起, 这种外套没有你要的颜色和尺码。

• 扩展 • **unavailable** *adj.* 难以获得的

The new timetable is unavailable. 新的时刻表现在还没有。

10　resist

vt. to try to prevent change or prevent yourself being forced to do sth.

抵抗，抵制（后接动词时，用动词的ing形式）

- 例句 • She could hardly resist laughing. 她几乎忍不住要笑。

  I can't resist baked apples. 我顶不住烤苹果的诱惑。

- 扩展 • **resistance** *n.* 抵抗，抵制

  There has been a lot of resistance to this new law. 抵制这一项新法律的人很多。

  resistant *adj.* 有抵抗力的，抵抗的

  This new type of infection is resistant to antibiotics. 这种新的传染病对抗菌素有抗药力。

11　distraction

n. sth. that makes you stop paying attention to what you are doing 使人分心的事物

- 例句 • There are too many distractions in the hotel for me to work properly.

  旅馆里使人分心的事物太多，使我难以集中精力工作。

  He found the noise of the photographers a distraction.

  他觉得摄影师们的嘈杂声分散了他的注意力。

- 扩展 • **distract** *vt.* 使分心；分散（注意力等）

  The noise in the street distracted me from my reading. 街上的嘈杂声使我不能专心读书。

12　temptation

n. a strong desire to have or do sth. even though you know you should not

劝诱，诱惑

- 例句 • As a young actress, she managed to resist the temptation to move to Hollywood.

  作为年轻的演员，她抵制住了去好莱坞的诱惑。

  The temptation to steal is greater than ever before—especially in large shops.

  偷窃的诱惑力比以往任何时候更强烈了，在大商店里尤其如此。

- 扩展 • **tempt** *vt.* 诱惑

  He was tempted into a life of crime by greed and laziness.

  他受贪婪和懒惰的驱使步入了罪恶的一生。

13　disturbance

n. sth. that stops you from being able to continue doing sth., or the act of stopping sb. from being able to continue doing sth. 扰乱，干扰

- 例句 • Phone calls are the biggest disturbance at work. 电话是工作时最大的干扰。

- 扩展 • **disturb** *vt.* 打扰；干扰

  Please don't disturb me while I'm working. 当我工作时，请不要打扰我。

  I'm sorry to disturb you with this question. 对不起打扰你了，我有个问题请教。

🌐 短语解析

1. thrive on　茁壮成长，蓬勃发展

【例句】Some people thrive on a stressful situation.

一些人在有压力的情况下发展很好。

He thrives on criticism. 他接受批评而不断进步。

2. have sth. in common (with sb./sth.) （和……）有共同的……

【例句】Jane and I have nothing in common. 简和我毫无共同之处。

He has much in common with most young people.

他跟大多数年轻人有很多共同之处。

3. compare... to... 把……和……相比；把……比作……

【例句】A beginner's painting can't be compared to that of an expert.

初学者的画不能与专家的相比。

A teacher's work is often compared to a candle. 教师的工作常被比作蜡烛。

4. put off 推迟，延迟

【例句】Don't put off until tomorrow what can be done today.

今日可做的事不要拖到明天。

She keeps putting off going to the dentist. 她老是拖延着不去看牙医。

5. end up doing 以……而告终

【例句】At first he refused to accept any responsibility, but he ended up apologizing.

最初他不承认有任何责任，到头来还是道了歉。

If you don't know what you want, you might end up getting something you don't want.

如果你不知道你想要什么，那你可能最终只得到你不想要的。

6. turn down 减弱，降低，压低（力量、声音等）；谢绝

【例句】Please turn the television down a bit. 请把电视机音量关小点。

He asked Jane to marry him, but she turned down his proposal.

他请求简嫁给他，但她拒绝了。

🌀 难句突破

1. (Para.1) ***While some people thrive on the independence and freedom offered through such classes, others find themselves regretting their decision and wishing they had enrolled at a traditional school instead.***

【解析】thrive on: 蓬勃发展，茁壮成长

regretting their decision 作find的宾补，后半句的主干应该是others find themselves regretting... and (find themselves) wishing (that) ...

【译文】有些人靠网络课堂提供的独立和自由而成功发达，有些人则后悔当初的选择，很希望自己进入的是传统学校而不是网络学校。

2. (Para.2) ***Successful distance learners do just as well, if not better, without people looking over their shoulders.***

【解析】1) as well 表示"也，同样……"。如：

He is a scientist, but is a poet as well. 他是一个科学家，但也是一个诗人。

as well as 用于肯定句中，起连接作用，表示"既……又……；不仅……而且……"。如：

He gave me clothes as well as food. 他既给我食物，又给我衣服。

2) if not better 为插入语，表示"如果不比……好"。If not + 比较级，表示"如果不比……，至少和……一样"。如：

Tom is as good as Jerry, if not better. 如果汤姆不比杰瑞好的话，至少和杰瑞一样好。

He is as tall as his brother, if not taller. 如果他不比他哥哥高的话，至少和他哥哥一样高。

【译文】 成功的网络学习者在没有人监督的情况下，也会做得一样好，甚至更好。

3. (Para. 2) *While some people need teachers to keep them motivated and on-task, distance learners are able to motivate themselves.*

【解析】 motivate: 激发，给某人动机

【译文】 有些人需要老师给他们动力，督促他们学习，而网络学习者能够自己激励自己。

4. (Para. 2) *These students enjoy the freedom of working at their own pace and appreciate the ability to complete their work in as much time as it takes them, instead of waiting for an entire class.*

【解析】 1) 句子的主干是 these students enjoy the freedom..., and appreciate the ability...，而后面用 of 短语和不定式来分别修饰和说明是什么样的 freedom 和 ability。

2) ... as much time as it takes them 中 it 指的是 work，them 指代 students。

【译文】 这些学生很享受按照自己的进度安排学习的自由，也很乐于在力所能及的时间内完成学习任务，而不是等着全班步调一致。

5. (Para. 2) *However, they understand that putting off their work too often can end up adding months, if not years, to their studies.*

【解析】 if not years 作为插入语，表示"如果不是几年的话"。

【译文】 然而，他们明白经常推迟完成作业最终会使得他们的学业延长几个月甚至几年的时间。

6. (Para. 2) *Although some distance learning courses offer video recordings and audio clips, most programs require that students understand a large amount of information that is only available through written text.*

【解析】 这句话的主干是although... most programs require that...，其中information又由一个定语从句修饰。

【译文】 尽管有些网络课程提供视听素材，但大部分教学还是要求学生仅仅通过阅读材料来掌握大量信息。

7. (Para. 2) *Whether it's the phone ringing off the hook, the kids screaming in the kitchen, or the temptation of TV programmes, everyone faces distractions.*

【解析】 the phone ringing off the hook 指电话铃不停地响；kids screaming in the kitchen 指孩子在厨房吵闹；the temptation of TV programmes 指电视节目的诱惑。

分词短语作定语时，放在被修饰的名词之后，单个分词作定语时，放在被修饰的名词之前。如：

China is a developing country. 中国是一个发展中国家。

The man standing at the window is our teacher. 那个站在窗户旁边的人是我们的老师。

【译文】 无论是电话铃声，厨房里孩子们的吵闹声，还是电视节目的诱惑，每个人都面临着很多

让他们分心的事物。

8. (Para. 2) ***They feel comfortable turning down an invitation or letting the machine pick up the phone when they know there is work to be done.***

【解析】 turn down sth. 表示"拒绝"。

feel comfortable turning down... 表示"在拒绝……的时候是自然而然的"。

【译文】 当他们意识到还有功课没有完成时,他们自然而然就会拒绝邀请,或者让答录机去接听电话。

9. (Para. 3) ***But if, after comparing your personality and habits to those of successful distance education students, you've discovered that you have a lot in common, online classes may be the perfect option for you.***

【解析】 1) compare A to B 表示"把 A 和 B 作比较"。如:

This road is quite busy compared to that one. 和那条路相比这条路相当繁华。

2) those指代那些优秀的远程学习者的personality and habits。

3) option 表示"选择,抉择"。

【译文】 但是,当你将自己的个性和习惯同那些优秀学生比较之后发现你们有很多共同点时,网络课程对于你将会是一个理想的选择。

🌑 参考译文

你适合网络学习吗?
——看看你是否具备网络学习者的四个素质

在你去网络学校注册上课之前,请务必想清楚自己是否真的适合网络学习。进修一个网络课程学位会是一次愉快而有益的经历,但并非人人都适合接受网络教育。有些人靠网络课堂提供的独立和自由而成功发达,有些人则后悔当初的选择,很希望自己进入的是传统学校而不是网络学校。

成功、愉快地进行网络学习的人具有一些共同特征。请你对照下面列出的几条,看看自己的个性和习惯是否适合选择网络课堂。

1. 成功的网络学习者在无人监督的情况下,也会做得一样好,甚至更好。有些人需要老师给他们动力,督促他们学习,而网络学习者能够自己激励自己。虽然有老师在网上给他们布置学习任务、为他们批改作业,但他们知道自己与老师之间不能进行面对面的交流,而他们也不需要别人鼓励。最成功的学生是能够自我激励并为自己设定目标的。

2. 成功的网络学习者从不(至少说是很少)拖延作业,也不会等到最后一刻才开始写论文。这些学生很享受按照自己的进度安排学习的自由,也很乐于在力所能及的时间内完成学习任务,而不是等着全班步调一致。他们明白经常推迟完成作业最终会使得他们的学业延长几个月甚至几年的时间。

3. 成功的网络学习者具有良好的阅读能力。大部分人通过听课、记笔记的方式学习,而多数网络学习者则只能通过阅读来掌握学习材料。尽管有些网络课程提供视听素材,但大部分教学还是要求学生仅仅通过阅读材料来掌握大量信息。即使没有老师的直接面授,这些学生也能够理解大学水平的课文。

4.成功的网络学习者能够抵制不断的干扰。无论是电话铃声，厨房里孩子们的吵闹声，还是电视节目的诱惑。每个人都面临着很多让他们分心的事物。优秀的学生知道怎样排除那些影响他们进步的干扰因素。当他们意识到还有功课没有完成时，他们自然而然就会拒绝邀请，或者让答录机去接听电话。

如果你几乎不具备这些成功学生的素质，你大概要重新考虑是否应该申请网络学校了。需要记住的是网络学习并非适合于任何人，有些人会觉得这种方式很棒，而有些人将会一直苦苦挣扎在独立学习的困境中。但是，当你将自己的个性和习惯同那些优秀学生比较之后发现你们有很多共同点时，网络课程对于你将会是一个理想的选择。

语言拓展

日常用语

练习 选择补全对话的最佳答案。

1. 【答案】C

   【题解】当别人打电话来找某人而此人在时，可用"Hold on. I'll get him/her."意为"请别挂断，我去叫他/她。"若此人刚好不在，可用"I'm sorry. He/She isn't in."或"He/She is out."接下来可以说"Can I take a message for him/her?"请别人留言。A项和B项都不太礼貌，且不符合英语的习惯。D项不是打电话的语言，若你就是别人要找的人，可直接说"Speaking."或"It's Tom speaking."而不能说"I am Tom."或"Tom is me."

2. 【答案】B

   【题解】别人打来电话要求与某人通话而此人暂时无法接听时，需向对方说明无法接听的原因，否则是不礼貌的，故选B。意为"他正在另一条线上（与其他人通话）。"

3. 【答案】D

   【题解】只有D项符合用英语打电话的习惯，解答请参考第一题。

4. 【答案】C

   【题解】该题题干是请求接线员接通某人时所说的话，而选项是接线员说的话。请求时可用"Can you put me through to ××××(电话号码)?"接线员通常回答"Yes, I'll put you through."但尝试后接不通或对方号码占线时，应说"Sorry, the line/number is busy/engaged."也可再加上"Will you hold on?"意为"你能不挂断让我再拨一次吗？"

5. 【答案】B

   【题解】依据选项处的上下文来推断，一定是要找的人不在而打电话的人要求留言，故选B。而D项为请求对方留言，"我能帮他捎个口信吗？"故不能选。

阅读技巧

练习 略读以下这篇文章并回答问题。

1. 【译文】根据标题，这篇文章主要是关于什么内容的？

   【答案】It is about how to learn successfully through the Internet.

   【题解】注意题目的要求是 according to the title，即从文章的标题来看，这篇文章的大意是什么？文章的标题是 Successful Online Learning，即"成功的网上学习"，因此全文应该是关于如何成功地通过网络进行学习，也即是 how to learn successfully through the Internet.
注意：What's the main idea of this passage/article/paragraph? 和 What is this passage/article/paragraph mainly about? 是阅读理解中常见的题型，称为主旨题，要求我们归纳全文或某一段的大意。要做好这种题，通常需要通读全文或全段内容，从整体上把握它的主要内容，但有时也可从标题、开头段、结尾段或各段的主题句当中获得比较明显的提示。

2. 【译文】读了文章的第一段之后，你知道接下来的段落会谈到什么内容吗？

   【答案】The following paragraphs can be divided into two parts. One is the differences between online and traditional courses, while the other is tips for success with online learning.

   【题解】第一段当中明确提到了本文的两个主要内容，即 differences between online and traditional courses 和 some tips for success with online courses。

3. 【译文】分别读一下第二至第六段的首句。从这些句子当中，我们可以知道网络学习的哪些情况？

   【答案】From these sentences we know the main differences of online and traditional courses, the advantages and disadvantages of online learning, and the demands made of a student for successful online learning.

   【题解】第三段和第四段的首句分别概括了 traditional courses 与 online courses 各自的特点，即二者的主要区别。第五段的首句说明 online courses 也有它的缺点，downfall 意为"下降、衰败、败落"。第六段的首句则指明网上学习需要学生有管理时间的能力和技巧，即对学生的要求。

4. 【译文】网络学习的关键点有哪些？

   【答案】They are: to participate, to be persistent, to think before you send, and to share tips, help and questions.

   【题解】这题要求我们找出 "the key points for online learning"。答案很明显，即带着重号，大写并加下划线的几点。

5. 【译文】这篇文章的大意是什么？

   【答案】This article talks about the differences between online and traditional courses, and suggests some tips for success with online courses.

   【题解】这道题要求我们在通读全文的基础上归纳文章大意。全文的内容可以总结为两点，即 differences（网络课程与传统课程的区别）和 tips（作者提出的有效进行网上课程学习的建议）。

写作技巧

练习

1. 指出本册书中的以下课文分别是以什么方法开头的。

答案：1. 直叙法　2. 故事法　3. 提问法　4. 举例法

2. 回顾该单元所学习的写作技巧，给题为"远程学习之我见"的文章写一个开头。

样文：

My View on Distance Learning

With the popularization of computer and information technology, distance education, though a new comer, has developed at a rather surprising speed in China and proved to be an effective way of learning.

Thanks to distance learning, many people in the poor areas could enjoy equal opportunities as their counterparts in the richer areas do. What's more, students in China are able to have access to the instruction that the students abroad have. Besides, online education gives adult students the flexibility to continue working, or take care of their families while further pursuing their study. On the whole, online education has distinctive advantages over traditional education. All you need is a computer to attend lectures and earn a degree.

In spite of its enormous achievements, compared to that in rich countries, distance learning in China is still far from perfect and thus should be improved in the following two aspects. First, the needed facilities like computers, information network for distance learning are still lacking in some rural areas and should be installed. Second, more knowledge and courses should be available through distance education so as to meet varied learners' needs.

语法知识

——形容词和副词

练习 选择最佳答案补全下列句子。

1. 【答案】D

   【题解】该题考查的是as... as结构的一种形式，即"as much + a +名词+as+分句"。如：George is as much a worker as Jack. 乔治与杰克一样是个工人。

   【译文】人们普遍认为教书与科学一样是一门艺术。

2. 【答案】B

   【题解】how often 多久一次，指频率；how soon 多久以后，指需要多长时间；how long 多长，多长时间，只能与延续性的动词连用，如：How long will you stay there? 你会在那儿呆多久？how many 多少，指数量。

   【译文】你还要多久才能完成这幅画？

3. 【答案】D

   【题解】so much 作副词"太，非常"时通常后置修饰动词。如：I love her so much. 我太爱她了。too much 可后置修饰动词，意为"太多"。如：He talked too much. 他说得太多了；也可前置修饰名词，意为"太多的"。如：There is too much salt in the soup. 汤里的盐太多。very 和so 不连用。much too 可以前置修饰形容词，指"非常，太……"。如：Amanda is much too young to get married. 阿曼达太年轻，结婚还太早。本题需要一个副词前置修饰形容词cold，故只能选D。

   【译文】我不会和你一起去的。今天实在太冷了。

4. 【答案】B

   【题解】much 是程度副词，放在形容词比较级的前面，指"……得多"。如：Henry's room is much bigger than mine. 亨利的房间比我的大得多。本题中less与后边的expensive 构成形容词的比较级，前面再加much，意为"便宜得多"。

   【译文】这种布料与丝绸一样柔软光滑，但却比丝绸便宜得多。

5.【答案】C

【题解】twice the size of 相当于twice as large as；类似地，four times the length of 相当于four times as long as。如：This river is twice the width of that one. 这条河是那条河的两倍宽。The new library is three times the size of the old one. 新图书馆是旧图书馆的三倍大。

【译文】这个小镇现在已经发展成为一个现代都市，面积也达到了原来的两倍。

6.【答案】D

【题解】本题考查形容词的次序。多个形容词作定语修饰一个名词，它们的次序往往比较固定。限定词一般都置于第一位，其他修饰语则常常根据其与名词的亲疏关系依次排列。它们的排列顺序一般是：限定词（包括冠词、物主代词、指示代词、不定代词等）→数词（先序数词、后基数词）→描绘形容词（短词在前，长词在后）→表特征的形容词（包括大小、形状、新旧、年龄等，词序也大致如此）→表颜色的形容词→表类属的形容词（包括专有形容词和表材料质地的形容词）+ 名词性定语 + 被修饰的名词。故D为正确答案。

【译文】屋子中央有一张漂亮的圆木桌。

7.【答案】A

【题解】本题仍然考查much +形容词比较级的结构，解答同第四题。much better 不合句意。需注意的是bad 的比较级是worse。badly 指"严重地、恶劣地"。

【译文】尽管约翰在考试中很努力，但还是考得比弟弟差得多。

8.【答案】C

【题解】本题主要考查farther 和further 作形容词时意义的区别。这两个词作形容词都可以表示"更远的"，但further还可表示"更进一步的"，有抽象的意义。而farther一般用于具体意义。如：We have decided to take no further action. 我们已经决定不采取进一步的行动。注意：这时不能用farther 替代further。

【译文】如果足球赛推迟进行的话，会有进一步的通知。

9.【答案】A

【题解】silent 沉默的，无声的；secret 秘密的；quiet 安静的，静止的；calm 平静的，沉着的。

【译文】我试图从他嘴里得到关于这项新技术的一些信息，但他却保持沉默。

10.【答案】A

【题解】enough作副词通常紧接在它所修饰的形容词的后面，故排除B、C、D。a long enough holiday 指"足够长的假期"。

【译文】如果我的假期够长的话，我会去欧洲游览，并在一些有趣的地方停留。

11.【答案】B

【题解】副词so 和such 修饰带有名词的形容词时，语序有所不同。后面是可数名词单数时，用"so+形容词+a+名词"；或"such+a+形容词+名词"。如：so nice a girl或such a nice girl. so强调形容词，such 强调名词。后面是可数名词复数或不可数名词时，用such。如：They're such nice people. 他们是这么好的人。such clear water 这么清的水。本题的music是不可数名词，故用such。

【译文】你曾听过如此美妙的音乐吗？

12.【答案】B

【题解】as well as表示同级比较，用于肯定句，表示"与……程度一样"。注意：在否定句中该结构要变为not so well as。如：John doesn't play basketball so well as David.

【译文】约翰篮球打得和大卫一样好，甚至比他更好。

13.【答案】D

　【题解】lately *adv.* 近来，最近；latter *adj.* 后面的，后者的；later *adj.* 更迟的，更后的，*adv.* 稍后，随后；late *adj.* 迟的，晚（期）的，已故的，新近的；*adv.* 晚，迟，最近，在晚期。本题需要副词修饰get up，意为"起床晚"，故选D。

　【译文】今天早上她起得晚。

14.【答案】C

　【题解】hardly... when...句型，意为"一……就……"。如：Hardly had she sat down when the phone rang. 她刚坐下电话铃就响了。Hardly had I opened the door when he told me. 我刚开开门，他就告诉了我。注意hardly 引起的句子用过去完成时并倒装，when引起的句子用一般过去时。

　【译文】他刚一进办公室就意识到自己把报告给忘了。

15.【答案】B

　【题解】本句需要在feel的后面补充一个词构成系表结构，形容词sleepy意为"困乏的，欲睡的"；形容词asleep通常出现在动词后面，意为"睡着的，睡熟的"，如fall asleep "睡着"。而A是动词"睡着，睡觉"，D是sleep的过去式。

　【译文】那个懒孩子总是在上课的时候犯困。

每课一练

Part I　Vocabulary & Structure

Directions: *There are 30 incomplete sentences in this part. For each sentence there are four choices marked A), B), C) and D). Choose the ONE that best completes the sentence.*

1. The accident was _____ to careless driving.

　A) for　　　　　B) likely　　　　　C) due　　　　　D) because

2. The news made the old lady very _____.

　A) sadder　　　　B) sad　　　　　C) sadly　　　　D) sadness

3. He stressed that the disadvantages of the change would _____ its advantages.

　A) overtake　　　B) outweigh　　　C) overcome　　　D) beyond

4. I can't find _____.

　A) a coat enough large　B) a large enough coat　C) a large coat enough　D) an enough large coat

5. Over a third of the population was estimated to have no _____ to the health service.

　A) assessment　　B) assignment　　　C) exception　　　D) access

6. —In our English study reading is more important than speaking, I think.

　—I don't agree with you. Speaking is _____ reading.

　A) as important as　B) so important as　C) the most important　D) the same as

7. His lectures on Roman history would do credit _____ a real expert.

　A) in　　　　　B) to　　　　　C) of　　　　　D) with

8. Someone is knocking at the door _____.

   A) aloud   B) loud   C) loudly   D) aloudly

9. I fail to _____ ever meeting her.

   A) recall   B) pretend   C) plan   D) hope

10. I was _____ by their kindness and moved to tears.

   A) preoccupied   B) embarrassed   C) overwhelmed   D) counseled

11. Doesn't the clown look _____?

   A) fun   B) laugh   C) laughter   D) funny

12. My camera can be _____ to take pictures in cloudy or sunny conditions.

   A) treated   B) adjusted   C) adapted   D) remedied

13. The football game comes to you _____ from New York .

   A) lively   B) alive   C) live   D) living

14. I try to _____ a few dollars each month in order to buy a new bike.

   A) set up   B) set out   C) set off   D) set aside

15. With _____ three inches of rain falling in a six-month period, the farmers found it necessary to irrigate the land.

   A) less than   B) fewer than   C) little than   D) less few than

16. Clark felt that his _____ in one of the most dramatic medical experiments of all time was worth the suffering he underwent.

   A) apprehension   B) appreciation   C) presentation   D) participation

17. He bought a _____ carpet yesterday.

   A) large beautiful green Chinese   B) Chinese beautiful large green

   C) beautiful large green Chinese   D) Chinese green beautiful large

18. He said that the driver must have had an accident; otherwise he _____ by then.

   A) would have arrived   B) must have arrived   C) should arrive   D) arrived

19. —I will give you some picture books.

   —The _____, the _____.

   A) more; better   B) many; better   C) most; best   D) much; better

20. It's very _____ of you not to talk aloud while the baby is asleep.

   A) concerned   B) careful   C) considerable   D) considerate

21. Don't blame the youth. I think the young generation is _____ of trust.

   A) worth   B) worthy   C) worthless   D) worthwhile

22. A healthy life is frequently thought to be _____ with the open countryside and home growth food.

   A) tied   B) bound   C) involved   D) associated

23. The new edition of this book is _____ expensive than the old one.

   A) fewer   B) more much   C) less   D) a little

24. Being deaf hasn't stopped Karen _____ her ambition to be a hairdresser.

   A) fulfilling   B) finishes   C) fulfills   D) finishing

25. This street is much _____ than that one.

   A) straight   B) straighter   C) straightest   D) more straighter

26. There are few scientific and technical books that are not _____ at our university library.

    A) available   B) bought   C) determined   D) valuable

27. Thomas said that he was late because he was caught in a traffic jam. That was a(n) _____ story.

    A) like   B) alike   C) likely   D) liking

28. You see the lightning _____ it happens, but you hear the thunder later.

    A) the instant   B) for an instant   C) on the instant   D) in an instant

29. When his wife and two little children left him, he was very _____.

    A) alone   B) along   C) lonely   D) lonelier

30. They regard these men as their _____ enemies.

    A) death   B) dead   C) deadly   D) deadlines

Part II   Reading Comprehension

Directions: *Read the following two passages. Answer the questions of each passage by choosing A), B), C) or D).*

Passage 1

    Soccer is played by millions of people all over the world, but there have only been few players who were truly great. How did these players get that way—was it through training and practice, or are great players born, not made? First, these players came from places that have had famous stars in the past—players that a young boy can look up to and try to imitate. In the history of soccer, only seven countries have ever won the World Cup—three from South America and four from Western Europe. Second, these players have all had years of practice in the game. Alfredo Di Stefano was the son of a soccer player, as was Pele. Most players begin playing the game at the age of three or four.

    Finally, many great players come from the same kind of neighborhood—a poor, crowded area where a boy's dream is not to be a doctor, lawyer, or businessman, but to become a rich, famous athlete or entertainer. For example, Liverpool which produced the Beatles (甲壳虫乐队), had one of the best English soccer teams in recent years. Pele practiced in the street with a "ball" made of rags. And George Best learned the tricks that made him famous by bouncing the ball off a wall in the slums (贫民窟) of Belfast.

    All great players have a lot in common, but that doesn't explain why they are great. Hundreds of boys played in those Brazilian streets, but only one became Pele. The greatest players are born with some unique quality that sets them apart from all the others.

1. According to the author, which of the following statements is TRUE?

    A) Great soccer players are born, not made.

    B) Truly great players are rare.

    C) Only six countries have ever had famous soccer stars.

    D) Soccer is the least popular sport in North America and Asia.

2. The word "trick" at the end of Paragraph Two is closest in meaning to "_____".

    A) experience   B) cheating

    C) skills   D) training

3. Pele is cited as an example in the second paragraph to illustrate that _____.

   A) famous soccer players live in slum areas

   B) people in poor areas are born with some unique quality

   C) children in poor areas start playing football at the age of three or four

   D) many great soccer players come from poor areas

4. From the statement "only one became Pele" in the last paragraph, we can learn that _____.

   A) Pele is the greatest soccer player

   B) the greatest players are born with some unique quality

   C) Pele's birthplace sets him apart from all the other players

   D) the greatest players practice with "balls" made of rags

5. Which of the following is NOT included in the factors of a soccer player's success?

   A) His family background.

   B) His neighborhood.

   C) His practice.

   D) His height.

Passage 2

If you want to stay young, sit down and have a good think. This is the research finding of a team of Japanese doctors, who say that most of our brains are not getting enough exercise—and as a result, we are aging unnecessarily soon.

Professor Taiju Matsuzawa wanted to find out why otherwise healthy farmers in northern Japan appeared to be losing their ability to think and reason at a relatively early age, and how the process of aging could be slowed down.

With a team of colleagues at Tokyo National University, he set about measuring brain volumes of a thousand people of different ages and varying occupations.

Computer technology enabled the researchers to obtain precise measurements of the volume of the front and side sections of the brain, which relate to intellect and emotion, and determine the human character. (The rear section of the brain, which controls functions like eating and breathing, does not contract with age, and one can continue living without intellectual or emotional faculties.)

Contraction of front and side parts was observed in some subjects in their thirties, but it was still not evident in some sixty and seventy-year-olds.

Matsuzawa concluded from his tests that there is a simple remedy to the contraction normally associated with age—using the head.

The findings show in general terms that contraction of the brain begins sooner in people in the country than in the towns. Those least at risk, says Matsuzawa, are lawyers, followed by university professors and doctors. White collar workers doing routine work in government offices are, however, as likely to have shrinking brains as farm workers, bus drivers and shop assistants.

Matsuzawa's findings show that thinking can prevent the brain from shrinking. Blood must circulate properly in the head to supply the fresh oxygen the brain cells need. "The best way to maintain good blood circulation is through using the brain," he says. "Think hard and engage in conversation. Don't rely on pocket calculators."

6.The team of doctors wanted to find out _____.

   A) why certain people age sooner than others

   B) how to make people live longer

   C) the size of certain people's brains

   D) which people are most intelligent

7.On what are their research findings based?

   A) A survey of farmers in northern Japan.

   B) Tests performed on a thousand old people.

   C) The study of brain volumes of different people.

   D) The latest development of computer technology.

8.The doctor's tests show that _____.

   A) our brains shrink as we grow older

   B) the front section of the brain does not shrink

   C) sixty-year-olds have better brains than thirty-year-olds

   D) some people's brains have contracted more than other people's

9.The word "subjects" in Paragraph Five means _____.

   A) something to be considered

   B) branches of knowledge studied

   C) persons chosen to be studied in an experiment

   D) any member of a state except the supreme ruler

10.According to the passage, which people seem to age slower than others?

   A) Lawyers.　　　　 B) Farmers.　　　　 C) Clerks.　　　　 D) Shop assistants.

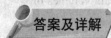 **答案及详解**

第一部分　词汇与结构

1. 【答案】C

   【题解】due to是固定搭配，意为"由于，因……而产生"。

   【译文】这起事故起因于粗心驾驶。

2. 【答案】B

   【题解】此题考查形容词作补语；而且very不能修饰比较级；在这里sad作宾语补语。

   【译文】这消息让老妇人非常伤心。

3. 【答案】B

   【题解】outweigh 比……重要，胜过，强过；overtake 赶上，追上；overcome 克服；beyond 是介词表示"超过"。

   【译文】他强调改变带来的问题可能多过它带来的好处。

4. 【答案】B

   【题解】此题考查enough的位置。enough *adv.* 表示"足够地，充分地"，放在所修饰的形容词后。

   【译文】我找不到一件足够大的外套。

5. 【答案】D

【题解】access to 使用，接近，或进入之途径或权利；assessment *n.* 估价；assignment *n.* 任务；exception *n.* 例外。

【译文】估计有1/3以上的人口享受不到医疗健康服务。

6. 【答案】A

【题解】此题考查"同等比较"的用法，句式中的"as... as..."结构意为"……和……一样"，其中的形容词或副词用原级。

【译文】——我认为英语学习中读比说重要。

——我不这么认为。说和读是同等重要的。

7. 【答案】B

【题解】do credit to 表示"为……带来光荣（荣誉）"。

【译文】他关于罗马史的讲座成就了他的专家美誉。

8. 【答案】C

【题解】此题考查副词的辨析。aloud *adv.* 大声地，与cry，call，shout一类动词连用；loud *adv.* 高声地，与talk，speak，laugh，read等动词连用，放在动词之后；loudly *adv.* 响亮地，大声地，使用范围较广，有时有"喧闹"的意味。

【译文】有人在大声敲门。

9. 【答案】A

【题解】此题考查动词的辨析。recall 后面有宾语时，要接动名词形式；pretend 假装；plan 计划；hope 希望。

【译文】我想不起曾经见过她。

10. 【答案】C

【题解】此题考查动词词义辨析。preoccupy 使全神贯注；embarrass 使窘迫；overwhelm 使不知所措；counsel 劝告。

【译文】他们的善意深深地感动了我，使我热泪盈眶。

11. 【答案】D

【题解】此题考查形容词作表语。感官，感觉动词后面要求用形容词作表语，常见的有see，appear，look，sound，smell，taste，feel等。

【译文】这个小丑看上去不滑稽么？

12. 【答案】B

【题解】此题考查动词词义辨析。treat 对待，处理；adjust 调整，调节；adapt 使适应；remedy 治疗，纠正。

【译文】我的照相机可以调节，不论阴天还是晴天都可以照相。

13. 【答案】C

【题解】此题考查形容词辨析。lively 活泼的,活跃的；alive 活着的,活泼的；live 活的,生动的,精力充沛的,实况转播的；living 活的,起作用的,逼真的,现存的。

【译文】这场足球赛是从纽约实况转播的。

14. 【答案】D

【题解】set aside 留出（专用的时间或金钱）；set up 建立；set out 出发，开始；set off 出发，动身。

【译文】为了买一辆新的自行车，我试着每个月都留出一些钱。

15. 【答案】A

【题解】此题考查比较级的用法。C和D两个选项是错误的表达。A选项中less为little的比较级，通常与不可数名词连用。B选项中fewer为few的比较级，与可数名词连用。less than意思是"少于……"，属于固定搭配。此句中rain为不可数名词，因此选A。

【译文】由于在六个月里的降水量只有不到三英寸，农民们感到有必要灌溉农田了。

16. 【答案】D

【题解】此题考查后缀 -tion和 -sion构成的名词辨析。apprehension 理解；appreciation 欣赏；presentation 陈述；participation 参与。

【译文】克拉克认为能参加有史以来最令人激动的医学实验，再苦也值得。

17. 【答案】C

【题解】此题考查数个形容词同时修饰一个名词时的排序。一般是"表示特性的词（nice, good, etc.）＋大小＋年龄＋形状＋颜色＋国籍、地区、出处"，如：the tall young American policeman。

【译文】他昨天买了一大块非常漂亮的绿色中国地毯。

18. 【答案】A

【题解】otherwise 引出与过去事实相反的虚拟语气。

【译文】他说司机一定出事了，要不然那时他应该已经到了。

19. 【答案】A

【题解】此题考查"the ＋比较级……，the ＋比较级……"结构的用法。

【译文】——我会给你一些图画书。
——越多越好。

20. 【答案】D

【题解】此题考查形容词的辨析。considerate 考虑周到的；be concerned for/about/with 对……关心；be careful of/about/with 对……当心；considerable 相当大（多）的，值得考虑的。

【译文】婴儿睡着了你就压低了音量，你真是考虑得太周到了。

21. 【答案】B

【题解】此题考查worth及其同根词的辨析。worth *adj.* 有某种价值，值得（做某事），be worth (doing) sth.; worthy *adj.* 值得……的，应……的，be worthy of sth.; worthless *adj.*无价值的，无益的；worthwhile *adj.* 值得做的，值得出力的，be worthwhile doing/to do sth.。

【译文】不要责怪年轻人。我认为年轻一代应该得到信任。

22. 【答案】D

【题解】tie 和involve不与with搭配，bound可以作"联系"讲，但是搭配是be bound up with。

【译文】人们常常把健康的生活与开阔的乡村和自家种的食物联系在一起。

23. 【答案】C

【题解】此题考查形容词比较级。

【译文】这本书的新版本比旧版本便宜。

24. 【答案】A

【题解】fulfill 实现；finish 完成。

【译文】耳聋并没有能阻碍凯伦实现她的目标成为一名理发师。

25.【答案】B

【题解】此题考查much，even，still，far，a lot，a great deal等程度副词(短语)修饰形容词或副词比较级的用法，句中常用"程度副词（短语）+形容词/副词的比较级+than..."结构。

【译文】这条街比那一条直多了。

26.【答案】A

【题解】available 可用到的, 可利用的；bought 是buy的过去分词；determine 决定，下决心；valuable 有价值的。

【译文】在我们大学的图书馆，几乎没有什么科学技术方面的书是找不到的。

27.【答案】C

【题解】此题考查词语辨析. like *n.* 同样的人（或物）, *adj.* 相似的；alike *adj.* 相似的；likely *adj.* 很可能的, 有希望的；liking *n.* 爱好, 嗜好。

【译文】托马斯说他是因为交通堵塞才迟到的。这是很有可能的。

28.【答案】A

【题解】the instant 相当于when的用法。on the instant 立即, 马上；for an instant 有一会儿。

【译文】闪电一发生你就看到光, 但过一会你才听到雷声。

29.【答案】C

【题解】此题考查alone和lonely的辨析。alone 独自一人的, 孤单一人的, 通常用作表语形容词；lonely 孤独的, 寂寞的, 通常用作定语形容词。

【译文】妻子和两个孩子离他而去后, 他很孤独。

30.【答案】C

【题解】此题考查词语辨析。death *n.* 死, 死亡；dead *adj.* 死的, 无感觉的, 呆板的；deadly *adj.* 致命的, 势不两立的；deadline *n.* 最终期限。

【译文】他们把这些人看作他们的死对头。

第二部分　阅读理解

1.【答案】B

【题解】推断题。根据文章第一段第一句 "... but there have only been few players who were truly great"（真正伟大的足球运动员毕竟是少数）, 选 B。

2.【答案】C

【题解】推断题。tricks本义是指"诡计", 从上下文可以推断出在句中指踢球的技巧, 所以C项符合题意。

3.【答案】D

【题解】推断题。根据文章第二段中 "many great players come from the same kind of neighborhood—a poor, crowded area..."（很多优秀的足球运动员都来自于贫穷的社会底层）, 选D。

4.【答案】B

【题解】细节题。根据文章最后一句话 "The greatest players are born with some unique quality that sets them apart from all the others."（最伟大的运动员拥有让他们不同于其他人的特有的天赋）, 选B。

5.【答案】D

　　【题解】细节题。文章第一段中"these players have all had years of practice in the game"（这些球员常年踢球，经验很丰富），符合C选项。而第二段中"many great players come from the same kind of neighborhood—a poor, crowded area"则告诉读者"很多优秀的足球运动员都来自同样的聚居区——贫困，嘈杂的社会底层"，这与A，B两项的内容相吻合。只有D项没有被提及，故选D。

6.【答案】A

　　【题解】细节题。根据第二段中"Professor Taiju Matsuzawa wanted to find out..."（教授试图找出为什么生活在日本北部身体健康的农夫们似乎正在丧失思考和推理的能力，以及如何能够减慢衰老的过程），选A。

7.【答案】C

　　【题解】推断题。根据第四段第一句话"Computer technology enabled the researchers to obtain precise measurements of the volume of the front and side sections of the brain..."（计算机技术的发展使我们可以准确地测量人脑的容积，但是研究者的研究基础并不是计算机的发展而是对人大脑容积的测量研究），选C。

8.【答案】A

　　【题解】细节题。从文章的第五段中"Contraction of front and side parts was observed..."和第六段中"... the contraction normally associated with age—using the head"，可知随着年龄增大，大脑容积会有萎缩，故A正确。D答案比较有迷惑性，但是文中第七段指出有些人的大脑萎缩得比较早，而不是有些人的大脑萎缩得比较多。

9.【答案】C

　　【题解】推断题。根据 subjects 后面出现的"in their thirties, ... some sixty-and-seventy-year-olds"，可以推断出 subjects 指参加实验的研究对象。

10.【答案】A

　　【题解】推断题。根据文章的第七段中"Those least at risk, says Matsuzawa, are lawyers, followed by university professors and doctors"，律师是这几类人中衰老最慢的，所以选A。

2 Culture Shock

单元导读

当一个人到达一个全新的地方，接触一种全新的文化，突然发现一切都与过去熟悉的事物迥然不同，以往的生活经验不管用了，这时绝大多数人都会经历一种心理上的迷惑，生理上的震撼，这就是"文化冲击"。任何一个在异国学习、生活或是工作的人都会不同程度地感受到文化冲击。面对这样的冲击，需要去调整适应的方面很多，从饮食、语言到风俗文化，甚至包括诸如打电话、使用取款机这样的小事。不管你有多么好的耐心，也不管你适应能力有多么的强，有时候，适应一种新的文化的过程可能会非常困难且令人沮丧。你很容易就会产生失落感，意志消沉，思乡心切。你甚至想要回家。

尽管这一过程会让你感到痛苦，但同时这也是了解不同文化的机会，更是看到一个全新的自己、激发创造力的机会。

课文精讲

文章导读

瑞安五年前来到了中国，成为了一名外籍客座教师。在这个历史悠久的国度里，瑞安也体验到了来自于方方面面的文化冲击。可是最大的挑战却在他的本质工作——课堂上。文章中瑞安回忆了自己在中国的教学经历：从第一次上课的尴尬，到取得突破性进展。作者以事情的发展顺序记录、描写了这一过程。

背景知识

中国教育思想和传统与西方存在着较大差异。关键源于文化价值取向的不同。如西方社会高度推崇个人主义、个人自由，所以在西方国家的课堂里，往往是老师讲得少，学生讲得多。而中国的传统文化则提倡个人服从群体的利益，把个人融入到群体之中。所谓"一日为师终身为父"，师生关系是父子关系的外化，是极受重视的人伦关系，而且也有一系列师生伦理的行为准则。在这样的文化背景中，要建立起完全在形式上平等的师生关系是很不容易的。由此，在课堂文化生活中，中国的孩子更愿意深思熟虑，让别人先讲，先听听别人的意见，即使别人说错了，也不愿意直截了当地指出别人的错误，而是婉转地表达自己的意见。

文章写作风格及结构

本文为一篇记叙文，作者身为在中国教英语的外籍客座教师，叙述了五年前其学生如何在课堂上遭遇文化冲击，他又是如何帮助学生应对文化冲击，改变思维方式，把英语视为活生生的语言来学习，从而取得进步的。选材贴近生活，为个人亲身体验，故行文流畅，条理清晰，语言生动而不失诙谐。

Parts 部分	Paragraphs 段落	Main Ideas 大意
Part I	1	Visiting teachers in China must deal with a lot of challenges. 外籍客座教师在中国难免要应对众多挑战。
Part II	2—6	The great challenge "I" have been faced with: Classroom Culture Shock. 追述"我"所面临的挑战：课堂上的文化冲击。

词汇点睛

1 challenge

n. sth. that tests strength, skill or ability especially in a way that is interesting 挑战

• 例句 • She refused to take up the challenge that was offered. 她拒绝了别人向她提出的挑战。

The government will have to meet the challenge of rising unemployment.

政府将不可避免地面对失业人口增加的挑战。

2 belief

n. an idea that you believe to be true, especially one that forms part of a system of ideas 信仰，信念

• 例句 • He acted in accordance with his beliefs. 他按照自己的信念行事。

He came to me in the belief that I could help him. 他到我这里来，相信我能帮助他。

• 反义词 • **disbelief** *n.* 不相信，怀疑

She looked at him in disbelief. 她怀疑地看着他。

He listened in disbelief to this extraordinary story. 他满腹疑惑地听着这个离奇的故事。

3 initial

adj. of or at the beginning, first 开始的，最初的

• 例句 • "D" is the initial letter of the word "day". "day" 一词的首字母是 "d"。

My initial reaction was to refuse. 我最初的反应是拒绝。

4 ponder

v. to spend time thinking carefully and seriously about a problem, a difficult question, or sth. that has happened 沉思，考虑

• 例句 • You have pondered long enough; it is time to decide. 你考虑的时间够长了，该作决定了。

He spent the day pondering the steps to be taken. 他一整天都在思索该采取的步骤。

• 同义词 • **meditate** *vt.* 考虑，思索

It is important to meditate on the meaning of life. 思考人生的意义很重要。

5　effectiveness

n. success of sth. in the way that was intended　有效性，效力

• 例句 • There are doubts about the effectiveness of the new drug in treating the disease.
关于这款新药治疗这种疾病的有效性，大家还存有疑虑。
I doubt the effectiveness of the medicine. 我怀疑这个药的疗效。

• 扩展 • **effect** *n.* 效果，作用
It failed to bring about the desired effect. 它未能产生预期的效果。
effective *adj.* 有效的
The government should take effective measures to reduce unemployment.
政府应该采取有效措施来减少失业。

• 辨析 • **efficiency** *n.* 效率，功效
The program was implemented with great efficiency and speed.
这个项目实施的效率和速度极高。

6　approach

n. a method of doing sth. or dealing with a problem　方法，途径

• 例句 • That player's approach to the music is quite different from anyone else's.
那个演奏者处理乐曲的方式跟别人很不同。
The problem needs a new approach.
这个问题需要用新的方法解决。

7　implement

vt. to take action to achieve sth. that you have decided should happen　执行，贯彻

• 例句 • We have decided to implement the committee's suggestions.
我们已决定实施委员会提出的建议。

8　forthcoming

adj. 1) willing to give information or an explanation about sth.　坦率的

• 例句 • The secretary at the reception was not very forthcoming. 接待处的秘书不太主动。

　　　　2) about to appear or take place　即将出现或发生的

• 例句 • He is a potential vote-winner in the forthcoming election.
他在即将举行的选举中很可能获胜。

9　minor

adj. small and not very important or serious, especially when compared with other things 较小的，
较少的

• 例句 • He received only minor injuries. 他只是受了些轻伤。
He left most of his money to his sons; his daughter received only a minor share of his wealth.
他把大部分的钱都留给了他的几个儿子；他女儿只拿到了其中的一小部分。

• 反义词 • **major** *adj.* （较）重要的；（较）大的；主要的
The car needs major repairs. 这辆车该大修了。
Liverpool is a major British port. 利物浦是英国的一个重要港口。

10   confess

v. to admit sth. that you feel embarrassed about 坦白，供认；承认

• 例句 • He confessed that he had done it. 他承认他干了这件事。

The man in the corner confessed to having told a lie to the manager of the company.

角落里那个人承认自己对公司经理撒了谎。

She confessed herself to be guilty. 她承认自己有罪。

• 辨析 • **acknowledge, admit, confess**

acknowledge为普通用语，着重公开承认某事的真实性，承认事实或某事的存在。

admit常含有被迫或不情愿之意，指因屈服于外界某种压力或者受到良心的谴责等而承认。

confess主要指承认自己的过错、罪行或隐私等，有"坦白"的含义。

They acknowledged having been defeated. 他们承认已经被打败了。

She admitted having read the letter. 她承认读过那封信。

We have to admit that he's a highly competent man. 我们不得不承认他是一个能力很强的人。

She finally confessed to having stolen the money. 最后她招认偷了那笔钱。

11   assign

vt. to give sb. a particular job or make them responsible for a particular person or thing

分配，指派

• 例句 • The hardest work was assigned to the strongest laborers. 最繁重的工作被分配给最强壮的劳工。

The teacher has assigned each of us a holiday task. 老师给我们每个人都安排了假期的任务。

They've assigned their best man to the job. 他们选派了他们中最优秀的人做那项工作。

• 扩展 • **assignment** *n.* （分派的）任务，（指定的）作业

You must complete this assignment by tomorrow. 你必须在明天前完成这个任务。

• 辨析 • **assign, allocate, divide, distribute**

assign 是正式用语，多指上级给下级或当权人给其控制的人分配工作、任务等。

allocate是正式用语，尤其指某执政团体为某个政府计划拨出专款。

divide含义广泛，表示根据计划或目的将某物分成若干份分发，常是平等的。

distribute指将一定数量的东西分成若干份，通常各份的量不一定相等，然后按预定计划进行分发。

A portion of the budget was allocated for the education of each student.

预算的一部分被划分出来留作每一个学生的教育费用。

The estate will be divided among the heirs. 财产将被分发到继承者手中。

In the 19th century the government distributed land to settlers willing to cultivate it.

在19世纪，政府将土地分发给愿意耕种的定居者。

12   acknowledge

vt. 1) to show sb. that you have noticed them or heard what they have said 注意到

• 例句 • I was standing right next to her, but she didn't even acknowledge my presence.

我就站在她旁边，可是她连个招呼都不跟我打。

    2) to admit or accept that sth. is true or that a situation exists 承认

• 例句 • I acknowledge the truth of your statement. 我承认你所说的是事实。

He acknowledged his faults. 他承认了错误。

13　breakthrough

n. important, or significant, progress in sth. you are studying or doing, especially that made after trying for a long time 突破

- 例句 • The company looks ready to make a significant breakthrough in China.
  这家公司看起来已经准备好要在中国进行重大突破。
  It's a major breakthrough in computer technology. 这是电脑技术上的一项重大突破。

14　awareness

n. knowledge or understanding of a particular subject or situation 意识，知道

- 例句 • Do you have any awareness of your ignorance? 你意识到自己的无知了吗？
  Health officials have tried to raise awareness about AIDS.
  健康官员尽力来提高公众对艾滋病的了解。

- 扩展 • **aware** *adj.* 意识到的
  It was several minutes before I was aware of what was happening.
  过了几分钟，我才意识到出事了。
  Is he aware that what he is doing is illegal? 他意识到自己做的事是违法的了吗？

短语解析

1. be in full swing　正在积极进行

【例句】The meeting was in full swing when we arrived. 当我们到达时，会议进行得正热闹。

2. be determined to　下定决心做……

【例句】Tom is working hard because he is determined to pass the exam.
汤姆正在用功学习，因为他决心要通过考试。
I left him, determined never to set foot in that house again.
我离开了他，决心再也不进那个房子了。

难句突破

1. (Para.1) *Many of them are expected—language barrier, different values and beliefs, chopsticks.*

【解析】句中的them指代前文提到的challenges，而非teachers。

【译文】其中很多挑战是预料之中的——语言障碍、价值观和信仰不同、以及如何使用筷子等。

2. (Para.1) *Others are surprising—the hazards of crossing the street, the stares, chou doufu.*

【解析】others此处指代other challenges。

other 与others的区别：

　　other泛指"另外的"，用作定语，常与复数名词或单数不可数名词连用。例如：other teachers, some other time。但如果前面有the, this, that, some, any, each, every, no, none, one, or以及形容词性物主代词时，则可与单数名词连用。例如：all other rice, no other way, every other day等等。如：

He likes traveling abroad and learning about other people's customs and traditions.

他喜欢去国外旅游，了解别人的风俗和传统。

I've no cash. Is there any other way of paying? 我没有现金，有没有其他的支付方式呢？

　　others意思是其他的人或物，作代词泛指"别的人或物"（但不是全部）。如：

Don't lend the book to others. 别把书借给其他人。

Some are carrying water; others are watering the trees. 一些人在挑水，其他人在给树浇水。

【译文】但另外一些却是始料不及的——如过马路时的危险、路人注视的眼光、臭豆腐等。

3. (Para.2) *I recall walking confidently to my first Oral English class five years ago, armed with all the modern methodology I learned in school and a lesson plan stolen from an ESL expert.*

【解析】1) arm... with...: 用……武装，向……提供，带着

armed with... 过去分词作伴随状语，表示我是怀揣着从专家那里"窃"来的教案走进教室的。

2) modern methodology由定语从句(that) I learned in school修饰，其中连接词that省略。and连接两个并列的成分modern methodology和a lesson plan，而a lesson plan又由后置的分词短语stolen from an ESL expert修饰。

【译文】我还记得五年前我第一次走进"英语口语课"课堂的情形。当时我已掌握了学校里学到的所有的现代教学方法，怀揣着从一位二语习得专家那里"窃"来的教案，信心十足地走进了教室。

4. (Para.2) *My initial instructions were greeted by wide-eyed wonder and silence, followed by giggles, ending in nervous chatter that didn't sound completely friendly.*

【解析】ending in nervous chatter... 现在分词作状语表结果。其中chatter又被定语从句that didn't sound completely friendly修饰。

【译文】我在上课之初向学生发出指令，得到的反应是：大家先是目瞪口呆、鸦雀无声，接着是阵阵窃笑，最后是神情紧张地私语，听上去还不怎么友好。

5. (Para.2) *All I had asked them to do was throw their books in the corner, push all the desks away, and put their chairs in a circle.*

【解析】本句的主语是all I had asked them to do，是主语从句。

主语从句通常由从属连词that，whether，if 和连接代词what，who，which，whatever，whoever以及连接副词how，when，where，why等词引导。如：

That the volleyball match will be put off is certain now.

排球赛要被推迟这件事已经确定下来了。

Whether Mr. Smith will go to attend the meeting depends on the weather.

史密斯先生是否要去参加会议取决于天气情况。

What Mr. Wang has said has nothing to do with the case. 王先生说的和本案无关。

Who will go to attend the meeting to be held in Beijing hasn't been decided yet.

还没有确定谁将去参加在北京召开的会议。

【译文】我让他们所做的只不过是把书丢到角落里，把桌子推到一旁，再把椅子围成一个圈而已。

6. (Para.4) *I took it upon myself to observe some more "traditional" English classes and saw very few traces of the techniques I planned to use.*

【解析】 1) 本句是由and连接的并列句，主干结构为I took it... and I saw...；其中techniques由省略了that的定语从句I planned to use修饰。

2) sb. take sth. upon oneself: 某人决定自己做某事，承担某事

【译文】 我毅然决定对一些更为"传统"的英语课堂进行观察，却没有找到任何有关我打算运用的教学方法的影子。

7. (Para.4) *My first class had been a shock, to students and teacher, so for the next class I was more forthcoming in what I expected, and why.*

【解析】 ... in what I expected是由what引导的宾语从句，作介词in的宾语。why同样引导宾语从句作介词in的宾语，这里是省略形式，其完整形式应该是in what I expected, and why I expected。

如果宾语从句作介词的宾语，则引导词只限于who, why, how等疑问词，不能用that连接。如：

William hasn't the least interest in what the chemistry teacher is saying.

威廉对于化学老师在讲什么一点也不感兴趣。

The decision depends on who will carry it out. 这个决定取决于谁来执行。

【译文】 我的第一堂课不管对学生还是对老师来讲都带来了某种冲击，所以接下来的那堂课上我更为坦率地向学生们说明了我的要求，也解释了提出这些要求的原因。

8. (Para.4) *This all took a little more chewing than expected, but they seemed to swallow it and were willing to try things my way.*

【解析】 1) expected 是省略形式，本句完整的形式应该是 ... than I had expected，表示比"我原来预想的时间要长一些"。

2) be willing to do sth.: 愿意做某事

3) seem to表示"看上去好像……"。如：

I can't seem to get the story straight. 我好像不能理解这个故事。

I can't seem to stop coughing. 我的咳嗽看来止不住了。

【译文】 学生们领会这些话所花的时间比我预想的要长一些，但是，他们似乎勉强接受了我的方式，而且愿意试着按我的方式来做。

9. (Para.6) *What I found was a group of intelligent young people with all the skills to speak proper English and none of the confidence.*

【解析】 1) 句子的主语是一个what引导的主语从句，and引导并列的两个介词短语修饰young people，这两个介词短语分别是：with all the skills to speak proper English和(with) none of the confidence。

2) none作为代词一般和of连用表示完全否定，文中用以指代后文的confidence。如：

None of the money is mine! 这笔钱没有一点是我的。

None of my children has/have blonde hair. 我的子女中没有一个是金发。

【译文】 结果我发现，这些年轻人都很聪明，而且具备了讲出一口地道英语的所有技能，但他们都没有自信。

10. (Para.6) *Understanding this, I took a more nurturing tone in the classroom.*

【解析】understanding this现在分词短语作状语表原因。解析详见Unit 1，Text B难句突破3。

【译文】了解这一点之后，我在课堂上采用了更加循循善诱的口吻。

11. (Para.6) *I became more of a kind-hearted coach than a teacher.*

【解析】1) 句子结构中包含一个比较的成分more... than...，表示我变得更像是一个教练而非一个老师。

2) "be + of + 名词"的结构中，名词表示种类、数量、度量等时，表示不同的人或物的共同特征，此时名词前通常带有冠词。如：

We are of the same age. 我们同岁。

The twin sisters are of a size and the skirt fits each of them exactly.

双胞胎姐妹的身材一样，这件裙子两个人穿都非常合适。

【译文】我更像是一个好心的教练，而不是老师了。

12. (Para.7) *More and more of them realize their time and effort spent studying English has little value if they do not use it to communicate.*

【解析】本句主语是 more and more of them，谓语动词是 realize；their time and effort... use it to communicate 是复合句作 realize 的宾语。在这个复合句中包含一个由 if 引导的条件状语从句，以及过去分词 spent studying English 充当的定语修饰 time and effort。

【译文】越来越多的学生认识到，英语如果不用来交流，那么他们在英语学习上所花费的时间和精力就没有多大的价值。

参考译文

课堂里的文化冲击
瑞安·斯莱克

外籍客座教师在中国难免要应对众多挑战。其中很多挑战是预料之中的——如语言障碍、价值观和信仰不同、如何使用筷子等。但另外一些却是始料不及的——如过马路时的危险、路人注视的眼光、臭豆腐等。我们学习一些中文词语，研究过马路的策略，并且躲开卖臭豆腐的小摊。然而，最大的挑战还是在课堂里。

我还记得五年前第一次上"英语口语课"的情形。当时我已经掌握了学校里学过的各种现代教学方法，怀揣着从一位二语习得专家那里"窃"来的教案，信心十足地走进了教室。然而情况却极度糟糕。我在上课之初向学生发出的指令，得到的反应是：大家先是目瞪口呆、鸦雀无声，接着是阵阵窃笑，最后是神情紧张地私语，听上去还不怎么友好。我不明白哪里出了问题。我让他们所做的只不过是把书丢到角落里，把桌子推到一旁，再把椅子围成一个圈而已。

第一次课是两个课时，而实际上肯定至少持续了四个课时。下课之后，我感到有必要回到家里，躺下来，去思考这些意料之外、从未经历过的事情。当时我想到了许多。首先，我仍有很多东西要学。其次，这次是学生而不是我遭遇到了文化冲击。

我毅然决定对一些更为"传统"的英语课堂进行观察，但却没有找到任何我原来打算要用的教学方法的影子。尽管我仍然认为以学生为中心的交际教学法是有效的，但我也意识到要将此方法付诸实践却很难。我的第一堂课不管对学生还是对老师来讲都带来了某种冲击，所以接下来的那堂课上我更为坦率地向学生们说明了我的要求，也解释了提出这些要求的原由。我不了解中国是怎样的情况，但我知道在美国，如果我强迫学生开口讲话，我就会被炒鱿鱼，所以我向他们解释道，能否开口说英语是只有他们自己才能负责的事情。然后，我坦言我没有什么新东西教给他们，而且我会尽可能地少说话。我的这些话又让他们感受到了小小的文化冲击。学生们领会这些话所花的时间比我预想的要长一些，但是，他们似乎勉强接受了我的方式，而且愿意试着按我的方式来做。

于是他们围坐成一圈听我讲本节课的安排，并不时地认真点着头。接着，学生们分成了几组，任务也安排了下去。现在，热烈的讨论和激烈的辩论随时都可以展开了。但是，教室里却又一次陷入了沉寂。没人愿意说话。

我取消了接下来的那节课，改为在我的校区公寓里单独和每位学生面谈。我决心要弄明白这究竟是怎么回事。结果我发现，这些年轻人都很聪明，而且具备了讲出一口地道英语的所有技能，但他们都没有自信。了解这一点之后，我在课堂上采用了更加循循善诱的口吻。我更像是一个好心的教练，而不是老师了。对于他们最细小的成功，我都予以肯定和赞扬。而针对错误，我只是记下来，并不当着全班的面给予纠正。每个人都在鼓励之下参与课堂活动，就连坐在角落里的那些害羞的女生们也愿意说上几句英语了。期末的时候，我在走进教室之前就能听见学生们讲英语了。我的课终于取得了突破性的进展。

五年来，我注意到中国的大学生逐渐对英语有了更深的认识。越来越多的学生认识到，英语如果不用来交流，那么他们在英语学习上所花费的时间和精力就没有多大的价值。虽然仍然有同学哀叹说英语不过是工具而已，但同时他们也知道有了斧子未必就能成为好木匠这个道理。大家把英语作为活生生的语言来学习，这是一个巨大的进步。要是现在我也喜欢上臭豆腐就好了。

习题全解

文章大意

1. 根据课文用适当的词填空。

【答案】
1) five
2) effectiveness
3) students
4) individually
5) intelligent
6) breakthrough

【解析】 seem to...：看上去；似乎

according to sb.: 对某人而言，某人认为

find sb./sth. + adj. 是find＋宾语＋形容词作宾补的结构，表示"发现某人/某事具有……的特性/特征"。

take responsibility for: 对……负责

【译文】 作者五年前开始在中国教英语。然而刚开始他的学生似乎并不接受他的教学方法。在经过大量的思考与观察之后，作者仍然相信以学生为中心的交际法是有效的。他认为能否开口说英语是只有学生自己才能负责的事情。为了说服学生接受他的方法，作者单独和每位学生面谈。他发现他的学生都很聪明。他们仅仅是在说英语的时候没有自信——这就是他们

为什么在他的英语口语课上保持沉默的原因。为了让学生开口说英语，作者作了大量努力，终于取得突破性进展。

文章细节

1. 根据课文回答下列问题。

【答案】

1) The language barrier, different values and beliefs, the hazards of crossing the street, the stares, etc. (Para. 1)

2) The author began to teach in China five years ago, and the subject he taught was Oral English. (Para. 2)

3) Something went terribly wrong in his first Oral English class. It seemed that his students didn't like his modern teaching methodology. (Para. 2)

4) He went home, lay down, and pondered the unusual happenings in his first class. He also observed some "traditional" English classes. However, he still believed in the effectiveness of the communicative approach and was not ready to change his teaching method. (Para. 3)

5) He told them what he expected and explained why. According to him, speaking English was something only the students could take responsibility for. The students, although finding it hard to understand at first, were willing to accept his teaching method. (Para. 4)

6) They were intelligent people with all the skills to speak proper English. However, they had no confidence and, therefore, they just kept silent in his Oral English class. (Para. 6)

7) He took a more nurturing tone in the classroom. Even the smallest successes were acknowledged and praised. Mistakes were noted, but not publicly corrected. Everybody was encouraged to participate. (Para. 6)

【译文】

1) [问题] 对于作者来说外籍客座教师在中国要应付哪些挑战？
   [答案] 语言障碍、价值观和信仰不同、过马路时的危险、路人注视的眼光等。

2) [问题] 作者何时开始在中国教书的？他教什么课程？
   [答案] 作者五年前开始在中国教书，他教授的课程是英语口语。

3) [问题] 在他的第一堂口语课上发生了什么？他的学生喜欢上他的课么？
   [答案] 他的第一堂英语口语课极其糟糕。他的学生似乎不喜欢他的现代教学法。

4) [问题] 课后他做了什么？他准备改变他的教学方法么？
   [答案] 他回到家里，躺下来，思考第一堂课上不同寻常的状况。他也对一些传统的英语课进行观察，但仍然相信交际法是有效的，并且不准备改变他的教学方法。

5) [问题] 在第二堂课上他对学生说了什么？这一次学生们接受了他的方法么？
   [答案] 他向学生们说明了他的要求，也解释了提出这些要求的原由。作者认为能否开口说英语是只有学生自己才能负责的事情。虽然学生们觉得一开始难于理解，可是他们还是愿意接受他的教学方法。

6) [问题] 作者发现他的学生们问题何在？他们为什么在口语课上总是保持沉默？
   [答案] 这些年轻人都很聪明，而且具备了讲出一口地道英语的所有技能，但他们都没有自信，因此他们在英语口语课上仅仅保持沉默。

7) [问题] 为了让他的学生们用英语会话作者作了哪些努力？他是如何成功取得突破性进展的？
   [答案] 他在课堂上采用了更加循循善诱的口吻。对于学生最细小的成功，他都予以肯定和赞

扬。而针对错误，他只是记下来，并不当着全班的面给予纠正。每个人都在鼓励之下参与课堂活动。

词汇练习

1. **请用下面所给词汇或短语的适当形式填写句子。**

 1) 【答案】initial

 【译文】我初次与这家公司联系是在三年前。

 2) 【答案】assigned

 【译文】乔治被分配到这家报社的巴黎办事处。

 3) 【答案】cancel

 【译文】由于生病，这位歌手不得不取消下周的演出。

 4) 【答案】acknowledges

 【译文】美国承认台湾是中国的一部分。

 5) 【答案】minor

 【译文】吉姆的汽车出了点小问题，但他自己修好了。

 6) 【答案】implemented

 【译文】比尔执行了他的投资计划，很快他的资金翻了一番。

 7) 【答案】was determined to

 【译文】那个年代，葡萄牙人一直试图绕非洲航行至印度，但哥伦布决定证明向西航行可抵达印度。

 8) 【答案】challenge

 【译文】抚育孩子对大多数人来说是最艰难的挑战。

 9) 【答案】approach

 【译文】这是解决这个问题最简单的方式。

 10) 【答案】confess

 【译文】我琢磨着找个最佳时间去跟父母坦白。

2. **正确选用以下单词完成句子。**

 1) 【答案】communication

 【译文】与北方的所有通讯均被暴雪阻断了。

 2) 【答案】communicate

 【译文】年轻人有时抱怨和父母无法交流。

 3) 【答案】communicative

 【译文】语言能力必须在有针对性的交流情景下反复锤炼。

 4) 【答案】confident

 【译文】我认为被指定为该墙报的编辑是件光荣的事。我有信心把它做好。

 5) 【答案】confidently

 【译文】我很确信未来的自然资源将会越来越少。

 6) 【答案】confidence

 【译文】你应该用响亮清晰的声音来表现自信，而非盛气凌人。

3. 根据上下文用下列单词的正确形式填空。

1) 【答案】alive

【译文】古代的传统在乡村地区仍很盛行。

2) 【答案】living

【译文】她是这个家庭在世成员中年纪最大的。

3) 【答案】living

【译文】为了有效地学习语言，我们必须把外语当作一门现行语言，使学生们在日常生活中都用得上。

4) 【答案】more lively/livelier

【译文】患者比今天早上看上去活跃多了。

5) 【答案】alive

【译文】当他们找到他时，他已经不省人事了，但还活着。

6) 【答案】lively

【译文】重要的是先理清思路，然后用生动的语言把它写清楚。

7) 【答案】live

【译文】今晚将直播这场足球赛。

8) 【答案】lively

【译文】他已经八十多岁了，但还是很精神。

语法结构

1. 仿照例句改写下列句子。

1) 【答案】Suddenly an idea occurred to me.

【译文】我忽然想到一个主意。

2) 【答案】It never occurred to me to ask her why she said this to me.

【译文】我从未想过问她为何对我说这个。

3) 【答案】It occurred to him that he could submit the paper on line.

【译文】他想起他能够在网上提交论文。

4) 【答案】It did not occur to Cathy to attend the meeting herself.

【译文】凯西没有想起她要参加这个会议。

5) 【答案】Has it ever occurred to you that it might be your fault?

【译文】你是否想过这可能是你的错？

2. 仿照例句用 **if only...** 改写下列句子。

1) 【答案】If only the English examination were that simple!

【译文】要是这次英语考试这么简单就好了！

2) 【答案】If only I hadn't gone to the US at that time!

【译文】要是那时我没去美国该多好啊！

3) 【答案】If only I could fly freely in the sky, just like a bird.

【译文】要是我能像只鸟儿在天空自由飞翔就好了。

4) 【答案】If only I had a digital camera.

【译文】要是我有个数码相机就好了。

5) 【答案】If only they hadn't missed the train!

【译文】要是他们没错过这趟火车就好了!

综合练习

1. 完型填空。

1) 【答案】A

【解析】in many ways 为固定搭配,意为"在许多方面";后半句又是一个定语从句,根据固定搭配,只能用 in which。

2) 【答案】A

【解析】本题考查动词辨析。decline 拒绝,谢绝;reject 拒绝,丢弃,驳回……观点;make 制造,使成为;give 给予。本句意为"什么时候接受,什么时候拒绝邀请",故用 decline。

3) 【答案】C

【解析】本题考查动词辨析。feel 感觉;come 来,来到;suffer 忍受;recover 恢复,弥补。本句意为"当一个人正忍受着文化冲击时,某些重要的症状可能会显现出来。"故用 suffer。

4) 【答案】B

【解析】accept 接受;reject 思想上的拒绝,排斥;refuse 行为上的拒绝;like 喜欢。本句意为"首先,他会排斥引起文化冲击的新环境。"故用reject。

5) 【答案】B

【解析】host country 为固定搭配,意为"东道国"。

6) 【答案】B

【解析】根据上下文,这里需要使用被动语态;同时,根据时态的要求,应该使用一般现在时,故答案只能选B。

7) 【答案】D

【解析】根据上下文,本句意为"在国内所经历过的艰难困苦都被遗忘了,脑海里只记得愉快的事情。"故答案选D。

8) 【答案】A

【解析】固定搭配,concern通常和介词over搭配,意为"对……的担忧"。

9) 【答案】C

【解析】固定搭配,physical contact 指身体接触。

10) 【答案】A

【解析】固定搭配,动词depend通常和介词on搭配,表示"依靠……",同样,名词dependence也和介词on搭配。本句意为"还有一些由于文化冲击而引发的症状,……渴望依赖定居已久的国内同胞。"

【译文】

　　文化冲击是因失去社交活动中人们熟悉的标志和信号而引发焦虑所造成的。这些信号包含了我们熟悉的日常生活情景的很多方面:该何时握手,怎样购物,什么时候接受别人邀请,什么时候又该谢绝,什么时候该严肃对待别人的话,什么时候又不用放在心上。

　　当一个人正在经受文化冲击时,可能会出现些显著的症状,首先,他排斥带来冲击的新环境。他抱怨所在国及当地的人。另一症状是回归，自己国家突然变得无比重要。对他而言，家乡的一切都变得不合逻辑的美好。在家乡经历过的一切问题和麻烦全抛在脑后，心里留下的全是美好的记忆。文化冲击还有些其他症状：如过于频繁地洗手，过分在意饮水、食物和床上用品，害怕与服务员肢体接触，发呆，无助，以及渴望依赖定居已久的国内同胞等等。

2. 用括号中的词汇和短语将下列句子译成英语。

1) 【答案】 It never occurred to her that such a minor mistake would cause her to lose her job.

2) 【答案】 If you are determined to be an IT engineer, you must arm yourself with plenty of knowledge about computers and the Internet.

3) 【答案】 The visiting professor had to acknowledge the effectiveness of traditional teaching methods.

4) 【答案】 No matter what barriers we may come across, we should face up to the challenge confidently.

5) 【答案】 If only I could take back my initial words!

文章泛读

文章导读

在一个崭新的文化环境中，文化冲击使得受冲击者无所适从，甚至整个的心理平衡和价值判断标准完全丧失。心理学家邓肯先生告诉我们文化冲击有五个不同的阶段，他本着它们出现的先后顺序，用形象生动的语言向我们解释说明了每一个阶段的特点，以及受冲击者可能的感受。

背景知识

文化具有非常深沉、非常持久的力量，在本国生活时一般很难理解，只有到了一个文化背景非常不同的国家生活，才能真正体会。文化冲击或文化震撼 (culture shock)，主要是因不同文化间的差异而引起。当一个人到达一个全新的地方，突然发现一切都与过去熟悉的事物迥然不同，以往的生活经验不管用了，不知道该怎样表现才恰当，不知道自己的角色是什么，觉得很不舒服，很不自在，很是困惑时，就是遇到文化冲击或文化震撼了。可以说，文化冲击是一个人从一种文化和物质环境转到另一种文化和物质环境，在心理感受、举止行为，乃至生理等方面发生的震动与失调现象。

文化冲击有很多阶段（phases/stages）。每一阶段可能一直发生或者只在特定时间出现，而每个人在每个阶段都会有自己的反应方式。你可能会发现度过某些阶段比其他人更长、更难。这是因为，有很多因素造成了文化冲击的持续性和影响性。例如：你的心理健康、人格特质、以往的经验、社会经济状况、语言熟练程度、家庭及教育水准等。

文章写作风格及结构

本文为一篇说明文，作者按照"总—分—总"的结构，详细阐述了文化冲击五个阶段的具体表现及几个阶段间的逻辑关系，让读者从心理上对文化冲击有了更深的了解。文章内容详实，脉络清晰。

Parts 部分	Paragraphs 段落	Main Ideas 大意
Part I	1	To give a general picture of culture shock. 概述"文化冲击"。
Part II	2—8	To elaborate on the five phases (or stages) of culture shock. 详述文化冲击的五个阶段。
Part III	9	To give yourself time to adjust to the new culture. 给自己时间适应新文化。

词汇点睛

1　overseas

adj. coming from, existing in, or happening in a foreign country that is across the sea 在海外的，在国外的

- 例句 • We get a lot of overseas visitors here. 我们这里有许多外国游客。

adv. to, or in, a foreign country that is across the sea 在海外

- 例句 • The coach has recommended several young players as candidates to go overseas.
  教练已推荐了几名年轻的球员赴海外学习。
- 辨析 • **students overseas** 指正在海外学习的留学生。

  overseas students 指已从海外学习归来的学生，归国留学生。

2　likewise

adv. in the same way 同样地

- 例句 • I'm going to bed and you would be well advised to do likewise.
  我要睡觉了，你最好也睡吧。

  "I'm very pleased to meet you." "Likewise."
  "我见到你非常高兴。" "我见到你也一样地高兴。"

3　shape

vt. to influence sth. such as a belief, opinion, etc., and make it develop in a particular way 塑造，决定

- 例句 • You'll have to shape the clay before it dries out. 你必须在黏土变干之前把它塑造成型。

  His attitudes were shaped partly by early experiences.
  他的态度在一定程度上是由他早期的经历决定的。
- 扩展 • **shape** *n.* 形状，样子

  He's a devil in human shape. 他是披着人皮的魔鬼。

4 identity

n. 1) *the qualities and attitudes that a person or group of people have, that make them different from other people* 个性，身份

- 例句 • He has lost his identity card. 他遗失了他的身份证。

  The police are still uncertain of the murderer's identity. 警察尚未证实杀人犯的身份。

  2) *the individual characteristics by which a thing or person is recognized or known* 特点，特性

- 例句 • She was asked to fill in a form about the identity of her lost bag.

  她被要求填表写明她遗失提包的特点。

- 扩展 • **identify** *vt.* 识别，辨认出，认同

  The dead body was identified as the missing pilot. 尸体被认出是失踪的飞行员。

  He identified himself with the masses. 他和群众打成一片。

  identical *adj.* 同一的，完全相同的

  This picture is identical with that one.

  这幅画跟那幅画一样。

- 辨析 • **identity, status**

  identity指的是身份，即姓名、出生、住址、职业等信息。

  status指的是地位，即在社会群体中的地位或法律地位。 如：

  The car is a status symbol to them. 这车对于他们是社会地位的象征。

5 distinct

adj. clearly different or belonging to a different type 不同的

- 例句 • Those two suggestions are quite distinct from each other. 这两个建议截然不同。

  Although they look similar, actually these plants are quite distinct.

  这些植物看起来很相似，实际上却完全不同。

- 短语 • **be distinct in... from...** 在……方面与……不同

  Silk is distinct from rayon in every respect. 在各个方面真丝跟人造丝都截然不同。

- 辨析• **distinct, various, different**

  distinct指两个或更多个东西各自有其特点，不容混淆，含有"明显"和"性质上不同"的意思。如：things similar in form but distinct in nature 形式相似，实质不同的东西。

  various强调种类或性质的不同与多，而不强调其本质的差别。如：representatives from various parts of the country 全国各地的代表。

  different普通用语，指事物间的区别，侧重"相异的"。如：

  The two boys are different in their tastes. 这两个男孩的兴趣是不同的。

6 concern

n. a feeling of worry about sth. important 担心，担忧

- 例句 • Our main concern is that they are not receiving enough help.

  我们最担心的是他们一直没有得到足够的帮助。

  vt. if an activity, situation, rule etc. concerns you, it affects you or involves you 涉及，关系到

- 例句 • This concerns the healthy growth of the children. 这事关系到孩子们的健康成长。

- 短语 • **concern oneself about/with/in** 忙于某事，关切某事

  There's no need to concern yourself about this matter; we're dealing with it.

  你不用管这事了，我们正在处理。

be concerned about/with/over/for sth. 为某事忧虑

We're rather concerned about father's health. 我们相当担心父亲的健康。

- 扩展 • **concerned** *adj.* （前置定语）关切的；（后置定语）有关的

It's a challenge to everyone concerned. 对每一位相关人士来说，这都是一个挑战。

concerning *prep.* 关于

I spoke to him concerning his behavior. 我和他就他的行为谈了话。

7　rejection

n. the act of not accepting, believing in, or agreeing with sth. 排斥，拒绝

- 例句 • Her proposal met with continual rejections. 她的建议一再遭到拒绝。

Be prepared for several rejections before you land a job.

找到工作前，先做好遭到几次拒绝的准备。

- 扩展 • **reject** *vt.* 拒绝，抵制

She rejected the offer of that position. 她拒绝接受那个职位。

- 辨析 • **reject, decline, refuse**

reject指以否定、敌对的态度而当面拒绝。如：

They rejected damaged goods. 他们拒收损坏的货物。

decline指较正式地、有礼貌地谢绝。如：

He declined the nomination. 他谢绝提名。

refuse普通用语，指坚决、果断或坦率地拒绝。如：

He refused to take the money. 他拒绝接受此款。

8　survive

vt. 1) *to continue to live after an accident, war, or illness* 幸存，生还

- 例句 • There's little chance that mankind would survive a nuclear war.

人类经历一场核战争还能幸免于难的可能性很小。

　　2) *to continue to be successful* 经受得住

- 例句 • The house survived the storm. 这所房屋并未在暴风雨的袭击中倒塌。

- 用法 • survive本身已表示"幸存，幸免于"，因而不要再加多余的in或from。如：

[译] 在地震中，镇上没有几个人幸存下来。

[误] Few people in the town survived from the earthquake.

[正] Few people in the town survived the earthquake.

- 扩展 • **survival** *n.* 生存

We need food and water for survival. 我们为了生存需要食物和水。

survivor *n.* 幸存者

9　recovery

n. the process of returning to a normal condition after a period of trouble, illness, or difficulty 恢复，还原

She made a quick recovery after her illness. 她病后恢复得很快。

He's happy about the team's recovery from defeat. 他为这个队失败后的重新振作而感到高兴。

recover *vt.* 恢复，重新获得

The skater quickly recovered his balance. 那个滑冰的人很快恢复了平衡。

10 reverse

adj. the opposite order, etc., to what is usual or to what has just been stated 逆向的，相反的

- 例句 - Statistics showed a reverse trend to that recorded in other countries.
  统计数字表明这种趋向与其他国家所示情况迥异。

vt. to change sth., such as a decision, judgment, or process so that it is the opposite of what it was before 颠倒，倒转

- 例句 - The normal word order is reversed in passive sentences. 被动句中，正常的语序被颠倒了。

n. the exact opposite of what has just been mentioned 相反，反面

- 例句 - Eddie is afraid of Angela, and the reverse is also true. 埃迪怕安琪拉，反之亦然。

11 emotional

adj. relating to your feelings or how you control them 情绪的，情感的

- 例句 - I needed this man's love, and the emotional support he was giving me.
  我需要这个男人的爱，以及他给予我的情感支持。

  Sometimes emotional problems might lead to serious results.
  有时候情绪问题会导致严重的结果。

- 扩展 - emotion *n.* 情感，情绪

  The speaker appealed to our emotions rather than to our minds.
  演讲者激发了我们的情感而不是启发了我们的思考。

  emotionless *adj.* 没有情感的，冷漠的

  emotionally *adv.* 在情绪上；情绪上地

短语解析

1. show off 炫耀

【例句】 You're just lucky; there's no need to show off. 你只是幸运而已，没必要炫耀。

She is busy showing off her engagement ring. 她正忙着炫耀自己的订婚戒指。

2. be known as 被称为

【例句】 Shakespeare is known as one of the greatest playwrights in history.
莎士比亚被称为历史上最伟大的剧作家之一。

They are known as the House of Representatives and the Senate.
它们被称为众议院和参议院。

3. at ease (with...) （对……）感到自在

【例句】 She has only come to America for a few weeks, but already she felt completely at ease with the American way of life. 虽然她才到美国几周，但她对美国人的生活方式已完全适应了。

I never feel at ease in his company. 我跟他在一起总是感到很不自在。

难句突破

1. (Para.1) *One of the reasons that we feel like a fish out of water is that we do not know all of the cues that are used in the new culture.*

【解析】 句子主干是 one of the reasons is that we... 。句中有三个 that 引导的从句，分别为定语

从句 (that we feel like a fish out of water) 修饰 reasons；表语从句 (that we do not know all of the cues)，充当 is 的表语；定语从句 (that are used in the new culture)，修饰 cues。

　　在复合句中修饰名词或代词的从句叫定语从句。被修饰的名词或代词叫先行词，引导定语从句的关系代词有who，whom，whose，which，that等和关系副词where，when，why等。如：

This is the man who helped me. 这就是那个帮过我的人。

This is the book which you want. 这就是你想要的那本书。

　　在引导限定性定语从句时可以用which，可以用that，其中that可以省略，而引导非限定性定语从句时必须用关系代词which不能用that。如：

I have lost my pen, which I like very much. (非限定性定语从句)

我把我很喜欢的那只笔丢了。

The letter which/(that) I received was from my father. (限定性定语从句)

我收到那封信是我父亲寄来的。

　　句中作表语的从句叫表语从句。引导表语从句的关联词通常有从属连词that, whether, if 和连接代词what, who which, whatever, whoever以及连接副词how, when, where, why 等。表语从句位于系动词之后，有时还会用as if引导。如：

The problem is who can get there to take the place of Ben. 问题是谁可以到那里接替本。

The fact remains that we are far behind the developed countries in science and technology.

事实仍然是我们在科学和技术方面远远落后于发达国家。

That is how he managed to overcome the difficulties. 这就是他如何成功克服困难的过程。

【译文】　我们之所以感觉像是如鱼离水，其中一个原因就是我们不完全了解那些在新文化中使用的提示标符。

2. (Para.3) ***The newcomer is excited about being in a new place where there are new sights and sounds, new smells and tastes.***

【解析】　1) 句中包含一个where引导的同位语从句（where there are new sights and... tastes），对place进行解释说明。

2) be excited about sth./doing sth. 对……感到很兴奋。由于后面要接名词或者动词的ing形式，因此这里要用being in a new place，表示置身于一个新的地方。

【译文】　初来乍到者因其置身于一个新地方而感到兴奋。因为这里有新的景象，新的声音，新的气息和新的味道。

3. (Para.4) ***It may start to seem like people no longer care about your problems.***

【解析】　1) seem的常用结构为：seem+形容词或分词；seem+名词；seem+介词短语；seem+不定式；it seems that+从句。如：

He's 16, but he often seems younger. (seem+形容词)

他16岁，但是他常常看上去要比实际年龄小些。

There seems no reason to reject it. (seem+名词) 似乎没有理由拒绝它。

The children seemed as if/as though/like they were tired. (seem+介词短语)

孩子们看上去很累。

I seem to know more about him than anyone else. (seem+不定式)

我似乎比其他人更了解他一些。

It seems that she can't come. (it seems that+从句) 她似乎不能来了。

2) no longer相当于not... any longer，意为"不再……"。如：

It is no longer raining. Let's play football. (＝It is not raining any longer. Let's play football.)

已经不下雨了，我们踢足球吧。

【译文】你可能会开始觉得人们似乎不再关心你遇到的问题了。

4. (Para.4) *They may help, but they don't seem to understand your concern over what they see as small problems.*

【解析】1) 句中what引导宾语从句（what they see as small problems）作介词over的宾语。

2) concern作名词时表示担心、焦虑，一般会用搭配 concern for/about/over sth./sb. 如：

The public has a concern for their safety. 公众对他们的安全很担心。

concern还可以作动词，表示"关于……"。如：

It is a report concerned about drug abuse. 这是一篇关于滥用毒品的报道。

另外，concern还被用于一些固定的搭配中，如：as/so far as sb./sth. is concerned表示"就某人、某事而言"。如：

As far as I'm concerned you can do what you like. 就我个人而言，你怎么做都可以。

The car is fine as far as the engine is concerned but the bodywork needs a lot of attention.

这辆车发动机还不错，但车身需要大修。

【译文】他们也许会帮忙，但他们似乎并不了解你的顾虑，因为你的问题在他们看来都是小问题。

5. (Para.5) *It is so called because it is at this point that the newcomer starts to reject the host country, complaining about and noticing only the bad things that bother them.*

【解析】1）句中含有一个强调句it is at this point that the newcomers...。it is... that... 是一个强调句型，如果要强调除谓语动词之外的其他成分时都可以用这种句型，它的具体用法是"it is (was) + 被强调部分 + who (that)..."。如果强调的部分是人可用who，whom代替that。如：

The parents will never forget that it was he who had saved their child's life.

这对父母永远也不会忘记是他挽救了他们孩子的生命。(强调主语)

It was the kind of work that I liked. 我喜欢的就是这种工作。(强调宾语)

It was at twelve o'clock that BBC gently informed its listeners that it was an April Fool trick.

12点钟，英国广播公司才温柔地告诉听众们这是一个愚人节的玩笑。(强调状语)

It is all because you're a fool that I'm often ill.

正是因为你很愚蠢我才经常生病。(强调状语从句)

2）句中的complaining和noticing现在分词作伴随状语，表示在排斥的同时抱怨和注意到那些烦心事。详见Unit 1, Text B难句突破3。

【译文】之所以叫"排斥期"，是因为正是从这个阶段起，新来的人开始排斥他所在的国家，开始抱怨，并只注意到那些令人讨厌的烦心事。

6. (Para.6) *Your homeland may suddenly seem marvelously wonderful; all the difficulties that you had there are forgotten and you may find yourself wondering why you ever left.*

【解析】 1) find + sb./sth. + *n.* / *v.*-ing /*adj.* 发现某人/某事……。如：

Do you find David difficult to talk to? 你觉得与大卫交谈很难么？

I don't find him an easy person to get on with. 我觉得他是个很好相处的人。

She doesn't find it easy to talk about her problems. 她发现很难谈论她的问题。

2) ever用于否定句和疑问句，或者用于含有表示怀疑或条件成分的句子中，置于动词之前表示强调，相当于at any time。如：

Nothing ever happens in this village. 这个村里从未发生过任何事。

Do you ever wish you were rich? 你曾希望自己很富有吗？

If you ever visit London, you must come and stay with us.

你要是到伦敦来，一定要到我们这里住。

【译文】 祖国突然间似乎变得美妙非凡，曾在国内遭遇的困顿都在脑海中荡然无存，你甚至会想不通自己为什么要离开祖国。

7. (Para.7) *With this complete adjustment, you accept the food, drinks, habits and customs of the host country, and you may even find yourself preferring some things in the host country to things at home.*

【解析】 1) with this complete adjustment是一个介词短语作状语。类似的用法还有介词without。如：

With the exams approaching, it's a good idea to review your class notes.

考试临近了，不妨复习一下课堂笔记。

With your contribution, that makes a total of $45. 由于你的贡献，一共赚了45美元。

Without a doubt, this is the best Chinese food I've ever had.

毫无疑问，这是我吃过的最好吃的中国菜。

2) host country指"东道国"，host表示"主人"。

【译文】 经过这一番彻底调整，你已经接受了东道国的饮食和风俗习惯，你甚至会觉得与自己的家乡相比，你更喜欢这里的一些东西了。

参考译文

文化冲击：一条离水之鱼

邓肯·梅森

　　旅居海外的人就像是"离水之鱼"。同鱼一样，他们一直都在自己的文化中畅游。鱼不知水为何物，同样，我们对于孕育自己的文化也常常缺乏充分的思考。我们的文化使我们形成了自身的特性。很多人际交流中的提示标符（如肢体语言、词汇、面部表情、语调、成语、俚语等）都因文化不同而有所不同。我们之所以感觉像是如鱼离水，其中一个原因就是我们不完全了解那些在新文化中使用的提示标符。

　　心理学家告诉我们，文化冲击有五个不同的阶段（或者时期）。

　　在刚到一个国家的头几天里，通常一切都进展得非常顺利。初来乍到者因其置身于一个新地方而感到兴奋。因为这里有新的景象，新的声音，新的气息和新的味道。他们可能会遇到一些问题，但他们通常把这些问题视为新鲜事物的一部分。他们要么是住在宾馆里，要么是住在居民家里，这些家庭都很乐于接待外国人。初到异国他乡的人也许会发现，迎接他们的"红地毯"已经铺开，他们也许会受邀去餐馆，看电影或外出观光。新朋友乐于领着他们去很多地方，向他们"显摆一番"。这就是文化冲击的第一阶段，称为"蜜月期"。

遗憾的是，这段蜜月期通常结束得很快。新来的人不得不开始处理交通问题、购物问题或者交流问题。你开始觉得人们不再关心你遇到的问题了。他们也许会帮忙，但他们似乎并不了解你的顾虑，因为你的问题在他们看来都是小问题。你甚至会开始认为东道国的人们不喜欢外国人。

这时候就进入了文化冲击的第二阶段，即"排斥期"。之所以叫"排斥期"，是因为正是从这个阶段起，新来的人开始排斥他所在的国家，开始抱怨，并只注意到那些令人讨厌的烦心事。在这个阶段，这些人要么变得坚强并且留下来，要么变得脆弱而回到国内。

如果你不能顺利地度过第二个阶段，你会发现自己进入了第三个阶段："回归期"。在这段时期里，你的大部分时间都在讲母语、看国内的影碟、吃本国的食物。你也会发现你整日和一群讲母语的学生呆在一起。大部分时间你都在抱怨东道国和它的文化，你一心只记得自己国家的好。祖国突然间似乎变得美妙非凡，曾在国内遭遇的困顿都在脑海中荡然无存，你甚至会想不通自己为什么要离开祖国。

成功地度过了第三个阶段，你将进入文化冲击的第四个阶段："恢复期"。在这一阶段，你更加适应了东道国的语言和习俗。此时的你独自外出也不会有焦虑感。你仍然会遇到一些问题。但现在你对这种新文化已经适应了90%，并且开始意识到一个国家与另一个国家相比并不会好到哪儿去——只是生活方式不同，以及对生活中的问题的解决方法不同而已。经过这一番彻底调整，你已经接受了东道国的饮食和风俗习惯，你甚至会觉得与自己的家乡相比，你更喜欢这里的一些东西了。你终于能够非常自在地生活在新的环境里了。

一段时间之后，你可能会回到自己的国家，猜猜会怎么样？——你会步入文化冲击的第五阶段，即"反向文化冲击期"。在离开祖国的这一长段时间里，你已经适应了新生活方式中的习惯和习俗，回来之后也许反倒不能完全适应这里的生活了。在你出国期间，或许很多东西都发生了变化，所以你需要稍稍经过一段时间才能适应本国文化中的提示标符、符号和标志。

在文化冲击的诸多阶段，你都有可能遇到疾病或者情感问题。记住：时刻善待自己，并给自己一些时间去适应。做自己最好的朋友。做到了这些，恭喜你，你将成为世界公民！

🔘 习题全解

1. 根据课文，请选出最合适的答案。

1) **【答案】** A

【题解】 细节题。根据文章的第一段最后一句 "One of the reasons that we feel like a fish out of water is that we do not know all of the cues that are used in the new culture"（我们之所以感觉像是如鱼离水，其中一个原因就是我们不完全了解那些在新文化中使用的提示标

符），因此选A。

2) 【答案】C

【题解】细节题。根据文章的第三段中 "During the first few days of a person's stay in a new country, everything usually goes fairly smoothly. The newcomer is excited about being in a new place where there are new sights and sounds, new smells and tastes." "This first stage of culture shock is called the 'honeymoon phase'" （在刚到一个国家的头几天里，通常一切都进展得非常顺利。初来乍到者因其置身于一个新地方而感到兴奋。……这就是文化冲击的第一阶段，称为"蜜月期"），因此选C。

3) 【答案】B

【题解】细节题。根据文章的第五段中 "This may lead to the second stage of culture shock, known as the 'rejection phase'. It is so called because it is at this point that the newcomer starts to reject the host country, complaining about and noticing only the bad things that bother them" （这时候就进入了文化冲击的第二阶段，即"排斥期"。之所以叫"排斥期"，是因为正是从这个阶段起，新来的人开始排斥他所在的国家，开始抱怨，并只注意到那些令人讨厌的烦心事），因此选B。

4) 【答案】D

【题解】细节题。根据文章的第五段最后一句 "At this stage the newcomer either gets stronger and stays, or gets weaker and goes home" （在这个阶段，这些人要么变得坚强而留下来，要么变得脆弱而回到国内），因此选D。

5) 【答案】D

【题解】推断题。根据文章的第六段中 "If you don't survive stage two successfully, you may find yourself moving into stage three: the 'regression phase'. In this phase of culture shock, you spend much of your time speaking your own language, watching videos from your home country, eating food from home" （如果你不能顺利地度过第二个阶段，你会发现自己进入了第三个阶段："回归期"。在这段时期里，你的大部分时间都在讲母语、看国内的影碟、吃本国的食物）因此选D。

6) 【答案】B

【题解】细节题。根据文章的第七段中 "If you survive the third stage successfully you will move into the fourth stage of culture shock called the 'recovery phase'. In this stage you become more comfortable with the language and the customs of the host country" （成功地度过了第三个阶段，你将进入文化冲击的第四个阶段："恢复期"。在这一阶段，你更加适应了东道国的语言和习俗），因此选B。

7) 【答案】B

【题解】推断题。根据文章的倒数第二段可知，一个人在离开祖国的这一长段时间里，已经适应了新生活方式中的习惯和习俗，而且国内很多东西也都发生了变化；所以回国之后也许反倒不能完全适应那里的生活了。因此选B。

2. 请用下面所给词汇或短语的适当形式填空。

1) 【答案】identity

【译文】警察仍然不太确定凶手的身份。

2) 【答案】distinct

　　【译文】你的学业取得了明显的进步。

3) 【答案】survived

　　【译文】他的家人中只有一位在地震中幸免于难。

4) 【答案】reverse

　　【译文】连续几届总统曾试图扭转这种趋势，但都失败了。

5) 【答案】show off

　　【译文】他一坐在钢琴前，我们就知道他又准备卖弄琴技了。

6) 【答案】emotional

　　【译文】在我最困难的时候，是她给予了我精神上的支持。

7) 【答案】sights

　　【译文】尼亚加拉瀑布是世界著名风景名胜地之一。

8) 【答案】is known as

　　【译文】四川被誉为"天府之国"。

9) 【答案】prefer

　　【译文】与咖啡相比我更喜欢茶。

10) 【答案】concern

　　【译文】诗人在她生命的最后时日里，表达了对父亲的担忧。

3. 将下列句子译成中文。

1) 初来乍到者因其置身于一个新地方而感到兴奋。因为这里有新的景象，新的声音，新的气息和新的味道。

2) 这个阶段之所以被称为"排斥期"，是因为正是从这个阶段起，新来的人开始排斥他所在的国家，开始抱怨并只注意到那些令人讨厌的烦心事。

3) 你仍然会遇到一些问题。但现在你对这种新文化已经适应了90%，并且开始意识到一个国家与另一个国家并没有好坏之分——只是生活方式不同，以及对生活中的问题的解决方法不同而已。

4) 在你出国期间，或许很多东西都已经发生了变化，所以你可能需要稍稍经过一段时间才能适应本国文化中的暗示、符号和标志。

文章泛读

TEXT **C**

📖 文章导读

　　生活在异国文化氛围中会让我们既兴奋又好奇。但当这最初的新奇感消失后，我们又会有失落、孤独或不安的感觉。这种失落和不安是经历文化冲击的过程中一种很自然的现象。本文中，作者以激励的口吻提出了五条小诀窍以帮助受到文化冲击的人们度过难关。

背景知识

　　一般来说，几乎每个在国外的人都会经历文化冲击或文化震撼，但所感受到的冲击与震撼程度却因人而异，有些人可能感觉轻微些，有些人则会有较强烈的反应。文化冲击会使人觉得不安、害羞或难堪，有时会使人觉得挫折、生气或失望。而且，也不是经历一次就会结束，在最初一段时间内可能有密集的、反复的被冲击和被震撼的感觉。而从遭遇文化冲击开始到结束，实际就是一个适应新文化的过程。

　　文化冲击是一种正常现象，我们不必惊慌。当我们逐渐熟悉周围环境，逐渐适应外国人的生活态度之后，一切就会恢复正常。面对必需经历的文化冲击，我们要学会调整自己，保持积极主动的精神和乐观的态度，以度过难关。

文章写作风格及结构

　　本文为一篇说明文，作者列举了应对文化冲击的五个小诀窍。文章结构一目了然，语言浅显易懂，让读者读起来兴趣盎然。

Parts 部分	Paragraphs 段落	Main Ideas 大意
Part I	1	To point out that it's hard to avoid culture shock. 指出文化冲击难以避免。
Part II	2	To list tips on dealing with culture shock. 列举应对文化冲击的小诀窍。
Part III	3—4	To suggest that we adjust to a new culture with an optimistic attitude. 建议我们应以乐观的心态适应新文化。

词汇点睛

1　abroad

adv. in or to a foreign country 在外国，在海外

- 例句 • He lived abroad for many years. 他在国外住了许多年。

　　　 Are you going abroad for your holidays? 你打算去国外度假吗？

- 辨析 • **abroad, aboard**

　　　 aboard *adv./prep.* 在船(飞机/车)上，上船(飞机/车)

　　　 All aboard! 请大家上船（飞机/车）！

2　flexible

adj. able to change or be changed easily to suit any new situation 灵活的，易适应的

- 例句 • We can visit you on Monday or Tuesday; our plans are fairly flexible.

　　　 我们可以在星期一或星期二去看你，我们的计划是相当灵活的。

　　　 Your attitude to money must be more flexible. 你对钱的态度得更灵活一些。

3 frustrating

adj. making you feel annoyed, upset, or impatient because you cannot do what you want to do 令人泄气的，让人沮丧的

• 例句 • After three hours' frustrating delay, the train at last arrived.
经过三个小时令人厌烦的耽搁后，火车终于到达了目的地。

I find it frustrating that I can't speak English. 我为我不会说英语而感到沮丧。

• 扩展 • **frustrate** *vt.* 使灰心，挫败

The lack of money and hands frustrated him. 缺乏资金和人手使他灰心丧气。

frustrated *adj.* 沮丧的，失意的

Film directors are sometimes frustrated actors. 电影导演有时是失意的演员。

frustration *n.* 挫败，灰心，失望

Every job has its frustrations. 每种工作都有让人不称心的地方。

4 depressed

adj. very unhappy 情绪低落的，沮丧的

• 例句 • He was depressed because he had not passed his examination. 因为没有通过考试，他很沮丧。

I am depressed about the election results. 我对选举的结果感到很沮丧。

• 扩展 • **depress** *vt.* 使沮丧，使情绪低落

Wet weather always depresses me. 阴雨天总是使我情绪低落。

depression *n.* 沮丧、消沉、萧条

He committed suicide during a fit of depression. 他一时想不开，自杀了。

depressing *adj.* 令人沮丧的

The current situation is very depressing. 现在的局面很令人沮丧。

5 normal

adj. usual, typical, or expected 正常的

• 例句 • The normal price of a ticket is $230. 一张票的正常价格是230美元。

Weeping is a normal response to pain. 哭泣是对痛苦的正常反应。

• 反义词 • **abnormal** *adj.* 不正常的

• 辨析 • **normal, ordinary, regular**

normal指"正常的，正规的，常态的"，如：the normal temperature of the human body 人的正常体温。

ordinary指"平常的，普通的"，与 extraordinary 相对。如：an ordinary day's work 日常工作。

regular指"有规律的，正规的，定期的"，与 irregular 相对。如：He kept regular hours. 他过着有规律的生活。

6 reaction

n. sth. that you feel or do because of sth. that has happened or been said 反应

• 例句 • It's difficult to guess what her reaction to the news would be. 很难想象她将对此消息作何反应。

Her arrest produced an immediate reaction from the press. 她被捕的事立即在新闻界引起反应。

• 扩展 • **react** *vi.* 起反应，起作用

How did your mother react to the news? 你妈妈对这个消息的反应怎样？

The audience reacted readily to his speech. 观众对他的讲演立即起了反应。

7 opportunity

n. a chance to do sth., or an occasion when it is easy for you to do sth. 机会，时机

- 例句 - We'll have another opportunity to visit the exhibition next year.
  明年我们还会有一次机会参观展览。
  It would be foolish to let such an opportunity slip, it is the chance of a lifetime.
  让这样千载难逢的机会溜掉，实在是太愚蠢了。
- 辨析 - **opportunity, chance**
  opportunity 带有适逢机会，正好行事的意味（= good chance）。如：
  I had no opportunity to discuss it with her. 我没有机会和她谈这件事。
  chance强调其偶然性。如：It happened quite by chance. 这完全是偶然发生的。

8 confuse

vt. 1) to think wrongly that one person, thing, or idea is sb./sth. else 误解，混淆

- 例句 - I can't see how anyone could confuse you with another!
  我不明白别人怎么可能将你和其他人混淆起来。
  Don't confuse Austria with Australia. 不要把奥地利与澳大利亚弄混淆了。
- 短语 - **confuse sb./sth. with sb./sth.** 将此人或此物误当成彼人或彼物
  2) to make someone feel that they cannot think clearly or do not understand 使迷惑，搞乱
- 例句 - They confused me by asking me so many questions. 他们问了一大堆问题，把我问糊涂了。
- 扩展 - **confused** *adj.* 糊涂的，困惑的
  The old lady easily gets confused. 这位老太太容易迷糊。
  confusing *adj.* 莫名其妙的，难以理解的
  The instructions on the box are very confusing. 盒子上的使用说明含混不清。

🔵 短语解析

1. get through 度过

【例句】It's hard to see how people here will get through the winter.
很难想象这儿的人们怎么度过冬天。
We have managed to get through some very tough times.
我们已设法度过了几段非常艰难的时期。

2. come across 偶然遇到或找到

【例句】I came across his name in the newspaper. 我无意中在报纸上发现了他的名字。
We've just come across an old friend we haven't seen for ages.
我们刚碰到了一位多年不见的老朋友。

3. keep sth. in perspective 正确判断……

【例句】We must keep the problem in perspective; it's not really that serious.
我们必须对这个问题有个正确的认识；事情其实并不那么严重。
Remember to keep things in perspective. 记住要正确判断事情。

4. look back on 回顾

【例句】When she looked back on 1992 at the end of the year, she was overwhelmed with gratitude.
年末回顾1992年时，她不胜感激。

Looking back on my past, I just wish I'd have studied a lot more.

回望过去，要是我当年多学了很多东西该多好啊。

5. take advantage of 充分利用

【例句】 They took full advantage of the hotel's facilities. 他们充分利用了旅馆的设备。

Parents hope that their children will take advantage of this opportunity to fully develop their abilities. 父母希望他们的孩子能充分利用这次机会全面发展自身的能力。

难句突破

1. (Para.1) *This period of cultural adjustment involves everything from getting used to the food and language to learning how to use the telephone.*

【解析】 from getting used to the food... to use the telephone作定语修饰everything。get used to sth./doing sth.也可用作be used to sth./doing sth.，表示"习惯于……"。另外要注意这个词组和used to do的区别，used to do表示"过去曾经做某事（而现在已经不做了）"。如：

My dad used to smoke when he was young.

我爸爸年轻的时候抽烟（他现在已经戒烟了）。

I don't mind the heat. I'm used to hot weather. 我不介意炎热，我已经习惯炎热的气候了。

He's not used to working long hours. 他还不习惯工作这么长时间。

【译文】 这一阶段的文化调节涵盖方方面面，从适应饮食和语言到学会怎样使用电话。

2. (Para.1) *No matter how patient and flexible you are, adjusting to a new culture can, at times, be difficult and frustrating.*

【解析】 1) 句子的主干是adjusting to a new culture can be difficult and frustrating。其中主语是动名词短语adjusting to a new culture。

动名词由动词 + ing构成，具有名词和动词的性质，在句中起名词作用，可作主语、宾语、表语和定语。如：

Seeing is believing. 眼见为实。(作主语)

He is fond of playing football. 他喜欢玩足球。(作宾语)

My job is teaching English. 我的工作是教英语。(作表语)

The reading room of our school library can hold 800 people.

我们学校的阅览室可容纳800人。(作定语)

2) no matter how引导让步状语从句。状语从句放在主句之前时，常用逗号分开；放在主句之后，一般不用逗号。让步状语从句由although (though)，as，even if，however，whatever，no matter who (how...) 等词引导。如：

Clever as he is, he doesn't study well. 尽管很聪明，但是他学习不好。

Although it is rained heavily, they kept on working. 即使雨下得很大，他们还是继续工作。

I never seem to lose any weight, no matter how hard I try.

无论我怎么努力，似乎都没办法瘦下来。

【译文】 不管你多么有耐心，也不管你适应能力有多强，有时候，适应一种新的文化可能会非常困难并且令人沮丧。

3. (Para.2) ***Start a journal of the new things you come across every day and your reactions to your new home.***

【解析】1) 本句是一个祈使句，其中包含一个省略了引导词that的定语从句。and连接的两个并列成分是a journal of the new things和(a journal of) your reactions。

祈使句一般用以表达命令、请求或建议，主语通常省略。说话对象为第二人称时，一般省略主语。肯定式中，谓语动词用原形；否定式中，用don't (never) + 动词原形。如：Get up! Don't be afraid. 站起来！别害怕。

2) 句中的定语从句省略了引导词that。补充完整是：the new things (that) you come across every day。关于定语从句的详细解释参见本课Text B 难句突破1。

【译文】开始记下你每天遇到的新事物以及你对新家的反应。

4. (Para.2) ***... it is easy to feel stupid and get down on yourself, but there is no reason to.***

【解析】1) get down on: 开始不喜欢……

2) 本句中真正的主语是to feel stupid and get down on yourself，it是形式主语。

3) 后半句是一个省略用法，完整的说法是there is no reason to (feel stupid and get down on yourself)。在英文表达中，如果上文中曾经出现过的内容在下文又被提及则可以采用省略的用法。

【译文】认为自己很愚蠢，看不起自己是很容易的事情，但没有必要这样做。

5. (Para.3) ***Adjusting to a new culture can be difficult and frustrating, but it can also be a wonderful, thought-provoking time of your life during which you will grow as a person.***

【解析】1) adjust to: 适应……

2) 本句是由but连接的并列句，前半句的主语是动名词短语adjusting to a new culture。后半句的主语it指代的也是adjusting to a new culture。句中还包含一个which引导的宾语从句作介词during的宾语。（介词后接宾语从句的解释参见本课Text A 难句突破7）

【译文】适应新的文化也许十分困难而且令人沮丧，但那是你人生成长道路上一段非常美妙、值得回味的时光。

6. (Para.4) ***... all international students share in what you are going through; you are not alone.***

【解析】本句谓语动词为share，介词in引导share的内容，what引导宾语从句，作介词in的宾语。

【译文】所有的留学生都会和你有相似的经历，你并不是孤军作战。

7. (Para.4) ***Even more importantly, it is only a matter of time before you are adjusted and comfortable in your new home.***

【解析】1) 本句的主干是it is only a matter of time；其中it指you are adjusted and comfortable in your new home；before引导时间状语从句。

2) It is all/only/just a matter of time (before)... 表示"尽管不见得马上发生，但是一定会发生；只是迟早的事"。如：

It's only a matter of time before he's forced to resign. 他被迫辞职只是迟早的事。

It's simply a matter of time before the company is bankrupted. 这个公司倒闭只是迟早的事。

【译文】 更为重要的是，要适应你的新家并在新家中感到舒适自在不过是个时间问题罢了。

参考译文

应对文化冲击的小诀窍

在国外学习、生活或工作的人几乎都会经历某种程度的文化冲击。这一阶段的文化调节涵盖方方面面，从适应饮食和语言到学会怎样使用电话。不管你多么有耐心，也不管你适应能力有多强，有时候，适应一种新的文化可能会非常困难并且令人沮丧。你很容易就会产生失落感，意志消沉，思乡心切。你甚至想要回家！

不要惊慌……这些都是完全正常的反应，并不只是你一个人才有。有时候你很难记起当初为何要离开祖国。你在进行一项冒险活动——一个成长、学习的绝佳机会——但似乎事情不总是如此。尽管不能完全避免文化冲击，但下面的几条小诀窍可以帮你度过难关：

- 开始记下你每天遇到的新事物以及你对新家的反应。记录下你的所见所想有助于你更好地理解它们，今后回忆起来你也会感到其乐无穷。
- 不要把讲一门新语言的能力误解为与自己的智力有关；认为自己很愚蠢，看不起自己是很容易的事情，但没有必要这样做。每个人都需要一段时间调整才能适应一种新的语言。
- 积极进行体育锻炼！走路、游泳、跑步、打网球或者做一些你平常喜欢做的其他体育运动。你会感觉好一些，而且能认识新朋友，还可以保持体形。
- 保持幽默感。尽量在新体验和新挑战中找寻有意义的东西，不管这样做有多困难。现在就笑对人生，不要迟疑！
- 充分利用大学、教堂或社区提供的服务。联系留学生办公室的顾问、校学生宿舍的住宿指导员（如果你住学生宿舍的话）、教堂的工作人员……如果你遇到什么问题，一定要告诉相关人员。他们会很乐意帮助你，而你在有人支持的时候也会舒心很多。不要害怕开口。

适应新的文化也许十分困难而且令人沮丧，但那是你人生成长道路上一段非常美妙且值得回味的时光。在异国他乡生活的经历，会为你开启多扇新的大门，引领你体验新的思维方式，给你提供机会结交终身好友。

记住：所有的留学生都会和你有相似的经历，你并不是孤军作战。更为重要的是，适应你的新家、并在新家中感到舒适自在不过是个时间问题罢了。

记住：笑口常开！

语言拓展

日常用语

练习 选择补全对话的最佳答案。

1. 【答案】C
   【题解】 听到对方向你表示感谢时，你可用 "Not at all./You are welcome./Don't mention it./That's all right./It's my pleasure." 应答。

2. 【答案】C
   【题解】 同上。

3. 【答案】A
   【题解】 "Shall I help...?" 是提供帮助的交际用语，如果接受他的帮助应该在表示同意的同时表达感谢，如 "Yes, please.（好啊，麻烦你了。）Yes, I hope so.（好啊，希望你能帮忙。）Thank you.（谢谢。）Great.（好极了。）That's very kind/nice of you, thanks.（你真好，谢谢。）" 反之可以说明拒绝的原因，并表达感谢，如 "It's all right, thanks, I can manage.（不必了，谢谢，我还可以应付。）No, don't bother, really.（不必了，真的不用麻烦你。）No, it's OK.（不必了。）Thank you, but it's OK.（谢谢，但不必了。）Not at the moment, thank you.（暂时不用，谢谢。）" 等。

4. 【答案】B
   【题解】 此题考查有关 "感谢与应答" 的方法。对别人赠送的礼物，不论轻重，都要表示感谢，此时听话人也应该礼貌回答，此处的 "You're welcome." 意为 "不用谢。"

5. 【答案】A
   【题解】 当对方说 "非常谢谢你能载我一程" 时，可以回答 "At your service." 表示 "乐意为你效劳。" 同时，也可用 "Any time." 表示 "愿随时为你效劳。"

阅读技巧

练习 速读下面这篇文章并回答问题。

1. 【译文】 父亲节是哪一天？
   【答案】 The third Sunday in June.
   【题解】 从第一段的第二句话可以推断出。

2. 【译文】 谁是父亲节最有力的推动者？
   【答案】 Mrs. Bruce John Dodd of Spokane, Washington, USA.
   【题解】 见文章第三段第一句。

3. 【译文】 在什么时候她第一次为父亲庆祝了节日？
   【答案】 On June, 19, 1909.
   【题解】 见文章第六段第一句。

4. 【译文】 早期，在父亲节佩戴红玫瑰和白色花朵有什么不同？
   【答案】 In early times, people wore the red rose to honor a father still living, or a white flower to honor a deceased dad.
   【题解】 见文章第七段第二句。

5. 【译文】 从什么时候开始父亲节成为了美国的法定节日？
   【答案】 In 1966.

【题解】见文章倒数第二段第二句。

写作技巧

练习 回顾该单元所学的写作技巧，给题为"远程学习之我见"的文章写一段结尾。

样文：

Personally, I appreciate long-distance learning. It's indeed a helpful complement to the traditional schooling. It can provide learners with more flexible and versatile ways of learning. With online education, we can stick to our work and at the same time study and absorb the latest knowledge. Most of all, it is a way to construct a lifelong educational system in the learning-type society.

语法知识

——冠词

练习 选择最佳答案补全下列句子。

1. 【答案】D

   【题解】不定冠词＋序数词表示"another（再，又）"。

   【译文】她的实验失败了七次，但她仍然要尝试第八次。

2. 【答案】A

   【题解】定冠词放在序数词前表示顺序。

   【译文】这是我第二次去香港了。

3. 【答案】D

   【题解】不定冠词用在可数名词前表示一类事物。

   【译文】马是一种有用的动物。

4. 【答案】A

   【题解】定冠词用在表示计量单位的名词前。

   【译文】这个公司的工作人员按星期领工资。

5. 【答案】C

   【题解】含有普通名词的专有名词，其专有名词在普通名词前，且不用冠词。

   【译文】北海公园是北京一处美景。

6. 【答案】D

   【题解】不定冠词a/an有不确定的意义，与单数可数名词连用，表示同类中的"任何一个"、"其中之一"。

   【译文】尽管杰西卡的父母希望她能从商，但她想成为一名医生。

7. 【答案】C

   【题解】in front of 在……前面；in the front of 在……的前部。

   【译文】他坐在教室的前排，做他的家庭作业。

8. 【答案】B

   【题解】不定冠词表示"同一"，但不如"the same"语气强。

   【译文】我们外套的大小、颜色和款式都相似。

9. 【答案】C

   【题解】在与by连用的交通工具名称前不用冠词。by air 乘飞机。

【译文】他乘飞机去的上海。

10.【答案】C

【题解】"the＋身体各部位"结构。表示身体某部位接受外来的动作，通常不用部位当直接宾语，而以人当宾语，其后再接"介词+the+身体的部位"结构。

【译文】罪犯被枪击中了头部，当场死亡。

11.【答案】D

【题解】在构成一个整体的两个并列的名词之前不用冠词。

【译文】为了促销这种新产品，他们挨家挨户地去推销。

12.【答案】B

【题解】表示上文提到过或谈话双方都知道的人或物时用定冠词，泛指时不用。不定冠词和hundred, thousand, dozen以及数目及数量连用时，表示"one"的含义。

【译文】每个星期天他都去教堂。他常去的那个教堂有一千多个座位。

13.【答案】B

【题解】冠词用在"so（as, too, how）＋形容词"之后。如：She is as clever a girl as you can wish to meet. It is too difficult a book for us.

【译文】他是一个很诚实的男孩，我们都喜欢他。

14.【答案】A

【题解】定冠词用在西洋乐器名词之前，而表示球类、棋类运动的名词之前不用冠词。

【译文】汤姆喜欢踢足球，而他的姐姐喜欢弹钢琴。

15.【答案】C

【题解】在形容词最高级之前用定冠词。

【译文】这是我看过的最精彩的电影。

16.【答案】D

【题解】代词most（大部分）与of一起组成most of结构，在most of结构前，通常不加任何冠词。

【译文】大多数的游客来自欧洲。

每课一练

Part I   Vocabulary & Structure

Directions: *There are 30 incomplete sentences in this part. For each sentence there are four choices marked A), B), C) and D). Choose the ONE that best completes the sentence.*

1. Eventually he _____ the judgment and set the prisoner free.

    A) refused   B) returned   C) reversed   D) recovered

2. Don't worry. The problem is _____, and will be quickly overcome.

    A) unclear   B) serious   C) minor   D) major

3. I'd like to take _____ of this trip to buy the things I need.

    A) advantage   B) adventure   C) advice   D) advance

4. Beijing is well _____ its beautiful scenery and the Great Wall.

    A) known as   B) known to   C) known with   D) known for

5. There are concerns that the refugees may not _____ the winter.

   A) survive   B) survive from   C) survival   D) survive to

6. He actually enjoys his new hair style and likes _____ to everybody.

   A) showing up   B) showing off

   C) showing out   D) showing of

7. Reducing the gap between rich and poor is one of the main _____ facing the government.

   A) chances   B) challenges   C) chains   D) changes

8. Missing school to watch the football match is _____.

   A) out of question   B) out of the question

   C) out of a question   D) out question

9. I had _____ in my secretary; she would do the right thing.

   A) dependence   B) confidence   C) knowledge   D) responsibility

10. I _____ an old school friend in Oxford Street this morning.

   A) come into   B) come across   C) come out   D) come off

11. We have different approaches _____ gathering information.

   A) for   B) by   C) through   D) to

12. They refused to _____ that they were defeated.

   A) knowledge   B) acknowledge   C) aware   D) awake

13. She did me such a big favor. _____ I knew her name.

   A) If   B) Only   C) If only   D) Only just

14. She has a _____ interest in everything around her.

   A) lively   B) alive   C) live   D) living

15. The changes are an improvement _____.

   A) in way   B) in the way   C) in a way   D) by a way

16. It suddenly _____ to me that we could use a computer to do the job.

   A) happened   B) occurred   C) agreed   D) presented

17. I became a teacher because I _____ books to business.

   A) wanted   B) liked   C) preferred   D) had

18. To him, music is _____ a way of life _____ just an interest.

   A) more... than   B) as... as   C) not... as   D) less... than

19. Cells do not have _____ of their own.

   A) intelligence   B) intelligent   C) intention   D) intellectual

20. I am _____ go and nothing will stop me.

   A) determine to   B) determining to   C) determined to   D) determination to

21. There's no clue to the _____ of the thief.

   A) identify   B) identity   C) identical   D) ideal

22. I haven't much _____ his honesty.

   A) believe in   B) believe for   C) belief in   D) belief for

23. The footprints are quite _____; they must be fresh.

   A) distant   B) district   C) distinguish   D) distinct

24. Don't _____ Austria with Australia.

   A) confuse   B) mistake   C) regard   D) view

25. The manager's only _____ is how to improve the quality of the products.

   A) concernedly   B) concerned   C) concerning   D) concern

26. She is too shy to feel _____ at such a party.

   A) at the ease   B) on her ease   C) for ease of her D) at ease

27. Each _____ leaf is different and unique to each other.

   A) personal   B) individual   C) separable   D) private

28. If only the message _____ in time.

   A) arrives   B) is arriving   C) has arrived   D) had arrived

29. You should be _____ for your own faults.

   A) responsible   B) present   C) popular   D) watchful

30. —How did you pay the workers?

   —As a rule, they were paid by _____.

   A) the hour   B) an hour   C) hour   D) a hour

Part II   Reading Comprehension

Directions: *Read the following two passages. Answer the questions of each passage by choosing A), B), C) or D).*

Passage 1

It was a normal summer night. Humidity hung in the thick air.

I couldn't go to sleep, partly because of my cold and partly because of my expectations for the next day. My mum had said that tomorrow was going to be a surprise.

Sweat stuck to my aching body. Finally, gathered enough strength to sit up. I looked out of my small window into the night. There was a big bright moon hanging in the sky, giving off a magic light.

I couldn't stand the pressure anymore, so I did what I always do to make myself feel better. I went to the bathroom and picked up my toothbrush and toothpaste. I cleaned my teeth as if there was no tomorrow. Back and forth, up and down.

Then I walked downstairs to look for some signs of movement, some life. Gladiator, my cat, frightened me as he meowed his sad song. He was on the old orange couch, sitting up on his front legs, waiting for something to happen. He looked at me as if to say "I'm lonely, pet me. I need a good hug." Even the couch begged me to sit on it.

In one movement I settled down onto the soft couch. This couch represented my parents' marriage, my birth, and hundreds of other little events.

As I held Gladiator, my heart started beating heavily. My mind was flooded with question: What's life? Am I really alive? Are you listening to me? Every time I moved my hand down Gladiator's body, I had a new thought; each touch sang a different song.

I forgot all about the heat and the next day's surprise. The atmosphere was so full of warmth and silence that I sank into its arms. Falling asleep with the big cat in my arms, I felt all my worries slowly move away.

1. The author could NOT go to sleep partly because _____.

    A) it was too cold   B) it was too humid   C) he had a cold   D) he had a fever

2. The weather that night was probably _____.

    A) freezing   B) fine   C) rainy   D) cloudy

3. The author kept brushing his teeth so as to _____.

    A) whiten his teeth   B) soothe his toothache

    C) relieve himself of the pressure   D) shake off the cold

4. Gladiator was the name of a _____.

    A) movie   B) song   C) couch   D) pet

5. What may the "couch" in the passage symbolize?

    A) Happy memories.   B) Wonderful songs.   C) A comfortable life.   D) A new perspective.

Passage 2

    Differences in American schools compared with those found in the majority of other countries lie in the fact that education here has long been intended for everyone—not just for a privileged elite. Schools are expected to meet the needs of every child, regardless of ability, and also the needs of society itself. This means that public schools offer more than academic subjects. It surprises many people when they come here to find high schools offering such courses as typing, sewing, repair of radio, computer programming or driver training, along with traditional academic subjects such as mathematics, history, and languages. Students choose their curricula depending on their interests, future goals, and level of ability. The underlying goal of American education is to develop every child to the utmost of his or her own possibilities, and to give each one a sense of civic and community consciousness.

    Schools have traditionally played an important role in creating national unity and "Americanizing" the millions of immigrants who have poured into this country from many different backgrounds and origins. Schools still play a large role in the community, especially in the small towns.

    The approach to teaching may seem unfamiliar to many, not only because it is informal, but also because there is not much emphasis on learning facts. Instead, Americans try to teach their children to think for themselves and to develop their own intellectual and creative abilities. Students spend much time, learning how to use resource materials, libraries, statistics and computers. Americans believe that if children are taught to reason well and to research well, they will be able to find whatever facts they need throughout the rest of their lives. Knowing how to solve problems is considered more important than the accumulation of facts.

6. Which of the following best states the goal of American education?

    A) To train every student to be a person of integrity.

    B) To give every student the opportunity to fully develop his ability.

    C) To equip every student with profound knowledge.

    D) To offer practical skills to every students.

7. Which of the following can be inferred from the passage?

A) Every high-school student takes some practical training courses.

B) All high-school students take the same subjects.

C) The subjects every student takes may vary.

D) All public schools offer the same subjects to students.

8. American education puts great emphasis on the learner's _____.

A) collection of first-hand information B) acquisition of knowledge

C) ability to be creative D) capability of working with his hands

9. Based on the passage, American education satisfies the needs of all the following EXCEPT _____.

A) the brilliant students B) the dull students

C) the immigrants D) the overseas students

10. According to the passage, what feature of American education sets it apart from education in other countries?

A) The special consideration given to immigrants.

B) The underlying goal to fully develop every child's abilities.

C) The wide coverage of its school districts.

D) The variety of the courses offered in its schools.

答案及详解

第一部分　词汇与结构

1. 【答案】C

【题解】本题考查动词辨析。reverse 颠倒，扭转；refuse 拒绝； return 归还，回报；recover 恢复，重新获得。

【译文】最终他推翻原判，释放了囚犯。

2. 【答案】C

【题解】minor在此作形容词，意为"较小的，次要的"；而其他三个选项unclear 不清楚的，serious 严重的，major 主要的，较大的，都与句意不符，排除。

【译文】别担心，问题不大，很快就能被克服的。

3. 【答案】A

【题解】take advantage of是固定短语，意为"利用"。而 adventure 冒险，advice 建议，advance 前进，都没有这样的搭配。

【译文】我想趁这次旅行的机会，买些需要的东西。

4. 【答案】D

【题解】短语be known for是"因……而著名"；而be known as是"作为……而知名，被称为"。

【译文】北京因其美丽的景色及长城而闻名。

5. 【答案】A

【题解】survive 在此用作及物动词，不接from，意为"幸免于难"。而 survival 是它的名词形式。

【译文】人们担心那些难民可能熬不过冬天。

6. 【答案】 B

　　【题解】 此题考查短语show off，意为"炫耀"；而show up意为"出现"。

　　【译文】 他确实喜欢自己的新发型，逢人便炫耀。

7. 【答案】 B

　　【题解】 challenge 挑战；chain 链条；chance 机会；change 变化。

　　【译文】 缩小贫富之间的差距是政府面临的主要挑战之一。

8. 【答案】 B

　　【题解】 本题考查用冠词与不用冠词导致词义不同的情况。out of the question 不可能，不值得讨论的；out of question 毫无疑问。

　　【译文】 为看足球比赛而旷课，那可不行。

9. 【答案】 B

　　【题解】 confidence与in 连用表示"相信，信任"；knowledge与of连用表示"了解"；dependence与on 连用表示"依靠"；responsibility 责任。

　　【译文】 我相信我的秘书，她会把事情办好的。

10. 【答案】 B

　　【题解】 本题考查come的短语搭配。come cross/across 偶然遇见或发现某人（某事）；come out 出现；come off 离开；come into 进入。

　　【译文】 今天早上我在牛津大街碰到了从前的校友。

11. 【答案】 D

　　【题解】 approach意为"道路，方法"时，常与介词to 搭配。如：the new approach to language teaching 语言教学的新方法。

　　【译文】 我们通过各种不同途径来收集情报。

12. 【答案】 B

　　【题解】 acknowledge *vt.* 承认，供认；knowledge *n.* 知识；aware *adj.* 意识到的（常和of搭配）；awake *vt.* 唤醒。

　　【译文】 他们拒不承认失败。

13. 【答案】 C

　　【题解】 if only用以表示对现时或未来的愿望。如：If only I could swim. 真希望我会游泳；If only he wouldn't eat so noisily. 但愿他吃东西不这样大声就好了。而only just表示"刚刚，恰好"。如：I've only just moved to London. 我刚刚搬到伦敦。

　　【译文】 她帮了我的大忙。要是我知道她的名字就好了。

14. 【答案】 A

　　【题解】 此题考查形容词辨析。lively 活跃的，有生气的；alive（作表语）活着的，活泼的；live 活的，生动的，实况转播的；living 活的，起作用的，现存的。

　　【译文】 她对周围的一切都有浓厚的兴趣。

15. 【答案】 C

　　【题解】 本题考查不定冠词和定冠词用于固定词组意义不同的情况。in a way 有几分，在某种程度上；in the way 造成不便或阻碍。

　　【译文】 这些变化从某种意义上说是一种进步。

16. 【答案】B

【题解】本题考查句型It occurs to (sb.)...，表示"（某人）想起，想到……"。如：It has never occurred to her to ask anyone. 她从未想到去问问他人。

【译文】我突然想到我们可以用计算机来做这项工作。

17. 【答案】C

【题解】prefer sth. (to sth.) 选择某事物（而不选择他事物）；更喜欢某事物。如：I prefer walking to cycling. 我愿意步行，不愿意骑自行车。而其他选项都不和to搭配。

【译文】我当教师是因为，与经商相比，我更喜欢书本。

18. 【答案】A

【题解】本题考查比较级more than的特殊用法，在这意为"与其……不如……"。如：She screamed, not loudly, more in surprise than terror. 她叫了一声，声音不大，与其说出于恐惧，不如说出于惊讶。

【译文】与其说音乐是他的兴趣，不如说是他的生活方式。

19. 【答案】A

【题解】intelligence n. 智力，智能；intelligent adj. 聪明的，有才智的；intention n. 目的；intellectual n. 知识分子，adj. 智力的。

【译文】细胞自身没有智能。

20. 【答案】C

【题解】本题考查短语be determined to do sth. 意为"决意做某事"。

【译文】我已下定决心要去，什么也拦不住我。

21. 【答案】B

【题解】identity n. 身份，identity card 身份证；identify vt. 确认，鉴别；identical adj. 完全相同的，同一的；ideal n. 完美的人或事，adj. 理想的。

【译文】没有确定窃贼身份的线索。

22. 【答案】C

【题解】have belief in sb./sth. 表示"对某事物/某人所具有的信心、信赖"。

【译文】我不太信赖他的诚实。

23. 【答案】D

【题解】此题考查形近词的辨析。distinct adj. 清晰的，明显的；distant adj. 遥远的；district n. 地区，区域；distinguish vt. 区别，辨析。

【译文】足迹清晰可辨，一定是不久前才留下的。

24. 【答案】A

【题解】confuse... with... 混淆，将……误当作……；而其他选项的搭配分别是mistake... for... 将……误当作……；regard... as... 把……看作……；view... as... 把……视作……。

【译文】不要把奥地利跟澳大利亚搞混了。

25. 【答案】D

【题解】concern在此作名词，表示"担心，关切的事"；concerning prep. 有关，关于；concerned adj. 担心的，涉及的；concernedly adv. 担忧地。

【译文】这经理唯一关心的是如何提高产品质量。

26.【答案】D

【题解】本题考查短语at ease "自在，安逸" 的用法。其他三项表达均不成立，但可以说at one's ease with sb.表示 "和某人在一起很自在"，with ease表示 "轻而易举地"。

【译文】她过于害羞，在这样的晚会上感到拘束。

27.【答案】B

【题解】此题考查形容词词义辨析。individual意为 "个别的，单个的"，与collective "集体的" 相对而言；personal意为 "个人的"，与 "他人的" 相对而言；separable意为 "可以分开的"；private意为 "私人的"，与 "公共的" 相对而言。

【译文】每片树叶都各不相同，各有特色。

28.【答案】D

【题解】if only表示 "但愿，要是……就好了"。若表示对将来的愿望，用 "would/could+动词原形"；若表示与现在事实相反的愿望，用动词的一般过去式，be动词用were；若是以前没实现的愿望，用had done。

【译文】要是这个信息能按时送达就好了。

29.【答案】A

【题解】be responsible for 是固定词组，意为 "对……负责"。present adj. 出席的；popular adj. 流行的，受欢迎的；watchful adj. 警惕的。

【译文】你应该对你自己的过错负责。

30 【答案】A

【题解】此题考查定冠词在表示计量单位的名词前的用法。

【译文】——你以什么方式支付工人报酬？
——通常他们按小时领取报酬。

第二部分　阅读理解

1.【答案】C

【题解】细节题。根据见文章的第二段中 "I couldn't go to sleep, partly because of my cold and partly because of my expectations for the next day" （我无法入睡，一是因为我感冒了，二是因为我对明天充满了期待）。my cold 是 "我的感冒"，不是寒冷，所以选C。

2.【答案】B

【题解】推断题。文章的第三段中 "There was a big bright moon hanging in the sky, giving off a magic light" （一轮明亮的满月挂在空中，发出神奇的光芒），可推断那天晚上天气很好，所以选B。

3.【答案】C

【题解】推断题。问题问及作者一直不断刷牙的原因，文章第四段出现了toothbrush（牙刷）和toothpaste（牙膏），根据前一句话 "I couldn't stand the pressure anymore, so I did what I always do to make myself feel better" [受不了这样的压力，于是我像往常一样（以刷牙释压），好让自己感觉好过一点]，可以推断出答案是C，原因是为了 "relieve himself of the pressure （缓解压力）"。

4.【答案】D

【题解】细节题。利用题干中的特征词Gladiator作为答案线索，可发现文章的第五段出现了同位语结构"Gladiator, my cat, frightened me..."。Gladiator是"猫",因此选项D(宠物)是答案。

5. 【答案】A
   【题解】细节题。根据见文章的第六段中"This couch represented my parents' marriage, my birth, and hundreds of other little events"(这沙发代表了父母的婚姻,我的出生,还有生活中无数的小插曲)。只有选项A(快乐的回忆)与之吻合。

6. 【答案】B
   【题解】细节题。问题问及美国教育的宗旨。根据见文章的第一段中"The underlying goal of American education is to develop every child to the utmost of his or her own possibilities"(美国教育的根本目标是要培养孩子发挥他们最大的潜力)。因此正确答案是B(让每个孩子有机会全面发展)。

7. 【答案】C
   【题解】推断题。借助前一题的解答得知美国教育的根本目标是在于学生能力的培养,因此推断C(学生学习的科目因人而异)是答案。根据也可见文章第一段中"Students choose their curricula depending on their interests, future goals, and level of ability"(学生根据他们的兴趣、将来的目标和能力水平来进行课程的选择)。

8. 【答案】C
   【题解】细节题。根据见文章的第三段中"Instead, Americans try to teach their children to think for themselves and to develop their own intellectual and creative abilities"(美国教育试图培养孩子们的独立思考能力及创造力)。因此C选项正确。

9. 【答案】D
   【题解】推断题。借助第6题,了解到美国教育致力于培养每个学生的能力,因此判断无论选项A(聪颖的学生)还是选项B(迟钝的学生)都应该是美国教育能满足的对象。而文章第二段的"Schools have traditionally played an important role in... Americanizing the millions of immigrants..."(学校一向扮演着推进数百万移民美国化的角色),间接暗示美国教育能满足移民者的需要,因此只有D(留学生),没有提到。

10. 【答案】B
    【题解】细节题。根据见文章开头"Differences in American schools compared with those found in the majority of other countries lie in the fact that education here has long been intended for everyone",该句强调了"同其他多数国家相比,美国教育的不同在于它是面向每个学生的普及教育",所以选B。

3 Love

单元导读

什么是爱？不同的人对爱有不同的理解。多数情况下，我们对爱的定义是基于我们个人的感受和经历：

"爱是对亲人的情感，也是爱人间的温柔。它是依恋、热爱和敬重。"

"我的奶奶因为关节炎而无法弯下腰去涂脚指甲。于是爷爷就一直为她涂，即使在他的手也得了关节炎后。那就是爱。"

"当你们一起去吃饭，你把自己的薯条分一大半给他，而不想着去分他的。那就是爱。"

"看着臭汗淋漓的老爸，妈妈还说他是最帅的。那就是爱。"

"你告诉一个家伙说你喜欢他的衬衫，于是他就每天穿着它。那就是爱。"

……

爱是神秘而难以理解的力量。它可以精彩、不同寻常，可能是上天的恩赐，也可能是痛苦，是悲剧。而在更多的时候它是一次经历。没有爱的生活是乏味的，毕竟让地球转动的是爱，而不是金钱或其他的什么。

课文精讲

TEXT **A**

📖 文章导读

朋友的热恋让安妮特重新审视自己的爱情。是什么让这份爱情延续至今？这里不仅有那些显而易见的原因：责任感、共同的兴趣、沟通……还有其他更多。安妮特将和我们分享她温情脉脉的爱情故事。

🔘 背景知识

莫扎特（Walfgang Amadeus Mozart）：（1756—1791）奥地利作曲家，维也纳古典乐派的代表人物。1756年1月27日生于萨尔茨堡，1791年12月5日卒于维也纳。莫扎特出生在一位宫廷乐师的家庭。3岁起显露音乐才能，4岁跟父亲学习钢琴，5岁作曲，6岁又随父亲学小提琴，8岁创作了一批奏鸣曲和交响曲，11岁写了第一部歌剧。他仅仅活了36岁。繁重的创作、演出和贫困的生活损害了他的健康，使他过早地离开了人世，他的音乐作品成为世界音乐宝库的珍贵遗产。

7 文章写作风格及结构

本文为记叙文（narration），通过列举让爱情保鲜的方法来叙说一个温情脉脉的爱情故事。

Parts 部分	Paragraphs 段落	Main Ideas 大意
Part I	1—3	My friend fell in love, and claimed she was young again, while I took a look at my love again, and found, although my husband became older and older, he was still attractive to me. 我的朋友恋爱了，她觉得自己年轻了。与此同时，我审视自己的爱情，发现虽然我的丈夫老了，可是仍然很吸引我。
Part II	4—10	From my own love story, I concluded seven main reasons for the question "What will make this love last". 从我自己的爱情故事中我总结出了七点保持爱情的要素。
Part III	11	Our love lasts because it is comfortable. Our love and experience didn't make us younger but contributed to our growth and wisdom and created our memories. 我们的爱情长久是因为这种感情让我们双方都很舒服。我们的爱和经历并没有让我们更年轻，却让我们更加成熟、更加睿智，并丰富了我们的回忆。

词汇点睛

1 claim

vt. to state that sth. is true 声称，断言

• 例句 • He claims he was at home alone at the time of the murder. 他声称案发时他独自呆在家里。

No one claimed responsibility for the bombing. 没有人声称对这起爆炸事件负责。

n. a statement that sth. is true 声称，断言

• 例句 • The government says they have reduced personal taxation, but I would dispute this claim.

政府声称已经减收了个人税，但我对这种说法持有异议。

2 recede

vi. if sth. you can see or hear recedes, it gets further and further away until it disappears 后退

• 例句 • The tide was receding. 潮水退去。

As the tide receded from the shore, we were able to look for shells.

潮水（自岸边）退去，我们就能寻找贝壳了。

3 commitment

n. sth. that you have promised you will do, or that you have to do 承诺，责任

• 例句 • He is under a commitment to finish the task by May 1. 他应允5月1日以前完成这项工作。

He has made a commitment to pay off all his debts. 他作出了还清所有债务的承诺。

She's got family commitments. 她承担着家庭的责任。

• 扩展 • **commit** *vt.* 犯（错误、罪行等），干（蠢事、坏事等）；使承担义务，使承诺

Anyone caught committing an offence will be punished. 任何人被发现违法都要受到惩处。

He refused to commit himself to any sort of promise. 他拒不作出任何承诺。

He has committed himself to support his brother's children. 他已答应抚养他弟弟的孩子。

4 unselfishness

n. the quality of not caring only, or primarily, about yourself 无私，慷慨

- 例句 - In their lessons at school, boys and girls may learn about such virtues as unselfishness, courage, and discipline.

  在校学习期间，孩子们可以学到很多品德，诸如无私、勇气、纪律。

- 反义词 - **selfishness** *n.* 自私

  selfish *adj.* 自私的

  He's too selfish to think of lending me his car. 他很自私，不想把汽车借给我。

5 spontaneous

adj. sth. that is spontaneous has not been planned or organized, but happens by itself 自然的，自发的

- 例句 - Hearing the joke, we burst into spontaneous laughter. 听到笑话，我们不由自主地大笑起来。

  There is a spontaneous cheer from the crowd. 人们自发地喝彩。

6 playfully

adv. not intended seriously 开玩笑地，顽皮地

- 例句 - She playfully made a bitter face and groaned, "It's really tough, you know."

  她顽皮地做着鬼脸，抱怨道，"你知道吗，这太难了。"

- 扩展 - **playful** *adj.* 爱嬉戏的，顽皮的

  She is as playful as a kitten. 她像小猫一样顽皮。

7 all-out

adj. involving a lot of energy, determination, or anger 全面的，竭尽全力的

- 例句 - That was the time to launch an all-out war against terrorism.

  是时候对恐怖主义发动全面的战争了。

  Official calls out all-out effort to ensure stability. 政府官员呼吁大家竭尽全力维护社会稳定。

8 nonstop

adj. without any stops or pauses 不间断的，不停的

- 例句 - There is a nonstop flight to Los Angeles. 有一个航班直达洛杉矶。

  After six hours nonstop searching, finally he found what he wanted.

  经过六个小时不间断地寻找，他终于找到了他想要的。

9 household

adj. relating to looking after a house and the people in it 家庭的

- 例句 - Microwave ovens are now a common household appliance.

  微波炉现在是普通的家用器具。

  n. all the people who live together in one house 一家人；家庭

- 例句 - On Sunday, the whole household went to the beach in the south. 星期天全家去了南方的海滩。

  I grew up as part of a large household. 我是在一个大家庭里长大的。

- 扩展 - **housing** *n.* （总称）房屋，住宅

More housing is needed for old people. 需要为老年人提供更多的住宅。

She came to college early to look for housing. 她早早到校去寻找住房。

10　parental

adj. relating to being a parent and especially to being responsible for a child's safety and development 父（母）亲的

- 例句 • Some fathers are trying to share the housework and parental responsibilities.

某些父亲正在尽力地分担家务事以及为人父的责任。

Parental love should include discipline, and so the teenager will receive guidance.

父母的爱应该包括惩戒，这样孩子们才能得到引导。

11　burden

n. sth. difficult or worrying that you are responsible for 负担，重担

- 例句 • It is a burden to the people. 这对人民是一种负担。

The developing countries bear the burden of an enormous external debt.

发展中国家负担着大量外债。

12　historical

adj. describing or based on events in the past 历史（上）的，史学的

- 例句 • Prof. Johnson has a wide range of historical knowledge. 约翰逊教授有着广博的历史知识。

Qu Yuan is a historical play written by Guo Moruo. 《屈原》是郭沫若写的一部历史剧。

- 辨析 • **historic** *adj.* 历史上著名的，具有重大历史意义的

There are a lot of historic spots in China. 中国有许多古迹。

It is here that the historic campaign took place. 这场历史性的战役就是在这里展开的。

13　exchange

vt. 1) *to discuss sth. or share information, ideas, etc.* 交流

- 例句 • We hardly exchanged a word during breakfast. 早餐时我们几乎没有交谈过一句话。

　　　2) *to give someone sth. and receive sth. different from them* 交换

- 例句 • Teachers should usually exchange ideas with their students. 老师应该常常和学生们交换意见。

Ali exchanged seats with Ben. 阿里和本调换了座位。

n. the act of giving someone sth. and receiving sth. else from them 交换，互换，调换

- 例句 • Let's have an exchange of views on the matter. 我们交换一下对这件事的意见吧。

He gave me an apple in exchange for a piece of cake. 他用一个苹果和我换了一块蛋糕。

14　forgiveness

n. the act of forgiving 原谅，宽恕

- 例句 • He asked for our forgiveness. 他请求我们的原谅。

- 扩展 • **forgive** *vt.* 原谅，饶恕

Please forgive me for being late. 请原谅我来晚了。

She forgave him his thoughtless remark. 她原谅了他轻率的言语。

15　embarrassingly

adv. making you feel ashamed, nervous, or uncomfortable 令人尴尬地

- 例句 • That is an embarrassingly poor performance. 那场表演糟糕得令人尴尬。

- 扩展 • **embarrass** *vt.* 使困窘，使尴尬

I was embarrassed by his comments about my clothes. 他对我的衣服的评论使我很尴尬。

Meeting strangers embarrasses Tom. 会见陌生人使汤姆局促不安。

embarrassing *adj.* 令人为难的，令人尴尬的

She asked a lot of embarrassing questions. 她问了不少令人尴尬的问题。

This incident is deeply embarrassing for the government. 这一事件真让政府难堪。

16　savings

n. (pl.) all the money that you have saved, especially in a bank 存款，储蓄

• 例句 • Dick has £100 in his savings. 迪克有100英镑的存款。

He lost all his savings. 他失去了全部积蓄。

17　sensitivity

n. the ability to understand other people's feelings and problems 感性，易受感动，敏感（性）

• 例句 • She has always shown a sensitivity to audience needs and tastes.

她总是对观众的需求和喜好很敏感。

• 扩展 • **sensitive** *adj.* 敏感的

Don't shout at her—she's very sensitive. 别对着她大声喊，她很敏感。

She is sensitive to criticism. 她对别人的批评很敏感。

• 辨析 • **sensible** *adj.* 明智的，合情理的

It was sensible of you to keep it a secret. 你不把这件事情说出来是很明智的。

That was a sensible idea. 那是一个明智的主意。

18　recover

vi. to get better after an illness, accident, shock, etc. 痊愈，复原

• 例句 • Jason was slow to recover from the car accident. 杰森车祸后复原很慢。

The country is recovering from an economic crisis. 这个国家正在从经济危机中恢复过来。

• 扩展 • **recovery** *n.* 恢复，痊愈

He made a very quick recovery from his operation. 他手术后很快就痊愈了。

19　appointment

n. an arrangement for a meeting at an agreed time and place, for a particular purpose 约会，预约

• 例句 • He will only see you by appointment. 只有事先预约，他才能见你。

An appointment was made for the following morning. 约会定在第二天上午。

• 扩展 • **appoint** *vt.* 约定，指定（时间，地点）

He wasn't there at the appointed time. 在约定的时间里他不在那里。

He appointed the school house as the place for the meeting. 他指定校舍为开会的地点。

20　contribute

v. 1) *to help to bring about* 有助于，促成

• 例句 • Plenty of fresh air contributes to good health. 多呼吸新鲜空气对健康有益。

Various factors contributed to his downfall. 许多因素导致了他的垮台。

2) *to join with others in giving help, money, etc.* 捐赠，捐助；贡献

• 例句 • He contributed a large sum to the hospital. 他给这家医院捐赠了一笔巨款。

Everyone contributed food for the picnic. 人人都为野餐贡献了些食物。

🔵 短语解析

1. make it to 及时到达……

【例句】She had to get a move on if she was going to make it to the city before noon.

如果她要在中午之前到达那个城市，那她必须要出发了。

With blood pouring from his leg, he made it to a nearby hospital.

带着满腿的鲜血，他及时到达了附近的一家医院。

2. shed tears 流泪，哭泣

【例句】She shed no tears for her friend's death. 面对朋友的逝去，她没有流一滴眼泪。

3. on a regular basis 经常

【例句】We hear from him on a regular basis. 我们经常收到他的来信。

4. take its toll 造成损失（伤亡等）

【例句】Years of civil war and drought have taken their toll, and the population of the region is greatly reduced. 连年的内战和干旱已经造成了损失。这个地区的人口锐减。

Bad working conditions eventually take a toll on staff morale.

糟糕的工作环境最终会对员工的士气造成影响。

🔵 难句突破

1. (Para. 3) *As my friend raves on about her new love, I've taken a good look at my old one.*

【解析】1) as作连词，引导时间状语从句，具体用法见Unit1，Text A难句突破9。

2) rave on: 热情洋溢地谈论

rave on about中的on about是双重介词。双重介词是两个介词的重叠使用，表达两个介词共有的更精确更明了的含义，从表达意义的角度分析，双重介词用在一个介词难以全面表达含义的场合，或者是需要从两个角度来描述其具体意义的场合。一般来说，前一个介词意义含糊，后一个介词比较具体或从另一个角度对前者进行补充完善。例如：

New shoots will come up from round roots. 新芽从旧根周围长出。

（from和round同属地点位置范畴，但任何一个介词均不足以全面表达意义。）

He won't come back until after sunset. 到太阳落山之后他才能回来。

（until与after同属时间范畴。）

【译文】朋友激情洋溢地谈论着她的新欢时，我也好好审视了我的老相好一番。

2. (Para. 3) *His hairline is receding and his body shows the signs of long working hours and too many candy bars.*

【解析】his body shows the signs of long working hours 是非常隐晦的描写手法，通过描写他的体形显现出长久工作的痕迹来暗示他已经上了年纪，略显沧桑；同样后半句and (his body shows the sign of) too many candy bars通过描写他的体形显出过多进食糖块的痕迹也就是说日渐发胖。

【译文】他的头发日渐稀少，体型也显露出长久工作的沧桑和过多进食糖块的痕迹。

3. (Para. 4) *Yesterday, after slipping the rubber band off the rolled up newspaper, Scott flipped it playfully at me, which led to an all-out war.*

【解析】1) after在此处作介词，后接sth.或v.-ing，表示"在……之后"。

2) which引导非限定性定语从句，指代整个主句Scott flipped it playfully at me。非限定性定语从句和先行词之间有逗号分开，而且两者之间的关系比较松散，只起补充说明的作用，即使省略了也不影响主句意义的完整。在非限定性定语从句中，关系代词只能用which而不能用that。which可以指代主句中的一个名词或名词性词组，也可以指代整个主句。例如：

I have lost my pen, which I like very much.

（关系代词which在从句中作宾语，指代主句中的pen。）

我把我很喜欢的那支笔弄丢了。

New Concept English is intended for foreign students, which is known to all of us. （关系代词which在从句中作主语，代表整个主句。）

众所周知，《新概念英语》是为非英语国家的学生编写的。

【译文】昨天，斯科特把原本捆扎着报纸卷的橡皮筋取下来，然后顽皮地把它弹向我，"战争"从此一发不可收拾。

4. (Para. 4) *Last Saturday at the grocery, we split the list and raced each other to see who could make it to the checkout first.*

【解析】1) split意为"分开，分割" 此处split the list表示把购物清单一分为二。

2) 句中的and连接两个并列的动作split和race；who引导宾语从句作动词see的宾语。

3) 此处的make it表示及时地做某事，此处指选好东西后到达收银台。

【译文】上周六在杂货店，我们把购物清单一分为二，比赛看谁在选好东西后先到达收银台。

5. (Para. 7) *Not only do we share household worries and parental burdens—we also share ideas.*

【解析】not only... but (also)... 意为"不但……而且……"，重点强调的是后一部分。并且需要注意的是not only放在句首时，需要用部分倒装的形式。例如：

Not only **is he himself interested in the subject**, but also his students began to show interest in it.

（正常的语序应该是he himself is interested in the subject）

不仅他自己对这个课题很感兴趣，而且他的学生也开始感兴趣了。

Not only **is your answer right**, but mine also is.

（正常的语序应该是your answer is right）

不仅你的答案是对的，我的也对。

【译文】我们不仅共同分担家务之忧和为人父母的责任，我们还分享各自的见解。

6. (Para. 7) *He touched my heart when he explained it was because he wanted to be able to exchange ideas about the book after I'd read it.*

【解析】1) 句子的主干是he touched my heart；when引导时间状语从句；because引导表语从句；after引导时间状语从句说明exchange ideas的时间。

2) he touched my heart表示我被他感动，相当于I was touched by him。

【译文】他解释说，那是因为他希望在我读完这本小说之后可以和我交流感想。我的心为之感动。

7. (Para. 9) *Last week he walked through the door with that look that tells me it's been a tough day.*

【解析】 1) 本句中出现了两个that。其中第一个that是代词，表示那种表情（that look），第二个that是关系代词，引导定语从句，修饰"look"。

2) look在此处作名词，表示表情，相当于appearance。例如：

She gave me a questioning look. 她脸上露出了质问的表情。

She had a worried look about him. 对于他，她露出了担忧的表情。

【译文】 上周，他回家进门时的表情告诉我他那天过得很糟糕。

8. (Para. 9) *How was he going to tell this husband of 40 years that his wife would probably never recover?*

【解析】 句子的主干是how was he going to tell this husband that...。that引导宾语从句作 tell 的直接宾语。

husband of 40 years: 相伴了40年的丈夫。

【译文】 他怎么忍心告诉这位与妻子相伴了40年的丈夫，他的妻子可能再也无法康复了呢?

9. (Para.9) *Because my husband is still moved and concerned after years of hospital rooms and dying patients.*

【解析】 本句涉及到指代的用法。用hospital rooms and dying patients指代我丈夫的医务工作。当甲事物同乙事物不相类似，但有密切关系时，可以利用这种关系，以乙事物的名称来取代甲事物。这种方式叫借代。类似的用法又如：以kettle喻指water（The kettle boils. 水开了。），以the crown喻指royal affairs（He succeeded to the crown. 他继承了王位。）。

【译文】 因为我的丈夫在经历了多年的医务工作，目睹过无数的垂死病人之后仍然会被感动，仍存怜悯之心。

10. (Para.11) *We don't feel particularly young: we've experienced too much that has contributed to our growth and wisdom, taking its toll on our bodies, and created our memories.*

【解析】 1) that在句中引导定语从句；先行词是不定代词much。注意当先行词是all，few，little，much，something，nothing，anything等不定代词时，必须用that引导定语从句，不能用which。例如：

All that we have to do is to practice every day. 我们所能做的就是天天练习。

2) taking its toll on our bodies是现在分词作状语表示伴随，其中its指代experience，表示"经历在我们的身上刻下岁月的痕迹"。

3) and连接的两个并列成分是：we've have experienced...和 (we've) created... 。

【译文】 我们也不再感觉年轻：我们已经历了太多，而这些经历在我们身上刻下岁月痕迹的同时，也让我们更加成熟、更加睿智，并丰富了我们的回忆。

参考译文

最美好的爱
安妮特·帕克斯曼·鲍恩

我有一个朋友，正处于热恋中。她坦言天空都好像比以前更蓝了。莫扎特的音乐让她感动得流泪。而且她的体重也减了15磅，看上去像个封面女郎。

"我又年轻了！"她激动地嚷着。

朋友激情洋溢地谈论着她的新欢时，我也好好审视了我的老相好一番。我的丈夫斯科特在同我结婚的将近20年间，体重增加了15磅。他曾经是个马拉松选手，而现在只有在医院大厅里奔来奔去。他的头发日渐稀少，体型也显露出长久工作的沧桑和过多进食糖块的痕迹。但在外出用餐的时候，餐桌对面的他仍能用某种特定的眼神打动我，让我立即结账，然后和他一起回家。

当朋友问我"是什么让这份爱情延续至今"时，我罗列了一堆显而易见的答案：责任感、共同的兴趣、无私、外表的吸引力，还有沟通。然而，除了这些，还有其他更多的原因。比如，我们到现在还相处得非常开心，心之所至，我们都可以开心一番。昨天，斯科特把原本捆扎着报纸卷的橡皮筋取下来，然后顽皮地把它弹向我，"战争"从此一发不可收拾。上周六在杂货店，我们把购物清单一分为二，比赛看谁在选好东西后先到达收银台。就是在洗碗的时候我们也可以大斗一番。只要在一起，我们就能开心不已。

我们常常给对方带来惊喜。有一次我回到家，发现前门上贴着一张小纸条，纸条指引我去找到另一张纸条，然后是下一张，就这样我一直走到储藏室。打开门，发现斯科特手里拿着"金罐子"（我烹调用的汤锅）和内装着"财富"的大礼包。有时候，我也会在镜子上给他留便条，把小礼物偷偷藏在他的枕头底下。

我们相互理解。我理解他为什么非要和老朋友们打篮球，而他也理解我为什么每年一定要离开家一次，抛下孩子甚至他，去和我的姐妹们聚会，连续几天，不停地聊啊笑啊。

我们共同分享。我们不仅共同分担家务之忧和为人父母的责任，我们还分享各自的见解。上个月，斯科特开会回来，递给我一本厚厚的历史小说。尽管他喜欢惊险和科幻小说，但他还是在飞机上把那本小说读完了。他解释说，那是因为他希望在我读完这本小说之后可以和我交流感想。我的心为之感动。

我们相互谅解。当我在聚会上令人尴尬地大声说话，做出疯狂举动时，斯科特原谅了我。而当他向我坦白用我们的积蓄炒股亏了钱时，我拥抱着他说："没关系的，钱财乃身外之物。"

我们都是性情中人。上周，他回家进门时的表情告诉我他那天过得很糟糕。等他和孩子们玩了一会儿之后，我问他发生了什么事。他告诉我一位60岁的老太太患了中风。当回忆起那位老太太的丈夫站在她床边，抚摸着她的手时，斯科特落泪了。他怎么忍心告诉这位与妻子相伴了40年的丈夫，他的妻子可能再也无法康复了呢？我听到这里也禁不住流泪了，因为那可怕的病，因为这世上还有维系了40年的婚姻，还因为我的丈夫在经历了多年的医务工作，目睹过无数的垂死病人之后仍然会被感动，仍存怜悯之心。

最后一个原因是，我们彼此了解。我知道斯科特常把他的衣服到处乱丢，大多数约会他都迟到，他会把盒子里最后一块巧克力吃掉。他也知道我睡觉时喜欢用枕头蒙着头，我时不时会因为忘记带钥匙而把一家人锁在门外，我也会吃掉最后一块巧克力。

我想我们的爱情之所以持久是因为这种感情让我们双方都很舒服。是的，天空并没有变得更蓝，还是以前我们熟悉的颜色。我们也不再感觉年轻：我们已经历了太多，而这些经历在我们身上刻下岁月痕迹的同时，也让我们更加成熟、更加睿智，并丰富了我们的回忆。

习题全解

文章大意

1. 根据课文用适当的词填空。

【答案】　1) almost 20　　　　2) unselfishness　　3) communication　　4) fun

　　　　　5) understanding　　6) forgiveness　　　7) knowing　　　　8) comfortable

　　　　　9) growth and wisdom　　10) memories

【解析】besides 除了……

　　　　enjoying being together 享受在一起的时光

　　　　contribute to 为……作贡献

【译文】　作者和她的丈夫已经结婚近 20 年了。她的丈夫斯科特比原来胖了许多，头发也日渐稀少，但是对于作者来说，仍然很有魅力。

　　　　当作者的朋友问她是什么让这份爱延续至今的时候，她告诉朋友，除了最显而易见的原因——责任感、共同的兴趣、无私、外表的吸引和沟通外，还有其他的原因。虽然结婚已经20年了，他们仍然相处得非常开心，并且很享受在一起的时光。他们常常给对方惊喜，他们互相理解、分享、谅解，他们都是性情中人，并相互了解。她认为他们的爱之所以持久是因为这种感情让他们双方都很舒服。他们不再感觉年轻，但是生活经历让他们更加成熟、更加睿智，并丰富了他们的回忆。

文章细节

1. 根据文章回答问题。

【答案】

1) She feels that the sky is bluer; Mozart moves her to tears; she looks more beautiful and feels young again.

2) Almost 20 years.

3) Commitment, shared interests, unselfishness, physical attraction, and communication.

4) They have fun, spontaneous good times; there are surprises, understanding, sharing, forgiveness, sensitivity, and knowing.

5) Using the stories of their everyday life as examples.

6) No. To the author, the sky is not bluer, but a familiar hue. They don't feel particularly young, but feel their love experiences have contributed to their growth and wisdom. Although their life has taken its toll on their bodies, their love gives them good memories.

【译文】

1) [问题] 当作者的那位朋友陷入爱河时她的感觉是什么?

   [答案] 她觉得天更蓝了,莫扎特的音乐让她感动得掉泪,她看上去更漂亮,也感觉更年轻了。

2) [问题] 作者与她丈夫结婚多久了?

   [答案] 差不多20年了。

3) [问题] 作者的爱情得以持续的明显原因是什么?

   [答案] 责任感、分享、无私、外表吸引和沟通。

4) [问题] 除了那些显而易见的原因,作者认为还有其他什么原因?

   [答案] 他们相处很开心,心之所至,都可以开心一番。生活中充满惊喜、理解、分享、谅解、感念和了解。

5) [问题] 作者如何例证那些使他们爱情持久的原因?

   [答案] 用他们的日常生活作例子。

6) [问题] 作者对爱的感觉和她朋友一样么?她对爱是什么样的感觉?

   [答案]不。对作者而言,天空并不是更蓝了,还是以前熟悉的颜色。他们不再感觉年轻,但感觉他们的爱情经历让他们更加成熟和睿智了,尽管生活在他们身上已留下岁月的痕迹,但爱给他们带来了美好的回忆。

词汇练习

1. 请用下面所给词汇或短语的适当形式填写句子。

1) 【答案】shed

   【译文】火车发动了,亲爱的朋友们在站台上流着泪,挥动着手绢,向我们告别。

2) 【答案】laundry

   【译文】她洗了衣服,并把它挂出去晾干。

3) 【答案】household

   【译文】微波炉现在是常见的家用电器了。

4) 【答案】contributes to

   【译文】充足的新鲜空气有利健康。

5) 【答案】slip

   【译文】你不能让机会溜掉。

6) 【答案】exchange

   【译文】我的家人在圣诞节时依然会交换礼物。

7) 【答案】made it to

   【译文】迄今为止,相对而言,为数很少的女性能在商界跻身前列。

8) 【答案】recovering

   【译文】这个国家正从经济危机中慢慢恢复。

9) 【答案】historical

   【译文】约翰逊教授有着广博的历史知识。

10) 【答案】on a regular basis

   【译文】我定期存钱。

2. 选用以下单词的适当形式完成句子。

1) 【答案】recede; weeping; tough; recover

   【译文】在夺走了差不多300人的生命后，洪水最终开始退去了。在清理受灾地区时，居民们也认识到要从灾难中恢复会经历一段艰苦的时间。

2) 【答案】embarrassment; confess; commitment; all-out

   【译文】这对他来说是件尴尬的事：堂堂六尺男儿居然怕黑。他要求他的朋友们许诺要保密。然而，朋友们的食言导致了他们之间的彻底决裂。

3) 【答案】sensitivity; unselfishly; stock; contributed; savings

   【译文】带着对孩子们深深的爱、感念和洞察，她无私地投身于教育事业。当其他人忙着将自己的钱投入股票市场时，她却将自己的部分积蓄拿来帮助那些辍学的学生。

4) 【答案】running through; claimed; burden

   【译文】将导致这个地区不稳定的所有可能因素匆匆考虑过后，她宣称唯一的解决办法是减轻穷人的赋税压力。

5) 【答案】caressed; hug; had forgiven

   【译文】芭芭拉把我拉到她身边，抚摸我的脸颊，紧紧抱住我。从她的笑容我知道她已原谅了我。

3. 学习表格里的词汇，推测其意义，并用所给词汇的适当形式完成句子。

1) 【答案】non-stop

   【译文】这儿每天都有一趟从伦敦到纽卡斯尔的直达列车。

2) 【答案】non-violence

   【译文】甘地是非暴力运动的忠实信徒。

3) 【答案】non-smokers

   【译文】这家饭店的这部分区域是禁烟的。

4) 【答案】non-profit

   【译文】非盈利机构用它获得的钱去帮助人，而不是用来盈利。

5) 【答案】non-agricultural

   【译文】当地政府正着手限制非农业性的耕地占用。

6) 【答案】parental

   【译文】作为一位单身妈妈，她竭力平衡着工作及作为母亲的责任。

7) 【答案】financial

   【译文】这是部精彩的电影，但票房收益并不高。

8) 【答案】natural

   【译文】这个年龄的孩子如此安静不合常理。

9) 【答案】racial

   【译文】社区的这一块需要保护，以避免种族歧视。

10) 【答案】emotional

   【译文】当我们不得不离开时，他非常伤感。

语法结构

1. 仿照例句用not only... (but) also改写下列句子。

1) 【答案】Not only does John read newspapers, he also reads magazines.

【译文】约翰不但读报，而且也看杂志。

2) 【答案】Not only did the students download a new computer game, they also downloaded some useful software.

【译文】学生们不但下载了一个新的电脑游戏，也下载了些有用的软件。

3) 【答案】Not only are we going to visit the Forbidden City, we are also going to visit the Summer Palace.

【译文】我们不但要去参观故宫，也要去游颐和园。

4) 【答案】Not only is Mary fond of playing basketball, she also likes skating.

【译文】玛丽不但喜欢打篮球，也喜欢滑冰。

5) 【答案】Not only did the boss blame the salesgirl, he also decided to dismiss her.

【译文】老板不但指责了这个女店员，而且还决定解雇她。

2. 仿照例句用with... 将下列句子中的中文部分译成英文。

1) 【答案】with people talking loudly around you

【译文】有人在你旁边大声说话，你还能睡着吗？

2) 【答案】with all the computers on

【译文】他离开了办公室，所有电脑都开着。

3) 【答案】with some documents under his arm

【译文】教授进入了讲演室，胳膊下夹着一些文件。

4) 【答案】with three questions unanswered

【译文】他交了试卷，有三个问题没回答。

5) 【答案】with all the other students staring at them

【译文】特里与他的数学老师争执着，其他所有学生都盯着他们。

综合练习

1. 完形填空。

1) 【答案】B

【解析】本题考查时态的运用。因为整个故事是用的过去时态，而且根据上下文可知he was carrying是一个定语从句，修饰前面的先行词books，这里需要用过去进行时态来表示"他背的所有书"，所以答案是B。

2) 【答案】C

【解析】take up 开始从事，着手处理；take on 呈现，具有；pick up 捡起，拾起。help sb. do sth. 是固定用法，所以只能用pick up动词原形。本句意为"马克跪下来，帮男孩拾起了散落在地上的东西。"

3) 【答案】A

【解析】同义词辨析。since 自从，因为；as to 关于；because of和for也可以表示"因为"，但because of和for后面通常跟名词或动名词短语，since则连接原因状语从句，所以答案选A。

4) 【答案】D

   【解析】本句意为"马克得知了……，但其他的功课都很糟……" have a trouble with... 是固定搭配，表示"在……方面很糟糕"。

5) 【答案】B

   【解析】relation 关系；contact 联系，接触；touch 身体接触；relationship 关系。本句意为"……期间他们也有短暂的联系。"

6) 【答案】C

   【解析】remind sb. of sth. 是固定搭配，表示"让某人忆起某事"。

7) 【答案】C

   【解析】clean out 是固定搭配，表示"彻底打扫"。

8) 【答案】B

   【解析】mass 大量，大多数；mess 混乱，一团糟；mix 使混合；mixture 混合，混合物。本句意为"……不想给后来使用的人留下一团糟。"

9) 【答案】C

   【解析】本题考查虚拟语气的用法。对过去的虚拟，从句用 had done...，主句用 would have done...。

10) 【答案】D

   【解析】might have done sth. 表示"对过去所发生的事情的推测"，因此答案选 D。

【译文】

　　一天，马克正走在从学校回家的路上，突然注意到前面的男孩绊倒了，他背的所有书，还有两件毛衣，一根棒球棒，一只手套和一个小磁带录音机都掉了下来。马克跪下来，帮男孩拾起了散落在地上的东西。由于同路，他帮他背了一部分行李。在路上，马克得知这个男孩叫比尔，喜欢打游戏、爱好棒球以及历史，但其他的功课都很糟，而且刚和女友分手。

　　马克把比尔送回家才走。他们在学校附近继续见面，偶尔会一起吃午饭，后来他俩都从初中毕业了，又进了同一所高中，期间也有过些短暂的联系；随后，等待了许久的高三生活来临了。在离毕业还有三周时，比尔问马克是否能出来谈谈。

　　比尔让马克回忆多年前他们初次见面的那一天。"你有没有想过为什么我那天带着那么多的东西？"比尔问道，"我清理了存物柜里的所有东西，是不想给后来使用的人留下一团乱。我存了些我妈妈用的安眠药，打算回家去自杀。但是在我们一起说说笑笑后，我发现如果我自杀了，我可能会错过那样的时光，以及以后很多那样的日子。马克，现在你知道了，你那天帮我时，你所做的远远不止那些。你救了我的命。"

2. 用括号中的词汇和短语将下列句子译成英语。

1) 【答案】He claimed that he could make it to the top of the mountain within two hours.

2) 【答案】George confesses that nonstop dating with his girlfriend has become a big burden to him.

3) 【答案】Exchanging ideas on a regular basis contributes to (building) a good relationship between husband and wife.

4) 【答案】Hearing the news that her mother had recovered from cancer, Linda was moved to tears.

5) 【答案】The couple share all the household chores, including everything from going to the grocery to doing the laundry.

文章泛读

📖 文章导读

    23岁是丹生命中的一个里程碑，结束校园生活的他将要开始对世界的探索。作为父亲的大卫，在即将与儿子告别的时候，会对丹说些什么呢？叮嘱？建议？祝福？……然而话到嘴边却又咽下。这样的情形已经不是第一次了——上学的第一天，大学生活的第一天。这次呢？大卫会如何表达一个父亲对孩子的爱呢？

💿 背景知识

    与母亲细碎宽广的爱相比，父爱似乎难以企及；但是，父爱的深沉，父爱的伟岸，父爱的宏远，同样给人启迪与教诲。世界上的第一个父亲节于1910年诞生在美国。1924年，美国总统柯立芝（Calvin Coolidge）支持父亲节成为美国的全国性节日；1966年，美国总统约翰逊（Lyndon Johnson）宣布当年6月的第三个星期日为美国父亲节；1972年，美国总统尼克松（Richard Nixon）签署正式文件，将每年6月的第三个星期日，定为全美国的父亲节，并一直沿用至今。虽然今天一般人对于父亲节不像对母亲节一般重视，庆祝活动也不如母亲节的热闹，但是父母的关爱却是一致的，当母亲含辛茹苦地照顾我们时，父亲也在努力地扮演着他的角色。或许当我们努力思考着该为父亲买什么样的礼物过父亲节之时，不妨反省一下，我们是否爱我们的父亲，像他们那样曾为我们无私地付出一生呢？

🔢 文章写作风格及结构

    本文为记叙文（narration），通过描写父亲在儿子临行前的思想活动，以及对往事的回忆，向读者刻画了一个平凡而又伟大的父亲，让读者深深感受到那份浓浓的父爱。

Parts 部分	Paragraphs 段落	Main Ideas 大意
Part I	1—3	My 23-year-old son, Dan, was going to Paris, and I wanted to provide him with some good advice that would last longer than just here and now, but I lacked courage to do so. 我23岁的儿子丹要去巴黎了，我想给他提一些不只是眼下对他有益的建议，但却没有勇气开口。
Part II	4—7	Many times I'd let such opportunity pass me by. 很多次我让这样的机会溜走。
Part III	8—14	Finally I managed to express my feeling; both of us find that was wonderful. 最终我表达出了我的感情，这样爱的表达让我们感觉非常美好。

词汇点睛

1 pack

vt. to put things into cases, bags, etc., ready for a trip somewhere 打包，捆扎

• 例句 • They packed their bags and left. 他们把行李打好包就动身了。

All these books need to be packed into boxes. 所有这些书都需要打点装箱。

• 反义词 • **unpack** *vt.* 打开包裹（或行李等）；卸货

She unpacked her clothes from the suitcase. 她打开衣箱拿出衣服。

2 transition

n. changes from one form or state to another 过渡，转变

• 例句 • The transition from childhood to adult life can be difficult to some extent.

在某种程度上，从童年到成年的过渡阶段可能是困难的。

His attitude underwent an abrupt transition. 他的态度突然转变了。

3 circle

v. to move in the shape of a circle around sth., especially in the air 环绕，盘旋

• 例句 • The plane circled the airport before landing. 飞机着陆前围绕机场盘旋。

The moon circled the earth every 28 days. 月亮每28天绕地球一圈。

n. 1) a completely round shape, like the letter O 圆圈，环状物

• 例句 • They sat in a circle round the fire. 他们围着火坐成一圈。

 2) a group of people who know each other and meet regularly, or who have similar interests or jobs （有共同兴趣、利益的人形成的）圈子，集团

• 例句 • In political circles there is talk of war. 在政治圈里，有关于战争的言谈。

4 penetrate

vt. to see through; to enter into 洞察，了解，看穿；渗入，刺入

• 例句 • It was impossible to penetrate the mystery. 当时要揭开那个谜是不可能的。

The knife penetrated his stomach. 刀刺进了他的腹部。

• 扩展 • **penetrating** *adj.* 敏锐的，有洞察力的；弥漫的

The cold is very penetrating today. 今天寒气逼人。

5 inspire

vt. to make sb. have a particular feeling or react in a particular way 鼓舞，激发

• 例句 • The young painter had the example of Picasso to inspire and guide himself.

这位青年画家以毕加索为榜样激励和引导自己。

The Muse does not inspire all poets equally. 女神谬斯并非一视同仁地赐给所有诗人灵感。

• 短语 • **inspire sb. with sth. / inspire sth. in/into sb.** 激起/鼓舞了某人的……

The news inspired us with courage. → The news inspired courage in us. 那消息给了我们勇气。

• 扩展 • **inspiration** *n.* 灵感，启示

inspired *adj.* （人、作品）得到灵感的，有灵感的

inspiring *adj.* 鼓舞人心的，启发灵感的

6 mumble

vt. to say sth. too quietly or not clearly enough 喃喃地说，咕哝

• 例句 • He mumbled something to me but I could not hear what he said.
他对我咕哝了几句，可是我没听清他说的什么。
He mumbled a few words and left. 他咕哝了几句便走了。

• 辨析 • **mumble, murmur**
mumble 指"含糊地说"。
murmur指"发低沉连续的声音"，特指"连续低声地说"。如：
murmur a prayer 低声祈祷

7　departure

n. an act of leaving a place 离开，出发，启程

• 例句 • The departure of the train was delayed. 火车开出的时间推迟了。
His departure was quite unexpected. 他的离去很出人意料。

• 短语 • **take one's departure** 动身，离开
• 扩展 • **depart** *vi.* 离开，背离
When does the next train depart? 下一趟列车什么时候开？
department *n.* 部门，系

8　perspective

n. 1) a way of looking at or thinking about sth. 视角，观点，看法

• 例句 • We must learn to see things in their right perspective and avoid making mistakes.
我们要学会从正确的视角来观察事物，以免犯错误。
Please see the events in their historical perspective. 请用历史的观点看待这些事件。

　2) a view, especially one in which you can see a long way into the distance 景色，景观

• 例句 • From the top of the hill you can get a perspective of the entire park.
从山顶上你能眺望整个公园的景色。

9　clumsy

adj. a clumsy action or statement is said or done carelessly or badly, and may be likely to upset sb.
笨拙的，不得体的

• 例句 • I'm clumsy! I knocked over your cup of coffee! 我真是笨手笨脚！把你的咖啡碰翻了。
He made a clumsy attempt to apologize. 他试着道歉，却显得很笨拙。

• 扩展 • **clumsily** *adv.* 笨拙地，粗陋地
clumsiness *n.* 笨拙

短语解析

1. round the corner　很近

【例句】His house is round the corner. 他家离此不远。
Good times are just round the corner. 好日子近在眼前。

2. come up with　提出，想出，想到

【例句】She came up with a new idea for increasing sales. 她想到了一个增加销量的新办法。
He couldn't come up with an appropriate answer at the time.
当时他想不出一个合适的答案。

3. let sb. down 让某人失望

【例句】Please come and support me. Don't let me down. 请支持我，别让我失望。

The singer we had engaged let us down at the last moment, so we had to find a quick replacement.

我们雇的歌手在最后一刻失约了，因此我们不得不急急忙忙找人顶替。

4. after all 终究，毕竟

【例句】So you've come after all! 你到底还是来了！

So you see I was right after all! 你看，毕竟还是我对吧！

🔵 难句突破

1. (Para.2) *When we were to say goodbye, I looked closely at his face. I would like to provide him with some good advice that would last longer than just here and now.*

【解析】1) "be to + 动词原形"，表示约定的、计划中的或按职责、义务要求即将发生的动作，还可以表示注定要发生的动作。例如：

We are to meet at the station at four this afternoon. 我们今天下午4点在车站会面。

Am I to wait for an answer? 我要等回复么？

2) 第二句话中的that引导定语从句修饰advice。

3) here and now意为"目前，此刻"。

【译文】在即将告别的时候，我仔细端详着他的脸，想给他提一些不只是眼下对他有益的建议。

2. (Para.3) *Inside I stood motionless and silent, looking into my son's green eyes with that penetrating look.*

【解析】1) 副词inside前置，表示强调，正常语序应该是I stood inside motionless and silent。

2) that并非引导词而是代词表示"那种"。

3) 本句中的第二个look作名词，表示目光、表情。

4) motionless and silent是形容词作状语，表示伴随状况、原因、结果等。例如：

He went to bed, cold and hungry.

【译文】屋内，我静静地站着，用那种洞悉一切的目光深深凝视着儿子那双碧绿的眼睛。

3. (Para.8) *Now I stood in front of him and recalled all the times when I hadn't made use of those opportunities.*

【解析】1) and连接两个并列的动作stood in front of him和recalled all the times。

2) when引导定语从句修饰times。

3) make use of意为"利用"。例如：

She makes use of people she meets as raw material for her fiction.

她把她所遇见的人们作为她创作小说的素材。

【译文】此时此刻，我站在儿子面前，回忆起过去我错过的一次又一次的机会。

4. (Para.9) *The night before his departure, I lay twisting and turning in bed, puzzling about what to tell him.*

【解析】twisting and turning 是现在分词作状语修饰 lay；puzzling 也是现在分词作状语表示伴随

状况。

【译文】丹出发前的那一夜，我在床上辗转难眠，实在不知道该跟他说点什么。

5. (Para.9) *Seen from the perspective of an entire life, how important is it that a father tells his son what he thinks of him deep inside?*

【解析】seen是过去分词作状语；句子的主干是how important is it；其中it是形式主语，而真正的主语是that引导的主语从句that a father tells his son what he thinks of him deep inside；在这个主语从句中又包含一个what引导的宾语从句what he thinks of him deep inside。

【译文】从孩子一生的角度来看，一个父亲告诉儿子自己内心对他的看法到底有多大意义？

6. (Para.10) *I felt my palms becoming moist, and my throat constricted.*

【解析】本句是由and连接的并列句，后半句省略了动词，其完整形式应该是and (I felt) my throat (becoming) constricted。

【译文】我感到手心冒汗，喉咙发紧。

参考译文

父爱无言
大卫·津曼

我23岁的儿子丹站在门口，准备与家人告别。他的背包已经收拾完毕，随时可以出发。两个多小时之后他就要飞往法国了。

丹此行至少要离开我们一年。这是丹生命中的一个里程碑，标志着从校园生活到成人世界的转变。在即将告别的时候，我仔细端详着他的脸，想给他提一些不只是眼下对他有益的建议。

然而话到嘴边却又咽下。此刻，我们的海边小宅里寂静无声。屋外，海鸥在瞬息万变、汹涌咆哮的海浪上空盘旋，我能听得见它们发出的尖叫声。屋内，我静静地站着，用那种洞悉一切的目光深深凝视着儿子那双碧绿的眼睛。

我知道我已不是第一次眼睁睁错过这样的机会了。丹尼尔小时候，在他上学前班的第一天，我带他去乘校车。当校车在拐角处出现时，他紧紧攥着我的手。从他的手中我感觉到他很兴奋。校车到站那一刻，我看到了他两颊漾开的红晕。他盯着我——就像现在这样。

爸爸，学校生活怎样啊？我能行吗？我能做好这一切吗？然后他登上校车，消失在我的视线中。车子开走了。我还是一句话也没说。

大约14年后，相似的一幕再次上演。我和丹尼尔的妈妈开车送他去即将就读的大学。第一天晚上，他和新朋友出去玩。等到早上我们去看他的时候，他病倒在床上。临别时，我努力想说点儿什么能够让他在新生活开始之际鼓起勇气、激起自信的话。

然而，我再一次语塞。我咕哝了几句诸如"祝你早点康复，丹"之类的话，就转身离开了。

此时此刻，我站在儿子面前，回忆起过去我错过的一次又一次的机会。而这样的事情我们大家又有多少人不曾经历呢？当儿子毕业或者女儿出嫁时，我们只是疲于应付种种仪式，却没有把孩子叫到一旁，亲口说出他们对我们有多么重要，或者与他们聊一聊未来的人生。

丹出发前的那一夜，我在床上辗转难眠，实在不知道该跟他说点什么。我的脑子里一片空白，于是乎就想也许根本没这个必要。从孩子一生的角度来看，一个父亲告诉儿子自己内心对他的看法到底有多大意义？

然而，当我站在丹面前时，我才明白这样的几句话是有意义的。我感到手心冒汗，喉咙发紧。为什么告诉儿子自己的想法有这么困难呢？我口干舌燥，意识到自己只能进出几个词来。

　　"丹，"我最终还是结巴着开口了，"如果当初我自己可以选择谁是我的儿子的话，我还是会选择你。"

　　我能说的仅此而已。我正揣测他是否明白了我的意思，他就走上前来，将我紧紧地抱住。那一刻，整个世界和世界上的万事万物都消失了，只有我和丹同在我们的海边小宅里。

　　他正要说什么，而我的双眼却已噙满泪水。我没听清他后来讲了些什么。我只感觉到他的胡茬扎着我的脸。几个小时过后，他带着女友乘飞机离开了。

　　我对丹说的那些话既笨拙又老套，虽一文不值，却又价值连城。

习题全解

1. 根据文章内容判断正误。

1) 【答案】F
　　【题解】从第二段第二句来看，去法国的这一年将是他走出校园踏入社会的过渡期。
　　【译文】作者的儿子丹尼尔准备前往法国过暑假。

2) 【答案】F
　　【题解】文章中作者就是因为没能给予儿子很好的建议而一直心存愧疚。
　　【译文】在丹尼尔动身前往法国之前，作者给予他很多好的建议。

3) 【答案】T
　　【题解】根据是第三段 " ... in our house by the sea"
　　【译文】作者居住的屋子离海边不远。

4) 【答案】T
　　【题解】根据第四段、第五段可知这句话是正确的。
　　【译文】在丹尼尔上学前班的第一天，他非常兴奋，但作者却一句话也没说。

5) 【答案】F
　　【题解】根据第六段、第七段，作者再一次语塞，错过了和儿子交流、沟通的机会。
　　【译文】在丹尼尔读大学的第一天，作者对他说了一些能鼓起勇气、激起自信的话。

6) 【答案】T
　　【译文】作者知道一个父亲告诉儿子自己在内心深处如何看待他，很重要，但站在儿子面前，他又觉得难于启齿。

2. 请用下面所给词汇或短语的适当形式填写句子。

1) 【答案】transition
　　【译文】事实证明向市场经济转变的过程是非常困难的。

2) 【答案】board
　　【译文】乘客需在飞机起飞前半小时登机。

3) 【答案】come up with
　　【译文】这就是你能想到的最好的借口吗？

4) 【答案】were about to
　　【译文】我们正准备离开，这时天开始下雨了。

5) 【答案】inspired

【译文】他的成功激励我向着既定目标更加努力地工作。

6) 【答案】ceremony

【译文】直到现在，我仍然记得在毕业典礼上老校长说的一番话。

7) 【答案】departure

【译文】在西蒙启程前往俄罗斯之前，我曾与他有过短暂的会晤。

8) 【答案】after all

【译文】囚犯们应该得到尊重，他们毕竟也是人。

9) 【答案】puzzles

【译文】让我想不通的是为何他的书会如此受欢迎。

10) 【答案】let you down

【译文】亨利绝不会让你失望，你随时可以向他求助。

3. 将下列句子译成汉语。

1) 屋外，海鸥在瞬息万变、咆哮不止的海浪上空盘旋，我能听得见它们发出的尖叫声。

2) 当校车在拐角处出现时，他紧紧攥着我的手。从他的手中我感觉到他很兴奋。

3) 我努力想说点儿什么，能够让他在新生活开始之际鼓起勇气，激起自信。

4) 我们只是应付这种种仪式，却没有把孩子们叫到一旁，亲口说出他们对我们有多么重要，也没有告诉他们对于未来应该有什么期待。

文章泛读

文章导读

秋天的异乡，两个曾经的恋人相遇了。往事已经久远，此时他们都已拥有各自或者幸福、或者不幸的生活。再次相遇，他们会说些什么？他们又会想些什么？

背景知识

兰斯敦·休斯（**Langston Hughes**）：（1902—1967）美国著名的黑人作家，以表现20世纪20年代至40年代的黑人生活而著名。他从高中时代开始写诗，代表作有1926年的《疲惫的布鲁斯》（*The Weary Blues*）、1931年的《黑人母亲》（*The Negro Mother and Other Dramatic Recitations*）、1932年的《守梦人》（*The Dream Keeper*）、1942年的《哈勒姆的莎士比亚》（*Shakespeare in Harlem*）、1947年的《奇异的原野》（*Fields of Wonder*）、1947年的《单程车票》（*One Way Ticket*）、和1961年的《最好的简单》（*The Best of Simple*）。

文章写作风格及结构

作者用婉约的语言向读者展示了在这个初秋的黄昏发生的故事。

Parts 部分	Paragraphs 段落	Main Ideas 大意
Part I	1	The love story between Bill and Mary. 比尔和玛丽间的爱情故事。
Part II	2—23	They met for the first time after their separation. 分手多年后他们第一次相遇。
Part III	24—29	With the coming of Mary's bus, they said goodbye again. 玛丽要乘的公车来了，他们再一次说再见。

词汇点精

1 impulsively

adv. doing things without considering the possible dangers or problems first 冲动地

• 例句 • He studied her face for a moment, then said impulsively: "Let's get married."

他盯着她的脸看了一会儿，接着冲动地说："我们结婚吧。"

He always makes decision impulsively. 他总是冲动地作决定。

• 扩展 • **impulsive** *adj.* 易冲动的；感情用事的

He's too impulsive to be a responsible Prime Minister. 他太过冲动，不能成为负责任的首相。

impulse *n.* 刺激，冲动

She bought the dress on impulse. 她一时冲动买了这件衣服。

2 unconsciously

adv. done without thinking or considering the consequences 无意中，不知不觉地

• 例句 • He unconsciously imitated his father. 他在不知不觉中仿效他的父亲。

He has offended her unconsciously. 他无意中冒犯了她。

• 扩展 • **unconscious** *adj.* 失去知觉的，没察觉到的 (+of)

She remained unconscious for several hours. 她有好几个小时不省人事。

He was unconscious of his mistake. 他没意识到自己的错误。

unconsciousness *n.* 无知觉，无意识

He is in a state of unconsciousness. 他处于失去知觉的状态。

• 反义词 • **consciously** *adv.* 有意识地，自觉地

3 frown

n. your facial expression when you are angry, unhappy, or confused 皱眉

• 例句 • She looked up from her exam paper with a worried frown.

她看完自己的试卷愁眉不展地抬起头来。

I noticed a slight frown of disapproval on her face.

我留意到她轻轻皱了下眉，流露出不赞成的表情。

vi. to make an angry, unhappy, or confused expression, moving your eyebrows together 皱眉

• 例句 • The teacher frowned angrily at the noisy class. 老师生气地对那班吵吵嚷嚷的学生皱起眉头。

• 短语 • **frown on/upon** 不赞成，不以为然

My parents always frown on late night out. 我父母向来不赞成深夜外出。

4　desperately

adv. doing sth. in a way that shows you need or want sth. very much 拼命地，不顾一切地

• 例句 • Thousands of people are desperately trying to leave their battered home.

成百上千的人拼命想离开他们破碎的家园。

He looked around desperately for somewhere to flee. 他四下打量，不顾一切地寻找逃脱的路。

• 扩展 • **desperate** *adj.* 不顾一切的, 拼死的, 令人绝望的

It is a characteristic of wisdom not to do desperate things. 智者的特点是不做孤注一掷之事。

desperation *n.* 拼命，（不顾一切的）冒险

In desperation I pleaded with the attackers. 绝望之下，我向攻击者哀求。

5　grin

vi. to smile widely 咧嘴而笑，露齿而笑

• 例句 • He grinned at me, as if sharing a secret joke. 他朝我龇牙一笑，好像彼此心领神会一个笑话。

He grinned his approval. 他咧嘴一笑，表示赞成。

6　chain

n. 1) people or things which are connected or next to each other forming a line 一连串，一系列

• 例句 • A chain of events happened yesterday. 昨天发生了一连串的事件。

There's a chain of mountains. 那儿有一列山脉。

2) a series of metal rings which are joined together in a line and used for fastening things, supporting weights, decoration, etc. 链子

• 例句 • She wore a gold chain around her neck. 她的脖子上戴了一条金项链。

v. to fasten someone or sth. to sth. else using a chain（常与up连用）用链子系住，束缚

• 例句 • The dog was chained (up) to the wall. 这只狗被一条链子拴在墙上。

7　blur

vi. to become difficult to see or to make sth. difficult to see, because the edges are not clear 使模糊，使看不清楚

• 例句 • Her eyes blurred with tears. 她泪眼迷离。

The windows blurred with rain. 窗子被雨水弄得模糊不清。

8　utter

vt. to say sth. 说（话）

• 例句 • He never uttered a word of protest. 他从来没说过一句反对的话。

He looked at me without uttering a word. 他看着我，一句话也没说。

adj. used to emphasize how great or complete sth. is 完全的；绝对的

• 例句 • What he is doing is utter stupidity! 他正在做的是完全愚蠢的事。

9　shriek

vi. to make a very high loud sound, especially because you are afraid, angry, excited, or in pain 尖叫

• 例句 • "I hate you," he shrieked. "我讨厌你，"他尖声叫道。

She shrieked in fear and dropped the pan. 她恐惧地尖声叫喊，把锅也扔了。

n. a loud high sound made because you are frightened, excited, angry etc. 尖叫声

• 例句 • A sudden terrible shriek froze the passenger to the spot. 突然一声可怕的尖叫吓得路人愣住了。

短语解析

lose sight of 看不见……，忽略

【例句】Our original aims have been lost sight of. 我们原来的目标已经无影无踪了。

In some cases, they have lost sight of customer needs in designing products.

有时，他们在设计产品时忽略了顾客的需要。

难句突破

1. (Para.1) *Bill went away, bitter about women.*

【解析】bitter about women是形容词短语作状语，表示结果。

形容词或形容词短语可以作状语，表示以下意义：

①表示行为方式或伴随状况。有时，它会像非限制性定语从句一样，表示意义上的增补，其逻辑主语是句子的主语。例如：

Crusoe stared at the footprint, full of fear. (=Curose, who was full of fear, stared at the footprint.)

克鲁索两眼死盯着脚印，内心里充满着恐惧。

② 表示原因。这种状语一般位于句首，有时也可位于句中。例如：

Angry at the girl oversleeping, Mr. Green went down to wake her up.

(=Mr. Green went down to wake up the girl because he was angry with her for oversleeping.)

格林先生下去叫醒女孩，对她睡过了头很是生气。

③表示时间或条件。这种状语通常位于句首，也可位于句末。例如：

Ripe, these apples are sweet. (=When/If these apples are ripe, they are sweet.)

这些苹果熟了，味道很甜。

④ 作让步状语。这种状语常由连词or连接的两个或两个以上的并列形容词构成，一般位于句首，有时也可位于句中。例如：

Wet or fine, he got up at six and took a walk in the park.

(= Whether it was wet or fine, he got up at six and took a walk in the park.)

不管是雨天还是晴天，他总是六点钟起床，并到公园里散散步。

⑤ 表示结果或存在的状态。这种状语在句中的位置比较灵活。例如：

For a moment she just stood there, unable to believe what had just happened.

她在那儿呆呆地站了一会儿，不敢相信刚才发生的事情。

⑥ 形容词或形容词短语可以在句首作状语，表示说话人的态度。例如：

Strange, he should have done such a thing. 奇怪，他居然做了这样一件事。

Worse still, the lion could even carry off the baby in its mouth.

更糟糕的是，狮子甚至能把婴儿叼走。

【译文】比尔走了，对女人充满了怨恨。

2. (Para.6) *Unconsciously, she lifted her face as though wanting a kiss, but he held out his hand.*

【解析】as though引导方式状语从句。

①在as if和as though引导的方式状语从句中一般用虚拟语气。例如：

The old man runs very fast as if/though he were a young man.

那个老人跑得很快，好像他是一个年轻人。

②只有当谓语是 look, seem, taste, smell等系动词时，as if/though 引导的从句不采用虚拟语气。例如：

It looks as if/though they are all in a terrible hurry. 看起来好像他们都非常匆忙似的。

The meat tastes as if/though it has already gone bad. 这肉吃起来好像已经坏了。

③当主句的主语和从句的主语一致，而且从句的谓语又是be时，从句的主谓可以省略。例如：

From time to time Jack turned around as though (he was) searching for someone.

杰克不时地转过头来好像是在找人似的。

He glanced as if (he was) in search of something.

他眼光扫了一下好像是在找东西似的。

【译文】下意识地，她抬起脸庞，似乎想要一个亲吻，而他却伸出了手。

3. (Para.29) *People came between them outside, people crossing the street, people they didn't know.*

【解析】people crossing the street是独立主格结构，表示方式和伴随状况。

独立主格结构有以下几种构成形式：名词/代词+现在分词/过去分词；名词/代词+形容词；名词/代词+副词；名词/代词+不定式；名词/代词+介词短语

独立主格结构的特点：1）独立主格结构的逻辑主语与句子的主语不同，它独立存在。2）名词或代词与后面的分词、形容词、副词、不定式、介词等是主谓关系。3）独立主格结构一般有逗号与主句分开。例如：

He put on his socks, wrong side out. (= ... with the wrong side out.)

他穿上袜子，穿反了。

Weather permitting, we are going to visit you tomorrow. 如果天气允许，我们明天去看你。

This done, we went home. 工作完成后，我们才回家。

He came into the room, his ears red with cold. 他走进房间，耳朵冻红了。

He came out of the library, a large book under his arm. 他夹着本厚书，走出了图书馆。

【译文】车外，人们从他们中间走过，穿过大街，都是些他们不认识的人。

参考译文

初秋

兰斯敦·休斯

当比尔还很年轻时，他们恋爱了。许多个夜晚他们都是在一起散步、聊天中度过。然后，一件无关紧要的事情使他们俩谁也不搭理谁。冲动之下，她嫁给了一个她自以为钟爱的男人。比尔走了，对女人充满了怨恨。

昨天，当她穿过华盛顿广场时，她遇到了他，这是许多年后她第一次看见他。

"比尔·沃克，"她喊道。

他停下脚步。刚开始他并没有认出她来，他觉得她看上去是那样的衰老。

"玛丽！你这是从哪来啊？"

下意识地，她抬起脸庞，似乎想要一个亲吻，而他却伸出了手。她握了一下。

"我现在住在纽约，"她说。

"哦"——他客气地笑了笑，紧接着眉宇间微微闪过一丝紧蹙。

"老惦记着你后来怎么样了，比尔。"

"我现在是个律师。在一家很不错的事务所，离市中心不远。"

"结婚了吧？"

"是的。有两个孩子。"

"哦，"她说。

来来往往的人们穿过公园，从他们身边走过，都是些他们不认识的人。时间已近傍晚，夕阳西下，凉意渐起。

"你丈夫呢？"他问她。

"我们有三个孩子，我在哥伦比亚大学财务处工作。"

"你看上去很……"（他本想说老）"……不错，"他说。

她明白他的意思。在华盛顿广场的树荫下，她发现自己拼命地回忆过去，完全沉浸在往事之中。当年还在俄亥俄时，她就比他大。时至今日，她早已青春不再，而比尔却风采依旧。

"我们住在中央公园大道西路，"她说。"有空过来坐坐。"

"一定，"他应道。"找个晚上，你和你丈夫上我家一起吃顿饭吧，随便哪天。我和露西尔非常愿意和你们会会。"

树叶从枝头缓缓飘下，落在广场上。无风自落。秋日的黄昏。她感到有些不舒服。

"我们也很愿意，"她回答说。

"你该见见我的小家伙。"他咧嘴一笑。

蓦然间，第五大道整条街的路灯都亮了，在蓝色的暮霭中凝成一圈圈的光晕。

"我的公车来了，"她说。

他伸出手说："再见。"

"什么时候……"她刚想说，但汽车已准备开动了。大街上的路灯时而模糊，时而闪烁，时而又模糊。她上车时不敢张嘴，害怕张嘴却又吐不出一个字来。

她突然非常大声地喊了一声"再见！"但车门已在那一刹那关闭。

车子开动了。车外，人们从他们中间走过，穿过大街，都是些他们不认识的人。空间和行人阻隔了他们。她看不见比尔了。这时她才想起她忘了给他留地址——也没有问他要地址——还忘了告诉他她最小的儿子也叫比尔。

语言拓展

日常用语

练习 选择补全对话的最佳答案。

1. 【答案】C

  【解析】当别人因为某事向某人道歉，接受道歉的时候要表示"没有关系"或者"可以原谅"一般会用"It's nothing./ It doesn't matter./ Forget it./ Never mind."等表达。而当别人表示感谢时，你可以用"Not at all./ That's all right./ You are welcome./ Don't mention it."等表达。

2. 【答案】A

  【解析】同上。选项C是不礼貌的回答。

3. 【答案】D

  【解析】别人向你道歉时，你可以回答"That's all right."相当于"It doesn't matter."或"Never mind."意为"没关系，不要紧"。别人向你表示感谢时，你也可以说"That's all right."相当于"You're welcome."或"Not at all."。"I don't mind..."表示"不介意……"。

4. 【答案】A

  【解析】That's OK!有以下几层意思：赞同别人的说法或观点时，说"That's OK!，"意为"是的"，相当于"That's right"；当别人向你道歉时，你说"That's OK!"意思是没关系；当别人向你表示谢意时，你说"That's OK!"意思是"没什么，不用谢"，相当于"That's all right."或"Not at all."

5. 【答案】B

  【解析】"It's nothing at all."意为"实在不算什么"表达"不用客气"的意思。不符合这里的语境。只有选项B是对别人道歉的回答。

阅读技巧

练习 确定以下几段文章的主旨。

1. 【答案】Chinese people often feel awkward talking to Americans.

  【译文】中国人常常觉得和美国人谈话很别扭。

  【解析】该段的第一句是主题句，从中可以知道段落的主旨。后面都是阐述出现这一现象的原因。

2. 【答案】No teaching method can satisfy all students at the same time.

  【译文】没有哪一种教学方法可以同时满足所有的学生。

  【解析】该段的最后一句是主题句。采用的是先分后总的写作手法。

3. 【答案】Ways of expressing good manners are different from country to country.

  【译文】不同的国家有不同的表达文明礼貌的方式。

  【解析】该段的第一句是主题句，其后的句子都是对这一主题的举例说明。

4. 【答案】Baby-sitting with my brother is not fun.

  【译文】照看我的弟弟可不是件好玩的事情。

  【解析】该段的主题句出现在段落的中间部分。

5. 【答案】Driving a bus is hard work.

  【译文】开公交车是一项艰苦的工作。

  【解析】该段没有出现明确的主题句，但是从段落中罗列的公交车司机需要应付的种种麻烦情况可以总结出段落的主旨。

写作技巧

练习 回顾本单元所学的写作技巧，写一篇不少于**120**词的作文，记述给你留下深刻印象的一段学校生活经历。

样文：

It was the morning of April 6th 2003. At about 7:30, I went to school by bike as usual. It was a rainy day and the road was slippery. On the way, I noticed a boy riding in front of me, talking loudly with his friends. He didn't wear a raincoat; instead, he held an umbrella in one hand, and rode with another hand. As he turned left to Guangming Road, he failed to see a car coming from behind a truck parked on the corner. Suddenly I heard a big noise and saw an umbrella thrown away. The boy was knocked down by the car. I was completely shocked.

I dialed "120". It was't long before an ambulance arrived. One doctor brought a blanket for the boy. Another doctor and I lifted him into the ambulance. When recalling the accident later, I was still scared, but learnt a great lesson from it.

语法知识

——动词时态（一）

练习 选择最佳答案补全下列句子。

1. 【答案】B

   【解析】题干中的时间状语yesterday说明动作是过去发生的，所以用一般过去时。

   【译文】昨天在回家的路上我遇到了一位老朋友。

2. 【答案】D

   【解析】过去进行时用于表示过去某一动作发生时，另一动作正在进行。

   【译文】昨晚我去看他的时候，他正在看足球比赛。

3. 【答案】B

   【解析】一般现在时时态可用于时间和条件状语从句中表示将来。

   【译文】在我去逛街的时候照顾好我的小狗。

4. 【答案】A

   【解析】过去进行时表示过去某一动作发生时，另一动作正在进行。

   【译文】我在街上走的时候遇到了约翰。

5. 【答案】C

   【解析】一般现在时可以在时间和条件状语从句中表示将来。

   【译文】当他听到这个好消息的时候，一定会很高兴的。

6. 【答案】A

   【解析】过去进行时表示过去某一动作发生时，另一动作正在进行。

   【译文】你昨晚给我打电话时，我正在洗澡。

7. 【答案】D

   【解析】将来进行时表示将来某一时刻或某一段时间正在进行的动作。

   【译文】约翰今晚不能去看电影了，因为他那时正在讲课。

8. 【答案】B

   【解析】现在进行时可以表示现阶段正在进行而说话此刻不一定进行的动作。

【译文】琼斯太太总是在抱怨家务事的辛苦。

9.【答案】A

【解析】表示真理、事实时用一般现在时。

【译文】他告诉我们诚实是成功的关键。

10.【答案】B

【解析】在表示将来某一时刻或某一段时间里发生的动作或情况时，用一般将来时。

【译文】我们的队伍很有可能会赢得比赛。

每课一练

Part I　　Vocabulary & Structure

Directions: *There are 30 incomplete sentences in this part. For each sentence there are four choices marked*
A), B), C) and D). Choose the ONE that best completes the sentence.

1. If you don't want to wash your jacket, you can send it to a _____.

   A) participant　　　　B) planet　　　　C) laundry　　　　D) ribbon

2. Look! Here _____ the famous player.

   A) comes　　　　B) come　　　　C) had come　　　　D) coming

3. He is preparing for a lecture on stock _____.

   A) estate　　　　B) exchange　　　　C) plague　　　　D) situation

4. The _____ from childhood to adulthood is always critical to everybody.

   A) conversion　　　　B) transition　　　　C) turnover　　　　D) transformation

5. Now that Bob is sharing child-raising and _____ tasks with his wife.

   A) household　　　　B) houseful　　　　C) house　　　　D) householder

6. If you want to see the chairman of the department, you'd better make an _____ with his secretary first.

   A) admission　　　　B) agreement　　　　C) appointment　　　　D) alphabet

7. I think we should let Mary to go camping with her boyfriend. _____ she is a big girl now.

   A) Above all　　　　B) First of all　　　　C) For all　　　　D) After all

8. We welcome our teachers _____ at the gate of our school.

   A) with flowers in our hands　　　　　　B) carry flowers in our hands

   C) flowers in our hands　　　　　　　　D) we carry flowers in our hands

9. My father _____ sixty next year.

   A) is going to be　　　B) is to be　　　C) will be　　　D) is about to be

10. The colleague _____ to have worked in several big companies before he joined our firm.

   A) confesses　　　　B) claims　　　　C) declares　　　　D) confirms

11. The task _____ much harder than we _____.

   A) is; expect　　　B) was; expected　　　C) was; had expected　　　D)was; were expecting

12. I felt somewhat disappointed and _____, until something occurred which attracted my attention.

   A) leaving　　　　B) was about to leave　　　　C) left　　　　D) had been leaving

13. Why he did it will remains a _____ for ever.

   A) strange　　　　B) pass　　　　C) public　　　　D) puzzle

14. Every country and every nation has its own _____ and cultural tradition, strong points and advantages.

   A) historian   B) history   C) historical   D) heroine

15. David's story gives us a(n) _____ of the information war.

   A) pack   B) pile   C) episode   D) parcel

16. Although the heavy rain stopped, it was at least an hour later that the flood began to _____.

   A) retire   B) recede   C) recline   D) retreat

17. Eating too much fat can _____ heart disease and cause high blood pressure.

   A) contribute to   B) attribute to   C) attend to   D) devote to

18. Not only _____ the gift, he _____ the sender.

   A) did he refuse; criticized   B) did he refuse; also criticized

   C) he refused; also criticized   D) he refused; criticized

19. The sound is so powerful that it can _____ the thick wall.

   A) penetrate   B) pardon   C) persuade   D) pursue

20. I showed him the pictures I _____ of the animals the day before, and told him the stories.

   A) was taking   B) had taken   C) have taken   D) was taken

21. During the graduation _____ the president gave a wonderful speech.

   A) evaluation   B) sign   C) individual   D) ceremony

22. If you _____ tears when you miss the sun, you also miss the stars.

   A) share   B) shed   C) urge   D) devote

23. _____ the biscuit in a strong box, or it will get smashed in the delivery.

   A) Lift   B) Split   C) Sweep   D) Pack

24. I hope to be _____ your teacher _____ your good friend.

   A) not; but   B) not only; but   C) if; not   D) rather; than

25. We must _____ the stolen goods at all costs.

   Λ) recover   B) revise   C) cover   D) rescue

26. Our _____ is London, but the plane took us to Paris.

   A) departure   B) destination   C) discount   D) destiny

27. The caterers John's, who are just _____, are very good.

   A) round the clock   B) round the bend   C) round the corner   D) round on

28. Did I say "a lot of dime"? I'm sorry, I meant to say "a lot of time". It's a _____ of the tongue.

   A) slip   B) throne   C) leap   D) fall

29. His father's death gives him a whole new _____ on life.

   A) motivation   B) perspective   C) impact   D) impression

30. He swears to his mother that he will never let her _____.

   A) on   B) down   C) alone   D) out

Part II   Reading Comprehension

Directions: *Read the following two passages. Answer the questions of each passage by choosing A), B), C) or D).*

Passage 1

   The dog, called Prince, was an intelligent animal and a slave to William. From morning till night, when

William was at home, Prince never left his sight, practically ignoring all other members of the family. The dog had a number of clearly defined duties and, like the good pupil he was, Prince lived for the chance to demonstrate his abilities.

At nine every morning, Prince ran off to the store in the village, returning shortly with William's daily paper and William's favorite tobacco. A gundog by breed, Prince possessed a large soft mouth specially evolved for the safe carrying of hunted creatures, so the paper and the tobacco came to no harm, never even showing a tooth mark.

William was an engine driver, and he wore a blue uniform which smelled of oil and oil fuel. He had to work at odd times: "days", "late days" or "nights". Over the years Prince got to know these periods of work and rest, knew when his master would leave the house and return, and he never wasted this knowledge. If William overslept, Prince barked at the bedroom door until he woke, much to the annoyance of the family.

One evening William slipped and fell on the icy pavement somewhere between the village and his home. He was so badly shaken that he stayed in bed for three days, and not until he got up and dressed again did he discover that he had lost his wallet. The house was turned upside down in the search, but the wallet was not found. However, five days after the fall, Prince dropped the wallet into William's hand. Very muddy, stained and wet through, the little case still contained fifty-three pounds, and William's driving license. Where the dog had found it no one could tell, but he had recognized it probably by the faint oily smell on the worn leather.

1. How did the dog perform his duties?
   A) He was delighted to show them off.
   B) He often messed things up.
   C) He was reluctant to do them.
   D) He had few opportunities to do them.

2. According the passage, gundogs _____.
   A) are the fastest runners of all dogs
   B) don't have teeth
   C) can carry birds, etc. without hurting them
   D) are loyal friends to their master

3. As a result of William's work, _____.
   A) he did not get enough sleep
   B) there was an oily smell from his clothes
   C) the dog grew used to traveling by train
   D) the dog was confused about the time of the day

4. It upset William's wife and family when _____.
   A) William was on his night shift
   B) the dog made too much noise in the house
   C) William made them all get up early
   D) the dog would only follow William's order

5. Why didn't William realize his loss for several days?

    A) Because he thought his wife had kept it for him.

    B) Because he lost his consciousness all that time.

    C) Because he thought the wallet was in the house.

    D) Because he had no occasion to feel in his pockets.

Passage 2

    About ten men in every hundred suffer from color blindness in some way; women are luckier with only about one in two hundred is affected in this manner. There are different forms of color blindness. A man may not be able to see deep red. He may think that red, orange and yellow are all shades of green. Sometimes a person cannot tell the difference between blue and green. In rare cases an unlucky man may see everything in shades of green—a strange world indeed.

    In certain occupations color blindness can be dangerous and candidates are tested most carefully. Color blindness in human beings is a strange thing to explain. In a single eye there are millions of very small things called "cones". These help to see in a bright light and to tell the difference between colors. There are also millions of "rods" but these are used for seeing when it is nearly dark. They show us shape but not color. Wait until it is dark tonight, and then go outside. Look round you and try to see what colors you can recognize.

    Birds and animals which hunt at night have eyes which contain few or no cones at all, so they cannot see colors. As far as we know, bats and adult owls cannot see colors at all, only light and dark shapes. Similarly cats and dogs cannot see colors as well as we can.

    Insects can see ultraviolet rays which are invisible to us, and some of them can even see X-rays. The wings of a moth may seem grey and dull to us, but to insects they may appear beautiful, showing colors which we cannot see. Scientists know that there are other colors around us which insects can see but which we cannot see. Some insects have favorite colors. Mosquitoes like blue, but do not like yellow. A red light will not attract insects but a blue lamp will.

6. Which of the following is TRUE about the people who suffer from color blindness?

    A) Some of them may see everything in shades of green.

    B) Few of them can tell the difference between blue and green.

    C) Few of them may think that red, orange and yellow are all shades of green.

    D) Very few of them may think that everything in the world is in green.

7. When millions of rods in our eyes are at work in darkness we can see _____.

    A) colors only   B) darkness only   C) shapes only   D) both A and C

8. According to the passage, bats and adult owls CANNOT see colors because _____.

    A) they hunt at night   B) they cannot see light   C) they have no rods   D) they have no cones

9. According to the passage, dogs and cats _____.

    A) as well as human beings cannot see some colors   B) have fewer cones than human beings

    C) have less rods than human beings   D) can see colors as well as human beings

10. Which of the following is NOT true about insects?

A) Insects can see more colors than human beings.

B) Insects can see ultraviolet rays which are invisible to men.

C) All insects have their favorite colors.

D) The world is more colorful to insects than to human beings.

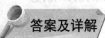 答案及详解

第一部分 词汇与结构

1. 【答案】C

【题解】本题考查单词词义。participant 参与者；planet 星球；laundry 洗衣店；ribbon 缎带，丝带。

【译文】如果你不想自己洗你的夹克，你可以把它送去洗衣店。

2. 【答案】A

【题解】本题考查动词的时态。英语中在某些以here, there开头的句子中用一般现在时表示现在发生的动作，又如：Here comes the bus! 车来了！There goes the bell! 铃响了！Here they are! 他们来了！

【译文】看！那位著名的演奏家来了。

3. 【答案】B

【题解】本题考查stock的固定搭配。estate一般会用搭配 real estate表示"房地产"，stock exchange 股票交易，plague 瘟疫。

【译文】他正在准备一篇关于股票交易的演讲。

4. 【答案】B

【题解】本题测试点为近义词辨析。conversion, transition, transformation 三词都有"改变，变化"之意，但transition "过渡（时期）"指在一段时间内从一种形式、状态、主题、地点向另一形式、状态、主题、地点的转变。conversion 指宗教信仰的改变和改变的行为。turnover意为"翻覆，翻折，流通量，营业额，周转"。transformation意为"变化，改革，转换"，指在形式、外表或性质方面的完全变化。

【译文】对每一个人来说，从孩提时代向成年人过渡的时期总是相当关键的。

5. 【答案】A

【题解】本题考查单词词义。household 家庭的；houseful 满屋，一屋子；householder 户主。

【译文】如今鲍勃和他的妻子共同养育子女和分担家务活。

6. 【答案】C

【题解】本题考查"约见、约定"的固定表达 make an appointment，此外为了和某人约见确定一个时间可以说fix a time，私人的约会可以说make a date。

【译文】如果你想见部门主管，你最好先和他的秘书预约一下。

7. 【答案】D

【题解】本题考查几个固定词组的使用。above all 最重要的是；first of all 首先；for all 尽管；after all 毕竟。

【译文】我认为我们应该让玛丽和他男朋友一起去野营，毕竟她是个大姑娘了。

8. 【答案】A

【题解】本题考查with表伴随的用法，一般以"with+名词"的形式出现。

【译文】我们手捧鲜花在校门口欢迎我们的老师们。

9. 【答案】C

【题解】本题考查表将来的几种说法的区别。be going to带有计划性，表示将来按计划某事应发生。be to do一般表示按计划进行或征求对方意见。will，shall 表示未事先计划的意图，或者一定会发生的事情。be about to do表示即将，马上要发生的事情。

【译文】我爸爸明年60岁。

10. 【答案】B

【题解】本题考查近义词辨析。confess (to) doing sth. 承认做过某事。declare后一般接名词短语或that从句，表示"声明，宣布"等。claim后可接名词短语、that从句，也可接不定式短语，不定式中的动作若在claim之前发生，则用不定式完成式，表示"声称，主张"等。confirm后接名词短语或that从句，表示"证实，肯定"等。

【译文】这个同事声称，他在加入我们公司之前曾在几个大公司就职。

11. 【答案】C

【题解】本题考查动词的时态。expect这一动作发生在前，因此expect的时态要比be的时态在前，四个选项中只有C符合这样的要求，be动词用的是一般过去时was，而expect用的是过去完成时had expected。

【译文】这项任务远比我们预期的难。

12. 【答案】B

【题解】本题考查动词的时态。此处表示我感到失望正准备走。be to do sth. 表示"将来要做……"。因此选B。

【译文】我感到有点失望并且准备走了，这时有事发生，引起了我的注意。

13. 【答案】D

【题解】本题考查puzzle的词义。pass 关口；puzzle 谜，难题。

【译文】他为什么做这件事会成为千古之谜。

14. 【答案】C

【题解】由题干中的and cultural... 可知，and表示并列结构，而cultural是形容词，因此本题可以排除作为名词的A、B和D选项。historian 历史学家；heroine 女英雄。

【译文】每一个国家和民族都有自己的历史及文化传统、优势和所长。

15. 【答案】C

【题解】本题考查episode的词义。a pack of 一包；a pile of 一堆；an episode of 一个……的片断。

【译文】大卫的故事展示给我们一个信息战的片断。

16. 【答案】B

【题解】本题考查 re- 为前缀的几个单词的词义。retire 退休；recede 后退，减退；recline 放置；retreat 撤退，退却。虽然recede和recline都有"退"的意思，recede强调减退，后退，而retreat强调撤回，撤退。

【译文】虽然大雨停了，洪水一小时后才开始减退。

17. 【答案】A

【题解】本题考查四个带to的搭配。contribute to 为……作贡献，致使……的发生；attribute to 归因于；attend to 关注，致力于；devote to 投身于。

【译文】摄入太多的脂肪可能导致心脏病和高血压。

18. 【答案】B

【题解】此题考查not only... but also... 连接分句的时候的倒装用法。当句子以not only开头的时候，要部分倒装。故可以排除C和D。并且需要后面的also和前面的not only相呼应，因此不能省略。故选B。

【译文】他不仅拒绝了礼物，并且批评了送礼的人。

19. 【答案】A

【题解】此题考查几个形近词的词义。penetrate 穿透；pardon 原谅；persuade 说服；pursue 追赶。

【译文】这声音如此有力以至于穿透了那堵厚墙。

20. 【答案】B

【题解】本题考查动词的时态。根据句义判断，我照照片在前，向他展示在后，show在题干中使用的是过去时showed，因此take picture应该用过去完成时 had taken，故选B。

【译文】我向他展示了我前一天给动物们拍的照片，并给他讲了那些故事。

21. 【答案】D

【题解】本题考查ceremony的词义。evaluation 评估；sign 标记；individual 个人的；ceremony 典礼，仪式。

【译文】在毕业典礼上，校长作了一场精彩的演讲。

22. 【答案】B

【题解】本题考查流泪的固定搭配 shed tears。share 分享；urge 催促；devote 投入于，献身于。

【译文】如果你为错过太阳而流泪，那么你也将错过群星。

23. 【答案】D

【题解】本题考查pack的词义。lift 举起；split 劈开；sweep 扫；pack 包装。

【译文】包装饼干需要硬一点的盒子，要不然在运输中就会被挤碎。

24. 【答案】B

【题解】本题考查not only... but (also)... 的用法。not only... but (also)... 表示"不仅……而且……"。not... but... 表示"不是……而是……"。

【译文】我希望自己不仅成为你的老师，也成为你的好朋友。

25. 【答案】A

【题解】本题考查recover表示"痊愈"之外的另一个意思："重新获得"。revise 修订，校订；cover 覆盖；rescue 援救，营救。

【译文】我们无论如何也要找回丢失的东西。

26. 【答案】B

【题解】本题考查几个形近词的词义。departure "出发，启程"。如果要表示出发地则要用departure point/place。destination 目的地；discount 折扣；destiny 命运。

【译文】我们的目的地是伦敦，但是飞机却把我们带到了巴黎。

27. 【答案】C

【题解】本题考查round的搭配，round the clock 昼夜不停；round the bend 疯狂的；round the corner 在拐角处；round on 责骂。

【译文】在街拐角的那家约翰餐饮非常好。

28.【答案】A

【题解】此题考查口误的固定搭配 slip of the tongue。throne 君主；leap 跳跃；fall 落下。

【译文】我说的是"a lot of dime"么？对不起，我本想说"a lot of time"。这是一个口误。

29.【答案】B

【题解】本题考查perspective的词义。motivation 动机；perspective 观点；impact 冲击；impression 印象。

【译文】他父亲的去世使他对生活有了一个全新的认识。

30.【答案】B

【题解】本题考查let和介词的搭配。let on 宣扬，承认；let sb. down 使某人失望；let alone 不干涉，更不用说；let out 终止，结束。

【译文】他向他妈妈发誓说他永远不会让她失望。

第二部分　阅读理解

1.【答案】A

【题解】细节题。根据见文章的第一段中"... lived for the chance to demonstrate his abilities"（它一有机会就展示它的本事），所以选A（它乐于炫耀）。

2.【答案】C

【题解】推断题。根据见文章的第二段中"... soft mouth specially evolved for the safe carrying of hunted creatures"（猎犬柔软的嘴巴使它们可以安全地叼着猎物而不至于伤害它们）。所以选C。

3.【答案】B

【题解】细节题。根据见文章的第三段第一句"Williams was an engine driver, and he wore a blue uniform which smelled of oil and oil fuel"（威廉是一个机车司机，因而他那蓝色的制服总是有一股燃油味），所以选B。

4.【答案】B

【题解】细节题。根据见文章的第三段最后一句话"... Prince barked at the bedroom door until he woke, much to the annoyance of the family"（普林思对着门吼叫，直到它的主人醒来，这让家里的其他人很是厌烦），所以选B（它在屋子里吠叫）。

5.【答案】D

【题解】细节题。根据见文章的第四段第二句话"... he stayed in bed for three days; and not until he got up and dressed again did he discover that he had lost his wallet"（他在床上躺了三天。直到起来了，穿衣服的时候，才发现钱包丢了），所以选D（他没有机会去摸口袋）。

6.【答案】D

【题解】细节题。根据见文章的第一段中"In rare cases an unlucky man may see everything in shades of green..."（很少有特别不幸的人看到的一切都是绿色的），所以选D（很少有色盲会以为世界上的一切都是绿色的）。

7.【答案】C

【题解】细节题。根据见文章的第二段中"There are also millions of 'rods' ... They show us shape but not color"（眼睛里有成千上万的"杆状细胞"……它们让我们看到物体的形状，但不能帮助我们辨别颜色），所以选C（只有形状）。

8. 【答案】D

　　【题解】细节题。根据见文章的第三段第一句"鸟类和夜间捕食类动物的眼睛只有很少的'圆锥细胞'，甚至没有，所以它们看不到颜色"，因此选D。

9. 【答案】B

　　【题解】细节题。根据文章的第三段可以判断。注意文中的cannot... as well as是"不如……好"的意思，是比较级的as... as形式，不是作为"也"意思讲的短语"as well as"，所以选B。

10. 【答案】C

　　【题解】根据文章的第四段第一句话"昆虫可以看到我们肉眼看不见的紫外线，有些甚至能看到X射线"，可以判断选项B为真；第二句话"我们看来灰暗的蛾子翅膀在它们眼里却美丽多彩，显示出我们看不到的色彩"，可以知道选项A、D为真。根据第四段的"Some insects have favorite colors"（一些昆虫有它们最爱的色彩），可以知道C选项符合题目要求。

4 Money

单元导读

众所周知，金钱可以让生活舒适些。它可以为我们提供基本的生活必需品，从而提高生活质量。这就是为什么那么多人做着成为百万富翁的美梦。更有甚者把金钱当作人生价值的体现。

但与此同时也有不少人因为对金钱的误解而身陷麻烦。他们忽略了家庭、朋友和自己的健康，认为人生目标就是对金钱的追求，从而变成了金钱的奴隶。而金钱可不是个好主人，甚至会把生活引向灾难。

没有钱确实会带来压力、悲哀，但拥有金钱也不能保证就一定会幸福。如果你的收入变成过去的两倍，你对生活的满意度可能会高一些，但是绝不是两倍。拥有100万的人不一定比只有1,000元的人更幸福。尽管金钱可以带来某种程度上的舒适，提供一定的安全感，但它绝不是生活的答案。

课文精讲

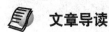

文章导读

文章以一个小故事开始，引出了本文的主题：当今社会对物质的崇拜。

文章从三个方面体现了当下的这一社会现象：从孩童到成人这一过程的社会熏陶；现代工业产品的制造；教育受到的影响。

作者以嘲讽的语气批判了这一不正常的社会现象，从而传达给读者这样的信息：钱并不是生命中最重要的东西。

背景知识

20世纪是人类有史以来最宏伟的造物世纪。人类创造的物质财富超过了过去的历史总和。或许是太多的物质财富成为人认识自己的障眼物，也许是人的自私性决定了人对物质财富的贪恋。但不能否认的是，物质财富毕竟给人类带来福音，人的生活一天比一天更好。

文章写作风格及结构

　　文章以一个小故事开始，引出了本文的主题：当今社会对物质的崇拜。在随后的文章里用简明扼要的语言说明、分析了这一现象，并表达了自己的态度。

Parts 部分	Paragraphs 段落	Main Ideas 大意
Part I	1	A romantic fable. 一个浪漫的故事。
Part II	2—3	Living in a materialistic society, we are trained from our earliest years to be acquisitive and obsessed with the idea of making money. 生活在崇尚物质的社会的我们，从小就培养了一种利欲心，一心想多赚钱。
Part III	4	This materialistic outlook has seriously influenced education. 崇尚物质的观念对教育产生了严重的影响。

词汇点睛

1　matter

vi. to be important or to have an effect on what happens 有关系，重要

- 例句 • It doesn't mater whether you go or not. 你去不去没有关系。

　　It doesn't matter if you are a few minutes late. 你迟到几分钟没有关系。

2　debt

n. sth. owed, such as money, goods, or services 债，债务

- 例句 • He managed to pay off his debts in two years. 他设法在两年内还清了债务。

　　The debt that he owed her could never be paid. 他欠她的人情永远也还不清。

- 短语 • **in debt** 欠债

　　He was deeply in debt. 他负债累累。

　　in sb.'s debt 欠某人的债

　　Thank you for helping. I'm in your debt. 感谢你的帮助。我欠你一份情。

3　acquisitive

adj. wanting to have and keep a lot of possessions 想获得的，贪婪的

- 例句 • He is acquisitive of new ideas. 他好求新知。

　　In an acquisitive society the form that selfishness takes is monetary greed.

　　在一个贪婪的社会里，贪财是自私自利的表现形式。

- 扩展 • **acquire** *vt.* 取得，获得；学到

　　We just acquired a dog. 我们刚得到了一只狗。

　　He spent years acquiring a good knowledge of Chinese. 他用了好几年时间掌握了中文。

4　possession

n.　1) (usu. pl.) sth. that you own or have with you at a particular time 所有物，财产

- 例句 • Check your possessions on arrival. 到达时检查一下你所带的物品。

2) *if sth. is in your possession, you own it, or you have obtained it from somewhere* 所有，占有

• 例句 • The possession of a degree does not guarantee you a job. 有了学位不能保证你找到工作。

They are in possession of a big orchard. 他们有一座大果园。

5 label

vt. to attach a label onto sth. or write information on sth. 贴标签于，标注标签

• 例句 • Be sure to label all the test tubes. 务必将所有试管贴上标签。

The bottle is labeled "Poison". 瓶子上贴着"毒药"的标签。

n. a piece of paper, etc. that is tached to sth. and that gives information about it 标签

• 例句 • I put labels on my baggage. 我在行李上贴上标签。

I don't know what is in this tin because it has no label.

我不知道这是个什么罐头，因为没有标签。

6 measure

vt. to find the size, length, or amount of sth., using standard units such as inches, metres, etc. 量，测量

• 例句 • We measured the room and found it was twenty feet long and fifteen feet wide.

我们测量了房间，它长20英尺，宽15英尺。

Time is measured by the hour, minute and second. 时间是以小时、分、秒计算的。

n. 1) sth. with which to test size, quantity, etc. 量度，测量

• 例句 • Exams are not necessarily the best measure of students' abilities.

考试不一定是衡量学生能力的最好办法。

2) *(usu. pl.) proceeding; steps* 措施，办法

• 例句 • We should take effective measures to solve the problem of pollution.

我们应该采取有效措施解决污染问题。

• 扩展 • **measurement** *n.* 衡量，测量

The measurement of individual intelligence is difficult. 一个人的智力很难衡量。

7 amusing

adj. funny and entertaining 有趣的

• 例句 • This is an amusing joke. 这是一个有趣的笑话。

The book is full of amusing stories about his childhood. 这本书里全是关于他童年的趣事。

• 扩展 • **amuse** *vt.* 逗乐，逗笑

His story amused everyone. 他的故事把大家都逗乐了。

We were all highly amused by the comedian's antics. 小丑的滑稽表演逗得我们哈哈大笑。

8 insurance

n. an arrangement with a company in which you pay them regular sums of money and they then pay the costs of anything bad happening to you 保险

• 例句 • He buys himself insurance each time he travels abroad. 每次出国旅行，他总为自己购买保险。

The insurance is very necessary. 保险是很必要的。

• 扩展 • **insure** *vt.* 给……上保险

Have you insured your new car yet? 你为你的新车投保了吗?

9 affluent

adj. having plenty of money, nice houses, expensive things, etc. 富裕的，丰富的

- 例句 • He was born to an affluent family. 他生在富裕人家。

  The land is affluent in natural resources. 该地自然资源丰富。

10 desirable

adj. sth. that is desirable is worth having or doing 希望得到的，值得拥有的

- 例句 • I envy Jane because her job is so desirable. 我羡慕简，因为她有一份那么称心的工作。

  It is most desirable that he should attend the conference. 他能参加这次会议，那是最好不过的了。

- 扩展 • **desire**

  1) *vt.* 向往，渴望

- 例句 • We all desire happiness and health. 我们都渴望幸福和健康。

  I have long desired to meet them. 我一直渴望见到他们。

  2) *n.* 愿望，欲望

- 例句 • I have little desire for wealth. 我对财富没有多大的欲望。

11 deliberately

adv. done in a way that is intended or planned 故意地，蓄意地

- 例句 • She broke my bicycle lamp deliberately. 她故意砸坏了我的自行车灯。

  He deliberately made trouble for me. 他故意找我麻烦。

- 扩展 • **deliberate** *adj.* 故意的；沉着的，从容不迫的

  He is deliberate in his speech. 他说话从容不迫。

  It was a deliberate lie. 那是故意撒谎。

12 discard

vt. to get rid of sth. 丢弃，抛弃

- 例句 • They discarded the empty bottles. 他们扔掉了空瓶子。

  This popular theory must now be discarded in the light of new findings.

  有了新的发现，这一流行的理论如今必须放弃。

13 outlook

n. 1) your general attitude to life and the world 观点，态度

- 例句 • His whole outlook on life has changed. 他的人生观已经完全改变了。

  They differ widely in outlook. 他们的观点极不相同。

  2) *view on which one looks out* 展望，前景

- 例句 • The economic outlook is bright. 经济前景光明。

14 personnel

n. 1) the people who work in a company, organization, or military force 人员，职员

- 例句 • Airline personnel can purchase flight tickets at reduced prices.
  航空公司的职员可以以优惠价购买飞机票。

  Army personnel are not allowed to leave the base. 军事人员不准离开基地。

  2) *the department in a company that chooses people for jobs and deals with their complaints, problems, etc.* 人事部门

- 例句 • Personnel has received your application form. 人事部门已经收到了你的申请。

• 辨析 • **personal** *adj.* 个人的，私人的

I cannot insist on my personal opinion. 我不能坚持个人意见。

15 compete

vi. to try to gain sth. and stop sb. else from having it 竞争

• 例句 • Several companies are competing against/with each other to get the contract.

几家公司正为争取一项合同而互相竞争。

She and her sister are always competing for attention. 她和她姐姐总是争着出风头。

• 扩展 • **competition** *n.* 竞争，比赛

The world's best players are here and the competition is fiercer than ever.

世界上的顶尖高手云集一堂，竞争空前激烈。

16 recruit

vt. to find new people to work in a company, join an organization, do a job, etc. 征募，招收

• 例句 • Our university recruits young people to the teaching profession every year.

我们学校每年都要招收一些年轻人担任教职。

Many government officials were recruited from private industry.

很多政府公务员都是从私人企业招收来的。

17 tempting

adj. sth. that is tempting seems very good and you would like to have it or do it 诱人的

• 例句 • The food looked tempting. 这种食品看上去真馋人。

I've recently received a very tempting job offer from IBM.

最近我收到了IBM公司提供的诱人的工作机会。

• 扩展 • **tempt** *vt.* 吸引，引起……的兴趣

The warm weather tempted them to go out on a picnic. 温暖的天气吸引他们外出野餐。

The offer tempted me. 这个提议很让我心动。

temptation *n.* 诱惑，引诱

There are many temptations in life. 生活中充满了诱惑。

18 tactic

n. a method that you use to achieve sth. 策略，战略

• 例句 • Tactics would be employed to speed up the peace process.

人们将采取策略来加速和平进程。

Republicans accuse Democrats of using delaying tactics to prevent a final vote on the bill.

共和党人指责民主党人采用拖延战术来阻止对这一提案的最后投票。

19 worship

vt. to show respect and love for a god 崇拜，尊敬

• 例句 • She worships her teacher. 她崇拜她的老师。

n. admiration and respect shown to or felt for sb. or sth. 崇拜，崇敬

• 例句 • They bowed their heads in worship. 他们崇敬地低下了头。

They gazed at the Chinese table tennis players with worship in their eyes.

他们用敬慕的眼光凝视着中国乒乓球运动员。

🔵 短语解析

1. pay off 还清（债务等）

【例句】After all these years, we've at last paid off all our debts.

经过这么多年，我们总算把债还清了。

You'll have to pay off your old loan before being allowed a new one.

你必须还清旧债，才能重新贷款。

2. in terms of 依据……，按照……；从……方面来说

【例句】She judges everyone in terms of her own standards. 她按照自己的标准评判每一个人。

In terms of customer satisfaction, the policy cannot be criticized.

从顾客满意这一点来看，这一方针无可指责。

3. keep up with 跟上

【例句】You are walking so fast that I can't keep up with you. 你走得太快，我跟不上了。

4. be bound to 必定……，一定会……

【例句】The weather is bound to get better tomorrow. 明天天气一定会变好。

Don't lie to her. She's bound to find out all about it.

别对她撒谎，她肯定会发现这一切的。

5. be obsessed with 被……困扰（或迷住）

【例句】He was obsessed with fear of death. 他被死亡的恐惧所困扰。

She was obsessed with the idea that she was being watched. 她总觉得受人监视而心神不宁。

6. set out to 着手做……，开始做……

【例句】When she was 18, Amy set out to find her biological parents.

艾米从18岁开始寻找她的亲生父母。

He set out to paint the whole house but finished only the front.

他动手油漆整栋房子，但是只漆完了房子的正面。

7. no sooner than 一……就……

【例句】I had no sooner entered the hall than the ceremony began. 我刚进入礼堂，仪式就开始了。

No sooner had he arrived that he began to complain. 他一到就开始发牢骚。

8. for one's sake 为了……起见，为了……

【例句】I did it entirely for your sake. 我这么做完全是为你好。

He changed into old shoes for the sake of comfort. 为了舒适，他换上了旧鞋。

🔵 难句突破

1. (Para. 1) *So the young people waited until they found good jobs with good prospects and they were able to get married.*

【解析】until引导时间状语从句，表示"一直到……"时，主句和从句都用肯定式；表示"直到……才……"时，主句用否定式，从句用肯定式。例如：

He worked until it was dark. 他一直工作到天黑。

He did not get up till his mother came in. 母亲进来时他才起床。

【译文】于是，这对年轻人一直等着，等到找到了好工作才结婚。

2. (Para. 1) ***And so ends another modern romantic fable.***

【解析】本句是一个全部倒装结构。当方式状语、频度状语等移至句首时，一般引起部分倒装，而如果主语较长，则使用全部倒装结构。例如：

Many a time has Mike given me good advice.

迈克给过我许多次很好的建议。（many a time放在句首引起部分倒装。）

Thus began the nice music between us and the Chinese.

就这样，我们和中国人民之间开始奏起了美妙的乐章。（thus放在句首引起倒装，并且因为主语the nice music between us and the Chinese太长，因此使用全部倒装结构。）

【译文】至此，又一个现代版的浪漫爱情故事结束了。

3. (Para. 2) ***When we grow old enough to earn a living, it does not surprise us to discover that success is measured in terms of the money you earn.***

【解析】1）本句的主干是it does not surprise us...，when引导时间状语从句。在句子的主干中it是形式主语，而真正的主语是后面that引导的从句that success is measured in terms of the money you earn。

2）in terms of意为"依据……"。

【译文】当我们长大成人，可以自食其力的时候，发现成功是根据你挣钱的多少来衡量的，这一点也不会让我们感到惊讶。

4. (Para. 2) ***The most amusing thing about this game is that the Joneses and all the neighbors who are struggling frantically to keep up with them, are spending borrowed money kindly provided, at a suitable rate of interest, of course, by friendly banks, insurance companies, etc.***

【解析】1）本句主干是the most amusing thing about this game is that...，其中that引导表语从句；而这个表语从句的主语是the Joneses and all the neighbors，谓语动词是spend；其中who引导的定语从句（who are struggling frantically to keep with them）修饰the Joneses and all the neighbors。

2）keep up with the Joneses意为"左邻右舍互相攀比"。

【译文】在这场游戏中，最有趣的一点是，邻里之间拼命进行攀比所花的钱，当然都是以合理的利率从那些友好的银行、保险公司等机构借来的。

5. (Para. 3) ***Gone are the days when industrial goods were made to last forever.***

【解析】1）当表语至于句首时，倒装结构为"表语＋系动词＋主语"。例如：

Present at the meeting were Professor White, Professor Smith and many other guests.

出席会议的有怀特教授，史密斯教授以及其他嘉宾。

Gone are the days when they could do what they liked to the Chinese people.

他们对中国人民为所欲为的日子已经一去不复返了。

Among the goods are Christmas tress, flowers, candles and toys.

物品当中有圣诞树，鲜花，蜡烛和玩具。

2）本句中还包含一个when引导的定语从句when industrial goods were made to last forever修饰the days。

【译文】把工业产品制造得经久耐用的年代已经一去不复返了。

6. (Para. 3) *"Built-in obsolescence" provides the means: goods are made to be discarded.*

【解析】1) built-in是复合词，通过类似的方法形成的词还有：slipup, slide-over, come-off等。

2) means在本句中意思是"方式"。例如：

They had no means of communication. 他们没有交流的方法。

We need to find some other means of transportation. 我们需要找到其他的运输方式。

【译文】而商品与生俱来的有限使用寿命使之成为可能：产品造出来就是用来丢弃的。

7. (Para. 3) *You no sooner acquire this year's model than you are thinking about its replacement.*

【解析】no sooner... than... 引导时间状语从句，表示"刚……就……"。主句中的动词一般用过去完成时，从句用过去时。主句一般倒装，把助动词had提到前面。表示同样意思和用法的还有"hardly... when..."。例如：

No sooner had I entered the room than I heard a loud noise.

我刚进房间就听到了巨大的噪音。

No sooner had I started mowing the lawn than it started raining.

我刚开始割草就开始下雨了。

The party had hardly started when she left. 晚会刚开始，她就走了。

【译文】你刚买到今年的新款，又在考虑升级换代了。

8. (Para. 4) *Fewer and fewer young people these days acquire knowledge only for its own sake.*

【解析】1) fewer and fewer 是"形容词比较级 + 形容词比较级"的用法，表示"越来越……"。例如：

The weather is getting colder and colder. 天气越来越冷了。

The city is becoming more and more beautiful. 城市变得越来越漂亮了。

2) for one's own sake 意为"为了……起见"。

【译文】现在，单纯为了获取知识而学习的年轻人越来越少。

9. (Para. 4) *Recruiting tactics of this kind have led to the "brain drain", the process by which highly skilled people offer their services to the highest bidder.*

【解析】本句中包含一个which引导的定语从句by which highly skilled people...，which在从句中作介词by的宾语。这种用法多见于正式语体。例如：

The room in which there is a machine is a workshop.

有一台机器的那个房间是一个工作间。

They tried to think of a plan by which they could fulfill their task ahead of time.

他们试图想一个方法可以提前完成任务。

【译文】这样的招聘策略导致了"人才流失"，使得高级技术人才去为出价最高的公司提供服务。

10. (Para. 4) *Mammon is worshipped as never before, the rich get richer and the poor, poorer.*

【解析】as never before表示"前所未有的，从前没有过的"，其中as作副词，表示"与……相同程度；与……等同"。as的用法详见本册Unit 1，Text A难句突破9。

【译文】财神受到了前所未有的崇拜，于是富的更富，穷的更穷。

参考译文

钱是生命中最重要的东西吗？

从前，有一位美丽的姑娘和一位英俊的小伙子。他们很贫穷，但彼此深爱着对方，希望永结同心。但是这对年轻人的父母摇头了。他们说："你们现在还不能结婚，你们必须先找到一份有前景的好工作才行。"于是，这对年轻人一直等着，等到找到了好工作才结婚。当然，他们还是很贫穷，没有房子，没有家具，但这些都没有关系。因为小伙子有份很好的工作，一些大的机构组织就借钱给他买房子，买家具，买所有最新式的家用电器，还有一部车。小两口还清欠债后，过上了幸福的生活。至此，又一个现代版的浪漫爱情故事就这样结束了。

我们生活在一个崇尚物质的社会，从小就培养了一种利欲心。从孩童时期起，我们的所有物品就被清晰地打上了"我的"、"你的"之类的标记。当我们长大成人，可以自食其力的时候，发现成功是根据你挣钱的多少来衡量的，这一点也不会让我们感到惊讶。我们一辈子都在同隔壁的张三李四相互攀比。如果我们买了台新电视，我们的邻居张三势必会买一台更大更好的。如果我们买了一辆新车，隔壁的李四肯定要超过我们，买两辆新车：一辆给妻子，一辆给自己。在这场游戏中，最有趣的一点是，邻里之间拼命进行攀比所花的钱，当然都是以合理的利率从那些友好的银行、保险公司等机构借来的。

并不只是生活在富足社会里的人才会一心想多赚钱。生活消费品到处都需要，而现代工业则有意开拓新市场。把工业产品制造得经久耐用的年代已经一去不复返了。工业的车轮必须要不停地运转下去，而商品与生俱来的有限使用寿命使之成为可能：产品造出来就是用来丢弃的。小汽车越来越中看不中用。你刚买到今年的新款，又在考虑升级换代了。

这种崇尚物质的观念对教育产生了严重的影响。现在，单纯为了获取知识而学习的年轻人越来越少。他们所修的每门课程都有明确的目的性：那就是得到更高的薪水待遇。市场对人才的需求远远超过人才的供给，大公司在学生们完成学业之前就开始竞相聘用，为他们提供诱人的薪水和"小恩小惠"。这样的招聘策略导致了"人才流失"，使得高级技术人才去为出价最高的公司提供服务。富裕的国家抢走了贫穷邻国的能人。财神受到了前所未有的崇拜，于是富的更富，穷的更穷。

习题全解

文章大意

1. 根据课文用合适的词填空。

【答案】1) acquisitive 2) money   3) neighbors 4) banks 5) discarded

6) education 7) bigger wage packet 8) exceeds 9) salaries 10) brain drain

【解析】in terms of 表示"根据，依据，从……方面"；struggle to do 表示"费力，尽力做……"；keep up with 表示"跟上……，与……攀比"；affluent society "表示富足的社会"；fringe benefit 表示"小恩小惠"；brain drain 表示"人才流失"。

【译文】　　我们生活在一个崇尚物质的社会，从小就培养了一种利欲心。当我们长大成人，可以自食其力的时候，发现成功是根据我们挣钱的多少来衡量的。我们用以合理的利率从那些友好的银行、保险公司等机构借来的钱拼命地和我们的邻居互相攀比。

　　在富足的社会中，工业产品造出来就是用来丢弃的，以便开拓新的市场。这种崇尚物质的观念对教育产生了严重的影响。所修的每门课程都是为了得到更高的薪水。市场对人才的需求远远超过人才的供给，大公司在学生们完成学业之前就开始竞相聘用，为他们提供诱人的薪水和"小恩小惠"。这样的招聘策略导致了"人才流失"。这样，富裕的国家抢走了贫穷邻国的能人。于是富的更富，穷的更穷。

文章细节

根据文章回答问题。

【答案】

1) Because they didn't have a good job with good prospects.

2) The young man had a good job with good prospects.

3) In terms of the money you earn.

4) No. Goods are made to be discarded.

5) Fewer and fewer young people acquire knowledge for its own sake. Every course of study must lead somewhere, i.e. to a bigger wage packet.

6) By offering tempting salaries and fringe benefits.

7) These recruiting tactics have led to the brain drain. The wealthier nations deprive their poorer neighbors of their most able citizens, thus the rich get richer and the poor get poorer.

【译文】

1) [问题] 当这对年轻男女准备结婚的时候，他们的父母为什么不同意？

　　[答案] 因为他们还没有找到一份有前景的好工作。

2) [问题] 为什么一些大机构借给他钱买房子？

　　[答案] 因为这个年轻人有一份有很好前景的工作。

3) [问题] 一个物质的社会如何评价成功？

　　[答案] 根据一个人赚钱的多少。

4) [问题] 在富足的社会里工业产品仍然经久耐用么？

　　[答案] 不是，产品造出来就是用来丢弃的。

5) [问题] 崇尚物质的观念对教育产生了怎样的影响？

　　[答案] 现在，单纯为了获取知识而学习的年轻人越来越少。他们所修的每门课程都有明确的目的性：那就是得到更高的薪水待遇。

6) [问题] 大公司怎样竞聘人才？

　　[答案] 提供诱人的薪水和"小恩小惠"。

7) [问题] 这些竞聘策略的最终结果是什么？

　　[答案] 这样的招聘策略导致了"人才流失"，富裕的国家抢走了贫穷邻国的能人。于是富的更富，穷的更穷。

词汇练习

1. 请用下面所给词汇或短语的适当形式填写句子。

1) 【答案】matter

   【译文】如果我错过了这辆公交车也没关系，我就走着去。

2) 【答案】exceeding

   【译文】他因为超速而被处以罚款。

3) 【答案】keep up with

   【译文】我们应该追赶上最新技术发展的速度。

4) 【答案】debts

   【译文】他没有足够的钱来还清债务。

5) 【答案】prospect

   【译文】关于史密斯先生的身体恢复情况，前景不容乐观。

6) 【答案】benefits

   【译文】这家公司给雇员提供丰厚的薪水报酬以及让人羡慕的福利制度。

7) 【答案】is bound to

   【译文】别对她撒谎，她一定会发现的。

8) 【答案】amusing

   【译文】整本书都记载了他童年时代的趣事。

9) 【答案】means

   【译文】电子邮件已成为日益重要的商业交流方式。

10) 【答案】set out / has set out

    【译文】新政府正着手实施更好的贸易政策。

2. 请选用适当的介词或副词填空。

1) 【答案】For

   【译文】为了安全起见，你必须得让孩子们远离所有的药品。

2) 【答案】in

   【译文】这工作很有发展前途，但起薪太低了。

3) 【答案】with

   【译文】他们发现自己不得不同外资公司争夺市场份额。

4) 【答案】out

   【译文】他正着手将纽卡斯尔队打造成全国最顶尖的球队。

5) 【答案】with

   【译文】我很难跟上班上其他同学的进度。

6) 【答案】off

   【译文】他提前六个月还清了全部贷款。

7) 【答案】of

   【译文】男孩的父母宣称学校的行为剥夺了他们儿子接受良好教育的权利。

8) 【答案】with

   【译文】许多年轻女孩总是被她们的体重问题困扰。

3. 辨析表格中容易混淆的几组词，请选用恰当的词填空。

1) 【答案】personal

【译文】坚持你个人的观点很重要。

2) 【答案】Personnel

【译文】你应该将申请表寄到人事部门。

3) 【答案】personal

【译文】我有些私人问题想和你讨论一下。

4) 【答案】personnel

【译文】在坠毁的那架飞机上有五位机组成员。

5) 【答案】means

【译文】毫无疑问，收音机和电视都是重要的传播信息的工具。

6) 【答案】mean

【译文】你究竟是什么意思？

7) 【答案】mean

【译文】字典会告诉你词的意思。

8) 【答案】means

【译文】考试不应该被当作是衡量学生学习水平的唯一方式。

语法结构

1. 仿照例句改写下列句子。

1) 【答案】It was the day before yesterday that John went to the cinema.

【译文】前天，约翰去看了电影。

2) 【答案】It was AIDS that killed him.

【译文】是艾滋病夺走了他的生命。

3) 【答案】It is my sister who helps me with my study.

【译文】姐姐在学习上对我帮助很大。

4) 【答案】It was by train that the expert came here.

【译文】专家是坐火车到这儿的。

5) 【答案】It was at the corner that a car knocked Bob down.

【译文】鲍勃是在拐角处被车撞倒的。

2. 仿照例句用no sooner... than... 改写下列句子。

1) 【答案】No sooner had I sat down than someone knocked on the door.

【译文】我刚一坐下就有人敲门。

2) 【答案】No sooner had I finished my homework than Mom called me for help.

【译文】我刚一做完作业妈妈就让我给她帮忙。

3) 【答案】No sooner had Laura hidden her jewelry than the robbers broke into the house.

【译文】劳拉刚把珠宝藏好强盗就破门而入。

4) 【答案】No sooner had the teacher recovered from illness than he began teaching.

【译文】老师病一好就开始给学生上课。

5) 【答案】David no sooner finds the answer to the first question than he is thinking of the second.

　　【译文】大卫刚找到第一题的答案，就开始思考第二题。

综合练习

1. 完型填空。

1) 【答案】D

　　【题解】根据上下文，此句意为"这次的旅行如何啊？"因此只能选D。

2) 【答案】D

　　【题解】固定搭配，achieve the purpose，意为"达到目的，实现目标"。get 获得，到达；arrive 到达；reach 延伸，到达。故选D。

3) 【答案】A

　　【题解】固定搭配，to sb.'s astonishment/to sb.'s surprise，意为"让某人感到吃惊"。只能选A。

4) 【答案】B

　　【题解】根据上下文，此句意为"我们有仆人服侍，他们却可以彼此照应，互相帮助。"each other 彼此，互相，因此选B。

5) 【答案】C

　　【题解】本题考查动词短语辨析。arrive to 到达……地方；lead to 导致……后果；reach to 作不及物动词，表示"延伸至……"，reach some place 作及物动词，表示"到达……地方"；get to 到达……地方。本句意为"我们有一个游泳池，但只到花园中央为止……"故选C。

6) 【答案】C

　　【题解】side 一边，侧面；edge 边缘；end 末端，尽头；line 线路，航线。本句意为"他们门前却有条小溪，一眼望不到头。"故选C。

7) 【答案】B

　　【题解】根据上下文，本句意为"你是富裕或者贫穷取决于你看待事物的角度，这难道不是真理？"连词whether（是否）符合句意，故选B。

8) 【答案】D

　　【题解】固定搭配，attitude towards life 对待生活的态度。

9) 【答案】A

　　【题解】本题考查代词辨析。any 任何一个；some 一些，有些；all 所有的；none 一个也没有。根据上下文，只能选A。

10) 【答案】D

　　【题解】本题考查代词辨析。something 某事物；anything 任何事物；everything 每件事；nothing 没有什么。根据上下文，只能选D。

　　【译文】

　　　　一天，一位很富有的父亲带着儿子来到乡下，他的目的是想让儿子了解穷人的生活。他们一整天都呆在当地很穷的一家人的农场里。当他们启程返家时，父亲问儿子："这次的旅行如何啊？"

　　　　"非常棒，爸爸！"男孩答道。

"这下你知道穷人过的是怎样的生活了吧？"父亲问道。

"是的。"儿子答道。

"那你从中学到什么了？"父亲问道，心想他的目的达到了。然而儿子的回答却令他吃惊。儿子说道："我们家只养了一只狗，他们有四只；我们有仆人服侍，他们却可以彼此照应，互相帮助；我们有一个游泳池，但只到花园中央为止，他们门前却有条小溪，一眼望不到头；我们的花园里虽然有进口的路灯，他们却拥有数不尽的星星；我们一出门只来到前院，他们一出门却可以看见整个地平线。"

小男孩说完后，父亲沉默无语。

随后儿子又补充道："谢谢，爸爸。您让我知道了我们有多穷。"

你是富裕或者贫穷取决于你看待事物的角度，这难道不是真理吗？如果你拥有爱情、友情、幸福的家庭、健康的身体，有幽默感，并且拥有积极的生活态度，那么你就拥有了一切。这些绝非金钱能买到。尽管你能拥有所有你想象得到的物质财富，但假如你心思枯竭，精神空虚，那么你仍然一无所有。

2. 用括号中的词汇和短语将下列句子译成英语。

1）【答案】It was the car accident that deprived her of a normal life.

2）【答案】If we can't keep up with technical developments, we are bound to be washed out.

3）【答案】He is rich in terms of money, but not in terms of happiness.

4）【答案】No sooner had he exceeded the speed limit than the police car appeared.

5）【答案】The two companies compete with each other for the sake of money.

文章泛读

文章导读

你是一个拜金主义者吗？你认为钱越多越好吗？在回答这些问题之前看看约翰·萨特的传奇故事吧。

旧金山原本只是一个有800名左右居民的小镇。因为"黄金"，这个宁静怡人的小镇，几乎在一夜之间就变成了一个喧嚣而又拥挤的城市。发生在这里的故事也引人入胜。

背景知识

淘金热与旧金山：旧金山，又译作圣弗朗西斯科或三藩市，是美国西部重要的海港城市，金融、贸易和文化中心。它地处加利福尼亚州西北部，太平洋和圣弗朗西斯湾之间半岛的北端，三面临海。市区面积约120平方公里。圣弗朗西斯科 (San Francisco) 是1847年墨西哥人以西班牙文命名的，当时这里的居民只有800多人。1848年这里发现金矿后，移民蜂拥而至，掀起了淘金热。许多华人作为"契约劳工"来此挖金矿，修铁路，备尝艰辛。此后大批华工在这里安家落户，他们称这座城市为旧金山（以区别澳大利亚的新金山）。

文章写作风格及结构

本文为记叙文（narration），通过讲述约翰·萨特的传奇人生，告诉我们简单的人生道理。

Parts 部分	Paragraphs 段落	Main Ideas 大意
Part I	1—2	With the discovery of gold, San Francisco was changed almost overnight. The same factors also changed the life of John A. Sutter. 随着金矿的发现，旧金山几乎在一夜之间改变了。所有这些改变了旧金山的因素，也改变了约翰·萨特的命运。
Part II	3—9	The story of John A. Sutter. 约翰·萨特的故事。

词汇点睛

1　independence

n. political freedom from control by the government of another country 独立，自主

- 例句 • Cuba gained independence from Spain in 1898. 古巴于1898年脱离西班牙而获得独立。
  Most young people want independence from their parents. 大多数年轻人不想依赖父母。
- 扩展 • **independent** *adj.* 独立的，自主的
  Mozambique became independent in 1975. 莫桑比克于1975年获得独立。
- 短语 • **be independent of** 不依赖；不受……限制
  They went camping so as to be independent of hotels. 他们去露营，免得受住旅馆的限制。
- 反义词 • **dependence** *n.* 依赖，依靠

2　declare

vt. to state officially and publicly that a particular situation exists or that sth. is true 宣布，宣称

- 例句 • He declared that he was in love with her. 他声称他已经爱上了她。
  I declared at the meeting that I did not support him. 我在会上声明我不支持他。
- 辨析 • **declare, publish, proclaim**
  三个词都含"明确地声明或宣布的意思"。
  declare 经常用于正式场合，指"清楚，有力地，公开让人知道"。如：
  He declared his intention to run for office. 他宣布了自己参加竞选的想法。
  publish 指"通过口头和书面方式让公众都知道，但主要是后者"。如：
  He'll publish a statement. 他将公布一项声明。
  proclaim 用于公共或正式场合，特别指"重大的事件"，着重"庄严地向广大群众宣布"或"严肃认真地申明"。如：
  proclaim the founding of a republic 宣告一个共和国的成立

3　inhabitant

n. a person who lives in a particular place 居民，住户

- 例句 • They are the oldest inhabitant of the village. 他们是这个村最早的居民。

  This is a city of 6 million inhabitants. 这是个有600万居民的城市。
- 扩展 • **inhabit** *vt.* 居住在，栖居于

  The island used to be inhabited. 这个岛过去曾经有人居住。

4　previously

adv. before now or before a particular time 先前，以前

- 例句 • I remember seeing him somewhere previously. 我记得从前在什么地方见过他。

  This record was previously held by John. 这项记录以前是由约翰保持的。
- 扩展 • **previous** *adj.* 先前的；以前的

  His previous attempt was successful. 他以前的尝试成功了。
- 短语 • **previous to (=before)** 在……之前

  I had collected material previous to writing. 我在写作以前先搜集了材料。
- 辨析 • **previous，preceding，prior**

  previous 指"时间上早于某事件或行动的"。如：

  He cannot go for he has a previous engagement. 他不能去，因他已事先有约会。

  preceding 指"此前的"，多用于指文章中某一处之前的。如：

  preceding chapter 上一章

  prior 指"除时间外，还可在顺序、重要性等方面在前的"，比previous多一层"优先"的意思。

  This task is prior to all others. 这项任务比所有其他任务都重要。

5　overnight

adv. 1) suddenly or surprisingly quickly 突然地，一夜间

- 例句 • Byron became famous overnight. 拜伦一夜间成名了。

  Don't expect it to improve overnight. 不要指望这事一下子就改善了。

  2) for, during the night 在晚上；整夜
- 例句 • We stayed overnight in London after the theater. 我们看完戏后在伦敦住了一晚。

6　rough

adj. using force or violence 粗野的，粗暴的

- 例句 • He's a rough-looking character. 他是个举止粗野的家伙。

  They complained of rough handling by the police. 他们抱怨受到警察粗暴的对待。

7　factor

n. one of several things that influence or cause a situation 因素

- 例句 • The closure of the mine was the single factor in the town's decline.

  矿山的关闭是这个镇衰落的唯一原因。

  Her friendly manner is an important factor in her rapid success.

  待人友好是她迅速获得成功的重要因素。

8　private

adj. for use by one person or group, not for everyone 私人的，私有的

• 例句 • This is private land, you can't walk across it. 这是私人土地，你不能通过。

The two leaders held a private conversation. 两位领导人举行了一次秘密会谈。

• 短语• **in private** 在家里，私下地

Make suggestion to your friends in private. Praise your friends in public.

劝告朋友要在无人地方，赞扬朋友可在人多场合。

• 扩展 • **privacy** *n.* 独处，隐私

We must respect other's privacy. 我们应该尊重别人的隐私。

9　intelligent

adj. an intelligent person has a high level of mental ability and is good at understanding ideas and thinking clearly 聪明的，有才智的

• 例句 • Can you say that dolphins are much more intelligent than other animals?

你能说海豚比其他动物聪明得多吗？

It is an intelligent dog, easily trained to control sheep.

它是一条有灵性的狗，稍加训练便可以看守羊群。

• 扩展 • **intelligence** *n.* 智力, 聪明, 情报

Use your intelligence, and you're sure to achieve something.

发挥你的聪明才智，你一定能取得成就。

Central Intelligence Agency (CIA) 中央情报局

intelligence quotient（IQ）智商

• 辨析• **intelligent, intellectual**

形容人时，intelligent是指聪明，头脑灵敏。而intellectual是指受过良好教育、对需要长期研究的学科感兴趣。一个小孩，甚至一条狗，可以用intelligent来形容，但不能称为intellectual。

10　establish

vt. to set up; to found 设立，建立

• 例句 • The company was established in 1860. 这家公司创办于1860年。

The club has established a new rule allowing women to join.

俱乐部制定了一条新规章，允许妇女入会。

11　descend

vi. if a large number of people descend on a person or a place, they come to visit or stay, especially when they are not very welcome 蜂拥而至

• 例句 • Hundreds of football fans descended on the city. 数百名足球迷蜂拥入城。

The whole family descended on us at Christmas. 圣诞节他们全家突然来我家做客。

vt. to come or go down 下来；下降

• 例句 • She descended the stairs. 她走下楼梯。

• 短语• **descend from sb.** 从……传下来

The title descends to me from my father. 这个头衔是由我父亲传给我的。

be descended from sb. 是某人的后裔

He claims to be descended from a Spanish prince. 他声称是一位西班牙王子的后裔。

- 扩展 • **descent** *n.* 下降，血统

We watched anxiously her descent from the tree. 我们焦急地看着她从树上下来。

Many Americans are of English descent. 许多美国人有英国血统。

12 poverty

n. the situation or experience of being poor 贫穷，贫困

- 例句 • She has lived in poverty all her life. 她一生都过着贫困的生活。

Poverty is not a shame, but the being ashamed of it is.

[谚]贫不足耻，耻贫乃耻。

- 反义词 • **richness**

13 suit

n. an argument that a person or company brings to a court of law to be settled 诉讼

- 例句 • He filed a divorce suit against his wife. 他对妻子提起离婚诉讼。

The victims have started a suit to get compensation for their injuries.

受害者已经开始起诉，要求得到损害赔偿。

vt. to be appropriate for 适合，适当

- 例句 • That dress suits you. 那套衣服你穿起来挺合适。

14 occupy

vt. to live or stay in a place 占据，占领

- 例句 • The bed seemed to occupy most of the room. 床似乎占据了大半个屋子。

The army occupied the enemy's capital. 军队占领了敌国首都。

- 短语 • **occupy oneself (in doing sth. / with sth.)** 忙于（做）某事

She occupied herself with routine office tasks. 她忙于办公室的日常工作。

- 扩展 • **occupation** *n.* 占据，占领，职业

He returned from Paris and found his office was under someone else's occupation.

他从巴黎回来，发现他的办公室被别人占了。

Please state your name, age and occupation. 请说明姓名、年龄和职业。

15 percentage

n. an amount expressed as if it is part of a total which is 100 百分比，部分

- 例句 • What percentage of the students were absent? 旷课的学生占百分之几？

A large percentage of school-books now have pictures. 现在大部分教科书都有插图。

- 用法• percentage 前不与数字连用，如：不直接说three percentage，而改为three percent或 a percentage of three。

- 扩展 • **percent** *n.* 百分比，百分数

Sixty percent of the pupils are boys means that of every hundred pupils, sixty are boys.

60%的学生是男孩是指每100个学生中，有60个是男孩。

16 property

n. the thing (especially land or buildings) or things that sb. owns 财产，所有物

- 例句 • The jewels were her personal property. 这些首饰是她的私人财产。

Don't touch those tools—they are not your property. 不要动那些工具——那不是你的东西。

17 hang

v. 1) to kill sb. by dropping them with a rope around their neck 绞死

• 例句 • He was the last man to be hanged for murder in this country.

他是这个国家中最后一个被处以绞刑的谋杀犯。

It's impossible for him to be hanged for such a crime.

他不可能因为犯这个罪而被绞死。

2) to attach sth., or to be attached, at the top so that the lower part is free or loose 悬挂，下垂

• 例句 • Hang your coat up on the hook. 把你的大衣挂在衣钩上。

Her hair hung down to her waist. 她的长发垂及腰际。

• 短语 • **hang about** 闲荡；缓缓行走

He hung about outside my house. 他在我家房子外面转悠。

hang on 紧握；（电话用语）别挂断；仔细听

Hang on to the strap. The bus is starting. 抓住皮带，汽车要开动了。

Hang on a minute；I'm just coming. 请稍等一下，我马上就来。

The boy hangs on his teacher's every word. 这小男孩专心听老师讲的每句话。

hang out 常去某处

Where does he hang out these days? 他这些日子都在什么地方来着？

18 blow

n. an action or event that causes difficulty or sadness for sb. 打击

• 例句 • It was a great blow when he failed to pass the exam.

他考试不及格对他是个重大的打击。

Being beaten by a young man came as a big blow to his pride.

败在一个年轻人手下，他的自尊心受到极大的打击。

v. to move sth., or to be moved, by the force of the wind or a current of air 风吹，吹动

• 例句 • The wind has blown my hat off. 风把我的帽子刮走了。

19 delay

n. when sb./sth. has to wait, or the length of the waiting time 耽搁，延迟

• 例句 • We apologize for the delay in answering your letter. 来信收悉，迟复为歉。

Report it to the police without delay. 赶快将此事报告警察。

v. to make or be slow or late 延迟；推迟

• 例句 • We decided to delay our holiday until next month. 我们决定将休假延至下个月。

Thousands of commuters were delayed for over an hour. 数千名乘车下班的人被耽搁了一个多小时。

🌐 短语解析

1. leak out （水）漏出；[口]（消息等）泄露出去

【例句】The details were supposed to be secret but somehow leaked out.

这些细节原属秘密，可是不知怎么给泄露出去了。

It has leaked out that they intend to increase the arms budget.

有消息透露，他们有意增加军备预算。

2．tear down 扯下，拆卸

【例句】These beautiful old houses are being torn down to make way for a new road.

这些漂亮的老房子正在被拆毁，以便修建新道路。

They are tearing down these old houses to build a new office block.

他们正拆除这些旧房子以便建新办公楼。

3. spring up 涌现，突然出现

【例句】New houses were springing up all over the town. 全镇各处很快盖起了新房子。

Doubts have begun to spring up in my mind. 我突然起了疑心。

4. far from... 远非……，远远不……

【例句】The problem is far from easy. 这问题绝非易事。

Your account is far from the truth. 你所说远非事实。

5. in sb.'s favor 有利于……

【例句】The exchange rate is in our favor today. 今天的兑换率对我们有利。

The court decided in his favor. 法庭的判决对他有利。

6. take over 接管

【例句】The firm has been taken over by an American conglomerate.

该公司已被美国一企业集团接管。

When she fell ill her daughter took over the business from her.

她患病期间生意曾由她女儿接管。

难句突破

1. (Para.1) *In all American history, there is no story stranger than that of John A. Sutter.*

【解析】that指代story。代词that常用来指前面提到过的名词。例如：

This book is not so interesting as that I read yesterday. 这本书没有我昨天读的那本有趣。

【译文】美国历史上，约翰·萨特的故事最富有传奇色彩。

2. (Para.1) *San Francisco was a small town of some 800 inhabitants.*

【解析】of用来引入名词的后置修饰语。类似的用法还有：a coat of many colors 一件彩色的大衣；a girl of 10 一个10岁的女孩；a child of strange appearance 一个外貌奇特的孩子。

【译文】当时的旧金山还只是一个有800名左右居民的小镇。

3. (Para.2) *San Francisco grew to three times its size in just a few weeks.*

【解析】three times its size表示扩大成原来的三倍。倍数表示可用以下方式表达：

A是B的几倍可表达为："A is... times as + 形容词（副词）原级 + as B" 或 "A is... times the size (length/height/amount etc.) of B"。例如：

这座桥是旧桥的三倍长。

This bridge is three times as long as the old one.

This bridge is three times the length of the old one.

【译文】在短短几周内，旧金山的面积扩大到原来的三倍。

4. (Para.2) ***Previously a quiet, pleasant town, San Francisco was changed almost overnight into a rough and crowded city, full of all kinds of adventurers and other strange characters.***

【解析】Previously a quiet, pleasant town是San Francisco的同谓语，指的就是San Francisco; full of all kinds of adventurers... 作定语修饰a rough and crowded city。

【译文】旧金山这个原本宁静怡人的小镇，几乎在一夜之间就变成了一个喧嚣而又拥挤的城市，冒险家和其他稀奇古怪的各色人物到处可见。

5. (Para.3) ***He had come, penniless, in the spirit of adventure to the United States.***

【解析】penniless 是形容词作主语补语，修饰he。in the spirit of表示"拥有……的精神"。

【译文】他来到美国时身无分文，有的只是冒险精神。

6. (Para.3) ***He obtained the rights to a large piece of land in the present area of Sacramento, some seventy miles north of San Francisco.***

【解析】in the present area of Sacramento表示现今的萨克拉门托。present 作定语时可以表示"现存的，现有的"。例如：the present difficulties 目前存在的困难；the present government 当今的政府。

【译文】他在旧金山以北约70英里处，即现在的萨克拉门托，获得了很大一片土地。

7. (Para.4) ***He became a very rich man by providing most of the ships that came to the harbor of San Francisco with supplies both for their own use and for export.***

【解析】句子的主干是he became a very rich man by providing... ships... with supplies...; that引导定语从句修饰the ships。

【译文】靠着向过往旧金山港口的船只提供补给以及出口物资，他变得非常富有。

8. (Para.6) ***On the site of his saw mill grew up the present city of Coloma.***

【解析】本句是全部倒装的结构。当句首状语为表示地点的介词词组时，会引起全部倒装。例如：
In this chapter will be found a partial answer. 答案的一部分可以在这一章找到。
From the valley came a strange sound. 一个奇怪的声音从山谷传来。

【译文】原先的萨特锯木场所在地则成为了今天的科洛马城。

9. (Para.7) ***Far from becoming the richest man in the world, as he had dreamed, Sutter was reduced to poverty.***

【解析】as引导状语从句，表示"以……方式，像……一样"。详解见Unit 1，Text A难句突破9。

【译文】萨特非但没有如愿成为世界上最有钱的人，反而变得一贫如洗。

10. (Para.7) ***In 1855 Sutter brought a suit in the Californian courts against the 1,700 settlers, who now occupied the lands he had previously owned.***

【解析】本句主干为Sutter brought a suit... against the... settlers；其中settlers由who引导的非限定性定语从句修饰；在这个定语从句中又套有一个定语从句（that）he had previously owned 修饰lands。

【译文】1855年，萨特在加利福尼亚州法院对那1,700名定居者提起诉讼，控告他们侵占了过去属于他的土地。

11. (Para.7) *He demanded $25 million from the state for the roads, canals, and bridges that he himself had built but which the state had taken over.*

【解析】本句的主干是he demanded $25 million from the state...；but连接两个并列的分句that he himself had built和which the state had taken over；其中的两个引导词that和which都引导定语从句修饰同样的先行词the roads, canals, and bridges。

【译文】他自己修建的道路、沟渠、桥梁被政府接管，他要求政府赔偿他2,500万美金。

12. (Para.8) *When the judge's decision was made public, 10,000 people, who were now established in the area and thought they might lose their homes, descended upon the court.*

【解析】本句的主干是public... descended upon the court；其中when引导时间状语从句when the judge's decision was made；10,000 people是pubic的同位语，对public 作出解释和说明；who引导非限定性定语从句who were now established in the area and thought they might lose their homes 修饰public。

【译文】法官的裁决被公之于众时，一万民众突袭了法院，这些人已在当地安居立业，唯恐失去了家园。

13. (Para.9) *He went back east and, in the courts of Washington, again brought a suit to recover what he claimed had been stolen from him.*

【解析】what引导宾语从句what he claimed had been stolen from him作recover的宾语；east在这里作副词用来表示"向东方地"，例如：
My window faces east. 我的窗户朝东。
We are traveling east. 我们向东方旅行。

【译文】他又回到了东部，并在华盛顿法院再一次提起诉讼，要求归还所有被盗财产。

14. (Para.9) *The "General", as he was once called, died alone in a small Washington hotel room, a broken and bitter man.*

【解析】本句主干是the "General"... died alone in a... room；此处as作连词，意为"正如……之事实"，具体用法详见Unit 1, Text A 难句突破；a broken and bitter man作the "General" 的同位语。

【译文】曾经被人称为"将军"的他，却在华盛顿一家小旅店的房间里孤独而终，死时穷困潦倒，满腔愤恨。

参考译文

招祸之财

美国历史上，约翰·萨特的故事最富有传奇色彩。1846年加利福尼亚州宣布独立，当时的旧金山还只是一个有800名左右居民的小镇。1848年，人们在离小镇不远的一处地方发现了黄金。这块土地当时归约翰·萨特所有。

紧接着，大批人群开始迅速涌向旧金山和金矿所在地。这就是著名的1849年淘金热。在短短几周内，旧金山的面积扩大到原来的三倍。旧金山这个原本宁静怡人的小镇，几乎在一夜之间就变成了一个喧嚣而又拥挤的城市，冒险家和其他稀奇古怪的各色人物到处可见。所有这些改变了旧金山，也改变了约翰·萨特的命运。

约翰·萨特早先是瑞士人。他来到美国时身无分文，有的只是冒险精神。在宾夕法尼亚州生活和工作了一段时间后，他最终于1839年在加利福尼亚州定居。那一年他才36岁。他在旧金山以北约70英里处，即现在的萨克拉门托，获得了很大一片土地。在那里，他建立起自己的私人领地。萨特非常有头脑，而且接受过良好的教育。他修建了一个城堡，并在其中建起了一个大型贸易站。

　　他种植了大量的果树以及上百亩的小麦。靠着向过往旧金山港口的船只提供补给以及出口物资，他变得非常富有。他定期雇用500名员工为他工作，大部分是墨西哥人和印第安人。

　　1848年，人们在萨特的地盘上发现了黄金。当时他正在城堡附近的一处地方修建锯木场。一个工人在从锯木场延伸至下游的小溪里发现了一些金块。起初，萨特竭力隐藏这个消息。他梦想变得更富有，或许成为世界上最富有的人。但是，几周之间，发现黄金的消息就泄漏了出去。人们从四面八方涌向萨特的地盘。

　　没过多久，人们从美国国内各地、甚至更远的地区来到这里。这些人宰杀掉萨特的所有家畜，偷盗他的农产品和工具，拆毁他的房子以获得木材，建造自己的家园。在萨特的贸易站所在地，萨克拉门托市迅速崛起。原先的萨特锯木场所在地则成为了今天的科洛马城。

　　萨特非但没有如愿成为世界上最有钱的人，反而变得一贫如洗。他最终只得离开此地，搬到了他自己地产的一个边远的地方，在那里东山再起。1855年，萨特在加利福尼亚州法院对那1,700名定居者提起诉讼，控告他们侵占了过去属于他的土地。他自己修建的道路、沟渠、桥梁被政府接管，他要求政府赔偿他2,500万美金。此外，他还要求得到所有已开采黄金的其中一部分，并索回其财产。

　　加州法院判决萨特胜诉。很快，萨特再一次富有，而且举足轻重。他又开始梦想建立自己的帝国，自己当国王和统治者。但紧接着风暴再次爆发。当法官的裁决被公之于众时，一万民众突袭了法院，这些人已在当地安居立业，唯恐失去了家园。他们烧毁了法院大楼，并试图绞死法官。他们捣毁了萨特更多的财产。后来萨特的家被人纵火烧毁，夷为平地。萨特的大儿子自杀了，二儿子也遭谋杀。

　　在这最后一连串的打击之后，萨特再也没有恢复过来。他又回到了东部，并在华盛顿法院再一次提起诉讼，要求归还所有被盗财产。从参议员到众议员，从一个政府部门到另一个政府部门，他就这样不知疲倦地劳顿奔波。但无论是国会还是法院，都把他的请求一而再再而三地延迟、搁置。萨特在这样的痛苦中度过了余下的15年。曾经被人称为"将军"的他，却在华盛顿一家小旅店的房间里孤独而终，死时穷困潦倒，满腔愤恨。

● 习题全解

1. 根据课文，请选出最合适的答案。

1) 【答案】B

　　【题解】细节题。根据文章的第一段第二句 "When the independence of California was declared in 1846, San Francisco was a small town of some 800 inhabitants" （1846年加利福尼亚州宣布独立，当时的旧金山还只是一个有800名左右居民的小镇），第二段第二句和第三句

"This was the famous Gold Rush of 1849. San Francisco grew to three times its size in just a few weeks" （这就是著名的1849年淘金热。在短短几周内，旧金山的面积扩大到原来的三倍），只有B是错误选项。

2) 【答案】D

【题解】细节题。根据文章的第三段可知，约翰·萨特曾经在瑞士，美国的宾夕法尼亚州和加利福尼亚州居住过，但文中并没有提到他曾经在洛杉矶居住过，因此选D。

3) 【答案】A

【题解】推断题。根据文章的第三段第三句"He lived and worked for a time in Pennsylvania and finally settled in California in 1839, when still a young man of thirty-six." （在宾夕法尼亚州生活和工作了一段时间后，他最终于1839年在加利福尼亚州定居。那一年他才36岁。）可推断得知约翰·萨特出生于1803年。

4) 【答案】A

【题解】细节题。根据文章的第四段第一句"He planted great numbers of fruit trees as well as hundreds of acres of wheat" （他种植了大量的水果树以及上百亩的小麦）可知约翰·萨特没有种植水稻，此外，其他三个选项都能在文中找到，因此只能选A。

5) 【答案】C

【题解】细节题。根据文章的第五段第三句"Here, in a stream leading from the mill, one of Sutter's workmen found some pieces of gold" （一个工人在从锯木场延伸至下游的小溪里发现了一些金块），因此选C。

6) 【答案】B

【题解】推断题。根据文章的第六段、第七段可知，当黄金在萨特的地盘上被发现后，他曾梦想成为世界上最富有的人，但汹涌而至的淘金人潮破灭了他的梦想，他变得一贫如洗。

7) 【答案】A

【题解】细节题。根据文章的第七段第三句"In 1855 Sutter brought a suit in the Californian courts against the 1,700 settlers, who now occupied the lands he had previously owned" （1855年，萨特在加利福尼亚州法院对那1,700名定居者提起诉讼，控告他们侵占了过去属于他的土地），因此选A。

8) 【答案】D

【题解】推断题。根据文章的最后两段可知，虽然法院判决萨特胜诉，但法不责众，民众烧毁了法院大楼，并试图绞死法官；他们捣毁了萨特更多的财产；后来萨特的家被人纵火烧毁，夷为平地，家人也被牵连。在这最后一连串的打击之后，萨特再也没有恢复过来。由此可见，财富最终只给萨特带来了灾难。

2. 请用下面所给词汇或短语的适当形式填空。

1) 【答案】factor

【译文】这两栋房屋我们都喜欢，但最后的决定因素在于它们的位置。

2) 【答案】took over

【译文】史密斯先生退休后，他的儿子接管了生意。

3) 【答案】recovering

【译文】这个国家正从经济危机中复苏。

4) 【答案】established

　　【译文】这所学校始建于1840年。

5) 【答案】springing up

　　【译文】网吧正迅速遍布整个城市。

6) 【答案】poverty

　　【译文】她一生都穷困潦倒。

7) 【答案】inhabitants

　　【译文】越来越多的城市居民从市中心迁往市郊。

8) 【答案】declared

　　【译文】琼斯被宣布获胜。

9) 【答案】descend

　　【译文】每年都有成百上千万的游客慕名来到该地区旅游。

10) 【答案】leaked

　　【译文】消息被泄漏了。

3. 将下列句子译成中文。

1) 【答案】旧金山这个原本宁静怡人的小镇，几乎一夜之间就变成了一个喧嚣而又拥挤的城市，冒险家和其他稀奇古怪的各色人物到处可见。

2) 【答案】靠着向来到旧金山港口的船只提供补给以及出口物资，他变得非常富有。

3) 【答案】1855年，萨特在加利福尼亚州法院对那1,700名定居者提起诉讼，控告他们侵占了过去属于他的土地。

4) 【答案】当法官的裁决被公之于众时，一万名已在当地安居立业的人唯恐失去家园，蜂拥而至，来到法院。

文章泛读

文章导读

　　金钱能够买到快乐吗？有钱人是否就更快乐呢？我们的幸福感是否伴随着经济发展的浪潮而增加了呢？你考虑过诸如此类的问题吗？作者将在本文中回答这些问题，具体的数据，理性的分析，都将让这些回答有据可依，更有说服力。

背景知识

　　福布斯：1917年，37岁的苏格兰记者福布斯独立创办了美国第一本纯粹报道商业新闻的杂志——FORBES，但他使用的报道方式却和那个时代截然不同。他反对当时盛行的堆砌枯燥的商业数字的方法，坚持关注掌控企业的人们。由于其明确的定位和独特的深度报道，《福布斯》成为今天美国主要商业杂志中唯一保持10年连续增长的刊物，其受众群在商业杂志中占据魁首，2003年达到500万。

📖 文章写作风格及结构

本为为说明文（expository），作者通过确切的数据、例证向我们说明了并不是金钱越多就越幸福。

Parts 部分	Paragraphs 段落	Main Ideas 大意
Part I	1	Most people believe money matters. 大多数人相信金钱很重要。
Part II	2—4	Wealth is like health: the utter absence can breed misery, but having it doesn't guarantee happiness. 财富就如同健康：一点没有，处境就会很凄惨，但是拥有了也未必幸福。
Part III	5—7	Our happiness has not floated upward with the rising economic tide. 我们的幸福感并没有伴随着经济发展的浪潮而增加。

🌐 词汇点睛

1 fantastic

adj. extremely good, attractive or enjoyable 极好的，极妙的

• 例句• She has made a fantastic achievement. 她取得了了不起的成就。

You've got the job? Fantastic! 你得到工作了？太好了！

• 扩展• **fantasy** *n.* 幻想，想象

Do you still remember your childhood fantasies about becoming a football player?
你还记得自己儿时想成为足球运动员的幻想吗？

2 essential

adj. extremely important and necessary 基本的，必须的

• 例句• Money is not essential to happiness. 金钱对于幸福并非必不可少。

Even in small companies, computers are an essential tool.
即使在小公司里，计算机也是基本工具。

• 扩展• **essence** *n.* 必需品，实质

I only had time to pack the essentials. 我只有时间装上那些必需品。

In essence, your situation isn't so different from mine. 从实质上讲，你我的情况并非相差很远。

3 financially

adv. relating to money or the management of money 财政上，金融上

• 例句• She is still financially dependent on her parents. 她在经济上仍然依靠父母。

Financially, I'm much better than before. 我的经济状况比过去好多了。

- 扩展 • **financial** *adj.* 财务的，金融的

Tokyo and New York are major financial centers. 东京和纽约是主要的金融中心。

finance *n.* 资金

Finance for education comes from taxpayers. 教育经费来自纳税人。

4 relatively

adv. in comparison with sth. else 相对地

- 例句 • I found the test relatively easy. 我觉得这次测试相对比较简单。

Relatively speaking, these jobs provide good salaries.

相对来说，这些工作报酬不低。

- 扩展 • **relative** *adj.* 与……相关的

The facts are relative to the case. 这些事实与此案有关。

relate *vt.* 把……联系起来

- 例句 • I found it difficult to relate the two ideas in my mind.

我觉得很难把这两种想法联系在一起。

5 shelter

n. a place to live, considered as one of the basic needs of life 住所，避难所

- 例句 • They found a shelter from the storm in a barn. 他们在谷仓里躲避暴风雨。

The basic necessities of life are food, clothing, and shelter. 衣、食、住是生活的最基本需要。

v. to provide cover or protection for 掩蔽，躲避

- 例句 • In the rain people were sheltering in the doorways of shops. 下雨时人们在商店门口躲雨。

- 短语 • **shelter… from…** 庇护……；以避……

take/find shelter from the rain 找到避雨处

You must not shelter him from the police. 你千万不可隐匿他而不报警。

6 afford

vt. to have enough money to buy or pay for sth. 买得起，担负得起

- 例句 • He can afford an apartment. 他能买得起一套住房。

I can't afford three weeks away from work. 我无法丢下工作三星期。

- 用法 • 常与can, could, be able to 连用。例如：

He told me that the firm could not afford to pay such large salaries.

他告诉我公司无法支付如此巨额的工资。

7 affluence

n. the state of having plenty of money, so that you can afford to buy more expensive things
富裕，富足

- 例句 • He lives in affluence. 他生活优裕。

He quickly rose to affluence. 他很快就富起来了。

- 扩展 • **affluent** *adj.* 富裕的

a very affluent neighborhood 富人区

8 diminish

vi. to become or make sth. become smaller or less 减少，变小

- **例句** The world's resources are rapidly diminishing. 世界资源正在迅速减少。

  His influence has diminished with time. 随着时间的推移，他的影响已不如从前了。

- **辨析** **diminish, decrease, reduce**

  三个词都含"减少"的意思。

  diminish 指"形状缩小，数量减少"，特指"看得出来的缩小或减少"。如：

  His income diminished. 他的收入减少了。

  decrease 指"渐渐地减少"。如：His temperature decreases. 他的烧退了。

  reduce 指"人为地减少、降低"。如：reduce speed 减速

9 slightly

adv. a little 轻微地，一点地

- **例句** I knew him slightly. 关于他我只知道一点儿。

  I was slightly wounded. 我受了点轻伤。

- **扩展** **slight** *adj.* 轻微的，微小的

  I have a slight headache. 我有点轻微的头疼。

  There's a slight possibility of success. 成功的可能性很小。

- **短语** **not in the slightest** 一点也不，完全不

  It doesn't matter in the slightest. 那一点都不要紧。

10 temporary

adj. continuing for only a limited period of time 暂时的，临时的

- **例句** More than half the staff are temporary. 半数以上的职员是临时工。

  They tend to believe defeat is just a temporary setback. 他们相信失败只是暂时的挫折。

11 absence

n. 1) the lack of sth. or the fact that it does not exist 缺乏，没有

- **例句** Darkness is the absence of light. 黑暗就是缺乏光亮。

  2) when you are not in the place where people expect you to be, or the time that you are away 不在，缺席

- **例句** She will be in charge of the office during my absence. 我不在的时候，办公室由她负责。

  Absence makes the heart fonder. [谚] 眼不见，心更念；别久情深。

- **短语** **in the absence of** 缺乏……时；当……不在时

  In the absence of any further evidence the police were unable to solve the murder.

  由于缺乏更确实的证据，警方破不了这宗谋杀案。

- **反义词** **presence** *n.* 出席，在场

  Your presence at the meeting is requested. 敬请光临。

- **扩展** **absent** *adj.* 不在的，缺席的，心不在焉的，茫然的

  He was absent from the meeting. 他今天开会缺席。

  She had an absent look on her face. 她看起来心不在焉。

  Long absent, soon forgotten. [谚] 别久情疏。

12 breed

vt. to cause a particular feeling or condition 滋生，造成

• 例句• Poor living conditions breed violence and despair. 恶劣的生活条件滋生暴力和绝望。

vi. if animals breed, they mate in order to have babies 繁殖

• 例句• Many animals breed only at certain times of the year. 很多动物只在一年的某个时候交配繁殖。

13 misery

n. great suffering that is caused by being very poor or very sick 痛苦，苦恼，不幸

• 例句• He bears misery best who hides it most. [谚] 最能掩盖自己痛苦的人是最善于忍受痛苦的。

Misery loves company. [谚] 同病相怜，同忧相救。

• 扩展• **miserable** *adj.* 痛苦的，悲惨的，可怜的

The child is cold, hungry, and tired, so of course he's feeling miserable.

这孩子又冷、又饿、又疲劳，当然他感到很痛苦。

14 guarantee

vt. to promise to do sth. or to promise that sth. will happen 保证，担保

• 例句• We cannot guarantee our flight will never be delayed. 我们不能担保所有航班均不误点。

We guaranteed to deliver your goods within a week. 我们保证一周内交货。

• 短语• **be guaranteed to do sth.** 肯定会，必定会

If we try to keep it a secret, she's guaranteed to find out. 如果我们试图保密，她肯定会发现。

15 float

vi. 1) to stay on the surface of a liquid without sinking 浮动

• 例句• Wood floats on water. 木头浮在水上。

2) to be carried by the liquid to another place 飘浮

• 例句• The boat floated down the river. 小船沿河漂流。

16 decline

vi. to decrease in quantity or importance 下降

• 例句• They wish that prices would decline. 他们希望物价能下降。

The price of 14 inches TV set declined from 400 to 320 *yuan* each.

14英寸的电视机每台从400元降到了320元。

His health is declining. 他的健康日渐衰退。

vt. to say no (to); to refuse (sth. offered) 谢绝，婉谢

• 例句• We asked them to come to our party, but they declined the invitation.

我们邀请他们来参加我们的聚会，但他们婉言谢绝了。

n. declining; gradual and continued loss of strength 下降，斜坡，衰落

• 例句• the decline of the Roman Empire 罗马帝国的衰亡

17 soaring

adj. increasing quickly to a high level 剧增的，高涨的

• 例句• Most of the students have already felt the pressure of soaring prices.

大多数大学生都已经感受到物价飞涨的压力。

Soaring temperatures make us feel uncomfortable. 迅速增高的温度让我们感到不舒服。

•扩展• **soar** *vi.* 急升，猛增

Prices are soaring again. 价格又在飞涨了。

18 shrink

vi. (shrank, shrunk) to become smaller 收缩，缩小

•例句• My sweater shrank in the wash.

我的毛衣洗后缩水了。

Television in a sense has shrunk the world. 从某种意义上说，电视把世界缩小了。

•短语• **shrink from sth.** 回避，畏避 (困难)

They did not shrink from doing what was right. 只要做得对，他们就无所畏惧。

19 excel

vi. to do sth. very well, or much better than most people 优秀，胜过他人

•例句• When it comes to singing, she really excels. 说到唱歌，她确实是好极了。

He never excelled at games. 他从来不擅长游戏。

•短语• **excel oneself** 胜过过去

His meals are always very good, but this time he's excelled himself.

他做的饭菜一直很拿手，但这一次做的更好。

•扩展• **excellent** *adj.* 优秀的；杰出的

The college has excellent sporting facilities. 这所学院有极好的体育设备。

20 prosperity

n. when people have money and the material goods needed for a good life 繁荣，兴旺，昌盛

•例句• Peace brings prosperity. 和平带来繁荣。

Prosperity makes friends, adversity tries them. [谚] 富贵交友易，患难显真情。

•扩展• **prosper** *vi.* 繁荣，昌盛

China is prospering with each passing day. 中国正在蒸蒸日上。

21 cherish

vt. if you cherish sth., it is very important to you, and you protect it or care for it 珍爱，珍惜

•例句• The old man cherished the girl as if she were his daughter.

老人疼爱那女孩，就好像她是他自己的女儿一般。

He cherished the memory of his departed youth.

青春年华一去不复返，他将回忆珍藏心底。

22 spiritual

adj. relating to your spirit or mind rather than to your body 精神上的，灵魂的

•例句• We're concerned about your spiritual welfare. 我们关心你精神上的幸福。

She's English, but India is her spiritual home.

她是英国人，但印度才是她精神上的归宿。

•扩展• **spirit** *n.* 精神；灵魂；心情

Don't let your spirits droop. 不要萎靡不振。

He is in good spirit. 他很愉快。

短语解析

1. be well off 生活富裕，处境良好

【例句】You don't need to look for another job—you're well off where you are.

你用不着另找工作——你现在的境况很不错了。

His family is not very well off. 他家不太富裕。

2. in the long run 从长远看

【例句】In the long run prices are bound to rise. 从长远看，物价肯定要涨。

It will be cheaper in the long run to use real leather because it will last longer.

使用真皮制品从长远看还是相对便宜的，因为真皮制品比较经久耐用。

3. yearn for... 渴望……，怀念……

【例句】He yearned for his home and family. 他怀念故国家园。

They yearned for his return. 他们盼望着他回来。

4. long for... 渴望……

【例句】The children are longing for the holidays. 孩子们盼望放假。

She longed for him to ask her to dance. 她巴不得他邀请自己跳舞。

难句突破

1. (Para.2) *Researchers have found that in poor countries, such as Bangladesh, being relatively well off does make for greater well-being.*

【解析】1) 本句主干是researchers have found that...；that引导从句作found的宾语，在这个宾语从句中being relatively well off是主语，关于动名词作主语的讲解详见Unit 2, Text C 难句突破2；does强调谓语动词make。

2) 强调句子中的谓语动词要在谓语动词前加助动词do（有数、时态的变化）的形式。例如：

I do hope you have a merry Christmas! 我真的希望你圣诞快乐！

But the family did manage to send him to a technical school.

他的家人确实做到了把他送去读技术学校。

【译文】研究者发现，在一些贫穷的国家，如孟加拉国，相对的富有确实能够带来较大的安康。

2. (Para.3) *But a surprising fact of life is that in countries where everyone can afford life's necessities, increasing affluence matters surprisingly little.*

【解析】本句的主干是a surprising fact... is that...；that引导表语从句；在这个表语从句又存在一个where引导的定语从句where everyone can afford life's necessities。

【译文】但是一个令人惊讶的事实是，在那些人人都衣食无忧的国家里，财富的增长所产生的影响却微乎其微。

3. (Para.3) *Once comfortable, more money provides diminishing returns.*

【解析】once引导时间状语从句，相当于as soon as。例如：

Once you understand this rule, you will have no further difficulty.

一旦明白了这条规则，就再也没有困难了。

How could we cope once the money had gone? 钱一用完，我们怎么办？

Once comfortable = Once it is comfortable，类似的用法又如：

When finished, we will let you know. = When it is finished, we will let you know.

【译文】一旦人们生活舒适，金钱越多，其所带来的幸福感却会越少。

4. (Para.4) *Happiness seems less a matter of getting what we want than of wanting what we have.*

【解析】1) 本句的主干是happiness seems less… than…；第一个what引导从句what we want作动词get的宾语；第二个what引导从句what we have作want的宾语；than of wanting…实际上是than (a matter of) wanting…

2) a matter of：（有关）……的问题、事情。

【译文】所谓幸福，与其说是得到我们想要的，还不如说是珍惜我们已有的。

5. (Para.7) *More than ever, we have big houses and broken homes, high incomes and low morale, secured rights and diminished civility.*

【解析】ever与比较级的词连用，置于than之后表示"在任何时候"（之前／直至现在）。例如：

It's raining harder than ever. 雨下得更大了。

He hated her more than ever, when he got that letter. 他接到那封信后，越发憎恨她了。

【译文】这种现象比以往任何时候都要明显：我们住着大房子但却家庭破裂；拿着高收入却道德水准低下；我们的权利得到了保障，但却丧失了礼仪的教化。

参考译文

金钱能够买到快乐吗？

大卫·梅尔斯

金钱能够买到快乐吗？不能！那么，钱多一点会不会令我们快乐多一点呢？很多人可能会同意。我们相信，有钱和精神愉悦之间存在着某种联系。大多数人会说，是的，我们希望富有。现在有四分之三的美国大学生认为，"在经济上很富足"对他们来说"十分重要"或者"不可或缺"。金钱确实重要。

那么，有钱人是否就更快乐呢？研究者发现，在一些贫穷的国家，如孟加拉国，相对的富有确实能够带来较大的安康。我们需要食物、休息、住房以及社会交往。

但是一个令人惊讶的事实是，在那些人人都衣食无忧的国家里，财富的增长所产生的影响却微乎其微。美国密歇根大学研究员罗纳德·英格利哈对16个国家的17万民众作了一项调查，结果表明，财富与快乐之间的联系"小得惊人"。一旦人们生活舒适，金钱越多，其所带来的幸福感却会越少。第二块饼永远不如第一块香，同样，得到第二个10万美金时的快感绝没有第一次那样强烈。

即使是彩票中奖者和《福布斯》榜上前100位美国富豪也表示，比起普通美国人，他们只是多了一点点快乐而已。发大财所带来的欣喜只是短暂的。但从长远来看，财富就如同健康：一点没有，处境就会很凄惨，但是拥有了也未必幸福。所谓幸福，与其说是得到我们想要的，还不如说是珍惜我们已有的。

我们的幸福感是否伴随着经济发展的浪潮而增加了呢？回顾1940年，那时，五分之二的家庭没有淋浴或者浴缸，取暖通常意味着要往炉子里添加木块或者煤块；35%的家庭没有洗手间。同那时相比，今天的我们是否更加快乐呢？

事实上，我们并没有比那个时候更快乐。从1957年开始，声称自己"非常快乐"的美国人数从35%降到了32%。与此同时，离婚率翻了一番；青少年自杀率增长了近两倍；暴力犯罪率几乎翻了两番（即使最近有所下降）；越来越多的人（尤其是青少年）感到苦闷沮丧。

我把这种财富暴涨而精神萎靡的现象称为"美国悖论"。这种现象比以往任何时候都要明显：我们住着大房子但却家庭破裂；拿着高收入却道德水准低下；我们的权利得到了保障，但却丧失了礼仪的教化。我们善于谋生，但却拙于生活之道。我们为物质的繁荣而欢欣鼓舞，但却渴望了解追求财富的意义。我们珍爱自由，却也渴望着与他人交流。在这个物质财富充裕的时代，我们感受到了精神上的饥渴。

语言拓展

日常用语

练习 选择补全对话的最佳答案。

1. 【答案】D

   【题解】在听到别人的赞美时，不能按中国人的习惯那样说"不，不"或者"哪里，哪里"，而应该说"谢谢"。

2. 【答案】C

   【题解】在听到他人的好消息时，要表示祝贺；而在收到他人的祝贺时，要表示感谢。

3. 【答案】A

   【题解】在得知他人要去旅游的消息时，应该祝对方旅途愉快。如："Have a good journey. Wish you a pleasant journey."

4. 【答案】B

   【题解】在收到他人的祝福时，可以用"The same to you."表示把同样的祝福也送给他人。

5. 【答案】B

   【题解】同上。

阅读技巧

练习 阅读以下文章并总结其主要内容。

1. 【答案】To avoid injury during an earthquake, keep calm and stay where you are.

   【题解】本文篇章结构为"总—分"式结构：作者开门见山地提出文章的主题，然后具体阐述。文章的主题出现在文章第一句话。

2. 【答案】A CAT scanner is a machine that can provide more accurate and detailed information of a patient's body than X-rays can do.

   【题解】本文篇章结构为"总—分—总"式结构：作者提出主题，然后列出具体的事实，最后作出总结。文章的主题在文章开头和结尾均能找到。

写作技巧

练习 根据提纲，写一篇不少于 **120** 词的题为 **The Internet** 的文章。

样文：

The Internet is the worldwide, publicly accessible network of interconnected computer networks that transmit data by packet switching using the standard Internet Protocol (IP).

It exerts a peculiar fascination on a great many people. Both the old and the youth can enjoy the civilized comforts which modern science brings to us. It really adds color to the dull routine of everyday life.

There is no doubt that for the youth the Internet is an important tool for study. Nothing can be compared with its convenient operation, high speed and varied information resources. As long as you type in what you need, you'll get a large number of information picked out in such a short time. Besides downloading information, at the same time, yon can upload your own works and send them to the Internet. In this way you can have more opportunities to share the tremendous spiritual excitement with the ones who have common goals.

No one can avoid being influenced by modern science and technology. Maybe we can use our intelligence to make more discoveries and create more inventions aiming at influencing more people.

语法知识

——动词时态（二）

练习 选择最佳答案补全下列句子。

1. 【答案】B
   【题解】现在完成时态可以表示动作过去已经开始，持续到现在，而且还可能继续下去的动作或状态。常常与for, since等引导的时间状语连用。
   【译文】这个月以来，很多天天气都很好。

2. 【答案】C
   【题解】同上题。
   【译文】自从上个世纪以来，他家世代都是老师。

3. 【答案】A
   【题解】将来完成时表示未来某时间点或未来某动作之前业已完成的动作。
   【译文】到下个星期天，你就已经和我们在一起呆了三个月了。

4. 【答案】C
   【题解】现在完成进行时表示从过去某时开始，一直持续到现在的动作。其特点在于强调动作的继续性质。
   【译文】因为连续几周持续的降雨，整个地区都被淹没了。

5. 【答案】C
   【题解】过去完成时在这里表示过去某个动作发生以前的动作。
   【译文】在得知这个消息后，她跑回家去告诉她的妈妈。

6.【答案】B
　　【题解】将来完成进行时表示从过去某时开始，迄今仍在进行，而于将来某时将完成的动作。
　　【译文】到第二年5月，他们就已经修桥九个月了。

7.【答案】B
　　【题解】现在完成时表示过去已经开始，持续到现在。常常与for, since等引导的时间状语连用，其后引导的动作发生在过去。
　　【译文】自从约翰离开这里以后，我就再也没有看到过他。

8.【答案】C
　　【题解】过去完成时表示过去某个动作发生以前的动作。
　　【译文】在我来之前，他在做家庭作业。

9.【答案】B
　　【题解】no sooner… than意为"一……就……"。no sooner所在的主句常用过去完成时，than引导的从句用一般过去时。no sooner… than搭配放在句首，句子倒装。
　　　　　 take to one's heels指"逃走"。
　　【译文】那小偷一看见警察，拔腿就跑。

10.【答案】C
　　【题解】and在这里连接两个并列的动词：step和ask。
　　【译文】老师一踏进教室，就让学生把窗户打开。

11.【答案】D
　　【题解】scarcely… when…意为"一……就……"，可引导时间状语从句，只用于过去时，主句动作发生在从句动作前，故用过去完成时。
　　【译文】我一锁门，钥匙就断了。

12.【答案】D
　　【题解】在完成时态里，时间状语一般由since 和for引导。since意为"自从……以来"，表示时间从一个点开始，延至到现在(在过去完成时中延至到过去)。for表示动作持续的时间。
　　【译文】我已经有三个星期没有看到她了。

13.【答案】C
　　【题解】have been (to)指"到过某地"，说话时此人很可能不在那里，已经回来，侧重指经历。have gone (to) 指"已经去了某地"，说话时此人在那里，或可能在路上。
　　【译文】青岛是我到过的最美丽的城市。

14.【答案】B
　　【题解】过去完成时表示过去某个动作发生以前的动作。
　　【译文】这次考试没有我们想象得那么难。

15.【答案】A
　　【题解】现在完成进行时表示从过去某时开始，一直持续到现在的动作，强调动作的继续性质。题干中的so far暗示了"写信"这一动作的延续。
　　【译文】别打扰我，我整个早上都在写信，到现在为止，已经写了10封了。

每课一练

Part I　Vocabulary & Structure

Directions: *There are 30 incomplete sentences in this part. For each sentence there are four choices marked A), B), C) and D). Choose the ONE that best completes the sentence.*

1. The change in work patterns could offer a(n) _____ of a better future for work.

   A) information　　　B) organization　　　C) prospect　　　D) imagination

2. No sooner had they got the goods covered up _____ it started raining hard.

   A) in　　　B) than　　　C) then　　　D) after

3. Many people are struggling at the _____ line, short of food and shelter.

   A) poverty　　　B) poor　　　C) hunger　　　D) hungry

4. There is an old saying that a little _____ will sink a great ship.

   A) blast　　　B) burst　　　C) leak　　　D) sneak

5. By no means _____ destroy or create energy.

   A) we shall　　　B) shall we　　　C) can't we　　　D) we can

6. Mother is ill. Who will _____ the housework?

   A) take after　　　B) take up　　　C) take out　　　D) take over

7. Flood caused billions of dollars worth of his _____ damage.

   A) property　　　B) treasure　　　C) goods　　　D) wealth

8. He talked about the _____ experience they had on the trip.

   A) amusing　　　B) forgetful　　　C) amused　　　D) missing

9. The pen I _____ I _____ is on my desk, right under my nose.

   A) think; lost　　　B) thought; had lost　　　C) think; had lost　　　D) thought; have lost

10. Cost as a _____ in supply is very important.

    A) way　　　B) method　　　C) factor　　　D) fact

11. The world's _____ mainly consist of the yellow race, the white race, and the black race.

    A) citizen　　　B) habitant　　　C) people　　　D) inhabitant

12. The leader of the town said that their financial _____ of next year is optimistic.

    A) vision　　　B) horizon　　　C) outlook　　　D) view

13. Those students expect their teacher to _____ from disease very soon.

    A) cure　　　B) treat　　　C) heal　　　D) recover

14. For some years after his graduation, he _____ some of his classmates, but as times went by, he dropped them one by one.

    A) kept on　　　B) kept up with　　　C) kept up　　　D) kept in touch with

15. The police will give you ticket, if you _____ the speed limit.

    A) expand　　　B) extend　　　C) spread　　　D) exceed

16. They are working together to _____ the whole society.

    A) benefit　　　B) behalf　　　C) boast　　　D) broaden

17. Since 1780, when the town's first hat factory _____ in Danbury, Connecticut, the town has been a center for hat manufacturing in the United States.

    A) were established　　　B) was establishing　　　C) had been established　　　D) was established

18. When I saw his smiling face, I knew he_____ good news of his parents.

    A) has had   B) had had   C) has having   D) has

19. _____ had he gone to sleep than the telephone rang once again.

    A) Hardly   B) Scarcely   C) Just   D) No sooner

20. I'm still looking for the best way, but here, I'd like to list some points _____ my own experience.

    A) in front of   B) in terms of   C) instead of   D) terms of

21. It was in the factory _____ produced TV sets _____ our friends were murdered.

    A) which; which   B) that; which   C) that; that   D) where; that

22. The Great West Development _____ a bridge between China and the rest world.

    A) is a matter of   B) is the case of   C) is bound to be   D) is exemplified by

23. Before 1920s, the American women were _____ the right to vote in a large extent.

    A) deprived of   B) depriving of   C) persuade of   D) persuading of

24. He asked who was the man _____ on.

    A) to be operating   B) operating   C) to operate   D) being operating

25. An unexpected guest _____ on us last night.

    A) decreased   B) descended   C) declined   D) dropped

26. She _____ soon after dark and arrived home an hour later.

    A) had set out   B) set out   C) have set out   D) had been set out

27. As the old empires were broken up and new states were formed, new official tongues began to _____ at an increasing rate.

    A) bring up   B) build up   C) spring up   D) strike up

28. It was not until 1920 _____ regular broadcast began.

    A) while   B) which   C) that   D) since

29. He was _____ with the fear of poverty, so he robbed the bank.

    A) obsessing   B) been obsessed   C) obsessed   D) being obsessed

30. Whereas the _____ competitive trading had been conducted by small rival firms then.

    A) previously   B) proceeding   C) ancient   D) respectively

Part II   Reading Comprehension

Directions: *Read the following two passages. Answer the questions of each passage by choosing A), B), C) or D).*

Passage 1

    The automobile has many advantages. Above all, it offers people freedom to go wherever and whenever they want to go. The basic purpose of a motor vehicle is to get from point A to point B as cheaply, quickly, and safely as possible. However, to most people, cars are also personal fantasy machines that serve as symbols of power, success, speed, excitement, and adventure.

    In addition, much of the world's economy is built on producing motor vehicles and supplying roads, services, and repairs for those vehicles. Half of the world's paychecks are auto-related. In the United States, one of every six dollars spent and one of every six non-farm jobs are connected to the automobile or related industries, such as oil, steel, rubber, plastics, automobile services, and highway construction.

In spite of their advantages, motor vehicles have many harmful effects on human lives and on air, water, land, and wildlife resources. The automobile may be the most destructive machine ever invented. Though we tend to deny it, riding in cars is one of the most dangerous things we do in our daily lives.

Since 1885, when Karl Benz built the first automobile, almost 18 million people have been killed by motor vehicles. Every year, cars and trucks worldwide kill an average of 250,000 people—as many as were killed in the atomic bomb attacks on Hiroshima and Nagasaki—and injure or permanently disable ten million more. Half of the world's people will be involved in an auto accident at some time during their lives.

Since the automobile was introduced, almost three million Americans have been killed on the highways—about twice the number of Americans killed on the battlefield in all U.S. wars. In addition to the tragic loss of life, these accidents cost American society about $60 billion annually in lost income and in insurance, administrative, and legal expenses.

Streets that used to be for people are now for cars. Pedestrians and people riding bicycles in the streets are subjected to noise, pollution, stress, and danger.

Motor vehicles are the largest source of air pollution, producing a haze of smog over the world's cities. In the United States, they produce at least 50% of the country's air pollution.

1. Besides its basic purpose, car also serves as a symbol of people's _____.

    A) occupation   B) status   C) character   D) reputation

2. According to the passage, the average number of people killed annually in traffic accidents around the world is _____.

    A) 60 million   B) 250,000   C) 3 million   D) 18 million

3. A serious environmental problem resulting from automobiles is _____.

    A) tragic loss of life   B) traffic jams   C) air pollution   D) mental stress

4. Which of the following can be inferred from this passage?

    A) Automobiles are an important part of the world's economy.

    B) Automobiles are becoming less dangerous.

    C) Automobiles will produce less air pollution in the future.

    D) Automobiles are killing more people in recent years than in the past.

5. The title that suits the passage best is _____.

    A) Automobile and Economy

    B) Automobile and the Environment

    C) The Problems with the Automobile

    D) Advantages and Disadvantages of the Automobile

Passage 2

I don't know how I became a writer, but I think it was because of a certain force in me that had to write and that finally burst through and found a channel. My people were of the working class of people. My father, a stone-cutter, was a man with a great respect and veneration for literature. He had a tremendous memory, and he loved poetry, and the poetry that he loved best was naturally of the rhetorical kind that such a man would like. Nevertheless it was good poetry, *Hamlet's Soliloquy*, *Macbeth*, Mark Antony's *Funeral Oration*, Grey's *Elegy*, and all the rest of it. I heard it all as a child; I memorized and learned it all.

He sent me to college to the state university.

The desire to write, which had been strong during all my days in high school, grew stronger still. I was editor of the college paper, the college magazine, etc., and in my last year or two I was a member of a course in playwriting which had just been established there. I wrote several little one-act plays, still thinking I would become a lawyer or a newspaper man, never daring to believe I could seriously become a writer. Then I went to Harvard, wrote some more plays there, became obsessed with the idea that I had to be a playwright, left Harvard, had my plays rejected, and finally in the autumn of 1926, how, why, or in what manner I have never exactly been able to determine. But probably because the force in me that had to write at length sought out its channel, I began to write my first book in London, I was living all alone at that time. I had two rooms—a bedroom and a sitting room—in a little square in Chelsea in which all the houses had that familiar, smoked brick and cream-yellow-plaster look.

6. We may conclude, in regard to the author's development as a writer, that his father _____.

   A) made an important contribution

   B) provided him with good education

   C) opposed his becoming a writer

   D) insisted that he memorize good poetry in order to learn how to be a writer

7. The author believes that he became a writer mostly because of _____.

   A) his special talent

   B) his father's teaching

   C) his study at Harvard

   D) a strong hidden wish within him

8. Which of the following is TRUE about the author?

   A) He began to think of becoming a writer in high school.

   B) He had always been successful in his writing career.

   C) He went to Harvard to learn to write plays.

   D) He worked as a newspaper man before becoming a writer.

9. The author really started on his way to become a writer _____.

   A) when he was in high school

   B) when he was studying at Harvard

   C) when he lived in London

   D) after he entered college

10. According to the passage, about the author's life in 1926 which of the following conclusions CANNOT be safely drawn?

    A) He lost the ability to determine in which direction he should go.

    B) He was depressed about having his plays rejected.

    C) He lived in a house which had smoked brick and cream-yellow-plaster look.

    D) He started his first novel.

答案及详解

第一部分　词汇与结构

1. 【答案】C

   【题解】本题考查名词词义辨析。information 信息；organization 组织；prospect 前景，前途；imagination 想象。

   【译文】工作模式的改变可能会带来一个前景更好的未来。

2. 【答案】B

   【题解】本题考查的是连词固定搭配。no sooner... than... 表示"一……就……，刚刚……就……"。

   【译文】他们刚刚把货物盖好雨就开始下大了。

3. 【答案】A

   【题解】poverty line，表示"贫困线"。

   【译文】很多人都在贫困线上挣扎，缺衣少食。

4. 【答案】C

   【题解】a little (small) leak will sink a great ship是固定搭配，表示"千里之堤溃于蚁穴"。

   【译文】俗语说：千里之堤溃于蚁穴。

5. 【答案】B

   【题解】本题考查by no means的用法。by no means 决不可能，但放在句首时需要部分倒装，故选B。

   【译文】我们决不可能消灭或创造能量。

6. 【答案】D

   【题解】本题考查take的词组搭配。take over 接管；take after 相似；take up 开始从事；take out 取出，拿出。因此选D。

   【译文】妈妈病了，谁来接管家务事呢？

7. 【答案】A

   【题解】本题考查几个近义词的辨析。property 财产，指个人拥有的东西；treasure 金银财宝，指储藏起来的或搜集起来的财富；goods 商品，货物；wealth 财富，指大量的东西或大笔的钱。

   【译文】洪水导致他损失了价值几十亿美元的财产。

8. 【答案】A

   【题解】本题考查词义辨析。amusing 有趣的；forgetful 健忘的；amused 愉快的，开心的；missing 丢失的，缺少的。虽然amusing和amused都表示有趣，愉快的意思，但是这里修饰的对象是experience，因此要用现在分词amusing，amused 一般用来修饰人。

   【译文】他谈了在旅途中的有趣经历。

9. 【答案】B

   【题解】本题考查动词时态。题干中几个动词的发生顺序应该是丢笔—认为笔丢了—现在发现笔在桌上。因此按照这个顺序时态应该是had lost (the pen), I thought, (the pen) is on my desk。故选B。

   【译文】我原以为丢了的那只笔竟然在我桌子上，就在我眼皮底下。

10. 【答案】C

【题解】本题考查名词的词义辨析。way 方法，道路；method 方式，方法；factor 要素，因素；fact 事实。

【译文】成本作为供应的一个因素是非常重要的。

11. 【答案】D

【题解】本题考查近义词辨析。citizen 强调公民；habitant 强调居住者，表示个体概念；people 仅仅指人；inhabitant也指居民，但却是一个集合名词。

【译文】世界上的居民主要包括黄种人、白种人和黑种人。

12. 【答案】C

【题解】本题考查近义词辨析。vision 视力，视觉，眼力；horizon 地平线，视野，范围；outlook 景色，前景；view 见解，观看。

【译文】镇长说他们对于明年的财政预期非常乐观。

13. 【答案】D

【题解】本题考查近义词的辨析。cure表示病的治愈，强调治疗的结果，一般用cure sb. of some disease；heal也强调治愈、康复，一般用heal sb. of some disease；treat强调治疗的过程；recover表示恢复，recover from 从……中恢复。

【译文】这些学生期望他们的老师能够早日康复。

14. 【答案】D

【题解】本题考查几个与介词keep搭配的词组含义。keep on 继续，后面一般接doing sth.；keep up with 赶上，跟上；keep up继续，维持；keep in touch with 与……保持联系。

【译文】他毕业后的最初几年还和他的一些同学保持联系，但随着时间的推移，慢慢地和他们一个个失去了联系。

15. 【答案】D

【题解】本题考查近义词辨析。虽然这四个词都有超出的意思，但expand强调立体的膨胀；extend强调平面的延伸；spread强调扩展及覆盖；exceed强调尤指数量上的超过、胜过。

【译文】如果你超速，警察将会给你开罚单。

16. 【答案】A

【题解】本题考查形近词辨析。benefit vt. 有益于，有助于；behalf n. 利益；boast vt. 自夸；broaden vt. 放宽。此处需要填动词，表示使社会受益。behalf通常会用作on behalf of，意为"代表……的利益"。

【译文】他们共同努力为社会作出贡献。

17. 【答案】D

【题解】本题考查动词的时态。由since的出现可知，主句是完成时（has been a center...），since引导的从句要用一般过去时。另外，制帽厂是被建立因此要用被动态，故选D。

【译文】自1780年镇上第一家制帽工厂在康涅狄格的丹伯里成立以来，这个镇已经发展成为美国制帽工业的中心。

18. 【答案】B

【题解】本题考查动词的时态。他有好消息在前而我知道在后，因此have good news的时态应该比knew在前，因此用过去完成时，故选B。

【译文】当我看到他微笑的脸庞，我知道他有了关于他父母的好消息。

19.【答案】D

【题解】本题考查no sooner... than... 的固定搭配及其倒装结构。

【译文】他刚睡着电话铃又响了。

20.【答案】B

【题解】本题考查和介词of搭配的词组含义。in front of 在……前面；in terms of 根据，按照；instead of 代替，而不是；terms of 不是固定的搭配。

【译文】我仍然在寻找最好的方法，但是在这里，我愿意根据我自己的经验列出一些观点。

21.【答案】C

【题解】本题考查强调结构it + be... that...。第一个that是关系代词指代 factory，引导定语从句；第二个that是强调句中的that。

【译文】正是在这个生产电视机的工厂，我们的朋友被谋杀了。

22.【答案】C

【题解】本题考查词组的含义。be bound to 必定，一定；a matter of sth./doing sth. 与……有关的情况或问题；be the case of 是……的问题；be exemplified by 这点反映在以下事实……

【译文】西部大开发必定成为连接中国和世界的桥梁。

23.【答案】A

【题解】be deprived of the right to vote 被剥夺选举权

【译文】在20世纪20年代以前，大多数的美国妇女都被剥夺了选举权。

24.【答案】C

【题解】本题考查动词的时态。operate表示"做手术"。A是将来进行时，如要用这个时态需要有明确的将来时间点。B如果要表达正在做手术要用being operated。D的表达不符合语法规范。因此选C，表示"那个将要做手术的人是谁"。

【译文】他问那个将要做手术的人是谁。

25.【答案】B

【题解】本题考查几个近义词的辨析。decrease强调数量上的减少；descend除表示"下来，下降"之外还表示"突然来访"，一般与upon/on连用；decline 下降，下倾；drop 落下，滴下。drop by/in/over/round也表示"顺便来访"。

【译文】昨天晚上一位不速之客突然来到我们家。

26.【答案】B

【题解】本题考查动词词组的时态。句子结构是由and连接的并列句，因此set out的时态应和arrive的时态相同。而arrive为一般过去时，因此选B。需要注意的是set的原形、过去式、过去分词同形。

【译文】她天一黑就出发，一小时后到家。

27.【答案】C

【题解】本题考查关于up的词组搭配。bring up 培养，养育；build up 建立；spring up 发生，出现；strike up 开始（与人结识、谈话），开始演奏（或唱歌）。

【译文】随着旧王朝的瓦解和新国家的建立，新的官方语言开始越来越快地涌现出来。

28.【答案】C

【题解】本题考查强调结构it + be... that...，强调时间状语。

【译文】直到1920年才有了定时广播。

29. 【答案】C

    【题解】本题考查obsess的用法。sb. be obsessed by/with表示"某人被……附上、缠住、迷住心窍"。obsessing *adj.*表示被困扰，后面一般不接介词。

    【译文】因为对贫穷的恐惧而鬼迷心窍，他抢劫了银行。

30. 【答案】A

    【题解】本题考查previously的词义。此处需要副词修饰competitive，因此可以先排除B和C，而respectively表示"各自地，分别地"。

    【译文】而先前颇具竞争性的贸易却已经被当时是竞争对手的小公司掌控了。

第二部分　阅读理解

1. 【答案】B

   【题解】推断题。从文章的第一段最后一句话"... serve as symbols of power, success..."（汽车也象征着权利、成功、速度、刺激和冒险）可以推断出正确答案是B（身份，地位）。

2. 【答案】B

   【题解】细节题。根据见文章第四段第二句话"Every year, cars and trucks worldwide kill an average of 250,000 people"（在全球，每一年汽车和卡车夺走25万条生命），所以选B。

3. 【答案】C

   【题解】推断题。从题干知道这里要求选择的是汽车带来的环境问题，根据文章的第三段第一句话可以知道选项C（空气污染）是正确答案。

4. 【答案】A

   【题解】推断题。根据第二段可以推断出A选项的说法（汽车工业是全球经济的重要组成部分），而其他三个选项都不符合文章所表达的意思。

5. 【答案】D

   【题解】主旨题。作者以"The automobile has many advantages"开篇，并从运输功能、经济作用等方面说明；然后以"In spite of their advantages..."引出了汽车带来的负面影响。所以最好的标题是选项D（汽车的好处和坏处）。

6. 【答案】A

   【题解】推断题。从文章的第一段对父亲的回忆可以推知作者父亲对诗歌的爱好对作者有很深的影响，所以选A（作出了重要的贡献）。

7. 【答案】D

   【题解】细节题。根据文章的第一段中"... because of a certain force in me that had to write and that finally burst through and found a channel"（我内心的一种力量让我无法停下写作，这力量最终爆发，找到了渠道），选D（他内心隐藏的愿望）。

8. 【答案】D

   【题解】细节题。根据见文章第三段中"I was editor of the college paper, the college magazine..."（我是大学校报、校园杂志的编辑），所以选D。

9. 【答案】C

   【题解】细节题。根据见文章最后一段中"... I began to write my first book in London"（在伦敦，我开始写我的第一本小说），所以选C。

10. 【答案】A

　　【题解】推断题。　从文章最后一段中 "… left Harvard, had my plays rejected…" 可以推断作者对于自己的剧作被拒感到沮丧；从 "… in which all the houses had that familiar, smoked brick and cream-yellow-plaster look" 可以推断他所居住的房子也是这样的；从 "… in the autumn of 1926" 以及 "I began to write my first book…" 可以推知在1926年作者开始写他的第一本书。而选项A在文章中是没有根据的。所以选A（他失去了决定前进方向的能力）。

UNIT 5

Holidays

单元导读

西方国家有很多的节日，诸如：新年、情人节、复活节、万圣节、感恩节、圣诞节等等。在这些节日中，有的是世界性的节日，有的有着浓重的宗教意义，有的是特定文化、人群的节日。作为英语学习者的我们，不仅要学习语言本身，也应该熟悉西方文化，而西方节日则是其重要组成部分。因此，我们有必要了解西方节日的传统，例如其起源、庆祝方式等等。

课文精讲

文章导读

穿着大红袍、驾着驯鹿、背着一口袋礼物的圣诞老人，真的存在吗？朱莉人生中的第八个圣诞节一天天临近了，可是朱莉对圣诞老人的疑惑也越来越深。她决定做一个小小的测试，看看到底有没有圣诞老人。面对孩子的童稚、天真，父母该做些什么、说些什么呢？朱莉的测试结果是什么呢？在这个圣诞节结束的时候，她还相信有圣诞老人吗？

背景知识

圣诞节（**Christmas**）：圣诞节是基督教世界最大的节日。一般认为12月25日作为圣诞节可能开始于公元336年的罗马教会。4世纪初，1月6日是罗马帝国东部各教会纪念耶稣降生和受洗的双重节日，即上帝通过耶稣向世人显示自己。这一天又是罗马历书的冬至节，意味着万物复苏的开始。后来，因为各地教会使用的历书不同，具体日期不能统一，于是就把12月24日到第二年的1月6日定为圣诞节节期（**Christmas Tide**），各地教会可以根据当地具体情况在这段节期之内庆祝圣诞节。在欧美许多国家里，人们非常重视这个节日，把它和新年连在一起，而庆祝活动之热闹与隆重大大超过了新年，成为一个全民的节日。12月24日平安夜、12月25日圣诞节的主要纪念活动都与耶稣降生的传说有关。

圣诞老人（**Santa Claus**）：圣诞老人的传说在数千年前的斯堪的纳维亚半岛即出现。北欧神话中司智慧、艺术、诗词、战争的奥丁神，寒冬时节，骑上他那八脚马坐骑驰骋于天涯海角，惩恶扬善，分发礼物。与此同时，其子雷神着红衣以闪电为武器与冰雪诸神昏天黑地恶战一场，最终战胜寒冷。据异教传说，圣诞老人为奥丁神后裔。也有传说称圣诞老人由圣·尼古拉斯而来，所以圣诞老人也称St. Nicholas。因这些故事大多弘扬基督精神，其出处及故事情节大多被淡忘，然而圣诞老人却永驻人们精神世界。每年圣诞日，圣诞老人骑在白羊星座上，圣童手持圣诞树降临人间。随着世事变迁，作家和艺术家开始把圣诞老人描述成我们今日熟悉的着红装，留白胡子的形象。同时不同的国度和文化对圣诞老人也有了不同的解释。

📖 文章写作风格及结构

本文为一篇记叙文，作者以事件发展的时间顺序向我们讲述了一个有关圣诞节的充满童趣的幽默故事。

Parts 部分	Paragraphs 段落	Main Ideas 大意
Part I	1—2	As Christmas approached, Julie's doubt about Santa Claus was increasing; however, her parents didn't tell her the truth. 随着圣诞节的临近，朱莉对圣诞老人是否存在心怀疑虑。但她的父母并没有告诉她事情的真相。
Part II	3—7	Julie thought out a way to test the existence of Santa Claus. Her father tricked her into believing it. 朱莉想出了一个办法来验证圣诞老人的存在，但爸爸用了一个小计谋让她相信了圣诞老人的存在。
Part III	8—16	Julie was excited about the existence of Santa Claus, which made her parents worried. 朱莉一整天都在为圣诞老人的存在而激动，这让她的父母有些担心。
Part IV	17—30	Julie's father told her the truth. 朱莉的爸爸告诉了她真相。

🔍 词汇点睛

1　approach

vi. if an event or a particular time approaches, or you approach it, it is coming nearer and will happen soon 临近，接近

• 例句 • With winter approaching, many animals are storing food.
随着冬天的临近，很多动物都在储存食物了。

The time is fast approaching when we will have to make a decision. 必须作决定的时候快到了。

2　announce

vt. to say sth. in a loud and confident way 宣布

• 例句 • The morning paper announced the death of Mr. Smith. 晨报发表了史密斯先生的死亡消息。

Jonathan announced that he had found a new job. 乔纳森宣布他已经找到了新工作。

• 扩展 • announcement *n.* 宣布；宣告
An announcement will be made soon. 即将发表一项公告。

The children were excited by the announcement that they could have an extra holiday.
孩子们听到通知说他们可以有一个额外的假日，都兴高采烈。

3 issue

vt. 1) to officially make a statement, give an order, warning, etc. 发布

- 例句 • The government issued a warning that the strikers should end their action.

  政府发出警告，罢工者应停止其行动。

  Jessie issued a statement denying all the charges. 杰西发表声明否认所有的指控。

  2) to officially produce sth. such as new stamps, coins, or shares and make them available to buy 发行

- 例句 • A new set of stamps in memory of the end of the civil war has been issued.

  为纪念内战结束，发行了一套新邮票。

  n. 1) a subject or problem that is often discussed or argued about 问题，争论点

- 例句 • David addressed the issue of child abuse in his speech.

  大卫在他的讲演中提到了虐待儿童的问题。

  2) a magazine or newspaper printed for a particular day, week, or month （报刊的）一期

- 例句 • Have you read the latest issue of the magazine? 你看过该杂志的最新一期吗？

4 tension

n. a nervous worried feeling that makes it impossible for you to relax 紧张，不安

- 例句 • Tension increased along the border. 边界一线的紧张加剧。

  The government tried to ease racial tension in inner cities.

  政府试图缓解内地城市种族间的紧张关系。

  Exercise is the ideal way to relieve tension after a hard day.

  结束了一天辛苦的工作，体育锻炼是舒缓紧张的好办法。

- 扩展 • **tense** *adj.* 紧张的

  She is tense because of tomorrow's examination. 她因为明天的考试而感到紧张。

5 innocence

n. 1) the state of sb. not having much experience of life or knowledge about evil in the world, so that he can be easily deceived 天真，无知

- 例句 • Don't destroy the innocence of a child. 不要伤害一个孩子的天真。

  2) the fact of being not guilty of a crime 无罪，无辜

- 例句 • The prisoner maintained his innocence. 犯人坚持认为自己无罪。

- 扩展 • **innocent** *adj.* 天真的，幼稚的，无知的；清白的，无罪的，无辜的

  Jack is still as innocent as a child and is easily taken in.

  杰克仍像孩子一般天真，他很容易上当受骗。

  He was set free after he was proved innocent. 当他被证实是清白的之后即被释放了。

6 unbearable

adj. too unpleasant, painful, or annoying to cope with 不堪忍受的

- 例句 • The pain was almost unbearable. 这种痛简直无法忍受。

  This heat is quite unbearable to me. 这种热度令我难以忍受。

- 同义词 • **intolerable** *adj.* 无法忍受的

7 insist

vi. to demand that sth. should happen 坚持，坚决要求

- 短语 • insist on/upon
- 例句 • Susan insisted on seeing her lawyer. 苏珊坚持要见她的律师。

  They insisted that everyone should come to the party. 他们坚决要求每个人都参加聚会。

8 trick

vt. to deceive sb. in order to get sth. from them or to make them do sth. 欺骗，哄骗

- 短语 • trick sb. into doing sth.

  trick sb. out of sth.
- 例句 • Don't try to trick me! 别想骗我！

  She tricked the young man out of his money. 她骗取了那个年轻男人的钱。

  Clients were tricked into believing their money was being invested.

  客户被骗以为他们的钱正用于投资。

  n. sth. you do in order to deceive sb. 诡计，花招，骗术
- 例句 • He cheated the old woman of money by a trick. 他用诡计骗取了这个老年妇女的钱。

9 deceit

n. behavior that is intended to make sb. believe sth. that is not true 欺骗，谎言

- 例句 • His deceit made her very unhappy. 他的欺骗让她很伤心。

  On April Fools' Day my classmate made a deceit on me. 我的同学在愚人节那天骗了我。
- 扩展 • **deceptive** *adj.* 欺骗性的

  Appearances are very often deceptive. 外表往往是靠不住的。

  deceive *vt.* 欺骗，蒙蔽

  They try to deceive themselves that everything is all right.

  他们企图自欺欺人，认为一切都顺利。

  We were deceived into believing that he could help us. 我们受骗了，还以为他能帮助我们。

10 imaginable

adj. that can be imagined 可想象的，可能的

- 例句 • Doctors have tried every imaginable treatment for her disease.

  医生已经采取了一切可能的办法来治疗他的病。

  We had the best vacation imaginable. 我们度过了能想象得到的最好的假期。
- 辨析 • **imaginary** *adj.* 想象中的，假想的，虚构的

  All the characters in this book are imaginary. 书中所有人物都是虚构的。

  The equator is an imaginary line. 赤道是一条实际上并不存在的线。

11 tear

vi. to run or drive somewhere very quickly, especially in a dangerous or careless way 飞奔，猛冲

- 例句 • He tore out of the house shouting "fire!" 他从屋子里飞奔出来，喊着："着火了！"

12 produce

vt. if you produce an object, you bring it out or present it, so that people can see or consider it 出示

- 例句 • The man produced a letter from his pocket. 那个人从口袋里掏出一封信来。

  The lawyer could not produce any convincing evidence. 那位律师拿不出有说服力的证据来。

13 proof

n. facts, information, documents, etc., that prove sth. is true 证明，证据

• 例句 • He produced documents in proof of his claim. 他出示文件以证明自己的要求是合法的。

His finger prints were a proof of his guilt. 他的指纹是他的一项罪证。

• 扩展 • **prove** *vt.* 证实，证明

Facts have proved these worries groundless. 事实证明这些担忧是没有根据的。

14 relative

n. a member of your family 亲戚

• 例句 • He is a close relative of the general manager. 他是总经理的一个近亲。

Her boyfriend is a distant relative of mine. 她的男朋友是我的一个远亲。

• 同义词 • **relation** *n.* 亲戚，亲属

15 mess

n. a situation where there are problems or difficulties, especially as the result of mistakes or carelessness 困境

• 例句 • Look at the mess you've got us into now. 看你把我们弄到了什么样的境地。

My life's such a mess. 我的生活一团糟。

16 lean

vi. to move or bend your body in a particular direction 倾斜，屈身

• 例句 • He leaned forward to hear what the chairman was saying. 他向前探着身子听主席在说什么。

The tower leaned a little to the right. 塔略微向右倾斜。

17 underneath

prep. directly under another object or covered by it 在……的下面

• 例句 • Put your name underneath the address. 把你的名字写在地址的下方。

18 relieved

adj. feeling happy because you are no longer worried about sth. 放心的

• 例句 • He was relieved at the news. 他听到那消息后感到放心了。

His mother was relieved to see him happy again. 看到他又高兴起来，他的妈妈就放心了。

I felt relieved that Ben would be there. 知道本会在那里，我就放心了。

• 扩展 • **relieve** *vt.* 缓解，减轻，解除

These pills will relieve your headache. 这些药丸会缓解你的头痛。

The doctor's explanation relieved me of my fear. 医生的解释消除了我的担心。

19 craving

n. an extremely strong desire for sth. 渴望

• 例句 • Children usually have a craving for chocolate. 孩子总是渴望得到巧克力糖。

20 disgusted

adj. very annoyed or upset by sth. that is not acceptable 厌烦的

• 短语 • **be disgusted at/by/with...** 对……感到厌烦

• 例句 • He was disgusted with the behavior of the selfish child. 他很讨厌那个自私孩子的行为。

I'm completely disgusted at the way his wife has treated him.

他老婆那样对待他，使我反感透了。

- 扩展 • **disgusting** *adj.* 令人作呕的，很讨厌的

  Smoking is a really disgusting habit. 吸烟的确是令人讨厌的习惯。

🔘 短语解析

1. on one's mind　惦记，挂在心上

【例句】Perhaps it is time for President to have soldiers on his mind instead of war on his mind.

现在大概是总统先生把士兵而不是战争挂在心上的时候了。

2. in case　以防，万一

【例句】Be quiet in case you (should) wake the baby. 轻点，别弄醒了婴儿。

Take an umbrella with you in case. 带把雨伞，以防万一。

In case I'm late, start without me. 要是我迟到了，你们就只管出发吧。

3. make a fuss about　大惊小怪，小题大做

【例句】I don't know why you're making such a fuss about it.

我不明白你为什么对这样的事大惊小怪。

She makes a fuss when I'm five minutes late. 我迟到了五分钟，她就小题大做。

4. opt for...　选择……

【例句】About 40 percent of Mazda MX-3 buyers opted for the V-6 engine.

40%的马自达MX-3系列的买主选择了V-6引擎。

5. head for ...　前往……，朝……走去

【例句】These people are heading for the city hall. 这些人正往市政厅那边走去。

🔘 难句突破

1. (Para.2) *We made a fuss about the fire being out in the fireplace so he wouldn't get burned.*

【解析】1) being out是现在分词作宾语补足语。分词除了作宾语补足语以外还可以作其他很多成分，如定语、状语、表语等。例如：

We saw the teacher making the experiment. 我们看见老师正在做试验。

2) 本句中的he指代前文中出现的Santa Claus (圣诞老人)。

【译文】我们故弄玄虚地说，要把壁炉里的火灭了，圣诞老人才不会被烧伤。

2. (Para.2) *And that fantasy of a fat jolly man who flies through the sky in a sleigh and arrives via chimney with presents—that single belief says everything about the innocence of children.*

【解析】句子的主干是that single belief says everything...；破折号的作用是归纳总结，that single belief实际上指的就是破折号前面的that fantasy；而that fantasy被一个of结构修饰，用来说明是什么样的fantasy (fantasy of a fat jolly man...)；在这个of结构中又含有一个who引导的定语从句who flies through the sky... via chimney with presents修饰a fat jolly man。

【译文】一个胖乎乎、乐呵呵的老人，驾着雪橇掠过天空，带着礼物从烟囱来到这儿——仅此想法就可以彻底说明小孩子的天真无邪。

3. (Para.3) *She insisted that on this letter each of us—her father, Adam and I—write the words 'Santa Claus', so if Santa were to sign it, she could compare our handwriting with his.*

【解析】两个破折号中间的内容her father, Adam and I是对前面提到的us进行解释；句子的主干是she insisted that..., 其中that引导宾语从句；在这个宾语从句中有一个so引导的结果状语从句so if Santa...；而这个结果状语从句其实是由一个if引导的条件状语从句构成的if Santa were to sign it, she could compare our handwriting with his。

【译文】她坚持让我们每个人——她父亲、亚当和我——都在这封信上写上"Santa Claus（圣诞老人）"几个字。这样如果圣诞老人签名的话，她就可以把我们的笔迹和他的进行比较，然后她就会知道自己是否被骗了。

4. (Para.10) *I know for sure, for really, really sure.*

【解析】for sure是一个固定搭配，表示肯定的或肯定地。如：

I know for sure that I won't be able to go to the party.

我非常确定地知道我不能去参加晚会了。

One thing's for sure—once the baby's born, your lives will never be the same again.

有一件事是肯定的——一旦孩子生下来，你们的生活将会和原来的不同。

【译文】我确定。非常、非常确定。

5. (Para.23) *I could see he was trying to think of a way, any way, to explain our behavior so it wouldn't sound quite as deceptive, wrong and stupid as it was.*

【解析】本句主干是I could see (that) he was trying to..., 在这个省略了引导词that的宾语从句中又包含一个结果状语从句so it wouldn't sound...；it指代our behavior。

【译文】我看到他正努力寻思着用某种方法来解释我们的所作所为，不管是什么方法，得让它听起来不是那么充满欺骗、谬误和愚蠢。

6. (Para.26) *He said he was wrong, that he shouldn't have tricked her, that he should have answered her questions about Santa Claus the week before.*

【解析】动词said后一共有三个宾语从句，第一个是省略了引导词that的宾语从句he was wrong，第二个是that引导的宾语从句that he shouldn't have tricked her，第三个也是that引导的宾语从句that he should have answered her questions about Santa Claus the week before。

【译文】他说他错了，不应该欺骗她，说他上个星期就应该回答她关于圣诞老人的问题。

参考译文

应付圣诞老人

迪莉娅·艾布朗

　　10月朱莉已经满了八岁。随着圣诞节日益临近，她越来越惦念圣诞老人。在圣诞之前的整整一周，每天晚上她都向父亲宣布："我知道礼物其实是谁送的。是你！"片刻之后，她又加上一句："对吗？"

杰里没有回答。无论他还是我都无法确定她是否真的想知道真相。而且我俩也都不愿意放弃圣诞老人。我们告诉朱莉和她的弟弟亚当，放些饼干在外面以防圣诞老人肚子饿。我们故弄玄虚地说，要把壁炉里的火灭了，圣诞老人才不会被烧伤。我们几次发出威胁，说圣诞老人手上有一份好孩子和坏孩子的名单。这就是圣诞前夜紧张而激动人心的一幕——梦幻成真的一夜：一个胖乎乎、乐呵呵的老人，驾着雪橇掠过天空，带着礼物从烟囱来到这儿——仅此想法就可以彻底说明小孩子的天真无邪。失去这个幻想多么令人难以忍受。对他们和对我们都是如此。所以杰里和我什么也没说。

圣诞前夜，朱莉拿着一张纸来到我们面前。在纸的顶端她已经写上："如果你是真的，就在这儿签名。" 她说，这是给圣诞老人的一封信。她坚持让我们每个人——她父亲、亚当和我——都在这封信上写上"Santa Claus（圣诞老人）"几个字。这样，如果圣诞老人签名的话，她就可以把我们的笔迹和他的进行比较，然后她就会知道自己是否被骗了。

杰里写了。我也写了。亚当只有五岁还不会写字，只写了一个字母"S"就放弃了。朱莉把纸折好，在外面写上"圣诞老人"，然后把它和两块圣诞饼干一起放进了烟囱。

一通折腾后，朱莉和亚当都被安顿好睡觉了。杰瑞和我拿出了礼物，却不知该怎么处理那封信。

短暂商量之后，我们决定选择欺骗。杰里拿出那张字条，用尽可能潦草的字迹写上"祝你圣诞快乐！圣诞老人。" 然后把字条放回壁炉里，把饼干吃了。

第二天清晨，很早，大约六点，我们听见朱莉和亚当冲进楼下的客厅。杰里和我躺在床上听着他们拿到礼物时狂喜的反应。 突然，我们听到一声尖叫，"他是真的！他确实是真的！！！" 我们房间的门突然打开了。"他是真的！！！" 她嚷道。并给我们看了写着潦草字迹的那张纸。

那天下午，我们的朋友蒂娜到家里来交换礼物。"圣诞老人是真的，" 朱莉说。

"哦。"蒂娜说。

"我确定。非常、非常确定。看！"朱莉出示了证据。

就在那个时候电话响了。朱莉知道那是亲戚打来祝贺圣诞节的电话，就跑过去接。"圣诞老人是真的！" 我听见她对我姐姐诺拉说。

"这是怎么回事？"诺拉问我。

我把整件事情告诉了她。

诺拉说："我们这样做可能不对。"她很委婉地把自己也扯进了这件麻烦事中。

"你说得没错！" 我说。"你觉得朱莉有可能会忘掉所有这一切吗？"当然，这才是我真正想要的——让整件事被抛之脑后。

"我有些怀疑。"诺拉说。

我们度过了愉快的一天——品尝美味的食物、收到精美的礼物、还有很多客人来访。然后到了睡觉时间。

"爸爸，"当杰里安顿她睡觉的时候朱莉说。

"什么？"

"如果圣诞老人是真的，那鲁道夫一定也是真的。"

"你说什么？"

"如果圣诞老人是真的——"

"你知道，朱莉，"杰里说，然后顿了一下。我看到他正努力寻思着用某种方法来解释我们的所作所为，不管是什么方法，得让它听起来不是那么充满欺骗、谬误和愚蠢。

"字条上的字是我写的。"杰里说。

朱莉放声大哭起来。

杰里道了歉。他一遍又一遍地道歉，而朱莉则把头埋在枕头下面抽泣。杰里说他错了，不应该欺骗她，说他上个星期就应该回答她关于圣诞老人的问题。

朱莉从床上坐起来。"我还以为他是真的，"她用责怪的口吻说。突然她趴到床上，从床底下抽出一本漫画书，又坐了起来。"我能看五分钟的书吗？"她说。

"当然可以。"杰里说。

事情就这样过去了。为圣诞老人的死难过了一分钟，生活又继续了。

杰里和我如释重负地走出了朱莉的房间。我马上觉得想吃火鸡，就走进了厨房。刚要把火鸡放回冰箱，就听到亚当哭了起来。我下楼来到客厅。他房间的门开着，我听到朱莉极其不耐烦地说："噢，亚当，你用不着哭，只有三岁小孩儿才相信有圣诞老人呢。"

习题全解

文章大意

1. 根据课文用适当的词填空。

【答案】

1) eight   2) innocence   3) handwriting   4) chimney

5) burst   6) apologized   7) relieved   8) babies

【译文】　当朱莉八岁的时候，她开始怀疑圣诞老人是否真的存在。然而她的父母不想告诉她真相，因为他们不想让她失去天真无邪的童年。圣诞前夜，朱莉拿出一张纸，让所有的家庭成员都在上面写上"Santa Claus（圣诞老人）"这几个字，以便比较他们和圣诞老人的字迹，这样她就可以知道她自己是否受骗了。然后朱莉折好纸，连同两块圣诞饼干一起塞进了烟囱。

　　朱莉和她的弟弟都上床以后，她的爸爸杰里拿出了那张字条，并且用尽可能潦草的字迹写上"祝你圣诞快乐！圣诞老人。"第二天早上，当朱莉从烟囱里找到字条时，她非常高兴地发现圣诞老人是真的，她把她的发现告诉她遇到的每一个人。

　　那天晚上，当杰里告诉朱莉事情真相的时候，朱莉放声大哭，杰里向她道歉说他本不该欺骗她。当杰里和他的妻子走出朱莉房间的时候，他们如释重负，原来朱莉已经准备好接受这个事实了。然而朱莉又把故事讲给她的弟弟亚当听，并且说只有三岁小孩儿才相信有圣诞老人呢。

文章细节

1. 根据课文回答下列问题。

【答案】

1) She guessed it was her father, but she was not sure. (Para. 1)

2) They did not answer her questions, because they were not sure whether Julie wanted the truth and they did not want to give up Santa Claus themselves. (Para. 2)

3) She took a sheet of paper and asked all the family members to write "Santa Claus" on it. (Para. 3)

4) Her father wrote "Merry Christmas, Santa Claus" on the paper, and put it back in the chimney. (Para. 6)

5) Because she believed she had the proof that Santa Claus had signed the paper she prepared. (Para. 7)

6) Yes. He told her that he wrote the note. (Para. 24)

7) She burst into tears and sobbed into her pillow. (Paras. 25-26)

8) Because Julie told him about the truth that Santa Claus was not real. (Para. 30)

【译文】

1) [问题] 朱莉八岁的时候，她真的知道是谁送来了圣诞礼物么？

   [答案] 她猜是她的爸爸，但是她不确定。

2) [问题] 作者和她的丈夫是如何回答朱莉关于圣诞老人的问题的？他们为什么要这样做？

   [答案] 他们没有回答她的问题，因为他们无法确定朱莉是否真的想知道真相，并且他们自己也不想放弃圣诞老人。

3) [问题] 朱莉是如何确定自己没有受骗的？

   [答案] 她拿出一张纸，让家里所有的人在上面写上"Santa Claus（圣诞老人）"。

4) [问题] 朱莉的父母是如何对待这张字条的？

   [答案] 她爸爸在字条上写了"祝你圣诞快乐！圣诞老人"并把字条放回了烟囱。

5) [问题] 第二天早上朱莉醒来，她为什么相信圣诞老人是真的？

   [答案] 因为圣诞老人在她准备的那张纸上签了字，她认为她有了证据。

6) [问题] 朱莉的爸爸告诉她圣诞老人的真相了么？他是怎么做的？

   [答案] 是的。他告诉她是他写的字条。

7) [问题] 当朱莉知道真相后她的反应如何？

   [答案] 她放声大哭，把头埋在枕头下面抽泣。

8) [问题] 朱莉的弟弟亚当为什么哭？

   [答案] 因为朱莉告诉了他圣诞老人不是真的这一真相。

词汇练习

1. 请用下面所给词汇或短语的适当形式填写句子。

1) 【答案】reluctant

   【译文】他非常不情愿承认他的错误。

2) 【答案】via

   【译文】你可以通过因特网进入我们的主页。

3) 【答案】produce

   【译文】他不能为警察提供任何有说服力的证据。

4) 【答案】disgusted

　　【译文】我十分厌恶他妻子对待他的方式。

5) 【答案】on my mind

　　【译文】这个旅游计划已在我的脑海里酝酿了很久。

6) 【答案】come true

　　【译文】但愿你的希望可以成为现实。

7) 【答案】announced

　　【译文】他们宣布危险已经过去了。

8) 【答案】approach

　　【译文】当你靠近这座城市时，见到的第一栋建筑是教堂。

9) 【答案】innocence

　　【译文】律师正试图证明这个可怜的人是无辜的。

10) 【答案】burst into tears

　　【译文】她钻进我怀里失声痛哭。

2.请用括号里的词的适当形式填写句子。

1) 【答案】issued; threat; reaction; insisted

　　【译文】政府发布了警告，罢工者必须立刻取消罢工，否则将被惩罚。这样的警告被罢工者视为威胁，并引发了愤怒的反应。他们坚持永不放弃，除非有人采取措施改善他们的工作环境。

2) 【答案】mess; disgusts; terribly

　　【译文】纽约地铁混乱不堪已经有些年头了，高温、噪音、臭味，地铁里的一切都使乘客感到恶心。显而易见，必须采取措施了。

3) 【答案】opted for; relatives; heading for

　　【译文】80%的美国人选择结束战争。对于卷入战争的家庭，亲人的安全是他们最大的担忧。他们宣称不仅他们的家庭，而且整个国家都卷入了战争的灾难。

4) 【答案】tension; approached; imaginable

　　【译文】随着作决定的最后期限的临近，城市里紧张情绪高涨，没人知道会发生什么，也许会有现在还无法想象的可能。

5) 【答案】deceptive, belief, innocence

　　【译文】我知道外表具有欺骗性，但杰弗里看起来不像谋杀犯，所以我始终坚信他是无辜的。

3.请学习表格中的词，然后选择适当的词，用其正确形式填写句子。

1) 【答案】relieved

　　【译文】病人听说自己没得癌症就放心了。

2) 【答案】deceived

　　【译文】我们受骗了，竟相信他可以帮助我们。

3) 【答案】grieved

　　【译文】这个家庭因失去他们的独生子而悲痛。

4) 【答案】believe

　　【译文】我们相信他会成功的。

5) 【答案】relief

【译文】令她宽慰的是她女儿是安全的。

6) 【答案】grief

【译文】我不知道忘记他生日会让他这么不高兴。

7) 【答案】proof

【译文】有没有任何证据证明被告在犯罪现场?

8) 【答案】belief

【译文】没有什么事比孩子对父母的信任更自然的了。

9) 【答案】proved

【译文】他已在战斗中证明了他的勇气。

10) 【答案】deceit

【译文】他靠欺骗搞到了钱。

语法结构

1. 仿照例句改写下列句子。

1) 【答案】Being a college student, you should know something about computers and the Internet.

【译文】作为一名大学生,你应该懂点有关电脑和因特网的知识。

2) 【答案】Hearing the news that the police had arrested her younger brother, she fell into a faint.

【译文】听到自己弟弟被警察拘捕的消息,她昏了过去。

3) 【答案】Determined to live free someday, he managed to get trained in iron molding.

【译文】为有朝一日能自由生活,他设法去接受有关铸铁的培训。

4) 【答案】Thus encouraged, we made a still bolder plan for the next year.

【译文】因为受到这样的鼓励,我们为明年制定了一个更大胆的计划。

5) 【答案】The children rushed into the garden quite excited.

【译文】孩子们很兴奋地冲进花园。

2. 仿照例句,将括号中的汉语译成英语。

1) 【答案】In case I'm late

【译文】要是我迟到了,别等我。

2) 【答案】In case I forget

【译文】如果我忘记了,请提醒我我的承诺。

3) 【答案】in case it is sunny this afternoon

【译文】带上你的帽子,以防下午出太阳。

4) 【答案】in case this one should not work

【译文】再找另外一个装置,以防这个装置不起作用。

5) 【答案】in case the flight is delayed

【译文】带上点吃的东西,以防航班延误。

综合练习

1. 完形填空。

1) 【答案】A

【解析】根据上下文,这里需要表示转折的词,因此只能选A。however 然而,但是。

2) 【答案】B

【解析】be ready to do sth. 即将做某事，预备做某事；为固定搭配。

3) 【答案】C

【解析】cut sth. in/into sth.（用刀等）切割某物；为固定搭配。

4) 【答案】A

【解析】as if 好像；even if 即使，纵然；as that 和 even that 均不是固定短语。

5) 【答案】D

【解析】which引导非限制性定语从句，对前半句话起到解释说明的作用。

6) 【答案】D

【解析】put away 放好，储存……备用；put off 关掉，熄灭；put up 举起，抬起；put on 穿上，戴上。

7) 【答案】C

【解析】act as 扮作；appear 显露，出现；look like 看上去像……；look at 看……。

8) 【答案】C

【解析】some 一些；all 所有的；each 每，各（自）；no 没有。

9) 【答案】A

【解析】ask for 寻求；long for 渴望；go for 努力获取；live for 为……而生活。

10) 【答案】D

【解析】they 他们（主格）；them 他们（宾格）；their 他们的（代词所有格／形容词性物主代词）；themselves 他们自己（反身代词，用以指人或动物所施的动作返回到本身）。

【译文】

　　万圣节前夕是美国人年年都会庆祝的秋季节日。它的意思是"神圣的夜晚"，在每年的10月31日，也就是万圣节前夜。但实际上这不是一个真正的宗教节日，而主要是孩子们的节日。

　　每年秋天蔬菜成熟可以食用的时候，孩子们就会挑出大个儿的橙色南瓜。然后在南瓜上刻上一张脸，把一根点燃的蜡烛放在里面。这个南瓜看起来就好像一个脑袋！这些灯就叫做"Jack-o-lanterns"，意思也就是"杰克的灯"。

　　每年万圣节前夕孩子们还戴上奇怪的面具，穿上吓人的服装。有些孩子把脸画成怪物。然后他们拿着盒子或袋子挨家挨户串门。每来到一个新房子他们就说："不款待就捣乱！给钱还是吃的！"大人们就会把用来招待的钱或糖放在他们的袋子里了。

　　一些孩子在万圣节这天也考虑到了别人。他们拿着为联合国儿童基金会筹款的盒子。他们筹集这些钱来帮助全世界的贫困儿童。当然，每次他们帮助联合国儿童基金会时，他们本人常常也受到款待。

2. 用括号中的词汇和短语将下列句子译成英语。

1) 【答案】When her dream finally came true, Jenny was so excited that she burst into tears.

2) 【答案】The failure in last year's game is still on Robert's mind, so he is reluctant to take part in the game this year.

3) 【答案】The captain insisted that the ship should head for Africa.

4) 【答案】You should have noticed her reaction to this proposal, but you didn't.

5) 【答案】The government announced that the launch would be canceled in case the weather was not good.

文章泛读

📖 文章导读

关于感恩节，你知道些什么呢？火鸡？清教徒？还是印第安人？作者将在文章中告诉我们关于感恩节的点点滴滴。

💿 背景知识

感恩节（**Thanksgiving Day**）：每逢11月第四个星期四，美国人民便迎来了自己最重要的传统民俗节日——感恩节。这个节日始于1621年。那年秋天，远涉重洋来到美洲的英国移民，为了感谢上帝赐予的丰收，举行了三天的狂欢活动。从此，这一习俗就沿续下来，并逐渐风行各地。1863年，美国总统林肯正式宣布感恩节为国家法定假日。

清教徒（**Pilgrim**）：16世纪下半叶从英国国教内部分离出来的宗教派别。16世纪上半叶，英王亨利八世与罗马教皇决裂，进行宗教改革，建立以英王为首领的国教会（圣公会），但保留了天主教的主教制、重要教义和仪式。60年代，许多人主张清洗圣公会内部的天主教残余影响，得名清教徒。

📝 文章写作风格及结构

本文为一篇说明文，作者从感恩节的起源、庆祝方式等方面让我们更加全面地了解这样一个充满意义的节日。

Parts 部分	Paragraphs 段落	Main Ideas 大意
Part I	1—2	Thanksgiving is celebrated every year on the fourth Thursday of November. 人们在11月的最后一个星期四庆祝感恩节。
Part II	3—8	The origin of Thanksgiving. 感恩节的起源。
Part III	9—10	Thanksgiving was declared as a national holiday because of the suggestion of the writer Sarah Josepha Hale. 由于作家萨拉·约瑟法·黑尔的建议，感恩节成为了国家法定节日。
Part IV	11—13	The dinner and celebration of Thanksgiving. 感恩节正餐和庆祝活动。
Part V	14—16	Over the years, Americans have added new traditions to their Thanksgiving celebration. 多年以来，美国人已经为他们的感恩节庆祝活动增添了新的传统。

词汇点睛

1 celebration

n. an occasion or party when you celebrate sth. 庆祝，庆典

•例句• Her triumph was a cause for celebration. 她的胜利是庆祝的理由。

The party was a celebration of his life. 这场聚会是他一生的庆典。

•短语• **in celebration of** 为庆祝……

They held a party in celebration of their fiftieth wedding anniversary.

他们为自己的金婚纪念日举行了一个庆典。

•扩展• **celebrate** *vt.* 庆祝，庆贺

How do people celebrate New Year in your country? 你们国家的人怎样庆贺新年？

2 religious

adj. 1) relating to religion in general or to a particular religion 宗教的

•例句• She has been holding to her religious faith. 她一直坚持自己的宗教信仰。

He received his religious education in the school in the past.

他过去曾在这所学校接受过宗教教育。

2) (of a person) believing in and practicing a religion; devout 信奉宗教的，虔诚的

•例句• Hans was a very religious man. He behaved in a Christian way to all people including his enemies.

汉斯是个虔诚的宗教信徒，所以他用基督教的方式对待一切人，包括他的敌人。

•扩展• **religion** *n.* 宗教，宗教信仰

Is there always a conflict between science and religion? 科学和宗教之间是否总是存在着冲突？

3 tradition

n. a belief, custom, or way of doing sth. that has existed for a long time, or these beliefs, customs, etc., in general 传统，惯例

•例句• James Joyce's *Ulysses* challenged the literary traditions of his day.

詹姆斯·乔伊斯写的《尤里西斯》是对他那个时代文学传统的挑战。

It is a tradition that the young look after the old in their family.

在他们家，年轻的照顾年长的是一个传统。

•短语• **break with tradition** 打破传统

They broke with tradition and got married quietly. 他们打破传统，毫不声张地结了婚。

by tradition 按照传统风俗

By tradition, children play tricks on 1 April. 按照传统风俗，孩子们在4月1日搞恶作剧。

in the tradition of 有……的风格

He is a politician in the tradition of Kennedy. 他是位具有肯尼迪风格的政治家。

•扩展• **traditional** *adj.* 传统的，惯例的

It is traditional in America to eat turkey on Thanksgiving Day. 感恩节时吃火鸡是美国的传统。

4 evidence

n. facts or signs that show clearly that sth. exists or is true 证据，证明（常与for, of连用）

•例句• There is not a shred of evidence that the meeting actually took place.

没有丝毫证据表明这个会议确已举行。

We found further scientific evidence for this theory.

我们找到了进一步证实这种理论的科学根据。

- 短语 • **in evidence** 显眼，显而易见

The police were much in evidence at today's demonstration.

在今天的示威集会上警察随处可见。

give/bear/show evidence of 证明，说明，表明

A smile gives evidence of her consent. 微笑表明她同意。

- 扩展 • **evident** *adj.* 显而易见的，显然的

The growing interest in history is clearly evident in the number of people who visited museums and country houses. 从参观博物馆和乡村住宅的人数明显看出人们对历史越来越感兴趣。

5 flee

vi. 1) (fled, fled) to leave somewhere very quickly, in order to escape from danger 逃避，逃跑

- 例句 • He fled to London after an argument with his family. 他与家人争吵以后离家去了伦敦。

She burst into tears and fled. 她突然哭了起来，跑开了。

2) to run or hurry away; to escape (especially from danger, threat, etc.) 逃跑，避开；（尤指遇到危险、威胁等）逃离

- 例句 • The enemy fled in disorder. 敌人溃逃了。

- 短语 • **flee (from) sb./sth.**

He was caught trying to flee (from) the country. 他企图逃离这个国家时被抓住了。

6 oppression

n. when sb. treats a group of people unfairly or cruelly and prevents them from having the same rights as other people have 压迫，镇压

- 例句 • The people are just starting to rebuild their lives after decades of oppression.

经受了几十年的压迫后，人们刚开始重建生活。

- 扩展 • **oppress** *vt.* 压迫，压抑，使烦恼

The gloomy atmosphere in the office oppressed her. 办公室的低沉气氛使她感到压抑。

oppressive *adj.* 压迫的，欺压的；闷热的，令人窒息的

He founded an oppressive regime. 他建立了一个残暴的政权。

The heat in the tropics can be oppressive. 热带气候的炎热让人难以忍受。

7 voyage

n. a long journey in a ship 航程

- 例句 • Going to college can be a voyage of self-discovery. 上大学可以算作是一次自我发现之旅。

The *Titanic* sank on its maiden voyage. 泰坦尼克号首航便沉没了。

8 observance

n. sth. you do as part of a ceremony, especially a religious ceremony 庆祝，纪念

- 例句 • The church is processing an observance. 教堂正在举行一个纪念仪式。

Many countries take the observance of New Year's Day as a public holiday.

很多国家有把元旦当作公众节日的习俗。

- 扩展 • **observe** *vt.* 看到，注意到，观察到

Have you observed any changes lately? 最近你注意到什么变化没有？

observant *adj.* 善于观察的，观察力敏锐的

Observant walkers may see red deer along this stretch of the road.

观察敏锐的步行者能在这一路段看到赤鹿。

• 辨析 • **observance，observation**

observance *n.* 指（对法律、习俗等的）遵守，奉行；（对节日的）纪念，庆祝。如：

the observance of school rules 对校规的遵守

the observance of the King's birthday 国王祝寿大典

observation *n.* 指观察、观察力等。如：

under observation 在观察中，在监视下

a man of keen observation 观察力敏锐的人

9　campaign

n. a series of actions intended to achieve a particular result relating to politics or business, or a social improvement （政治或商业性的）活动

• 例句 • He launched some advertising campaigns to promote his product.

他发起了一些广告宣传活动以推销其产品。

Today police launched a campaign to reduce road accidents.

警察今天发起了一场减少道路交通事故的运动。

vi. to take part in or lead a campaign, for example to achieve political change or in order to win an election 领导运动，参加活动

• 例句 • Jean is campaigning for equal rights for women. 吉恩在参加争取妇女平等权利的运动。

10　official

adj. approved of or done by sb. in authority, especially the government 官方的，正式的

• 例句 • An official inquiry has been launched into the cause of the accident.

当局已对事故的原因展开调查。

According to official statement, the rumor in the air proved true.

根据官方声明，谣传经证明是真的。

n. a person who is in a position of authority in a large organization 官员，高级职员

• 例句 • Palace officials are refusing to comment on the royal divorce.

宫廷官员拒绝对王室婚变发表意见。

• 反义词 • **unofficial** *adj.* 非官方的，非正式的

11　reunion

n. a social meeting of people who have not met for a long time, especially people who were at school or college together 团聚，重逢

• 例句 • A reunion is pleasant for each member of the family.

家人团聚对每位家庭成员来说是一件愉快的事。

Christmas is a time of reunion. 圣诞节是团聚的日子。

• 扩展 • **reunite** *vt.* （使）再结合，重聚

The family was reunited after the war. 战争过后，一家人又相聚了。

• 短语 • **reunite A with/and B** （使）A与B重逢，A与B再次相聚

Last night she was reunited with her children. 昨天晚上，她与她的子女再度团聚。

12　serve

vt. 1) to give sth., food or drink as part of a meal 摆出（餐食），上（菜）

- 例句 • They served a wonderful meal to more than fifty delegates.

  他们招待五十多位代表吃了一餐美味佳肴。

  She served us a delicious lunch. 她招待我们吃了一顿可口的午餐。

  2) to be enough for sb./sth. 够……吃

- 例句 • This dish will serve four hungry people. 这盘菜够四个饿汉吃。

  3) to work or perform duties for a person, organization or country, etc. 工作，服务，尽职

- 例句 • He served as a captain in the army. 他曾是一位陆军上尉。

  I wanted to work somewhere where I could serve the community.

  我想找一个能够为公众服务的工作岗位。

- 短语 • **serve sb. right (for doing sth.)** 咎由自取，罪有应得

  Left you, did she? It serves you right for being so selfish.

  她离开了你，是吗？那你活该——你太自私了。

  serve its/one's turn 发挥作用，派上用场，足以满足……的需要

  Your knowledge of history will serve your turn in the interview.

  你的历史知识在面试中会派上用场。

13　professional

adj. done by or relating to people who are paid to do a sport or activity 专业的，职业的

- 例句 • If it is a legal matter, you need to seek professional advice.

  如果这属于法律问题，你就需要进行专业咨询了。

  Most of the people on the course were professional women.

  参加本课程的大多数人是职业女性。

- 扩展 • **profession** *n.* 行业，职业（界），业内人士

  He was an electrician by profession. 他的职业是电工。

  The legal profession has/have always resisted change. 法律界向来抵制变革。

14　broadcast

vt. (broadcast, broadcast) to send out radio or television programs 广播

- 例句 • The concert will be broadcast live tomorrow evening. 音乐会明晚将现场直播。

  The BBC broadcasts every day. 英国广播公司每天广播。

  n. a radio or television program 广播，广播节目

- 例句 • The news broadcast will be at 7:00. 新闻广播将在7点开始。

🌑 短语解析

become/be known as 以……知名，被称为……

【例句】The city has been known as the heaven of music. 这座城市一直被称作音乐的天堂。

It had become known as the most dangerous part of the city. 那地方被称作是市内最危险的地段。

难句突破

1. (Para.8) ***Writings from that time say Pilgrim leader William Bradford set a date late in the year.***

【解析】say在本句的意思并非"说"而是指"（书、符号等）表示（信息或指示）"。类似的用法如：

a notice saying "Keep Out" 写有"禁止入内"的告示

The law says that this is quite legitimate. 法律上说这是合法的。

Tradition says Pilgrim settlers from England celebrated the first Thanksgiving in 1621. 传统的说法是，从英国来的清教徒移民于1621年举行了首次感恩节的庆祝活动。 (Para.3)

【译文】写于那个时候的一些文学作品说，是清教徒的领袖威廉·布拉德福德在年末确定了一个日期。

2. (Para.9) ***Yet it took 250 years before a national observance was declared.***

【解析】it指代时间、距离或天气，作句中主语。又如：

It's a long time since they left. 他们走后有很久了。

It's two miles to the beach. 离海滨有两英里远。

It was raining this morning. 今早下雨来着。

【译文】但把感恩节作为全国性的节日来庆祝，则是250年后的事情。

3. (Para.12) ***Other traditional Thanksgiving foods served with turkey are potatoes, a cooked fruit called cranberries and pumpkin pie.***

【解析】本句的主干是Other... foods... are potatoes, a cooked fruit... and pumpkin pie。主语foods由一个过去分词短语served with turkey修饰，宾语fruit也由一个过去分词短语called cranberries修饰。

【译文】与火鸡一起摆上餐桌的其他传统感恩节食物有土豆、一种叫越橘的煮过的水果，以及南瓜饼。

参考译文

火鸡背后：感恩节的故事

杰瑞琳·沃森

每年11月的第四个星期四人们庆祝感恩节。11月属于秋季，是收获庄稼的主要季节。

作家欧·亨利把感恩节称为纯粹的美国节日。感恩节并非宗教性的节日，但它却有宗教上的意义。

感恩节起源于首批到美洲定居的欧洲人。他们收获农作物后，举行庆祝活动，为得到了食物而感恩。

传统的说法是，从英国来的清教徒移民于1621年举行了首次感恩节的庆祝活动。但有证据表明：美洲其他地方的定居者对感恩节的庆祝还要更早一些。不过清教徒的感恩节故事流传最广。

清教徒因为宗教信仰不同，为躲避迫害，逃离了英国。他们最先到了荷兰，然后又离开那个国家前往北美建立殖民地。1620年，清教徒们在后来被称为马萨诸塞州普利茅斯的地方登陆。

他们横渡大西洋的航程很艰难，到达美洲后的最初几个月也在艰难中度过。大约一百名清教徒恰恰在秋冬换季之时登陆。在接下来几个月寒冷的日子里，他们中有一半没能熬过去。

冬去春来时，清教徒们开始种植农作物。一位名叫斯匡托的美洲印第安人帮助了他们。夏季结束时，清教徒们栽种的玉米、大麦获得丰收。他们有足够的食物度过整个冬季了。

清教徒们决定举行庆祝活动，感谢他们获得的丰收。写于那个时候的一些文学作品说，是清教徒的领袖威廉·布拉德福德在年末确定了一个日期。他邀请邻近一印第安人部落的成员来参加庆祝活动。食物种类繁多。正餐包括多种野生禽类，诸如鸭子、鹅，还有火鸡。那次的感恩节庆祝活动持续了三天。

随着美洲殖民地的拓展，很多城镇和居民点都举行了感恩节或收获季节的庆祝活动。但把感恩节作为全国性的节日来庆祝，则是250年后的事情。

19世纪20年代，一位名叫萨拉·约瑟法·里尔的作家发起了一场运动，争取将感恩节定为官方的正式节日。慢慢地有越来越多的人支持她的想法。终于，1863年，亚伯拉罕·林肯总统宣布11月最后一个星期四为全国性节日——感恩节。后来，议会宣布将在每年11月的第四个星期四庆祝这个节日。

有些美国人千里迢迢赶回去与家人团聚。大家共进丰盛的晚餐，这是感恩节庆祝活动的主要内容。对多数人来说，只有在感恩节，家庭的所有成员才共聚一堂。这个节日是家人团聚的时刻。

感恩节正餐的主角是一只硕大的烤火鸡。与火鸡一起摆上餐桌的其他传统感恩节食物有土豆、一种叫越橘的煮过的水果，以及南瓜饼。有些家庭除了火鸡，还上其他的肉食。也有一些美国家庭感恩节晚餐吃素。这意味着没有肉食。

进餐前，人人都要说几句话，内容是关于他们最感激的事物。很多美国人也会帮助那些可能还没有机会享受到感恩节大餐的人。在全美国，成千上万的宗教及服务团体都会为老人、无家可归者和穷人提供节日的盛餐。

多年以来，美国人已经为他们的感恩节庆祝活动增添了新的传统。比如，一些职业橄榄球赛或大学橄榄球赛都会在感恩节这天举行。有些赛事通过全国性的电视台进行转播。

也有许多人喜欢在电视上观看感恩节游行。一些城市的大商场会组织这样的游行。比如说，在纽约，就有著名的梅西百货公司组织的感恩节游行。

与过去一样，许多美国人会在星期四这天与家人、朋友团聚。我们会分享自己所有的东西，而且我们也会对过去一年中的好事表达感恩之情。

习题全解

1. 根据文章判断下列句子是正确或错误。

1) 【答案】F

　　【题解】根据文章第一、二段中"感恩节是纯粹的美国节日，每年11月的第四个星期四人们庆祝感恩节……"，因此这句话是错误的，人们并不是每两年才庆祝感恩节，日期也不是12月的第四个星期四。

2) 【答案】T

　　【题解】根据文章第五段中"清教徒为躲避宗教迫害，逃离了英国。1620年，清教徒们在后来被称为马萨诸塞州普利茅斯的地方登陆，并建立殖民地"，因此这句话是正确的。

3) 【答案】T

　　【题解】根据文章第七段中"冬去春来时，清教徒们开始种植农作物。一位名叫斯匡托的美洲印第安人帮助了他们。夏季结束时，清教徒们栽种的玉米、大麦获得丰收"，因此这句话是正确的。

4) 【答案】F

　　【题解】根据文章第八段中"清教徒们决定举行庆祝活动，感谢他们获得的丰收"可以得知，清教徒举行庆祝活动并不仅仅是为了感谢上帝，感谢神，所以这句话是错误的。

5) 【答案】F

　　【题解】根据文章第十段"1863年，亚伯拉罕·林肯总统宣布11月最后一个星期四为全国性节日——感恩节"可以得知，并不是清教徒的领袖威廉·布拉德福德宣布11月最后一个星期四为全国性节日——感恩节，这种说法只是文学作品中提到而已，所以这句话是错误的。

6) 【答案】T

　　【题解】这句话是说"在美国，感恩节是和家人、朋友团聚的时刻，大家共进丰盛的晚餐，晚餐的主角是一只硕大的烤火鸡"。根据文章第11段、12段，这种说法是正确的。

2. 请用下面所给出的词汇或短语的适当形式填写句子。

1) 【答案】celebrated

　　【译文】我们以一场舞会来庆祝新年的到来。

2) 【答案】evidence

　　【译文】警察掌握了证据，证明凶手是一个老妇人。

3) 【答案】broadcasts

　　【译文】BBC电台每天都会进行广播。

4) 【答案】established

　　【译文】这家公司成立于1860年。

5) 【答案】reunion

　　【译文】每年的元旦，全家都会团聚在一起。

6) 【答案】official

　　【译文】英语是许多国家的官方语言。

7) 【答案】serve

　　【译文】中餐馆总是能提供可口的食物。

8) 【答案】religious

　　【译文】她能开诚布公地和朋友探讨她的宗教信仰。

9) 【答案】traditional

　　【译文】在美国，传统上人们会在万圣节那天穿上化妆舞会的服装。

10) 【答案】oppression

　　【译文】他们忍受了长达数年的政治迫害。

3. 将下面这些句子译成汉语。

1) 【答案】传统的说法是，从英国来的清教徒移民于1621年首次举行了感恩节的庆祝活动。但有证据表明：美洲其他地方的定居者对感恩节的庆祝还要更早一些。

2) 【答案】随着美洲殖民地的拓展，很多城镇和居民点都举行了感恩节或收获季节的庆祝活动。但把感恩节作为全国性的节日来庆祝，则是250年后的事情。

3) 【答案】有些美国人千里迢迢赶回去与家人团聚。大家共进丰盛的晚餐，这是感恩节庆祝活动的主要内容。

4) 【答案】与火鸡一起摆上餐桌的其他传统感恩节食物有土豆、一种叫越橘的煮过的水果，以及南瓜饼。

文章泛读

文章导读

和圣诞节一样，情人节也已经悄悄渗透到了无数年轻人的心中，成为中国传统节日之外的又一个重要节日。然而情人节的来历和意义可能并不一定为大多数人所知。作者将在本文中告诉你关于情人节的故事。

背景知识

情人节（Valentine's Day）：又称"圣瓦伦丁节"。起源于古代罗马，于每年2月14日举行，现已成为欧美各国青年人喜爱的节日。关于"圣瓦伦丁节"名称的来源，说法不一。有的说是纪念一位叫瓦伦丁的基督教殉难者，他因反抗罗马统治者对基督教徒的迫害，被捕入狱，并在公元270年2月14日被处死刑。行刑前，瓦伦丁曾给典狱长的女儿写了一封信，表明了自己光明磊落的心迹和对她的一片情怀。自此以后，基督教便把2月14日定为"情人节"。

文章写作风格及结构

本文为一篇说明文，作者从有关情人节的小故事、人们的庆祝方式等方面向我们描述了一个浪漫的节日。

Parts 部分	Paragraphs 段落	Main Ideas 大意
Part I	1—2	St. Valentine's Day is a romantic holiday for people to express their love. 情人节是人们互诉爱意的浪漫节日。
Part II	3	The symbols of St. Valentine's Day. 情人节的象征。
Part III	4	Story about St. Valentine's Day. 关于情人节的故事。
Part IV	5	A song for Valentine's Day. 一首关于情人节的歌。

词汇点精

1　complicated

adj. difficult to understand or deal with, because many parts or details are involved 复杂的，难懂的

• 例句 • The new generation of video games is much more complicated than former ones.

新一代的影碟游戏比以前的更复杂。

The instructions look very complicated. 这说明书看起来很难懂。

• 扩展 • **complication** *n.* 复杂化，（使复杂的）因素

The bad weather added a further complication to our journey.

恶劣的天气给我们的旅行增加了更多的困难。

• 辨析 • **complicated，complex**

二者都含"复杂的"意思。

complex 指"包含许多（尤其是不同的）部分，因而比较难懂或难解释的"。如：

This is a complex problem. 这是一个复杂的问题。

complicated 指"各部分相互交错而变得错综复杂"。如：

What a complicated machine! I can't possibly use it.

这是一台多么复杂的机器！我可不会使用它。

2　decorate

vt. to make sth. look more attractive by putting sth. pretty on it 装饰，修饰

• 例句 • They decorated the room with flowers and balloons. 他们用花和气球装饰了房间。

They are decorating the Christmas tree. 他们在装饰圣诞树。

• 扩展 • **decoration** *n.* 装饰品

The decoration on the carved wooden door is quite elaborate. 木雕门上的装饰图案相当精美。

3　humorous

adj. funny and enjoyable 幽默的，滑稽的，有幽默感的

• 例句 • She had not intended to be humorous. 她本想要幽默一下。

He had a wide mouth and humorous grey eyes. 他有一张大嘴巴，一双滑稽的灰眼睛。

• 反义词 • **humorless** *adj.* 缺乏幽默感的

• 扩展 • **humor** *n.* 幽默，诙谐，滑稽；心情，脾气

The humor of it is not to be absorbed in a hurry. 其中的幽默不是一下子能领会的。

He has a good sense of humor. 他很富于幽默感。

I'm in a good humor today. 我今天心情不错。

4　sentimental

adj. 1) producing emotions such as pity, romantic love or sadness 伤感的，多愁善感的

• 例句 • Her book is honest without being sentimental. 她的书笔调朴实，不故作伤感。

He is not the sort of man who gets sentimental about old friendships.

他不是那种为旧日的友情唏嘘感伤的人。

　　2) connected with your emotions rather than reason 情感的（而非理性的）

• 例句 • He has a strong sentimental attachment to the place. 他对那个地方怀有深深的眷恋。

• 扩展 • **sentiment** *n.* 感伤，柔情

There's no place for sentiment in business. 做生意不能感情用事。

- 辨析 • **feeling，emotion，passion，sentiment** 都含"感情"、"感觉"的意思。

  feeling 指"生理上受到刺激产生的感觉，或对某事的主观的强烈的反应"；作"感情"解时，常用复数。如：

  I never like to hurt people's feelings. 我从不愿意伤害别人的感情。

  emotion指"精神上极强烈的感情"。如：

  The girl was overwhelmed with emotion and couldn't speak for a moment.
  这女孩非常激动，一时说不出话来。

  passion 语气比 emotion 强，特别用于"性爱或愤怒等使人失去理智或判断，以至不能自持"的情况。如：

  In a passion of rage he killed her. 一气之下，他把她杀了。

  sentiment含有较多的理智成分，特指"较长期稳定的高尚情感"，可指"优美的情操"，也可指"浪漫色彩的感情"或"矫揉造作的感情"。如：

  We are often swayed by sentiment. 我们经常受感情的支配。

5　anonymous

adj. unknown by name, not having a signature 匿名的

- 例句 • The money is donated by a local businessman who wishes to be anonymous.
  这笔钱是当地一位不愿透露姓名的企业家捐赠的。

  He had received more than twenty anonymous letters. 他已经收到二十多封匿名信了。

- 扩展 • **anonymity** *n.* 匿名，作者不明

  The defendants' anonymity was maintained until they were brought to court.

  被告人的姓名一直不公开，直到他们被带上法庭时才予以披露。

6　speculation

n. a guess about the possible causes or effects of sth. without knowing all the facts, or the guesses that you make 推测，推断

- 例句 • There was widespread speculation that she was going to resign. 人们纷纷猜测她将辞职。

  His private life is the subject of much speculation. 他的私生活引起诸多猜测。

- 扩展 • **speculate** *vt.* 推测，猜测

  It is useless to speculate why he did it. 对他为什么这么做妄加猜测毫无用处。

7　affectionate

adj. showing in a gentle way that you love sb. and care about them 充满深情的，关爱的

- 例句 • He is very affectionate towards his children. 他非常关爱他的孩子。

  Rosie gave her an affectionate kiss on each cheek. 罗西在她的脸蛋上每边亲昵地吻了一下。

- 扩展 • **affection** *n.* 喜爱，钟爱，爱情

  Children need lots of love and affection. 孩子需要多多疼爱和关怀。

8　symbol

n. sb./sth. that represents a particular quality or idea 象征，标志

- 例句 • White has always been a symbol of purity in Western cultures.
  在西方文化中，白色一向象征纯洁。

  The tree in the picture is the symbol of life and the snake is the symbol of evil.
  图中的树象征着生活，而蛇象征着邪恶。

- 扩展 • **symbolize** *vt.* 象征，代表

He came to symbolize his country's struggle for independence.

他逐渐成为祖国为争取独立而斗争的象征。

9　whatsoever

adv. (also whatever) used to emphasize a negative statement 无论什么

- 例句 • I won't back him whatsoever. 在任何情况下我都不会支持他。

There can be no doubt whatsoever about it. 这件事毫无疑问。

- 扩展 • **whatever** *pron.* 任何（事物），不管发生什么

They eat whatever they can find. 他们找到什么就吃什么。

Whatever the cause, the hate between these two men grew deeper and deeper.

不管是什么原因，他俩之间的仇恨越来越深了。

- 短语 • **or whatever** 或其他类似的事物

He'd have difficulty in learning any language—Greek, Chinese, or whatever.

他学习任何语言都会遇到困难，不论是希腊语、汉语、或是其他语。

10　whisper

vt. 1) to say sth. very quietly, using your breath rather than your voice 耳语，低语

- 例句 • She whispered the news in my ear. 她对我悄悄说了这个消息。

She whispered a warning to me and then disappeared. 她低声警告我一声就不见了踪影。

2) to suggest (sth.) or pass (information) secretly （私下）传说，秘密流传

- 例句 • It's whispered that he may resign. 有人私下传说他可能要辞职。

n. a very quiet voice, when you are whispering 耳语，低语

- 例句 • She spoke in a whisper, so I couldn't hear what she said. 她低声说话，所以我听不清她在说什么。

🌐 短语解析

1.　get/take/have (a day) off 请假（一天），休假（一天）

【例句】It is luxurious for me to have a day off. 休假一天对我来说是很奢侈的。

He can't afford to have a day off. 他没有请一天假的时间。

2.　come along 出现

【例句】When the right opportunity comes along, she will take it. 待适当的机会来临，她就能抓住。

Is she married? No. She is waiting for the right man comes along.

她结婚了吗？没有，她在等待着意中人的出现。

3.　go through 穿过，通过，经受

【例句】You should go through the official channels to get help instead of through private relationship.

你应该通过官方渠道而不是通过私人关系寻求帮助。

He's amazingly cheerful considering all that he's gone through.

鉴于他经历过的种种遭遇，他的乐天达观令人惊叹。

🌀 难句突破

1. (Para.2) *But in whatever form, the message is the same—"Will you be my valentine?"*

【解析】句子的主干是the message is the same；whatever在本句中作副词，表示"无论什么，不管什么"，相当于regardless of what。类似的用法又如：

Whatever happens, you know that I'll stand by you.

不论发生了什么，你知道我都会支持你。

You are right, whatever opinions may be held by others. 你做得对，别人怎么看不必理会。

【译文】但无论通过何种形式，所传递的信息都是一样的——"你愿做我的爱人吗？"

2. (Para.3) *Cupid is often printed on the card, he is a winged infant, not wearing anything, poised to shoot his arrow into a heart.*

【解析】本句的主干是Cupid is often printed on the card；其中not wearing anything和poised to shoot... 分别是现在分词和过去分词作伴随状语，对Cupid进行描述；而两个逗号之间的he is a winged infant是非正式插入语，在口语中和非正式的语体中，可以插入一个句子对要说的话进行补充和说明。

【译文】丘比特通常被印刷在卡片上，他的形象是一个长有翅膀的裸体婴儿，摆着一副随时准备把他的爱情之箭射向某人的心田的姿势。

3. (Para.3) *So on February 14th not only do we have pictures of the Christian St. Valentine but we also have pictures of the non-Christian Cupid, the Roman god of Love.*

【解析】本句是一个由not only... but (also)... 连接的并列句。

如果句子包含有两个或更多的主谓结构，就是并列句。并列句中的分句通常用一个并列连词来连接，其中各个分句的意义同等重要，联系密切，无从属关系。

①由and, not only... but (also)..., neither, nor, neither... nor...等词连接的并列句，在意思上主要对前一句作补充或引申，包括肯定和否定两方面的意义。如：

One day John was late, and his teacher was angry. 一天约翰迟到了，他的老师生气了。

（and连接并列句表示意义的增补、动作的先后、条件和结果等）

Not only is he himself interested in the subject, but also his students began to show interest in it. 不仅仅他自己对这个学科感兴趣，他的学生也开始对这个学科感兴趣了。（not only... but also... 表示"不但……而且"，重点强调的是后一成分，放在句首要倒装）

Neither does he work hard, nor does his brother. 不仅仅他工作不努力，他哥哥工作也不努力。（neither... nor表示否定意义的引申，放在句首要倒装）

②or, either... or... 连接并列句表示选择意义。如：

The children can go with us, or they can stay in. 孩子们可以跟我们走，或者留下。

Either you are mad, or I am. 不是你疯了，就是我疯了。

③but, yet, still, however, while, when等连接并列句，表示意义的转折及对比。如：

Mary was a nice girl, but she had one shortcoming. 玛丽是个好女孩，不过她有个缺点。

He said it was so, she was mistaken, however. 他说是这样的，然而她误会了。

He asked his father why he couldn't hatch chickens while hens could.

他问爸爸为什么他不能孵小鸡，而母鸡却可以。

④for，so，thus，therefore连接并列句表示因果关系。如：

Someone is coming, for the dog is barking. 有人来了，因为狗叫了。

My brother studied hard, thus he succeeded in passing the exam.

我哥哥学习努力，因此他成功地通过了考试。

【译文】因而在2月14日，我们不仅有基督教的"圣瓦伦丁"的画像，还有非基督教的罗马爱神丘比特的画像。

参考译文

情人节

2月14日这个节日复杂却又妙趣横生。首先，情人节不是一个休假日。没人得到一天的休假。情人节这一天，人们通常给自己所爱的人或想要从对方得到爱的人寄去充满浪漫情趣的卡片。这卡片叫"情人卡"。情人卡色彩鲜艳，常用心、花或鸟等图案装饰，里面还印有幽默亦或感伤的诗句。这些诗句传递的基本信息往往是"做我的情人吧"、"做我的'心上人'或'爱人'吧"。情人卡通常不署名，有时也可签上"猜猜我是谁"。收到卡片的人要猜是谁寄的。这样可以产生有趣的推测，这也正是情人卡的部分乐趣所在。

爱的讯息可以通过心形盒子包装的巧克力糖，或系有红丝带的一束鲜花来传达。但无论通过何种形式，所传递的信息都是一样的——"你愿做我的爱人吗？"

情人节的标志之一就是罗马爱情之神丘比特。丘比特通常被印刷在卡片上，他的形象是一个长有翅膀的裸体婴儿，摆着一副随时准备把他的爱情之箭射向某人的心田的姿势。他会把一支爱情之箭射入某个人的心中，而让这人立即坠入爱河，也许是和他（她）第一个见到的人。有时候，一支箭会穿过两颗心，把它们联结在一起。因而在2月14日，我们不仅有基督教的"圣瓦伦丁"的画像，还有非基督教的罗马爱神丘比特的画像。

但是我们大多数人所逐渐接受的有关情人节的传说是源于基督教徒。有个故事讲述的是一名基督徒，他名字的发音有些像"瓦伦丁"。他生活在公元250年前后。那时罗马皇帝克劳迪亚斯二世禁止罗马士兵以任何借口结婚。信奉基督教的夫妇就去找"瓦伦丁"主持结婚。"瓦伦丁"以基督教方式为他们举行婚礼。后来瓦伦丁被罗马皇帝发现，关进了监狱。传说他通过在树叶上做标记然后把叶子扔出监狱的窗外的方式给朋友传递信息，而这些叶子的形状就像是一颗心。

人们喜欢唱的情人节歌曲有很多。下面是其中一首：

让我叫你一声亲密爱人吧，

我已投入了你的情河，

请你悄悄地说一声，

你也爱上了我。

让爱之光照着我，

那是你眼中喷出的真挚情火，

让我叫你一声亲密爱人吧，

我已投入了你的情河。

语言拓展

日常用语

练习 选择补全对话的最佳答案。

1. 【答案】C

   【题解】当别人问到"想要些咖啡吗？"肯定回答应该是"Yes, please."否定回答应该是"No, thank you."

2. 【答案】B

   【题解】当别人问到"你想要做什么？"时，应该以"I want to..."（我想……）来作为回答。

3. 【答案】D

   【题解】当别人问到"你打算在这儿呆多久？"应该告知具体的时间。

4. 【答案】A

   【题解】当别人问到"你想呆在这儿吗？"肯定回答应该是"Yes, I do."否定回答应该是"No, I don't."

5. 【答案】A

   【题解】当别人询问"你准备做什么？"时，应该告知具体的计划。

阅读技巧

练习

1. 读下列句子，请猜出划线词的意思。

1) 【答案】乏味的

   【题解】由句中的 that is，可以根据定义推测词义。

   【译文】这部电影太乏味了，一点儿都没意思。

2) 【答案】熟练的

   【题解】adept 同 unskilled 是对比关系，因此可以根据对比关系推测词义。

   【译文】一个称职的管理者能立刻识别出工作中的熟手和生手。

3) 【答案】致癌基因

   【题解】这是根据同位语推测词义。

   【译文】早在20世纪70年代初期，研究者们取得了突破性进展，他们发现了致癌基因，这是一种能引起癌变的基因，是平时隐藏在身体正常细胞中的不活跃分子。

4) 【答案】青少年

   【题解】可以根据句中i.e.后面的阐释、说明推测词义。

   【译文】青春期，就是指介于童年和成年之间的那段时期，或短或长，主要依据个人的社会阅历以及社会对成熟和成年的界定。

5) 【答案】模糊的

   【题解】由句中的but，可知clear和hazy是对比关系，所以根据对比关系推测词义。

   【译文】就我看来，这项计划的主要观点还是很清楚，但是细节方面还有些模糊。

6) 【答案】坚决的

   【题解】这是根据阐释、说明推测词义，由句子的第二句话可推断划线词的意思。

   【译文】他是一个意志坚定的人，一旦他给自己定了目标，就绝不会轻言放弃。

2. 请选择一个最佳答案来解释划线词。

1) 【答案】A

　【题解】根据因果关系推测词义。

　【译文】由于找不到出口，这孩子一直在迷宫中徘徊，直到父亲找到她。

2) 【答案】B

　【题解】根据定义推测词义。

　【译文】这些数据资料，换句话说，也就是在研究中所收集的信息，只有经过仔细的核对才能保证其准确性。

3) 【答案】A

　【题解】根据因果关系推测词义。

　【译文】如果你站在出入口不让任何人通过，那你就会堵住出口。

4) 【答案】D

　【题解】根据阐释、说明推测词义。

　【译文】她向后猛拉我，拽着我向后退，直到我们都脱离轨道。

5) 【答案】C

　【题解】根据因果关系推测词义。

　【译文】那个夏天真是酷暑难耐，草地被阳光炙烤成焦黄色，花儿也都耷拉着脑袋。

写作技巧

练习 请根据提纲，以 Middle School Students Going Abroad 为标题写一篇120字左右的作文。

样文：

Middle School Students Going Abroad

In recent years, studying abroad has been popular in our country. More and more middle school students would like to go abroad to study through intermediary institutions. With the number of such students ever growing, it has raised a lot of concern—is it good or bad to study abroad?

Some people are in favor of it. According to them, if possible, young students should go abroad for study at their early age. Firstly, it is commonly accepted that the younger you are, the quicker and better you learn a foreign language. Most of the students staying abroad have good opportunities to master the foreign language. Secondly, as we know, competition in our national entrance examination for college is so fierce that a lot of students fail to get a chance to study further, while students who receive an advanced education abroad are more likely to fulfill their potential. Thirdly, on contrary to the popular notion, the life of young students studying abroad is actually full of hardship instead of idleness. They learn to live on their own and value what they have rather than being spoiled by their parents and grandparents at home.

However, just like one coin has two sides, studying abroad has its own disadvantages. For example, because of the lack of living experience and poor ability to take care of themselves, young students may feel lonely and homesick. In addition, high living expenses and tuition fees will become a heavy burden upon their parents.

Therefore, in my opinion, studying abroad is good but we should avoid making a blind decision. Whether or not to study abroad depends on one's personal and family situation. It is not right to just follow others. Remember, studying abroad is one way but not the only way to one's success.

语法知识

——语态（一）

练习 选择最佳答案补全下列句子。

1. 【答案】D

   【题解】本题考查被动句的进行时态，说明行为的进行。

   【译文】在城市的那一端，一条新路正在修建中。

2. 【答案】A

   【题解】take place 发生，不能用于被动式。

   【译文】夏季的犯罪率远远高于全年的其他时间。

3. 【答案】C

   【题解】be laughed at 被人嘲笑，被动句中用by来引导动作执行者。

   【译文】他被他最好的朋友们嘲笑。

4. 【答案】A

   【题解】有些及物动词（其主语大都指物）的主动语态可以表示被动意义，这些动词可以和 well，easily等副词连用。

   【译文】在夏季，空调都很畅销。

5. 【答案】C

   【题解】本题考查被动式的过去完成时态。

   【译文】当她得知这一消息后，赶忙跑回家告诉母亲。

6. 【答案】A

   【题解】本题考查情态动词的被动式用法。must be done 必须得……

   【译文】我认为你得在你的读音上花很多心思。

7. 【答案】D

   【题解】本题考查时间状语从句中动词主动语态的过去完成进行时态。

   【译文】在我等了将近半个钟头后，公共汽车终于来了。

8. 【答案】D

   【题解】动词make用于被动式，其后省略的不定式to要恢复于句中。主动语态：make do sth.；被动语态：be made to do sth.

   【译文】奴隶们得从早干到晚。

9. 【答案】D

   【题解】本题考查被动式的过去完成时态。

   【译文】他在午夜时分回到家，却发现有人破门而入。

10. 【答案】C

    【题解】本题考查被动式的过去时用法。

    【译文】昨天，彼得得到一张电影票。

每课一练

Part I   Vocabulary & Structure

Directions: *In this section there are 30 incomplete sentences. For each sentence there are four choices marked A, B, C and D. Choose the ONE that best completes the sentence.*

1. The new appointment of our president _____ from the very beginning of next semester.

   A) takes part   B) takes effect   C) takes place   D) takes turns

2. Although a teenager, Fred could _____ being told what to do and what not to do.

   A) persist   B) consist   C) insist   D) resist

3. Computer technology will _____ a revolution in business administration.

   A) bring around   B) bring out   C) bring about   D) bring up

4. The twentieth century has witnessed an enormous worldwide political, economic and cultural _____.

   A) transformation   B) tradition   C) transportation   D) transmission

5. Don't let the child play with scissors _____ he cuts himself.

   A) so that   B) now that   C) in case   D) only if

6. The teacher said that we _____ another chance some time next month if we failed in the exam.

   A) would be given   B) would give   C) will be given   D) were given

7. A really powerful speaker can _____ the feelings of the audience to the fever of excitement.

   A) work out   B) work up   C) work over   D) work at

8. _____, they immediately left the house.

   A) Being heard the noise   B) Hearing the noise

   C) They heard the noise   D) They were hearing the noise

9. He decided to make further improvements on the computer's design _____ the light of the requirements of customers.

   A) for   B) by   C) with   D) in

10. The traditional approach _____ with complex problems is to break them down into smaller, more easily managed problems.

    A) to dealing   B) in dealing   C) dealing   D) to deal

11. _____, Newton was thinking and thinking.

    A) He lied under the apple tree   B) Laying under the apple tree

    C) He laid under the apple tree   D) Lying under the apple tree

12. In the old days, children _____ by the mother because she did not work outside the house.

    A) took care of   B) were taking care of

    C) taken care of   D) were taken care of

13. "Do you know that girl with long hair?" "I don't think so, although she _____ me of someone else I know."

    A) remembers   B) recalls   C) reminds   D) suggests

14. If you want to know the times of buses, please _____ at the office.

    A) inform   B) inquire   C) require   D) request

15. No _____ woman would go alone to a bar like that one.

    A) respectful   B) respecting   C) respectable   D) respective

16. For centuries, the Atlantic Ocean kept the America from _____ by the people of Europe.

    A) discovering   B) being discovering

    C) being discovered   D) discovered

17. Her husband died in 1992, _____.

    A) left her with two children   B) being left her with two children

    C) leaving her with two children   D) being leaving her with two children

18. She ever being so kind to me. I felt _____ to help her when she was in trouble.

    A) generous   B) obliged   C) virtuous   D) detached

19. I'm glad _____ to look around your research center.

    A) to allow   B) having allowed   C) to be allowed   D) being allowed

20. He decided to go for a sailing holiday _____ the fact that he was usually seasick.

    A) in spite of   B) because of   C) in case of   D) as a result of

21. I regret having left the work unfinished, I _____ everything ahead carefully.

    A) should plan   B) should have planned

    C) planned   D) must plan

22. Ms. Wright demanded that the urgent report _____ on her desk by 5 p.m. today.

    A) should put   B) will be put   C) is put   D) be put

23. _____, Miss Brown decided to take a taxi.

    A) She thought she must be late   B) Being thought she must be late

    C) When thought she must be late   D) Thinking she must be late

24. The older New England villages have changed relatively little _____ a gas station or two in recent decades.

    A) in addition   B) except for   C) except to   D) besides

25. Herman's success is due to his hard work and his ability to _____ plans, which will get work done efficiently.

    A) fulfill   B) approve   C) employ   D) conduct

26. "You are very selfish. No _____ you are not the most important person in the world." Edgar said to his boss angrily.

    A) suspect   B) reason   C) doubt   D) cause

27. The soldier was accused of _____ the officials by rumoring that the enemy attacked.

    A) cheating   B) scolding   C) lying   D) punishing

28. Floods cause billions of dollars worth of property damage _____.

    A) annually   B) relatively   C) actually   D) comparatively

29. The director was critical _____ the way we were doing the work.

    A) at   B) in   C) of   D) with

30. At a press conference after the award ceremony, the 18-year-old girl spoke in a(n) _____ low voice.

    A) optionally   B) relatively   C) legally   D) identically

Part II   Reading Comprehension

Directions: *Read the following two passages. Answer the questions of each passage by choosing A), B), C) or D).*

Passage 1

Using a public telephone may well be one of the minor irritations of life, demanding patience, determination and a strong possibility of failure, together on occasion with considerable unpopularity.

The hopeful caller (shall we call him George?) waits till six o'clock in the evening to take advantage of the so-called "cheap rates" for a long-distance call. The telephone box, with two broken panes of glass in the side, stands at the junction of two main roads with buses, lorries and cars roaring past. It is pouring with rain as George joins a queue of four depressed-looking people. Time passes slowly and seems to come to a standstill while the person immediately before George carries on an endless conversation, pausing only to insert another coin every minute or so.

Eventually the receiver is replaced and the caller leaves the box. George enters and picks up one of the directories inside, only to discover that someone unknown has torn out the very page he needs. Nothing for it but to dial directory Enquiries, wait patiently for a reply down the number given.

At last George can go ahead with his call. Just as he is starting to dial, however, the door opens and an unpleasant-looking face peers in with the demand, "Can't you hurry up?" Ignoring such barbarity, George continues to dial and his unwanted companion withdraws. At last he hears the burr-burr of the ringing tone, immediately followed by rapid pips demanding his money, but he is now so upset that he knocks down the coins he has placed ready on the top of the box. Having at last located them, he dials again: the pips are repeated and he hastily inserts the coins. A cold voice informs him, "Grand Hotel, Chalfont Wells." "I've an urgent message for a Mr. Smith who is a guest in your hotel. Could you put me through to him? I'm afraid I don't know his room number."

The response appears less than enthusiastic and a long long silence follows. George inserts more coins. Then the voice informs him, "I've been trying to locate Mr. Smith but the hall porter reports having seen him leave about a minute ago."

Breathing heavily, George replaces the receiver, just as the knocking on the door starts again.

1. The main purpose of the passage is to provide _____.

   A) instructions about how to use a public call box

   B) advice about how to deal with public telephone problems

   C) criticism of the efficiency of telephone system

   D) an account of possible annoyances in using a public telephone

2. George can at least be thankful that _____.

   A) the telephone itself is working

   B) he can use the directory in the box to find the number

   C) the call box is in a convenient position

   D) he is able to give his message to the hotel receptionist

3. The reason for George having to dial a second time is that _____.

   A) he has used up all the money

   B) he can't find the number he wants in the directory

   C) he forgets to put the money in the box

   D) he has got to find the money to put in the box

4. How is George feeling when he completes his call?

A) He is very disappointed at missing his family and friends.

B) He feels hard to control his annoyance.

C) He is angry with himself for being so stupid.

D) He is depressed at the thought of having to try again to get through.

5. Which of the following is NOT TRUE about "cheap rate"?

A) People would like to use "cheap rate" to have a chat with a good friend in London.

B) People would like to use "cheap rate" to ask about a friend in hospital who has just had an operation.

C) People would like to use "cheap rate" to discuss the important project details with the colleagues.

D) People would like to use "cheap rate" to express Christmas greetings to cousins in Australia.

Passage 2

The writers of murder stories go to a great deal of trouble to keep us guessing right up to the end. In actual fact, people often behave more strangely in real life than they do in stories.

The following advertisement once appeared in a local newspaper: "An opportunity to earn $250 in a few minutes. A man who is willing to take chances is wanted for an out-of-the-ordinary job which can be performed only once." A reader found this offer very generous and applied to the advertiser, but a bit suspicious, he gave a false name. Soon afterwards, he received a reply. Enclosed in the envelope was a typed note instructing him to ring a certain number if he was still interested. He did so and learnt on the telephone that the advertiser wanted him to "get rid of somebody" and would discuss it more fully with him the next day. But the man told the police and from then on acted under their instructions. The police saw the two men meet and watched them as they drove away together. In the car the advertiser came to the point at once: he told the man he wanted him to shoot his wife. The reason he gave was that he was suffering from an incurable disease and wanted to live in a warmer country, but his wife objected to this. Giving the man some money, the advertiser told him to buy a gun and warned him to be careful of the dog which, though it would not bite, might attract attention. He also gave him a photograph of his wife so that he would be able to recognize her. After that, the advertiser suggested that the man should "do the job" next morning. Meanwhile, he would prepare his wife by telling her that a young man was going to call. After the murder, they would meet again outside a railway station and the money would be paid as arranged. The second meeting never took place, for the advertiser was arrested shortly afterwards and charged with attempting to persuade someone to murder his wife.

6. Which of the following statements can best express the meaning of the opening sentence?

A) The murder stories often prefer to leave the doubtful points to the readers.

B) While reading, the readers can easily guess who is the real murderer.

C) The heroes in the stories meet with a lot of trouble.

D) Usually the stories show the readers who is the murderer at the very beginning.

7. When a reader saw the advertisement _____.

A) he was sure he could get it

B) he could hardly believe it

C) he applied for the job with a false name

D) Both B and C

8. According to the passage, we CANNOT infer that _____.

A) the advertiser gave the man the first instruction through a letter

B) it was on the telephone that the man understood what the job was

C) the two men worked together to fulfill the plan

D) the man was scared when he knew what he was asked to do, so he reported the police at once

9. When the police received the report _____.

A) they arrested the advertiser at once

B) they sent a dog to keep watching on him

C) they didn't arrest him until they got enough evidence

D) they arrested him after his wife was killed

10. What did the advertisement in a local newspaper provide?

A) An unusual job with a high pay.　　　　B) A good job everyone wants to have.

C) A chance to be famous.　　　　D) A large sum of money.

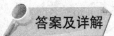 答案及详解

第一部分　词汇与结构

1. 【答案】B
   【题解】此题考查take 的词组辨析：take part (in) 参加，同participate (in)；take effect 生效，显露出效果；take place 发生；take turns 轮流。
   【译文】对校长的新任命在下学期初正式生效。

2. 【答案】D
   【题解】此题考查动词辨析：persist (in) 坚持不懈，执意；consist (of) 组成，包括，consist (in) 在于，存在于；insist (on) 坚持，坚决要求；resist 抵抗，抵制，后面接名词或动名词。
   【译文】虽然弗雷德只是一个十几岁的孩子，但他却能够自己决定什么该做，什么不该做。

3. 【答案】C
   【题解】此题考查bring 的词组辨析：bring around 说服，使信服，使恢复知觉；bring out 出版，激起；bring about 引起，导致；bring up 养育，提出（话题）。
   【译文】计算机技术将引发工商管理上的革命。

4. 【答案】A
   【题解】此题考查名词辨析：transformation 改变，变革；tradition 传统，惯例；transportation 运输，运输工具；transmission 播送，传送，传递。
   【译文】20世纪经历了全球政治、经济和文化的巨大变革。

5. 【答案】C
   【题解】so that 以便，引导目的、结果状语从句；now that 既然，引导原因状语从句；in case 以防，以免，引导目的状语从句；only if 只要，引导条件状语从句。
   【译文】不要让这孩子玩剪刀，以防他伤着自己。

6. 【答案】A
   【题解】主句谓语是过去时态，从句中next month提醒我们需要使用将来时态，根据句子意思，would be given 为被动态的过去将来时，是正确的选择。

【译文】老师说如果我们没有通过考试，下个月还会有一次机会。

7.【答案】B

【题解】此题考查work的词组辨析：work out 解决；work up 引起，激起；work over 彻底检查；work at 从事于。

【译文】一个真正有影响力的演讲者能够把观众的情绪激发到狂热的程度。

8.【答案】B

【题解】在没有and连接两个并列句的情况下，英语的一句话只能有一个谓语动词。原句的谓语动词是left，选项C和D都不能选；由于主语they和hear之间是主动关系，所以使用现在分词的主动形式，作时间状语。

【译文】听见噪音后，他们立刻离开了屋子。

9.【答案】D

【题解】in the light of 为固定搭配，意为：按照，根据。

【译文】他决定根据顾客的要求去进一步改进计算机的设计。

10.【答案】A

【题解】当名词approach的意思是"途径，方法，通路"时，与介词to构成"approach to + 名词/动名词"结构，表示"解决……的方法，进入……的途径"等。

【译文】处理复杂问题的传统方法是将其分解为更小、更容易解决的问题。

11.【答案】D

【题解】同第8题，缺少分词结构作时间状语，而lie的现在分词形式是lying，只能选D。

【译文】躺在苹果树下，牛顿一直都在思考问题。

12.【答案】D

【题解】根据题意，这句话的谓语动词应该使用被动语态，被动语态的构成是"be+动词的过去分词"形式，只能选D。

【译文】在过去，孩子们都是由母亲照顾，因为她不用外出工作。

13.【答案】C

【题解】此题考查动词辨析：remember 记得，常指"可以想起以前发生的事情"；recall与remember的意思相近，但较为正式，并且常指"自愿地回忆"；remind sb. of sth.是固定搭配，意指"使想起某事或某人，提醒某人做某事"；suggest 暗示，建议。

【译文】"你认识那个长发女孩吗？""不认识，尽管她使我想起我认识的另外一个人。"

14.【答案】B

【题解】此题考查动词辨析：inform 通知，告知，常用于短语inform sb. of sth.；inquire 询问，查询，常用于短语inquire sth. of sb.；require（正式）要求，命令；request（礼貌地）要求或请求。

【译文】如果想知道公共汽车的发车时间，请到办事处查询。

15.【答案】C

【题解】respectful adj. 尊敬的；respecting prep. 关于，至于；respectable adj. 受人尊敬的；respective adj. 各自的。

【译文】没有一个受人尊敬的妇女会独自去那样的酒吧。

16.【答案】C

【题解】介词后面都应该跟名词或动名词；根据题意，应该使用动名词的被动态形式，即being discovered，只能选C。

【译文】数个世纪以来，正是由于大西洋的存在，美洲才没有被欧洲人发现。

17. 【答案】C

【题解】根据句子结构，这里需要现在分词作状语，表伴随状态。句子主语同动词leave之间是主动关系，因此应该使用现在分词的主动态形式，即leaving，只能选C。

【译文】她的丈夫于1992年去世，就留下了她和两个孩子。

18. 【答案】B

【题解】generous 慷慨的；be obliged to do 有义务，应该；virtuous 善良的，有道德的，贞洁的；detached 冷静的，客观的。

【译文】她曾经对我很好，所以当她遇到麻烦的时候，我有责任帮她。

19. 【答案】C

【题解】be glad to do sth. 是固定搭配，不定式后面跟动词原型；根据题意，这里应该用不定式的被动态形式，即to be allowed，只能选C。

【译文】真高兴能获许参观你们的研发中心。

20. 【答案】A

【题解】in spite of 不管，不顾；because of 因为；in case of 假如，如果发生；as a result of 由于……。

【译文】就算会时常晕船，他还是决定要去航海旅行。

21. 【答案】B

【题解】根据题意，这里应该使用虚拟语气，should have done sth.表示"原本应该……"。

【译文】我真后悔没把工作做完，我应该提前计划好每件事。

22. 【答案】D

【题解】由demand引导的从句应该使用虚拟语气，其谓语动词应采用(should) do sth.的形式；而根据题意，从句谓语动词又需要用被动语态，因此只能选D。

【译文】怀特夫人要求今天下午5点前将这份亟需的报告放在她桌上。

23. 【答案】D

【题解】同第8题，现在分词作时间状语。

【译文】想到要迟到了，布朗小姐决定搭乘出租车。

24. 【答案】B

【题解】in addition同besides，此外，而且；except for 除了……以外，指除去整体中的一个细节；没有except to这样的表达。

【译文】近几十年来，古老的新英格兰村庄除了建了一两座加油站外变化不大。

25. 【答案】C

【题解】此题考查动词辨析：fulfill 履行；approve 赞成，同意，批准，通常与of搭配；employ 利用，雇用；conduct 指导，指挥。

【译文】赫尔曼的成功归因于他的努力工作以及他善于计划，而这些计划能使工作得以有效地完成。

26. 【答案】C

【题解】此题考查名词辨析：suspect 嫌疑犯；reason 理由；doubt 怀疑，疑问，no doubt 无疑；cause 理由，原因。

【译文】"你真自私。毫无疑问，你并不是世界上最重要的人物。"埃德加愤怒地对老板说。

27.【答案】A

【题解】此题考查动词辨析：cheat 欺骗；scold 责骂；lie 撒谎；punish 惩罚。

【译文】这个士兵因欺骗长官说敌人来进攻了而受到指控。

28.【答案】A

【题解】此题考查副词辨析：annually 每年；relatively 相对地，比较地；actually 实际上；comparatively 相对地，相比较地。

【译文】洪水每年都造成价值几十亿美元的财产损失。

29.【答案】C

【题解】critical 吹毛求疵的，批评的，决定性的，重要的；常用搭配：be critical of 对……不满。

【译文】主任对我们做这项工作的方法十分不满。

30.【答案】B

【题解】此题考查副词辨析：optionally 可选择地；relatively 相对地，比较地；legally 法律上地；identically 相同地，完全一样地。

【译文】在颁奖仪式后举行的新闻发布会上，那个18岁女孩发言的声音比较低。

第二部分　阅读理解

1.【答案】D

【题解】主旨题。从全篇文章内容来看，其主要目的不是关于如何使用公共电话，因为几乎人人都会使用公用电话，没有必要进行整篇论述，进行指导。也不是给人们提供如何处理公用电话问题的建议，而是使用时可能遇到的种种麻烦，并且举出了实例加以说明。文章一开头就提出了这个问题，第一个句子就是主题句，也是本文的主题思想，包含了本文的主要目的——证明使用公用电话时可能遇到的烦恼。因此选D。

2.【答案】A

【题解】细节题。本题可采用排除法。根据文章的第三段中 "George enters and picks up one of the directories inside, only to discover that someone unknown has torn out the very page he needs. Nothing for it but to dial directory Enquiries…"（当乔治走进电话亭拿起一本电话簿，才发现不知谁已把他需要的那一页给撕掉了，他不得不拨打问询处）。显然B项（他可以使用电话号码簿查号码）不符合题意。根据文章的第二段中 "The telephone box, with two broken panes of glass in the side, stands at the junction of two main roads with buses, lorries and cars roaring past"（电话亭设在来往汽车轰鸣嘈杂的主干道交汇处，玻璃窗也是破损的），这显然不是一个合适和方便的位置。所以C项不合题意。根据第四段和第五段，我们可以得知由于种种原因乔治未能向旅馆中的接待员传达到他的口信，所以D项也是错误的。纵观全文，有一点是肯定的，电话本身并没有停止工作，这起码能够给乔治一点点安慰，故A为本题的正确答案。

3.【答案】D

【题解】细节题。根据文章第四段中 "At last he hears the burr-burr of the ringing tone, immediately followed by rapid pips demanding his money, but he is now so upset that he knocks down the coins he has placed ready on the top of the box. Having at last located them, he dials again…"（最后他听到电话铃音的嗡嗡声，马上接着是急速的嘟嘟声，要他投币。但是由于他此刻非常懊恼，以致于把放在箱子上准备投进去的钱币弄掉了下来，因此，他不得不找到那些钱币投进箱子后再次拨号）。所以答案选D。

4. 【答案】B

【题解】推断题。乔治打完电话后的心情可以在文章的最后一句话中充分体现出来 "Breathing heavily, George replaces the receiver, just as the knocking on the door starts again" （乔治深深地吸了一口气，把话筒放好，这时扣门声又响了）。打电话中遇到了这么多不愉快的事情，自然不会给乔治带来什么愉快和欣慰，这种烦恼的心情从 "重重地吸了一口气" 中表现出来，故B符合本题题意。

5. 【答案】C

【题解】推断题。根据文章第一段中 "Using a public telephone may well be one of the minor irritations of life, demanding patience, determination and a strong possibility of failure, together on occasion with considerable unpopularity" 打公用电话（所谓的 "便宜价" 电话）是非常令人懊恼的，因为很难打出去，既费时又费力。由此可见对于一般性的问题可能会打 "便宜" 电话，例如和朋友聊天，问候病人或表示节日祝贺等，如A、B、D项中所述的情况。但对于重大事情或者紧急事情，人们就不会图 "便宜" 而耗掉自己的宝贵时间。所以C为正确答案，人们愿意打 "便宜" 电话和同事商讨重要的项目细节——这种说法是错误的。

6. 【答案】A

【题解】细节题。文章第一句的意思是凶杀案故事的作者总是喜欢留下一系列的疑点，让读者不断猜测，一直到故事的结局。理解该句要抓住 "keep us guessing right up to the end"，因此选A。

7. 【答案】D

【题解】细节题。根据文章的第二段中 "A reader found this offer very generous and applied to the advertiser, but a bit suspicious, he gave a false name" （有读者发现赏金很诱人，于是联系了打广告的人，但由于心存疑虑，他使用了假名），因此选D。

8. 【答案】C

【题解】细节题。选项A在第二段第四句可找到根据 "Enclosed in the envelope was a typed note instructing him to ring a certain number if he was still interested"；选项B在第二段第五句可找到根据 "He did so and learnt on the telephone that the advertiser wanted him to 'get rid of somebody' and would discuss it more fully with him next day"；选项D在第二段第六句可找到根据 "But the man told the police and from then on acted under their instructions"；只有选项C在文中毫无根据。

9. 【答案】C

【题解】细节题。根据文章最后一句，我们可以得知警察是在掌握所有证据之后才逮捕了那个买通凶手的人。

10. 【答案】A

【题解】细节题。根据文章第二段第一句中 "an out-of-the-ordinary job"（不平凡，不一般的工作），因此选 A。

6 Generation Gap

单元导读

　　成长背景不同的两代人在价值观念、思维方式上都有很大的不同，这一点在孩子和父母的关系上有明显的体现。老年人留念传统文化，而年轻人渴望创新；老年人乐于回顾，而年轻人喜欢展望；老年人严守着传统的严肃生活，而年轻人欣赏现代的生活方式。孩子们总是抱怨自己的父母思想守旧，而父母有时也看不惯孩子们的言行。父母希望孩子能听话，可孩子们却不管那一套。他们渴望能成为生活的主人：选择朋友、安排课程、规划未来、经济独立等等。而这些在父母的眼里都是不可能实现的。所有这些就是我们所说的"代沟"。

　　代沟的形成不仅仅是因为两代人在行为方式、道德标准等方面存在差异，缺乏沟通也是主要原因之一。所以，愈合这条鸿沟更多的取决于两代人之间的沟通。

课文精讲

文章导读

　　还记得你在春日迤逦的风景里放风筝的情景吗？那根连接着风筝的线，是应该紧紧握在手里，还是无私地将它放开？放出去的风筝、握在手里的线，悄悄地诉说着一个父亲与孩子的故事。

背景知识

　　社区学院：美国所谓的"Community College"，中文称为"社区大学"或"社区学院"，也可称为"两年制大学"。社区大学两年毕业后，学校会颁给学生副学士学位，即"Associate Degree"，如果学生想继续深造进修，也可以转学进入四年制大学，申请大三的课程，继续后两年的大学课程，因此越来越多国际学生申请美国社区大学，他们将社区大学视为进入四年制大学拿学位的一个重要跳板。另外，社区大学两年修课的主要目的也是为了帮学生打好之后在专业领域上进修的基础。

文章写作风格及结构

本文为一篇记叙文，作者站在一个孩子们的父亲的角度，向读者剖析了一位父亲面对孩子们走向自由和独立时的心理挣扎。

Parts 部分	Paragraphs 段落	Main Ideas 大意
Part I	1—3	When the author's children were young, he was sure he would never stand in the way of their becoming free and independent. 当作者的孩子都还年轻的时候，他确定他决不会成为儿女们走向自由和独立的绊脚石。
Part II	4—16	Fifteen years later, when the author's daughter and son tried to make their own decisions, the author wanted them to change their decisions, but eventually he realized he should let go of his pride and sit back and enjoy watching them soar. 15年后，当作者的女儿和儿子试图自己作决定时，作者却想要改变他们的决定。但最后作者还是意识到他应该不再那么看重自己的面子，而是以平和的心态高高兴兴地看着他们展翅高飞。

词汇点睛

1 loosen

vt. to make sth. less tight or less firmly fastened 放松，松开

- 例句 • He loosened his collar and tie. 他松开衣领和领带。

  The screws have loosened. 螺丝松了。

- 扩展 • **loose** *adj.* 松的，宽松的

  A screw has come loose. 有颗螺丝松了。

2 bind

vt. 1) to form a strong emotional or economic connection between two people, countries, etc. 联系，连接

- 例句 • Their shared experiences overseas helped to bind them together.

  海外的共同经历使他们结合在一起。

  A common history binds people together. 共同的历史把人们联系在了一起。

  2) to tie sb. so that they cannot move or escape 绑，捆

- 例句 • They bound my arms and legs with rope. 他们用绳子绑住我的手脚。

3 release

vt. 1) to let sb. or sth. go free 释放，松开

- 例句 • He was released from prison yesterday. 他昨天从监狱放出来了。

  He released the handbrake and drove off. 他松开手闸开车走了。

  2) to let news or official information be known and printed 发布，发行

- 例句 • No details of the murder were released to the press. 没有向报界公布谋杀案的细节。

4　independent

adj. able to do things by yourself in your own way, without needing help or advice from other people 独立的，自主的

• 例句 • Some of the students have an ability of independent thinking. 有些学生具有独立思考的能力。

An independent school is not controlled by the state. 独立的学校不受政府的控制。

This is independent of man's will. 这是不以人的意志为转移的。

5　pursue

vt. 1) to continue doing an activity or trying to achieve sth. over a lengthy period of time 继续努力去完成

• 例句 • He has been pursuing the study of physics for nearly 30 years.

他从事物理学的研究将近30年了。

She plans to pursue a career in politics. 她计划要在政界有一番作为。

2) to chase or follow someone or sth., in order to catch them, attack them, etc. 追赶，追踪

• 例句 • The police pursued the stolen vehicle along the highway. 警察沿着公路追赶那辆被盗的车辆。

• 扩展 • **pursuit** *n.* 追求，寻找；追赶，追逐

He went to the south in pursuit of work. 他去南方寻找工作了。

The pursuit of the murderer covered three provinces. 对杀人犯的追踪跨越了三个省。

6　attend

vt. 1) to go regularly to a school, church, etc. 上（学，教堂）

• 例句 • I am the first child in my family to attend college. 我是我们家第一个上大学的孩子。

2) to go to an event such as a meeting or a class 出席，参加

• 例句 • Who attended the meeting? 谁出席了会议？

7　transfer

vt. to move from one place, school, job, etc., to another 转学，转移，调动

• 例句 • The head office has been transferred from Chicago to New York.

总部办公室已由芝加哥移至纽约。

He is going to be transferred to another school soon. 他不久就要转到另一所学校。

8　reason

vi. to talk to sb. in an attempt to persuade them to be more sensible 劝导，讲道理

• 例句 • I reasoned with her on the matter for an hour, but she would not change her mind.

我就这件事和她理论了一个小时，但她不肯改变主意。

He reasoned with me for an hour about the foolishness of decision.

他同我争辩了一个小时，想让我明白我的决定是多么荒唐。

9　scarce

adj. if sth. is scarce, there is not very much of it available 缺乏的，稀有的

• 例句 • Food is scarce because of drought. 旱灾引起了食物匮乏。

Some animals are becoming scarce in Africa. 在非洲，有些动物越来越难得见到。

10　perform

vt. 1) to do sth., especially sth. difficult or useful 做，执行

• 例句 • He performed his experiment over and over again. 他把实验做了一次又一次。

He has performed all his duties. 他已履行了他全部的职责。

2) to do sth. to entertain people, for example by acting a play or playing a piece of music 演出，表演

• 例句 • Harry performed a little dance on the stage. 哈利在舞台上表演了一个小舞蹈。

The singer has never performed in New York before. 这位歌唱家以前从未在纽约演出过。

• 扩展 • **performance** *n.* 演出，表演；履行，执行

This is the old actor's last performance. 这是那位老演员的最后一次演出。

He is faithful in the performance of his duties. 他忠心耿耿地履行自己的职责。

11 unconvinced

adj. feeling uncertain that sth. is true 不信服的

• 例句 • However, many scientists remain unconvinced that he can succeed.

但是许多科学家仍然不相信他能够成功。

They are unconvinced of his decision. 他们对他的决定并不信服。

• 扩展 • **convinced** *adj.* 确信……的

I am convinced of the truth of my reasoning. 我确信自己的推理是正确的。

You will soon be convinced that she is right. 你不久就会相信她是对的。

12 former

adj. happening or existing before, but not now 以前的，从前的

• 例句 • He is my former classmate. 他是我从前的同班同学。

She is back to her former self again. 她又恢复到她从前的样子。

n. the first of two people or things that you have just mentioned 前者

• 例句 • Of the two possibilities, the former seems more likely.

在这两种可能性中，前者似乎更可能。

13 hesitation

n. the action of pausing before saying or doing sth. because you are nervous or not sure 犹豫，踌躇

• 例句 • He joined the army without the least hesitation. 他毫不迟疑地参军了。

After some hesitation one of them began to speak. 在一阵犹豫后，他们当中的一人开始说话了。

• 扩展 • **hesitate** *vi.* 犹豫，踌躇

Mike hesitated a moment before replying. 迈克犹豫了一会儿才作出回答。

Don't hesitate to contact me if you need any more information.

如果你想知道更多的情况，请及时与我联系。

🔖 短语解析

1. yearn for 渴望，向往

【例句】The people yearned for peace, and the chance to rebuild their lives.

人民渴望和平，渴望得到重建生活的机会。

He yearns for someone to talk to. 他渴望能有个人聊聊天。

2. in the distance 在远处

【例句】Church bells rang in the distance. 教堂的钟声在远处响起。

We can see the ancient ruins in the distance. 我们能看到远处的古建筑废墟。

3. stand/get in the way of 阻碍，阻止

【例句】Your social life must not stand in the way of your studies.

你的社交活动绝不能妨碍到你的学习。

He was angry at Mary for getting in the way of his dreams coming true.

他因为玛丽阻碍了他梦想的实现而忌恨她。

4. talk sb. out of sth. 劝说或说服某人放弃……

【例句】Can't you talk them out of selling the house? 你能否劝他不要卖掉房子？

Don't let anyone talk you out of pursuing your dream.

不要让任何人使你放弃梦想。

5. go at sth. 着手做，努力去做

【例句】They went at the job with enthusiasm. 他们干劲十足地做这项工作。

Once he decided to do something, he went at it for all he was worth.

他一旦决定要干什么事，就拼命地干起来。

6. talk some sense into sb. 劝某人理智行事

【例句】She hoped the teacher would be able to talk some sense into her son.

她希望老师能让她的儿子理智行事。

7. settle in/into... （使）习惯于……

【例句】It was the first time she had left home, so it took her a while to settle in.

她是第一次离开家，所以过了好一阵子才习惯。

To help you settle into your new work, here is the schedule for the first day.

为了帮助你适应新工作，这是第一天的工作安排。

8. be stuck in 陷入（困境等）

【例句】The car was stuck in the mud. 车陷入了泥地。

I'm stuck in the traffic jam. 我被堵车困住了。

9. sink in 被理解，被领悟

【例句】He paused a moment for his words to sink in. 他停顿了一下，以便让大家理解他的话。

It still hasn't sunk in that I'll never see her again.

我不会再和她见面了，但她还没有理解到这一点。

10. fix one's eyes on... 盯着……看，注视

【例句】She fixed her eyes on Mr. Johnson's face and waited for his answer.

她盯着约翰逊的脸等着他的回答。

Every eye was fixed on the new girl. 所有的眼睛都注视着这位新来的女孩。

11. all at once 突然

【例句】All at once there was a loud banging on the door. 突然传来了砰砰的撞门声。

12. let go of 放开，释放

【例句】Let go of his throat, as he was having difficulty breathing.

别掐着他的脖子了，他已经呼吸困难了。

Clare was in trouble, but he would not let go of Jenny.

克莱尔惹上了麻烦，但他也绝不会放过珍妮。

难句突破

1. (Para.1) *Seeing their excitement as the kite rose over the treetops, I wondered how I would feel when the day came that they yearned for their own freedom.*

【解析】本句的主干是I wonder how…，其中how引导宾语从句；when引导时间状语从句，而 seeing their excitement... over the treetops是现在分词短语作状语，表示时间。

【译文】看着风筝飞过树梢时孩子们的兴奋劲儿，我不禁在想，当有一天他们渴望独立自主时，我会是什么样的心情。

2. (Para. 2) *Back home that evening I wrote a poem called* Flying Kites.

【解析】在本句中back作时间状语，词性为副词，表示"（回到）以前的位置、状况或阶段"。类似的用法又如：

My aunt is just back from Paris. 我姨妈刚从巴黎回来。

Looking at her old photographs brought back a lot of memories. 老照片使她回忆起很多往事。

【译文】当晚回家后我写了一首诗，题为《放风筝》。

3. (Para.7) *None of my reasoning made any difference.*

【解析】none + of sb./sth. 可以用以预指后文，或复指前文的复数名词或代词、不可数名词或代词。本句中的用法是预指后文的不可数名词reasoning。如：

We had three cats once——none of them is/are alive now. 我们曾有三只猫——现在一个活着的也没有了。（复指前文的复数名词或代词）

I wanted some string but there was none in the house. 我需要一些绳子，但家里一根也没有。（复指前文的不可数名词或代词）

None of the guests wants/want to stay. 客人中没有一个想留下的。（预指后文的复数名词或代词）

None of this money is mine. 这笔钱没有一点是我的。（预指后文的不可数名词或代词）

【译文】我所有的劝导都毫无作用。

4. (Para.14) *Shame suddenly silenced me.*

【解析】本句中的silence是名词活用成动词表示"使……沉默"，在文学性的著作中，常常会用这种用法，使行文更加生动。如：

Try to silence a noisy crowd! 设法使喧闹的人群静下来！

This insult silenced him completely. 他受此侮辱后一言不发了。

【译文】我顿时羞愧得哑口无言。

参考译文

学会放手

刘易斯·摩尔

阳春三月一个有风的早晨，那时我的孩子还小，我带他们到一片开阔地上去放风筝。看着风筝飞过树梢时孩子们那兴奋劲儿，我不禁在想，当有一天他们渴望独立自主时我会是什么样的心情。

当晚回家后我写了一首诗，题为《放风筝》。诗中一位父亲把风筝放上天，然后把线交给儿子，嘱咐他要把线握紧。孩子放了几分钟风筝，然后突然松手让它飞走了。看着风筝越飞越高，小孩的眼中充满快乐，直到最后风筝变成了遥远天际一个舞动的斑点。父亲意识到，最终他也得松开拴在他和儿子之间的那根线。他想："我也会那样无私地将线放开吗？"

写完这首诗，我有点自鸣得意。我是绝不会成为儿女们走向自由和独立的绊脚石的。

15年后，我女儿琳达到了接受高等教育的年龄。我希望她到我和妻子任教的那所当地社区学院就读，但她却报考了100多英里以外的一所州立大学。

之后，我们的儿子加里作出了一个更加让人难以接受的决定。从社区学院毕业后，他转入了一所州立大学。但是大三刚上了一半，加里就宣布他要退学。他想回家，找份工作，然后跟他的未婚妻结婚。

我尽力说服他放弃这个念头。这个想法将会是个可怕的错误。他是个优秀的学生，能成大事。接受教育已彻底改变了我。我儿子怎么可能认识不到教育的重要性呢？

我所有的劝导都毫无作用。那个学期末加里就退学回家了。这令我相当失望。

我们这个山区小镇工作很难找，但他还是设法在一个苗圃谋到了一份工作，并投入了他一贯的热情。事实上，他喜欢在室外摆弄植物并且似乎精于此道。但我仍然无法释怀，堂堂大学教授的儿子居然在做一份连高中辍学生都能胜任的工作，算是哪门子事呢？

随着婚期日益临近，我最后一次努力劝他理智行事。我问他："你是否重新考虑过回学校？"

"没怎么想过。"加里说。

我不断地说出自己的观点。一旦他有了家庭，有了一份稳定的工作，他就再也回不了学校了。这会让他后悔一辈子的。他会因此而永远无法进入上流社会的行列。加里仍然没被说服。于是我决定来点硬的。

"看吧，"我说，"几年后你就会与你高中的同学重聚了，而他们都成了医生、律师、工程师和教师。"我稍事停顿，好让他能领悟我的话，然后问道："你觉得你能应付那种局面吗？"

"是的，爸爸，"他毫不迟疑地答道，"我能应付。"然后他咧开嘴笑了，盯着我的眼睛说："但是真正的问题是：你能吗？"

我顿时羞愧得哑口无言。我考虑的不是我的儿子，我考虑的是我自己以及我的朋友们会怎么想。问题不在于加里的自尊，而在于我的自尊。突然间我回忆起我的那首诗和诗中提出的问题："我也会那样无私地将线放开吗？"很明显我没有。我把儿子拴到了我自己的愿望和期待上。

就在那一刻，我明白我得放手了。加里已经长大，能够自己作主了。当然，大学教育非常重要，但也许上帝已经为我儿子作了别样的安排。

现在加里在这个城市工作，事业有成。他是好丈夫、好父亲。我为现在的他感到非常自豪。自从不再那么看重自己的面子以来，我就能以平和的心态高高兴兴地看着儿子展翅高飞了。

习题全解

文章大意

1. 根据课文用合适的词填空。

【答案】 1) fly　　　　2) poem　　3) loosen　　4) stand　　　　5) enrolled

6) schooling/studies　7) desires　8) pride　9) choices/decisions　10) proud

【译文】　　阳春三月一个有风的早晨作者带着他的孩子们去野外放风筝。回家以后写了一首题为《放风筝》的诗。诗中，一位父亲也是和他的儿子去放风筝，当父亲看到儿子让风筝在空中翱翔的时候，他意识到最终他也得松开他和儿子之间的那根线。当作者写完这首诗，他确信自己是绝不会成为儿女们走向自由和独立的绊脚石的。

　　　　然而几年后，当女儿报考一所州立大学时，作者却期望她能在当地的社区学院就读。之后，当儿子决定要退学，找份工作，回家结婚的时候，他又试图说服儿子放弃这个念头。在同儿子的争论中，他突然意识到了是他试图把儿子拴在自己的愿望和期待上。他决定放弃自己的自尊，让儿子作自己的决定。最终，他的儿子成为了一位出色的丈夫和父亲，作者为现在的儿子感到自豪。

文章细节

根据课文回答问题。

【答案】

1) He was wondering how he would feel when the day came that his children yearned for their own freedom. (Para. 1)

2) The father realizes that eventually he'll have to loosen the tie that binds him to his son. (Para. 2)

3) He felt a little smug because he was sure he would never stand in the way of his children becoming free and independent. (Para. 3)

4) The author expected his daughter to attend the local community college where he and his wife taught, but his daughter enrolled in a state college which was more than 100 miles away. (Para. 4)

5) He decided to find a job and marry his fiancée without finishing his schooling. (Para. 5)

6) He thought it was a terrible mistake for his son to give up his education, which he considered very important for his son's career and social position. (Para. 6)

7) He tried to make him change his idea and go on with his schooling. (Paras. 9-12)

8) He realized he was not thinking about his son but his own pride, and he should let his son make his own choices. (Paras. 14-15)

【译文】

1) [问题] 当作者在和孩子们一起放风筝的时候他想到了什么？

[答案] 他在想，当有一天他的孩子们渴望独立自主时他会是什么样的心情。

2) [问题] 在作者诗作《放风筝》中的那个父亲认识到了什么？

[答案] 那个父亲认识到最终他不得不松开拴在他和儿子之间的那根线。

3) [问题] 当作者完成诗作时感觉如何？为什么？

[答案] 他觉得有点自鸣得意，因为他确信自己绝不会成为儿女们走向自由和独立的绊脚石。

4) [问题] 作者希望自己的女儿读哪所大学？而他的女儿又是怎么做的？

[答案] 作者希望他的女儿到他和妻子任教的那所当地社区学院就读，但女儿却报考了100多英里以外的一所州立大学。

5) [问题] 在加里上大三上了一半的时候他作了什么决定？

[答案] 他决定放弃学业，找份工作，和他的未婚妻结婚。

6) [问题] 作者对他儿子的决定看法如何？

[答案] 他觉得儿子放弃学业将会是个可怕的错误，他认为教育对儿子的事业和社会地位而言是非常重要的。

7) [问题] 作者如何对待儿子的决定？

[答案] 他试图使儿子改变主意，继续学业。

8) [问题] 作者最终认识到了什么？

[答案] 他认识到他不是在为儿子着想，而是放不下自己的自尊，他应该放手，让儿子自己作决定。

词汇练习

1. 请用下面所给词汇或短语的适当形式填写句子。

1) 【答案】released

　【译文】他抓住了我的手却又很快放开了。

2) 【答案】pursuing

　【译文】史密斯教授致力于太空研究近30年了。

3) 【答案】transfer

　【译文】他希望转到艺术学院。

4) 【答案】hesitation

　【译文】他回答我问题前有一点迟疑。

5) 【答案】Eventually

　【译文】最终她得到了一份工作并搬到了伦敦。

6) 【答案】independent

　【译文】他的目标是在20岁时能不靠父母独立生活。

7) 【答案】enrolled

　【译文】比尔报名参加了一个三个月的英语培训课程。

8) 【答案】permanent

　【译文】交通事故对她的视力造成了永久的损害。

9) 【答案】bind

　【译文】两人在战争中的共同经历将他们联系在了一起。

10) 【答案】performing

　【译文】她由于未尽职而被解雇。

2. 在下面空格中填入适当的介词或副词。

1) 【答案】into

　【译文】查理并没花太长时间就适应了新工作。

2) 【答案】to

　【译文】无论她做什么都对我们的计划没有影响。

3)【答案】at

【译文】他们对这份工作投入了巨大的热情。

4)【答案】in

【译文】公共汽车陷在了泥里。

5)【答案】on

【译文】她盯着汤姆森先生的脸，等待着他的回答。

6)【答案】into

【译文】她希望他的父亲能够劝他理智行事。

7)【答案】for

【译文】人们渴望和平，渴望得到机会重建破碎的生活。

8)【答案】in

【译文】没人能阻碍进程。

9)【答案】in

【译文】远处是史密斯先生。

10)【答案】of

【译文】当妈妈带小玛丽去上学时，小玛丽不想放开妈妈的手。

3. 请学习下面表格中的构词，猜猜意思，然后选择适当的词再用其正确形式填写句子。

en- -en	Prefix en- and the suffix -en can be used to form verbs, meaning "to make sb. or sth. be in a particular state or have a particular quality". （前缀en-和后缀-en可以与形容词、名词一起构成新的动词。表示"让某人、某物处于一种特殊的状态或具有某种特别的性能"。）			
	large (大的)	enlarge (扩大)	dark (黑色的)	darken (使变黑)
	courage (勇气)	encourage (鼓励)	broad (宽的，广泛的)	broaden (使……变宽)
	sure (确信的)	ensure (保证，担保)	bright (明亮的)	brighten (使发亮)
	danger (危险)	endanger (使危险)	strength (力量，力气)	strengthen (加强，巩固)
	able (有能力的)	enable (使能够)	loose (宽松的)	loosen (放松)
	rich (富裕的)	enrich (使富裕)	weak (虚弱的)	weaken (削弱)

1)【答案】enable/encourage

【译文】这个项目旨在鼓励年轻人找到工作。

2)【答案】loosened

【译文】杰克脱下外套，松开领带。

3)【答案】weakened

【译文】朱莉娅由于长期患病而变得虚弱。

4)【答案】ensure

【译文】为保证他们的安全已经采取了所有必要的措施。

5)【答案】enrich

【译文】教育能极大地丰富你的生活。

6)【答案】brightened

【译文】当听到自己获得一等奖时，他脸上神采奕奕。

7) 【答案】strengthen

【译文】大学希望加强与当地政府的联系。

8) 【答案】enlarged

【译文】我要去放大两张照片。

9) 【答案】darkened

【译文】天色暗下来，有雨点落了下来。

10) 【答案】encouraged

【译文】我想感谢每个鼓励和支持过我的人。

语法结构

1. 仿照例句改写下列句子。

1) 【答案】After saying goodbye to us, Father went out.

【译文】父亲和我们说完再见就出去了。

2) 【答案】After clearing the table, Tina washed the dishes.

【译文】收拾完桌子，蒂娜洗了碟子。

3) 【答案】After quitting his job, the man opened a grocery store.

【译文】辞掉工作后，这人开了一家杂货铺。

4) 【答案】After mixing the flour and butter, my aunt added the eggs.

【译文】混合好面粉和黄油后，姨妈加入了鸡蛋。

5) 【答案】After traveling to Italy, Byron traveled to Greece.

【译文】结束了在意大利的旅行后，拜伦继续去希腊旅行。

2. 请仿照例句改写下列句子。

1) 【答案】Once I get him a job, he'll be fine.

【译文】一旦我给他事情做，他就会好起来。

2) 【答案】Once you understand the principle, you'll have no further difficulty.

【译文】你只要理解了原理，就不会再有困难。

3) 【答案】Once in the US, the drugs are distributed to all the major cities.

【译文】一旦运进美国，毒品就会被运到各大城市。

4) 【答案】Once you have finished your homework, you can watch television.

【译文】你只要完成了家庭作业就可以看电视。

5) 【答案】Once the children are addicted to video games, they will never concentrate on study.

【译文】一旦孩子们痴迷于电子游戏，就再也不会集中精力学习了。

综合练习

1. 完型填空。

1) 【答案】D

【解析】step into为固定搭配，表示"走进……，步入……"。

2) 【答案】C

【解析】so... that为固定搭配，中间用形容词或副词，表示"如此……以致……"；而such... that，中间用名词，表示"如此……以致……"。

3)【答案】A

　　【解析】aged 年老的；ancient 古老的，古代的；young 年轻的；middle-aged 中年的。

4)【答案】D

　　【解析】本题考查介词的用法。be shaking with laughter 笑得浑身发颤。

5)【答案】C

　　【解析】put on 穿上，突出"穿衣"这个动作；wear 穿着……，突出"穿戴的衣物"。

6)【答案】B

　　【解析】make for 倾向于；make up 化妆；make out 理解；make off 携……而逃。

7)【答案】C

　　【解析】be free from 为固定搭配，表示"免于……"。

8)【答案】A

　　【解析】本题考查介词的用法。beyond 超出，高于；live beyond their prime 活到老。

9)【答案】D

　　【解析】be sensitive to 为固定搭配，意为"对……敏感，易感受……"。

10)【答案】B

　　【解析】what if 即便……又怎样；even if 即使，纵然。

　　【译文】　　像7月的大多数日子一样，那天也很热。我走进一家小冷饮馆，买了一个巧克力冰激凌来解暑。这是家老店，最近刚装修过。

　　　　　　一走进店里，就看到一位老太太弓着背坐在靠门边的桌子上。也许是由于某些不幸，她的背弯曲得厉害，脸几乎都要碰到桌子上了。我面朝着她坐下，中间隔着几张桌子。

　　　　　　"可怜的人！"我想着，"她从生活中能得到什么呢？为什么老天会让人度过美好的青春年华后还活这么大岁数呢？"

　　　　　　我正想着，又一位老太太走进店内，和她坐在一起。随后，两人就聊起了童年往事，不一会儿，她们就笑得浑身发颤。

　　　　　　我再次望向第一个女人，这时从墙上的镜子里，我看到了我自己。

　　　　　　我穿着一件脏衬衫。

　　　　　　她却身着时下流行的白色上衣，脸也精心妆扮过。

　　　　　　我心情忧郁，她却在笑。

　　　　　　我一个人孤单单坐在那儿。

　　　　　　她却有朋友陪伴。

　　　　　　我为呆会儿不得不做的工作忧心忡忡。

　　　　　　她却不用为工作的最后期限以及交通的拥挤而发愁。

　　　　　　我潜意识里害怕自己变老。

　　　　　　她虽老了，但这并没让她变得脆弱。

　　　　　　我走出小店，一想到刚才的问题，就觉得自己好蠢。为什么她就能比我更有活力，更有朝气地面对生活？即便岁月使她腰背不再挺直，那又怎样呢？岁月没能使她向生活低头。

2. 用括号中的词汇和短语将下列句子译成英语。

1)【答案】Eventually, the policeman talked the girl out of jumping from the top of the building.

2) 【答案】I didn't want to stand in her way, so I left her without hesitation.

3) 【答案】He was determined to pursue his studies abroad after graduation, thinking that it would make all the difference to his future.

4) 【答案】The former president, who had been in prison for 5 years, was released yesterday.

5) 【答案】Only when you let go of your former lifestyle can you settle into the new environment.

文章泛读

文章导读

我们必须承认，孩子与父母之间存在"代沟"这个客观事实，两代人之间确实存在"差异"，不然怎么是"两代人"呢？但是，"代沟"不是不可以填充，"差异"不是不可以缩小。这需要父母有智慧，通过与孩子的交流与沟通，达到相互认同，相互理解。建立在这样基础上的教育才能产生正效应，否则，就会事与愿违。那么什么样的父母才是智慧型的父母呢？也许从本文中你能有所收获。

背景知识

反叛期的年纪众说纷纭，男女的反叛期都略有不同。根据心理学家的人生八阶梯理论，反叛期主要发生在13—18岁（成年初期）。青春期的叛逆刚开始是基于想要独立自主，这是身心发展的常态。正常的反叛可视为是成长的一种自然欲望，长成大人包括要开始自己作决定，青少年们需要对周围的世界提出问题，也开始拥有自己的信念和行动。由于他们缺乏经验，不可避免出错，但是，失败的经验其实在学习过程中扮演一个关键性的角色。

文章写作风格及结构

本文为一篇说明文，作者通过分析父母在孩子成长过程中可能出现的错误理念，向读者指出，在孩子成长的道路上，父母应该做的是通过允许他们走路（包括跌倒），允许他们说话（包括犯错），允许他们慢慢主宰自己的生活来帮助他们实现独立。

Parts 部分	Paragraphs 段落	Main Ideas 大意
Part I	1—2	Parents often believe they alone are responsible for how their children turn out. This misconception may cause the normal struggles between parents and children. 家长们通常相信他们对孩子的未来负有全部责任，这种错误的观点带来了父母和子女之间的斗争。

(to be continued)

(continued)

Parts 部分	Paragraphs 段落	Main Ideas 大意
Part II	3—9	The author lists three kinds of parents and the probable causes of their problems with their children. 作者列举出三类父母，并分析了他们和子女之间存在问题的可能原因。
Part III	10—12	Teens have to decide to lead their own lives. The task for children is to become independent and the task for parents is to help their children reach independence by allowing them to walk (and fall), to talk (and make mistakes), and to slowly take control of their own lives. 青少年必须决定过自己的生活。孩子的任务是变得独立，而父母的任务是通过允许他们走路（包括跌倒），允许他们说话（包括犯错），允许他们慢慢主宰自己的生活来帮助孩子实现独立。

词汇点睛

1　accompany

vt. 1) to happen or exist at the same time as sth. else 伴随，与……一同发生

- 例句 • Lightning usually accompanies thunder. 雷声常常伴随着闪电而来。

  The text is accompanied by illustrations. 正文附有插图。

  2) to go with sb. to a place 陪某人去某处

- 例句 • Four teachers accompanied the class on their skiing holiday.

  有四个教师陪同全班同学滑雪度假。

  3) to play a musical accompaniment for 为……伴奏

- 例句 • Mary sang and I accompanied her on the piano. 玛丽唱歌，我弹琴给她伴奏。

2　rear

vt. to look after a person or an animal until they are fully grown 培养，养育

- 例句 • He adopted and reared four children. 他收养抚育了四个孩子。

  She's rearing a large family. 她养着一大家人。

  n. (rather fml) the back （比较正式)后面，后部

- 短语 • **in/at the rear** 在后边

  The ball is in the rear of the building. 大厅在建筑物的后面。

  The storehouse is at the rear of the workshop. 仓库在车间后面。

  adj. at the back 后部的，背后的

- 例句 • The rear window is very dirty. 汽车的后窗太脏了。

3　misconception

n. wrong idea or understanding 误解

- 例句 • It is a popular misconception that all Scotsmen are mean.

  很多人误以为苏格兰人都很小气。

  It is a misconception on your part. 这是你的误解。

•扩展• **conception** *n.* 主意、计划、意图

You have no conception at all of how difficult my life was in those days.

你根本想象不出那些日子我的生活有多艰难。

4   peer

n. 1) *your peers are the people who are the same age as you, or who have the same type of job, social class, etc.* 同龄人，同辈人

•例句• Teenage girls and their male peers like this style of clothes.

十几岁的少女和同龄男孩喜欢这种款式的衣服。

He doesn't spend enough time with his peers. 他不大与其同龄人交往。

2) *male member of one of the ranks of nobility* 贵族

•例句• The queen created him a peer. 女王封他为贵族。

vi. to look closely at sth. because you cannot see well 仔细看（因看不清楚）

•例句• She peered at the tag to read the price. 她细看标签辨认价格。

I peered into the distance but I couldn't see anything because it was dark.

我凝视远方，可是因为天黑什么也看不见。

5   ensure

vt. to make it certain that sth. will happen 确保，保证

•例句• The role of the police is to ensure that the law is obeyed.

警察的作用是确保人人守法。

Great efforts ensure the success of our work.

巨大的努力确保了我们工作的成功。

•辨析• **ensure, assure, insure**

ensure意为确保某种行为或动因的结果一定会发生，常用搭配为：ensure that... 保证……；ensure sb. sth. 保证某人得到某物。

assure 意为"以十分肯定的语气告诉某人真相或实情使之放心"，常用搭配为assure sb. that/of 使某人确信，向某人保证……。如：

I assure you that the dog isn't dangerous. 我保证这条狗不咬人。

insure 意为"保险"，常用搭配为：insure against... 保……险。如：

My house is insured against fire. 我的房子保了火险。

比较：

To ensure the child's quick recovery, the doctor gave him some pills.

The doctor assured him that his child would recover from his illness.

6   maintain

vt. 1) *to make sth. continue in the same way or at the same standard as before* 维持，继续

•例句• If he can maintain this speed, he'll win the race.

他在比赛中要是能保持这种速度就能赢。

He failed again and again simply because he had maintained his defeatist attitude.

因为他一直坚持失败主义的态度，所以失败了一次又一次。

2) *to keep sth. working well* 保养或维修某物

•例句• The roads are well maintained. 这些路保养得很好。

Engineers are maintaining the turbines. 机修工们正在维修涡轮机。

3) to assert (sth.) as true 断言（某事）属实，坚持（认为）

• 例句 • The sociologist maintained that the theory is wrong.

这个社会学家坚持说那理论是错误的。

• 扩展 • **maintenance** n. 维护，保持

He took a course to learn about car maintenance.

他学习了汽车保养的课程。

• 辨析 • **support, uphold, sustain, maintain**

都含"支持"的意思。

support 系常用词，指"支撑，给某人（物）以积极援助或支持"。如：

We should support each other. 我们应互相支援。

uphold 指"对某人、某种活动、信仰等给予支持、道义上的支援或精神上的鼓舞"。如：

His words upheld me greatly. 他的话给我很大支持。

sustain 指"支撑，维持"。如：

His hope for future sustained him. 对未来的希望支撑了他。

maintain 指"使保持某种情况或状态而不受损害，使保持完整所给予的力量"。如：

The government maintains the law. 政府维护法律。

7   aspect

n. one part of a situation, idea, plan, etc., that has many parts 方面

• 例句 • Spelling is one of the most difficult aspects of English learning.

词语拼写是学习英语最困难的一个方面。

We should consider a problem in all its aspects. 我们应该全面地考虑问题。

8   assume

vt. 1) to take over control, responsibility, etc., or to start to do a particular job 取得，夺取

• 例句 • You must assume control. 你必须夺得控制权。

Although they were in the trouble at the beginning, they assumed success at last.

虽然他们在刚开始就陷入困境，但是他们在最后取得了胜利。

2) to think that sth. is true when you are not completely sure （无十分把握时）认为某事属实，假定，假设

• 例句 • Never assume, for it makes an ASS out of U and ME.

永远不要主观臆断，因为那会使你我成为蠢驴。

Joe is not here today, so I assume that she is ill. 乔今天不在，我看她是病了。

He's not such a fool as you assumed him to be. 他并非你所以为的那样愚蠢。

• 句型 • **assuming (that)...** 假定…… (= suppose/supposing that...)

Assuming that you are right about this, what shall we do?

假定在这件事上你是对的，那我们该怎么办？

• 扩展 • **assumption** n. 假定，假设

Their assumption that their project under way was something entirely new proved to be untrue.

他们以为他们正在进行的课题是崭新的，事实证明不是那样。

• 辨析 • **pretend, feign, assume**

都含"假装"的意思。pretend 指"感觉到某事，而在言行上装出是真的"。如：pretend not to hear 假装没听见。

feign 指"故意装作"。如：feign deafness 装聋。

assume 指"装出有某种感情的样子，以掩饰其真正的感情"。如：

She assumed a look of sorrow. 她假装着悲伤的样子。

9　defy

vt. to refuse to obey a law or rule, or refuse to do what sb. tells you to do 不服从，蔑视，公然反抗

• 例句 • She defied her parents and stayed out all night. 她不听父母的话，整夜都没回家。

If you defy the law, you may find yourself in prison. 如果不服从法律，就可能会坐牢。

• 短语 • **defy sb. to do sth.** 挑激某人做某事

They defied him to jump off the bridge. 他们激他跳下桥去。

• 辨析 • **deny** *vt.* 否认

He said that I had stolen his bicycle, but I denied it. 他说我偷了他的自行车，可是我否认了。

• 扩展 • **defiant** *adj.* 反叛的，目中无人的，挑剔

He is always defiant, so his colleagues don't like him.

他总是目中无人，所以他的同事不喜欢他。

He assumed a defiant attitude toward his employer. 他对雇主采取挑衅的态度。

10　reject

vt. 1) to refuse to give sb. any love or attention 丢弃，遗弃

• 例句 • We should reject weak plants. 我们应该剔除长得不好的植物。

We should reject all our shortcomings to make ourselves much better.

为了使我们变得更好我们应该丢弃所有的缺点。

2) *to say that you do not want sb. or sth.* 拒绝接受某人或某事物

• 例句 • He rejected my offer of help. 我主动提出帮忙，他拒不接受。

11　stressful

adj. a job, experience, or situation that is stressful makes you worry a lot 紧迫的，充满压力的

• 例句 • She finds her new teaching job very stressful. 他觉得新的教学工作充满压力。

I just went through a stressful week. 我刚过了紧张的一周。

• 扩展 • **stress** *n.*

1) 精神上或肉体上的痛苦、困难的情况等（所造成的压力或忧虑）

Worry over his job and his wife's health put him under a great stress.

对自己的工作及妻子的健康问题的忧虑使他陷于过分的紧张中。

2) 强调，重要性

We must lay stress on self-reliance. 我们必须强调自立更生。

stress *vt.* 强调

He stressed the point that we should be punctual. 他强调的一点是我们必须准时。

12　unrest

n. a feeling of being worried and uncertain about sth. 不安，动荡

• 例句 • Social unrest isn't a good thing. 社会动荡不是一件好事。

Community unrest is rapidly approaching the flashpoint.

群众的不安定情绪已接近一触即发之势。

• 扩展 • **unrestful** *adj.* 不安静的, 不能保持宁静的

13 discontent

n. a feeling of being unhappy and not satisfied with the situation you are in 不满

- 例句 • His discontent is just his weakness. 他的不满正是他的弱点。

  His speech caused our discontent. 他的言论引起我们的不满。

  vt. to make (sb.) discontented 使不满

- 例句 • A little criticism is enough to discontent him. 一点批评就足以令他不满了。

- 扩展 • **discontented** *adj.* 不满的，不愉快的

  He's discontented with his wage. 他不满于自己的工资。

  content *adj.* 知足的；满足的；满意的

  She is not content with the money she has—she wants more.

  她不满足自己现有的钱——她还想要多些。

  content *n.* 满足，内容

  It's the weekend, so you can sleep to your heart's content. 是周末了，你可以睡个够。

  I like the style of his writing but I don't like the content.

  我喜欢他作品的风格，但不欣赏其内容。

  content *vt.* 使满意，使满足

  Nothing contents her, she is always complaining. 没有什么能使她满意，她总是抱怨。

14 anxious

adj. 1) worried about sth. 焦虑的，担心的

- 例句 • There is no reason to be anxious about the result. 不必为这结果而担心。

  He was anxious for her safety. 他担心她的安全。

  2) strongly wishing sth.; eager for sth. 渴望的，急切的

- 例句 • He was anxious to meet you. 他急切地想与你会面。

  People all over the world were anxious to have peace. 全世界人民都渴望和平。

- 扩展 • **anxiety** *n.* 忧虑，焦急

  He was waiting for his brother's return with anxiety. 他焦虑地等着兄弟归来。

- 辨析 • **eager, anxious** 意思都含"渴望的"。

  eager指"以巨大的热情渴望实现愿望或达到目的的"，有时也指"由于其他感情影响而表现急不可耐的"。如：

  He was eager to see her. 他渴望见到她。

  anxious指"热切地希望实现愿望，并因顾虑愿望落空而心情不安，感到焦虑的"。如：

  I'm anxious to know the final result. 我急于想知道最后的结果。

15 despite

adv. used to say that sth. happens or is true even though sth. else might have prevented it 不管，尽管

- 例句 • We decided to go out despite the bad weather. 尽管天气不好，我们还是决定出去。

  He remains modest despite his achievements. 尽管有成绩，他仍然保持谦虚。

- 辨析 • **despite, although, though**

  首先，though是连词，despite是介词（通常情况下）；though后接句子，despite后接名词或名词性从句，从句作介词despite的宾语。其次，though表示让步的语气比despite轻。

  although和though 作连词时意思为"尽管，虽然"，用来引导让步状语从句，一般位于句首。它所引导的从句不能与并列连词 but, and, so 等连用，但可以与 yet, still 等词连用。

though 除了作连词外，还可以作副词，作"可是，然而"讲，而although 不行。 though 比 although 通俗，但不如 although 正式。 although 后只接句子，though 后可接形容词。

16　expectation

n. what you think or hope will happen 期待，指望

- 例句 • She tried hard to live up to her parents' expectations. 她努力不辜负父母的期望。

  He had high expectations of what university had to offer.

  他对大学所能给提供的一切期望很高。

- 扩展 • **expect** *vt.* 预料，期待（某事会发生或某人/事会来到）

  I expect he'll pass the examination. 我预料他会通过考试。

  Most of the parents expect much of their children.

  大多数父母都对自己的子女寄予很大希望。

  expectant *adj.* 期待的，怀有期望的

  The expectant crowds waited for the king and his queen to pass.

  期待的人群等候国王和王后经过。

17　trying

adj. annoying or difficult in a way that makes you feel worried, tired, etc. 难受的，恼人的

- 例句 • We've had a lot of problems in the office recently; it's been a very trying time for all of us.

  我们公司最近出了不少问题，对大家来说这都是一段十分烦恼的时期。

  He's a trying person to deal with. 他是个难对付的人。

18　function

v. to work in the correct or intended way 运转，运行

- 例句 • The engine will not function without oil. 发动机离开油就不能动了。

  The computer functioned well until attacked by the computer virus.

  这台电脑直到受到电脑病毒攻击一直都工作得很好。

  n. special activity or purpose of a person or thing 作用，技能，职责

- 例句 • The function of the heart is to pump blood through the body.

  心脏的功能是把血液输往全身。

- 短语 • **function as sth.** 起某物的作用，具有某物的功能

  The sofa can also function as a bed. 这沙发也可以当床。

短语解析

1. turn out 结果是……，证明是……

【例句】Things turned out to be exactly as what the professor had foreseen.

事情正如教授所预见的那样。

The plan turned out a failure. 这项计划结果归于失败。

2. be concerned about 关心，挂念

【例句】I'm concerned about their happiness.

我很关心他们的幸福。

We're all concerned about her safety. 我们都为她的安全担忧。

3. so far 迄今为止

【例句】He has had three sons so far. 到目前为止，他已经有了三个儿子。

I haven't met my new neighbor so far. 我至今没有见到我的新邻居。

4. take over 接管

【例句】I'm feeling too tired to drive any more; will you take over?

我累得开不动车了，你来开好吗？

Who do you think will take over now that the governor has been dismissed?

州长已被免职，你看会由谁来接任呢？

5. live up to/meet one's expectation 不辜负某人的期望

【例句】I usually enjoy his films, but the latest one didn't live up to my expectations.

我向来喜欢看他的影片，但他最近的一部片子辜负了我的期望。

The restaurant he recommended met my expectation.

他推荐的餐厅没有辜负我的期望。

6. lead a... life 过……的生活

【例句】He leads a happy life in the country. 他在乡村过着幸福的生活。

Nobody wants to lead a dog's life. 没人想过狗一般的生活。

🌀 难句突破

1. (Para.2) *This misconception may cause the normal struggles that occur between parents and teens to take on exaggerated importance.*

【解析】句中that引导定语从句修饰struggles；to take on... 是不定式作补语修饰struggle。

【译文】这种错误的理念可能会使父母和子女间原本普通的争斗显得过于严重。

2. (Para.3) *For many parents, the method used to ensure that a child will grow up "right" is to maintain control over many aspects of the child's life.*

【解析】本句主干是... the method... is to maintain control...；其中主语the method被过去分词短语 used to ensure... 修饰；that引导宾语从句，作ensure的宾语。

【译文】对许多家长来说，确保子女"健康"成长的办法就是一直控制孩子生活的方方面面。

3. (Para.4) *As the children grow older, they begin to realize they can never grow into adults without assuming control of their own lives.*

【解析】into是介词，此处表示"（在某过程中）直到某一点"。类似的例子还有：

He carried on working long into the night. 他一直工作到深夜。

She didn't get married until she was well into middle age. 她步入中年以后才结婚。

as作连词引导从句，具体用法见Unit 1，Text A难句解析9。

【译文】随着孩子们日渐长大，他们开始意识到没有生活的自主权他们将永远不能长大成人。

4. (Para.8) *For some middle-aged parents, the fact their children will soon be adults may be an unpleasant reminder that they, too, are aging.*

【解析】that引导同位语从句。由连接词that引导的同位语从句在句子结构上与由关系代词that引导的定语从句有相似之处，但是还有区别。如：

Did you hear the news that China National Women's Volleyball Team won the second place in

Atlanta? 你有没有听新闻说中国女排在亚特兰大奥运会上得了第二名？（that从句中本身的内容就是news内容本身，that在从句中不充当句子成分，只起连接作用）

Neither of us showed any interest in the news that John told us yesterday. 我们对昨天约翰告诉我们的消息都不感兴趣。（that从句说明是怎样的news，在从句中充当tell的宾语）

【译文】对一些中年家长而言，孩子们很快将长大成人这个事实可能会令他们感到不安，因为这让他们觉得自己也正在变老。

参考译文
与孩子共处：了解不断变化的父母与孩子的关系

许多家长都不堪承受抚养孩子带来的种种责任。家长们常常认为：自己的子女长大后会怎么样，他们负有完全的责任。很多父母都相信，要是他们不采取正确措施的话，他们的孩子在长大成人之后就会难以适应社会生活。

这种错误的理念可能会使父母和子女间原本普通的争斗显得过于严重。父母需要明白，虽然他们在孩子的生活中很重要，但其他的影响因素也同样重要。同龄人、老师、辅导员以及受欢迎的公众人物也会对成长中的青少年产生影响。

当青少年逐步迈向独立被他们自己或其父母看作是为了争夺控制权时，这就成了个问题。对许多家长来说，确保子女"健康"成长的办法就是一直控制孩子生活的方方面面。

这样的家长会决定孩子选择穿什么衣服，交什么朋友，发展什么兴趣爱好以及学习什么课程。随着孩子们日渐长大，他们开始意识到没有生活的自主权他们将永远不能长大成人。因此，他们开始为争取自主权而斗争。他们与父母争辩，公开反抗父母，要求自主权，而所有这些都会导致家庭矛盾的不断发生。对于这些孩子来说，走向成熟的道路是艰难的，因为父母和他们都要面临失去彼此曾经拥有的亲密关系的风险。正是由于这些行为威胁到他们之间的关系，家长和孩子都有可能觉得被抛弃，受到伤害。父母也很关心孩子是否有能力照顾好自己，是否能够作出正确的决定。

在某些家长看来，孩子的反叛行为证明他们作为父母是失败的。如果双方都对对方十分在意的话，那么这样的争斗就会加倍令人觉得压力重重。

很多研究家长与青少年关系的专业人士认为，家长自己的问题也会导致他们与孩子之间出现问题。通常，青少年的父母都是中年人。他们在中年时期可能会经历动荡、不满、变化和自我评价。

在这个时期，许多家长会问自己到目前为止自己在一生中做过些什么，以及在未来想要做些什么。有些成年人会因为尚未实现目标而感到沮丧。另一些人会感到担忧，因为他们不知道孩子长大成人离家以后他们该怎么办。

对一些中年家长而言，孩子们很快将长大成人这个事实可能会令他们感到不安，因为这让他们觉得自己也正在变老。这些中年家长会尽量保持孩子对他们的依赖，尽管事实上孩子们正日渐长大并越来越独立。

青少年经常抱怨他们无法实现家长的期望。很多父母已经为孩子选好了某种职业，某种着装规则，或者一所特别的大学。农民的孩子想当医师而不接管农场，或是律师的孩子希望作木匠而不进律师行，家长会失望或生气，因为孩子辜负了他们的期望。

青少年必须决定过自己的生活。可是，接受孩子们自己作的决定对家长来说可能极其难受。在孩子没有达到自己的期望时拒绝他们，这样的父母可能会与孩子疏远。

怎样才能改善你与青春期孩子的关系呢？首先，正如孩子们在从婴儿成长为儿童的过程中得学会走路和说话一样，他们要长大成人也必须学会独立。如果你意识到这一点的话，就会有所裨益。

离开父母那最初跟跄的几步，和第一句"不，我不愿意！"都是迈向独立的开始，是每个孩子必须完成的任务。只有当孩子学会离开父母独立行动时，他们才能完成这项任务。如果迈向独立是孩子的任务，那么家长的任务就应当是通过允许他们走路（包括跌倒），允许他们说话（包括犯错），允许他们慢慢主宰自己的生活来帮助他们实现独立。

🌑 习题全解

1. 根据课文，请选出最合适的答案。

1) **【答案】** T

【题解】 根据文章第一段第二句"家长们常常认为：子女长大后会怎样，父母负有完全的责任"，因此这句话是正确的。

【译文】 许多家长都认为他们应当对子女的未来负责。

2) **【答案】** F

【题解】 根据文章第二段第二句"父母需要明白，虽然他们在孩子的生活中很重要，但其他的影响因素也同样重要。同龄人、老师、辅导员以及受欢迎的公众人物也会对成长中的青少年产生影响"，因此这句话是错误的。

【译文】 作者认为，和同龄人、老师、辅导员以及受欢迎的公众人物相比，在孩子的生活中，父母并不重要。

3) **【答案】** T

【题解】 根据文章第四段第二句"随着孩子们日渐长大，他们开始意识到没有生活的自主权他们将永远不能长大成人。……父母也很关心孩子是否有能力照顾好自己，是否能够作出正确的决定"，因此这句话是正确的。

【译文】 随着孩子们日渐长大，他们公开反抗父母是为了争取生活的自主权；但父母也很关心孩子是否有能力照顾好自己，是否能够作出正确的决定。

4) **【答案】** T

【题解】 根据文章第六段第二、三句"家长自己的问题也会导致他们与孩子之间出现问题。通常，青少年的父母都是中年人。他们在中年时期可能会经历动荡、不满、变化和自我评价"，因此这句话是正确的。

【译文】 家长在中年时期所经历的动荡、不满、变化和自我评价是导致他们与孩子之间出现问题的原因之一。

5) **【答案】** F

【题解】 根据文章第八段第二句"这些中年家长会尽量保持孩子对他们的依赖，尽管事实上孩子们正日渐长大并越来越独立"，因此这句话是错误的。

【译文】 当孩子们日渐长大，家长会尽量帮助他们变得独立自主。

6) 【答案】F

　【题解】根据第九段第三句"农民的孩子想当医师而不接管农场，…… 家长会失望或生气"，因此这句话是错误的。

　【译文】农场主不想让孩子接管农场。

7) 【答案】T

　【题解】根据文章倒数第二段可知，孩子们要长大成人必须学会独立，这对改善父母与子女的关系非常重要。因此这句话是正确的。

　【译文】家长一定得意识到孩子们要长大成人必须学会独立，这对改善其与子女的关系非常重要。

8) 【答案】F

　【题解】根据文章最后一段第三句"如果迈向独立是孩子的任务，那么家长的任务就应当是通过允许他们走路（包括跌倒），允许他们说话（包括犯错），允许他们慢慢主宰自己的生活来帮助孩子实现独立"，因此这句话是错误的。

　【译文】孩子们的任务是迈向独立，家长的任务则是照顾好孩子。

2. 请用下面所给出的词汇或短语的适当形式填写句子。

1) 【答案】aspect

　【译文】你只是考虑到了问题的一个方面，但其实还存在许多其他方面的问题。

2) 【答案】assume / take over

　【译文】哪个政党将控制议会，昨晚还未见分晓。

3) 【答案】are concerned about

　【译文】现在人们很看重自身的健康。

4) 【答案】maintain/ensure

　【译文】要想在沙漠中维持生命不是一件容易的事。

5) 【答案】fulfilled

　【译文】畅游迪斯尼乐园实现了他童年时的梦想。

6) 【答案】took over

　【译文】自我从父亲手里接管公司后，玛丽亚就一直是我的工作伙伴。

7) 【答案】despite

　【译文】尽管医生叮嘱她休息，她还是去了西班牙。

8) 【答案】depressed

　【译文】一想到未完成的一堆工作，我就很沮丧。

9) 【答案】turned out

　【译文】让我吃惊的是，结果竟然是我错了。

10) 【答案】accompany

　【译文】不管儿子去到哪儿，她都会陪伴左右。

3. 将下面这些句子译成汉语。

1) 【答案】家长们常常认为，子女长大后会怎么样，父母负有完全的责任。

2) 【答案】对许多家长来说，确保子女"健康"成长的办法就是控制孩子生活的方方面面。

3) 【答案】随着孩子们日渐长大，他们开始意识到没有生活的自主权他们将永远不能长大成人。

4) 【答案】对一些中年家长而言，孩子们很快将长大成人这个事实可能会令他们感到不安，让他们觉得自己也正在变老。

文章泛读

文章导读

　　汤姆，和16岁的女儿有共同的爱好，他们一起听音乐，饶有兴趣地谈论流行文化。而这一切在汤姆小时候从没发生过。"我和父母之间有很大的隔阂"。的确，他小时候，从衣着发型，到音乐欣赏、各种娱乐活动以及对生活的期盼，与父母都无法沟通。但到了今天，这个鸿沟在美国的许多家庭变得越来越小。可这样的变化带来什么呢？让我们和作者一起思考吧。

背景知识

　　宾夕法尼亚州（**Pennsylvania**）：为纪念开创人威廉·宾（William Penn）之父而得名。州名的意义为"宾氏林地"。从1843年起，瑞典、荷兰、英国先后统治这一地区。独立战争期间，这里是全国政治、经济核心地区，先后召开了第一、第二次大陆会议，签署了《独立宣言》。1787年经联邦政府批准，宾夕法尼亚州成为加入联邦的第二个州。州府是哈里斯堡（Harrisburg），位于费城之西，人口六万。本州最著名的大学是1740年创立于费城的宾夕法尼亚大学（University of Pennsylvania）。

文章写作风格及结构

　　本文为一篇说明文，作者简要介绍了当今社会代沟问题的现状，从专家学者的角度分析了这一变化可能产生的问题，并在文章结尾处给出了相应的建议和意见。整篇文章内容清晰，写作要点简单明了。

Parts 部分	Paragraphs 段落	Main Ideas 大意
Part I	1—3	It seems that the earlier generations of parents and children always have generation gap. 老一辈的父母和孩子之间似乎总有代沟。
Part II	4—6	Today, the generation gap is shrinking in many families. This brings an easy camaraderie that can continue into adulthood. 而今代沟在许多家庭中正在缩小，这带来了一种轻松自在的友情，这种友情可以一直延续到孩子长大成人。
Part III	7—10	But family experts caution that the new equality may also cause diminishing respect for parents and overindulgence of the children. 但家庭问题专家警告说这种新型的平等关系也有可能导致对父母尊重的削弱，以及子女的过度放任。

(to be continued)

(continued)

Parts 部分	Paragraphs 段落	Main Ideas 大意
Part IV	11	Parents have to be careful not to totally be their kid's buddy, because they still have to be the authoritarian and disciplinarian. 父母们也得小心，不要彻底成为自己孩子的密友，因为他们仍然需要担当权威和训导者的角色。

词汇点睛

1 distant

adj. 1) unfriendly, showing no emotion 疏远的，冷漠的
- 例句 - Pat sounded very cold and distant on the phone.
  从电话里听起来帕特非常冷淡和疏远。
  Instead of stopping to speak, she passed by with only a distant nod.
  她没有停下来谈话，只是冷冷地点了一下头走了过去。
  2) far away in space or time 远的
- 例句 - The time we spent together is now a distant memory.
  我们一起度过的时光现已成为久远的记忆。
- 扩展 - **distance** *n.* 距离，间距
  What's the distance between New York City and Boston?
  纽约市离波士顿有多远？
  The beach is within walking distance of my house.
  海滩离我家很近，走几步路就到了。

2 revolve

vi. to move around a fixed point outside the body 旋转，转动
- 例句 - The fan revolved slowly. 电扇缓慢地转动着。
  The earth revolves around the sun. 地球绕太阳公转。
- 扩展 - **revolving** *adj.* 旋转的
  The theatre has a revolving stage. 剧院有一个旋转舞台。

3 discipline

vt. to teach sb. to obey rules and control their behavior 训练，调教
- 例句 - This is a guide to the best ways of disciplining your child.
  这是管教子女的最佳指南。
  The officers were disciplined for using racist language.
  这些军官因使用种族歧视性语言而受到惩罚。
  n. 1) training, especially. of the mind and character, aimed at producing self-control, obedience, etc. 训练，锻炼
- 例句 - Strict discipline is imposed on army recruits. 新兵受到严格的训练。
  2) result of such training; ordered behavior, e.g of schoolchildren, soldiers 纪律，风纪
- 例句 - The soldiers showed perfect discipline under the fire of the enemy.
  在敌人的炮火下，那些士兵显示了良好的纪律。

4 caution

vt. to warn sb. that sth. might be dangerous, difficult, etc. 警告

• 例句 • I would caution against getting too involved. 我想告诫说，别陷得太深。

The policeman cautioned the prisoners not to play any tricks.

警察正式告诫罪犯不要耍花招。

• 短语 • **caution (sb.) against sth.** 警告或劝告（某人）防止某事物

Sam cautioned him against making a hasty decision.

萨姆告诫他不要草率作出决定。

n. care that you take in order to avoid danger or mistakes 谨慎，小心，慎重

• 例句 • Statistics should be treated with caution. 对待统计数字要小心。

• 扩展 • **cautious** *adj.* 谨慎的，小心的

He was cautious when he was riding the bicycle. 他骑自行车的时候很小心。

5 equality

n. a situation in which people have the same rights, advantages, etc. 同等，平等

• 例句 • Don't you believe in equality between men and women? 难道你不相信男女平等吗？

We have the equality of opportunity. 我们的机会均等。

• 扩展 • **equal** *adj.* 相同的，同样的

There is an equal number of boys and girls in the class. 这个班男女生人数相等。

equal *n.* 同等的人，相同物

She treats the people who work for her as her equals. 她以平等的身份对待为她工作的人。

equal *vt.* 等于

A meter equals 39.38 inches. 1米等于39.38英寸。

6 downside

n. the negative part or disadvantage of sth. 不利方面

• 例句 • There are some downsides to us. 对我们来说有一些不利因素。

One major downside of the area is the lack of public transportation.

这个地区的一大不便之处就是缺少公共交通工具。

7 appropriately

adv. correctly or suitably for a particular time, situation, or purpose 适当地

• 例句 • The government has been accused of not responding appropriately to the needs of the homeless.

政府未采取恰当的措施以应无家可归者的需要，为此已受到谴责。

The chain of volcanoes is known, appropriately enough, as the "Ring of Fire".

人们把这链状火山群很恰当地称作"火环"。

• 扩展 • **appropriate** *adj.* 合适的，恰当的

Now that the problem has been identified, appropriate action can be taken.

现在既已找出问题的症结，即可采取适当行动。

8 guilt

n. a strong feeling of shame and sadness because you know that you have done sth. wrong 内疚

• 例句 • She had feelings of guilt about leaving her children and going to work.

她因离开自己的孩子去工作而感到内疚。

Many survivors were left with a sense of guilt. 许多幸存者都有内疚感。

- 反义词 • **innocence** *n.* 清白

The accused man proved his innocence of the crime. 被告人经证实无罪。

- 扩展 • **guilty** *adj.* 感到内疚的

I felt guilty about not visiting my parents more often. 我因没有常去看望父母而感到内疚。

9   impose

vt. if sb. in authority imposes a rule, punishment, tax, etc., they make people accept it 强加

- 例句 • A new tax was imposed on fuel. 当局开始对燃油征收一项新税。

The system imposes additional financial burdens on many people.

这个制度给很多人增加了额外的经济负担。

- 短语 • **impose on** 强加于，利用，欺骗

We are not to be imposed upon. 我们是不会上当的。

impose oneself on sb. 硬缠着某人，打扰某人

Don't impose yourself on people who don't want you.

不要强求和不需要你的人在一起。

10   argument

n. a situation in which two or more people disagree, often angrily 争吵，争论

- 例句 • We had an argument with the waiter about the bill. 我们和服务员就账单发生了争吵。

She got into an argument with the teacher. 她和老师争论了起来。

- 扩展 • **argue** *vi.* 争吵，争论

He argued with Mary about the best place for a holiday.

他和玛丽争论度假的最好地方。

They argued the case for hours. 他们就这件事争论了数小时。

11   resolve

vt. 1) to find a satisfactory way of dealing with a problem or difficulty 解决

- 例句 • Attempts are being made to resolve the problem of security in schools.

正在尝试解决校园安全问题。

Both sides met in order to try to resolve their difference. 双方会晤以努力解决分歧。

  2) to decide firmly; to determine 决定，决心

- 例句 • He resolved on (making) an early start. 他决定尽早出发。

- 扩展 • **resolved** *adj.* 下定决心的，坚定的

I was resolved not to see him. 我决意不见他。

resolution *n.* 解决，决议，决定

The lawyer's advice led to the resolution of this difficult problem.

律师的劝告帮助解决了这个难题。

The resolution was carried at the previous plenary session. 决议在上次全会上获得通过。

12   swing

vi. (swung, swung) to move back and forth 摇摆，摆动，回转

- 例句 • His arms swung as he walked. 他边走边摆着双臂。

A set of keys swung from her belt. 她腰上挂着一串钥匙摆来摆去。

  n.1) a swinging movement 摆动，挥动

- 例句 • He took a swing at the tree with his axe. 他挥斧砍树。

  2) a set, especially. for children, which is fixed from above by ropes or chains and one can swing backwards and forwards 秋千
- 例句 • The children are playing on the swings in the park. 孩子们在公园里荡秋千。
- 短语 • **in full swing** 热烈地进行

  The party was in full swing when the police burst in.

  在晚会进行得火热的时候，警察闯了进来。
- 辨析 • **swing, sway**

  都含"摆动"的意思。

  swing指"一端吊起、一面固定或两端都系住的物体摆动"。如：

  The pendulum swings. 钟摆摆动。

  sway 指"有伸缩性的物体受压后又恢复原位地摆动"。如：

  Branches sway gently in the wind. 树枝在风中微微摇动。

13　priority

n. the thing that you think is most important and that needs attention before anything else 优先，优先权

- 例句 • Club members will be given priority. 俱乐部成员享有优先权。

  The search for a new vaccine will take priority over all other medical research.

  研制新的疫苗将排在其他一切医学研究之前。
- 短语 • **give (first) priority to...** 给……以(最)优先权

  You must give priority to this matter. 你必须优先处理此事。
- 扩展 • **prior** *adj.* 在前的，优先的

  I have a prior engagement and so can't go with you. 我预先有约会，所以不能跟你去。

  This task is prior to all others. 这项任务比所有其他任务都重要。

🌐 短语解析

1. give way to 让位于……

【例句】As winter gave way to spring the days began to lengthen. 冬去春来，白昼开始变长了。

Give way to traffic coming from the right. 让右方驶来的车辆先行。

2. be aware of 知道，意识到

【例句】He was well aware of the problem. 他很清楚这个问题。

He doesn't seem to be aware of the coldness of their attitude towards his appeal.

他好像没有意识到大家对他的呼吁的冷淡态度。

3. as opposed to 相反，而不是

【例句】This exercise develops suppleness as opposed to strength.

这项锻炼不是增强力量，而是增强韧性的。

This is a book about business practice as opposed to theory.

这是一本讲商业实务，而不是讲理论的书。

4. on the part of 就……而言，在……方面

【例句】It was an error on the part of me. 那是我的过失。

It was a mistake on the part of Jones to sign the contract without reading it.

没看合同就签了字,那是琼斯的错误。

5. be viewed as 被看作……

【例句】When the car was first built, the design was viewed as highly original.

这辆车刚造好时,其设计被认为是独具匠心。

His action is viewed as a breach of trust. 他的行为被看作是背信弃义。

6. in great/good shape 处于良好状态,健康情况良好

【例句】I like to keep in good shape. 我喜欢保持健康。

Our garden is in good shape after all the rain. 下过那么多雨后,我们的花园情况良好。

难句突破

1. (Para.5) *And parent-child activities, from shopping to sports, involve an easy camaraderie that can continue into adulthood.*

【解析】本句的主干是parent-child activities... involve an easy camaraderie...;其中that引导定语从句修饰camaraderie;from shopping to sports是插入语,进一步说明activities。

【译文】而且父母和子女一起参与的活动——从购物到运动——都含有一种轻松自在的友情,这种友情可以一直延续到孩子长大成人。

2. (Para.9) *Yet, parents who don't set rules risk becoming "so powerless in their own homes that they feel out of control and sometimes afraid", cautions Dennis Lowe, a professor at Pepperdine University in California.*

【解析】1) 本句主干是parents... risk becoming...;who引导定语从句修饰parents;引号内的内容so powerless... sometimes afraid是Dennis Lowe警告的内容;a professor at... in California作Dennis Lowe的同位语。

2) yet此处作连词表示"然而,而"。如:

slow yet thorough 虽然慢但是彻底

She trained hard all year yet still failed to reach her best form. 她全年艰苦训练,然而仍未达到自己的最佳状态。

【译文】但是,不定规矩的家长会冒这样的风险,他们会变得"在自己家中没有权威,以至于觉得失控,有时甚至害怕",加州培普丹大学丹尼斯·洛教授警告说。

3. (Para.12) *"I don't think we're swinging back to the 'good old days', when parents ruled and children kept their mouths shut," says Robert Billingham, a family-studies professor at Indiana University.*

【解析】引号中的内容I don't think... kept their mouths shut是Robert Billingham所说的内容;when引导非限定性定语从句修饰说明good old days;a family-studies professor at Indiana University作Robert Billingham的同位语。

【译文】"我认为我们并不是要重回'过去的好时光',即父母处于统治地位,而子女没有发言权,"印第安那州立大学家庭学教授罗伯特·比林汉姆说。

🌑 **参考译文**

正在消失的代沟
玛里琳·加德纳

有时候，汤姆·克拉特梅克尔和他16岁的女儿霍兰一起做他们共同喜好的事：听摇滚乐和谈论流行文化，这时他就会回忆起自己小时候和父母疏远的关系。

"我从没对妈妈说过：'嘿，这张新专辑真的很棒——你喜欢吗？'"来自美国宾夕法尼亚的克拉特梅克尔先生说。"在鉴赏力与品味上我与父母之间存在绝对的鸿沟。"

音乐不是唯一有代沟的方面。从衣着、发式到活动、期望，老一辈的父母和孩子似乎总是各有一套。

现在，尽管代沟尚未消失，但它在很多家庭中正在缩小。过去独裁式的管束方式正让位于一种更加平等的关系。越来越多的父母更愿意采取"来，我们一起讨论讨论"的态度，而不是说"因为我这样说了，所以就应该这样"。

这样做的结果可能会形成家庭成员之间有益的亲密关系。过去的一代人可能不会谈到的话题——或者是那些令人尴尬的话题，如性和毒品等，现在不会令人感到不快，相反是见惯不惊了。这些谈话使家长们意识到孩子也许有重要的思想情感需要家长们了解。而且父母和子女一起参与的活动——从购物到运动——都含有一种轻松自在的友情，这种友情可以一直延续到孩子长大成人。

难怪现今的贺卡上会有这样的信息："给妈妈——我最好的朋友。"

但家庭问题专家警告说这种新型的平等关系也有可能产生负面影响——削弱对父母的尊重，以及过度放任子女。

很多家长已开始根据孩子的需求来作决定。他们关注的是如何使孩子高兴而不是恰当地引导孩子。而且父母工作的忙碌会令他们心中的负罪感增加，从而使得他们不再热心于花时间来管教孩子了。有些家长甚至担心，如果他们对孩子说不，或对孩子加以约束，就会伤害孩子的自尊心。

但是，不定规矩的家长会冒这样的风险，他们会变得"在自己家中没有权威，以至于觉得失控，有时甚至害怕"，加州培普丹大学丹尼斯·洛教授警告说。

他认为父母在急于维持和平，避免争执的同时，也就失去了教会子女怎样解决冲突，而不是简单避免冲突的机会。

专家说，父母们也得小心，不要彻底成为自己孩子的密友，因为他们仍然需要担当权威和训导者的角色。

"我认为我们并不是要重回'过去的好时光'，即父母处于统治地位，而子女没有发言权。"印第安那州立大学家庭学教授罗伯特·比林汉姆说。我们在趋于一种平衡，即父母重新被视为父母，而子女被看作是受到深爱和珍视的家庭成员。如果我们能取得这种平衡，而且父母及子女都能以家庭为重，那么我们就会和睦幸福的。

语言拓展

日常用语

练习 选择补全对话的最佳答案。

1. 【答案】C

   【题解】当别人邀请你参加某个聚会，接受邀请时回答："Yes, I'd love to." 拒绝邀请时回答："I'd love to, but..."，即应先表示自己是愿意去的，但因为某种原因而不能去，这样才有礼貌。

2. 【答案】C

   【题解】当别人邀你共进晚餐，接受/拒绝邀请时的回答，请参考第一题。

3. 【答案】C

   【题解】同上。

4. 【答案】B

   【题解】当别人邀请你看电影时，接受邀请时的回答还可以是："That's a good idea."

5. 【答案】C

   【题解】当别人问到"喝茶吗？"肯定回答："Yes, please." 否定回答："No, thank you."

阅读技巧

练习

1. 读下列句子，请猜出划线词的意思。

1) 【答案】过高估计

   【译文】他们高估了面试者的能力，问了他很多刁钻的题。

2) 【答案】宽敞的

   【译文】我们被告知我们的房间是宾馆里最宽敞的房间，这也是为什么我们得支付昂贵费用的原因。

3) 【答案】无条件的，绝对的；不挑剔的，无偏见的

   【译文】狗狗有着闪亮的棕色眼睛，摇个不停的尾巴，以及对主人无条件的爱。作为无偏见的听众，它们能让初级读者赢得自信。

4) 【答案】无私

   【译文】我们为他的无私感到自豪。

5) 【答案】不现实地

   【译文】我们不赞成他的意见，因为他的想法太过于理想主义。

2. 请猜出划线词的意思，并选择一个最佳答案填空。

1) 【答案】C

   【译文】应预先采取预防措施，以避免问题或困难的出现。

2) 【答案】B

   【译文】我写给史密斯教授的信一定寄错地方了，因为他根本就没收到。

3) 【答案】B

   【译文】演讲比赛每半年举行一次。

4) 【答案】C

   【译文】发生在意识表层下的思想活动被称为潜意识行为。

5) 【答案】A

【译文】很多非洲人都不适应寒冷的天气。

写作技巧

练习

1. 参照提供的中文信息写一张便条：

样文1：

Dear John,

  For the get-together tonight, I am terribly sorry that I am unable to make it owing to some emergency. Hope you guys will have a big time.

Tom Smith
May 31

2. 参照提供的中文信息写一则通知：

样文2：

The Influence of Culture on English Learning

Presented by

Henry Green

Visiting Professor at Southwest Jiaotong University

3:00-5:00 p.m. Thursday, June 8

Conference Room in the School of Foreign Languages

Sponsored by the School of Foreign Languages, Southwest Jiaotong University

语法知识

——动词不定式

练习 选择最佳答案补全下列句子。

1. 【答案】C

 【题解】本题考查expect to do sth. 不定式作宾语。

 【译文】你希望最快能什么时候去美国？

2. 【答案】D

 【题解】本题考查hope to do sth. 不定式作宾语。

 【译文】我希望我能来参加今晚的生日派对。

3. 【答案】D

 【题解】本题考查用 it 作形式主语，把真正的主语放在句尾；不定式的逻辑主语可以用 of 或 for 引导。

 【译文】让我们步行到那儿一定会迟到。

4. 【答案】B

 【题解】不定式的否定形式为"not to+动词原形"。

 【译文】他告诫我雨天时不要单独去游泳。

5. 【答案】C

【题解】在had better，would rather，except，but后面时，动词不定式的to要省略。

【译文】当国家需要你的时候，你必然要挺身而出。

6. 【答案】A

【题解】同上。

【译文】这懒惰的年轻人什么事都不做，整天只是玩。

7. 【答案】B

【题解】在had better后面时，动词不定式的to要省略，其否定形式为not do sth.

【译文】别告诉玛丽关于派对的细节，这是送给她的一个生日惊喜。

8. 【答案】D

【题解】本题考查used to do sth.的用法，表示"过去常常做某事"。

【译文】我年轻的时候，网球打得很好。

9. 【答案】A

【题解】用于感官动词feel，hear，listen to，look at，notice，see，watch之后作宾语补足语时，动词不定式的to要省略。

【译文】刚才，我听见一个女孩在隔壁房间唱歌。

10. 【答案】C

【题解】用于使役动词have，let，make之后作宾语补足语时，动词不定式的to要省略。

【译文】我已经很努力了，但还是没能弄懂这些英语句子。

11. 【答案】C

【题解】本题考查不定式的时态。不定式的完成式表示的动作发生在谓语动词所表示的动作之前，或表示过去未实现的动作。

【译文】很抱歉前几天冒犯了你。

12. 【答案】B

【题解】本题考查用it作形式主语，把真正的主语放在句尾；不定式的逻辑主语可以用of或for引导。

【译文】对我来说，改掉坏习惯并不太难。

13. 【答案】A

【题解】本题考查intend to do sth. 不定式作宾语。

【译文】去年，他曾打算出国，但他母亲却突然生病了。

14. 【答案】B

【题解】同12题。

【译文】对大学生来说，掌握一门外语十分必要。

15. 【答案】C

【题解】本题考查不定式作补语。

【译文】我还没能找到椅子坐下。

每课一练

Part I   Vocabulary & Structure

Directions: *There are 30 incomplete sentences in this part. For each sentence there are four choices marked A), B), C) and D). Choose the ONE that best completes the sentence.*

1. You'd rather _____ TV this evening, wouldn't you?

   A) watching   B) watch   C) to watch   D) watched

2. The employers _____ the employee's demand.

   A) gave up   B) gave way to   C) promised   D) comprised

3. He was not _____ the danger.

   A) know   B) realize   C) consider   D) aware of

4. The doctor _____ an operation on the patient.

   A) executed   B) acted   C) performed   D) conducted

5. The French pianist who had been praised very highly _____ to be a great disappointment.

   A) turned up   B) turned in   C) turned out   D) turned down

6. He hoped the firm _____ him to the Paris branch.

   A) exchange   B) transmit   C) transfer   D) remove

7. The development of industry must not be _____ at the expense of environmental pollution.

   A) projected   B) investigated   C) pursued   D) engaged

8. It's true that _____ you have a bad habit, you will find it difficult to give it up.

   A) since   B) because   C) as   D) once

9. When she fell ill her daughter _____ the business from her.

   A) took over   B) took up   C) took to   D) took out

10. I went to his room yesterday evening only _____ he was out.

    A) finding   B) found   C) to find   D) to have found

11. John _____ his experience in West Africa _____ an important part of his life.

    A) thinks... as   B) thinks... to be   C) views... to be   D) views... as

12. Don't _____ this news to the public until we give you the go-ahead.

    A) release   B) relieve   C) relate   D) retain

13. Most broadcasters hold that TV has been unfairly criticized and argue that the power of the medium is _____ .

    A) granted   B) exaggerated   C) implied   D) remedied

14. Teachers as well as parents impose all kind of tests and exams _____ middle school students.

    A) on   B) to   C) towards   D) for

15. He hated wandering about and expected to find a _____ position in the civil services of government.

    A) persevering   B) perfect   C) permanent   D) personal

16. He fell ill and _____ died.

    A) evidently   B) gradually   C) initially   D) eventually

17. The car _____ a lot of fuel.

    A) assumes   B) presumes   C) consumes   D) resumes

18. These pills should _____ you a good night's sleep.

    A) assure   B) ensure   C) insure   D) sure

19. It's easy to start friendship but difficult to _____.

    A) remain   B) maintain   C) retain   D) attain

20. Realizing that he hadn't enough money and _____ to borrow from his father, he decided to sell his watch.

    A) not wanted   B) not to want   C) not wanting   D) wanting not

21. I think we are _____ catching up with the developed countries in the not too distant future.

    A) capable to   B) able to   C) capable of   D) able of

22. The job will make him independent _____ his parents.

    A) on   B) for   C) of   D) to

23. The question is hard to _____.

    A) be answered   B) be answered for   C) answer   D) answer to

24. It was an error _____ my part.

    A) with   B) of   C) to   D) on

25. He wonder whom _____ advice from.

    A) asked   B) will ask   C) asks   D) to ask

26. They had a wonderful holiday, _____ the bad weather.

    A) inspite   B) despite   C) although   D) though

27. The badly wounded have _____ for medical attention over those only slightly hurt.

    A) principle   B) prize   C) praise   D) priority

28. It didn't take me long to _____ a new routine.

    A) set into   B) settle into   C) set up   D) settle up

29. The policeman _____ the prisoners not to play any tricks.

    A) cautioned   B) caught   C) coached   D) cornered

30. He said, "Time is running short. You _____ now."

    A) have better leave   B) better leave   C) had better leave   D) had better to leave

Part II   Reading Comprehension

Directions: *Read the following two passages. Answer the questions of each passage by choosing A), B), C) or D).*

Passage 1

To Whom It May Concern:

    My husband and I got married in 1965 and for the first ten years of our marriage I was very happy to stay home and raise our three children.

    Then four years ago, our youngest child went to school and I thought I might go back to work. My husband was very supportive and helped me to make my decision. He emphasized all of the things I can do around the house, and said he thought I could be a great success in business.

    After several weeks of job-hunting I found my present job, which is working for a small public relations firm. At first, my husband was very proud of me and would tell his friends, "My clever little wife can run that company she's working for."

But as his joking remark approached reality, my husband stopped talking to me about my job. I have received several promotions and pay increases, and I am now making more money than he is. I can buy my own clothes and a new car. Because of our combined incomes, my husband and I can do many things that we had always dreamed of doing, but we don't do these things because he is very unhappy. We fight about little things and my husband is very critical of me in front of our friends.

For the first time in our marriage, I think there is a possibility that our marriage may come to an end. I love my husband very much, and I don't want him to feel inferior, but I also love my job. I think I can be a good wife and a working woman, but I don't know how. Can you give me some advice? Will I have to choose one or the other or can I keep both my husband and my new career? Please help.

1. When was the letter most probably written?

   A) In 1965.　　　　　B) In 1975.　　　C) Four years ago.　　　　D) Around 1980.

2. What do you think shows the husband was supportive at the very beginning?

   A) He gave her encouragement.　　　　B) He made all the decisions for her.

   C) He took over all the housework.　　　D) All of the above.

3. Her husband _____ when she first landed her current job.

   A) was suspicious of it　　　　　　B) felt good about it

   C) felt a little bit disappointed　　　D) was happy but critical

4. Her husband stopped talking to her about her job when _____.

   A) she got promoted in her career

   B) she earned larger income than her husband did

   C) her husband was frustrated in his career

   D) both A and B

5. As her pay increased, _____.

   A) she bought a new house

   B) she found a gap emerged between her and her husband

   C) she did many things she had dreamed of

   D) she felt very proud of herself

Passage 2

Once in a television interview, I was chatting with the host about stay-at-home fathers. I made the point that one reason we're seeing more stay-at-home dads may be that it's no longer a given that a man makes more money than his wife. Many families now take earning power into account when deciding which parent will stay home.

At that point, one of the male crew members commented, "It should be the better parent who stays home." A lot of guys say things like that. Usually it's code for, "My wife（read: any woman）is the better parent."

I was a stay-at-home father for eight years, so his declaration made me bristle. It implied that our family's choice could only have been correct if I was a "better" parent than my wife.

I think men shoot themselves in the foot with this kind of thinking. When I began staying home my wife was the "better" parent: She had spent more time with Ry, could read him better and calm him more quickly. And given a choice, he'd have picked her over me. But as she was the more employable one, my wife went out to work and I looked after our son.

Know what? Because of the increased time I spent with him, I soon knew Ry well, understood what he needed and could look after him more or less as well as my wife could. Actually, the experience helped me unlock one of the world's great secrets: Women are good at looking after children because they do it. It's not because of any innate female aptitude—which I think is mostly learned anyway. It's because they put in the time and attention required to become good at the job.

Women obviously get a biological head start from giving birth and nursing. But over the long term experience is more important. When I got the experience myself, I was good, too. As good? I don't know. Who cares? Children are not made of glass. Other people are capable of looking after them besides Mom.

6. The first paragraph implies that _____.

A) the author works at a TV station

B) more and more women choose to stay at home to look after their kids

C) in more and more families the wife is earning more than the husband

D) many men are no longer given the opportunity to stay at home

7. The author decided to stay at home to look after their son eight years ago because _____.

A) he was earning less than his wife

B) it was easier for his wife to find a job

C) the son liked him better

D) he was the better parent

8. Which of the following is NOT mentioned as a thing that a good parent should do with his or her child?

A) Reading stories to him.

B) Understanding what he needs.

C) Spending more time with him.

D) Being able to calm him down.

9. Why are women generally better than men at taking care of children?

A) They were born with the capability.

B) They just enjoy doing it.

C) They have learned to do it at school.

D) They spend more time with them.

10. At the end of the article, the author concludes that _____.

A) he is as good as his wife at taking care of children

B) he is better than his wife at taking care of children

C) children prefer to be taken care of by their mother than by anyone else.

D) anyone can take good care of children as far as he has the experience

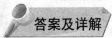 答案及详解

第一部分　词汇与结构

1. 【答案】B

【题解】would rather 后面接不带 to的动词不定式。

【译文】晚上你宁愿看电视，是吗？

2.【答案】B

【题解】此题考查动词或动词词组词义的辨析：give way to 指对要求等"屈从，让步"；compromise也有此意，用法为compromise with sb. on sth.；promise 意为"许诺"；give up意为"放弃"。

【译文】雇主对雇员提出的要求作出了让步。

3.【答案】D

【题解】be aware of是固定短语，意为"意识到"。其他选项均为动词，不能接在was not后面，可排除。

【译文】他还没有意识到危险。

4.【答案】C

【题解】本题考查动词词义辨析：execute 执行计划、命令；act 行动、表演；perform 表演、履行（职责），或以熟练技巧来完成复杂任务等（强调目的和结果）；conduct 实施进行（尤指对进行过程有指导和监督作用）。

【译文】医生为病人做了手术。

5.【答案】C

【题解】本题考查turn的短语搭配：turn out 原来是，结果是；turn up 出现，发生；（旋钮）开大，调大；turn in 上交；turn down 拒绝，关小。

【译文】受到高度赞扬的那名法国钢琴家结果却很令人失望。

6.【答案】C

【题解】本题考查动词词义辨析：transfer 调任；exchange 交换；transmit 传递，传导；remove 移去。

【译文】他希望公司把他调到巴黎的分支机构去。

7.【答案】C

【题解】本题考查动词词义辨析：pursue 寻求，从事；project 计划，投射；investigate 调查；engage 使从事于，使忙于。

【译文】工业发展不应以环境污染为代价。

8.【答案】D

【题解】once在这作连词，表示"一旦"的意思，符合句意。

【译文】事实上你一旦有了坏习惯就很难改正过来。

9.【答案】A

【题解】本题考查take的短语搭配。take over 接管，接任；take to 喜欢；take up 占据（时间、空间等），拿起；take out 拿出。

【译文】她患病期间生意曾由她的女儿代管。

10.【答案】C

【题解】本题考查的是"only+不定式"引导的结果状语，结果通常有悖期望。不定式作结果状语限于少数终止性动词，如find, hear, see, make, learn等。根据句意，不定式动作在句子谓语动作后发生，需用不定式一般式，不能用不定式完成式，故排除D。

【译文】昨天晚上我们去他房间却发现他不在。

11.【答案】D

【题解】固定搭配view... as = think of...as，意为"把……看作，把……认为"。

【译文】约翰把他在西非的经历当作他人生很重要的一部分。

12. 【答案】A

【题解】本题考查动词词义辨析：release 发布（新闻），泄露（消息）；relieve 缓解，使宽心；relate 讲述，使相互关联；retain 保温，保存。

【译文】在我们批准之前，不要把这消息公布于众。

13. 【答案】B

【题解】本题考查动词词义辨析：exaggerate 夸张，夸大；grant 给予；imply 暗示；remedy 纠正。

【译文】众多的电视播音员认为电视遭到了不公正的谴责，他们争辩说这种传媒的力量被夸大了。

14. 【答案】A

【题解】impose sth. on sb是固定搭配，意为"把……强加于某人"。

【译文】老师、还有家长把各种各样的考试强加于中学生身上。

15. 【答案】C

【题解】本题考查形容词词义辨析：permanent 永久的，持久的；persevering 坚忍的，不屈不挠的；perfect 完美的；personal 私人的。

【译文】他不喜欢四处漂泊，希望在政府行政机关找到一份固定的工作。

16. 【答案】D

【题解】本题考查副词词义辨析：eventually 最后，终于；evidently 明显地，显然；gradually 逐渐地；initially 最初，开头。

【译文】他患了病，最终去世了。

17. 【答案】C

【题解】本题考查动词词义辨析：consume意为"消耗"；assume 和presume的意思都是"假定，假设"；而resume指"（中断后）重新开始，继续"。

【译文】这辆车耗油量很大。

18. 【答案】B

【题解】ensure意为"确保某种行动或动因的结果一定会发生"，常用句型为：ensure that...或ensure (sb.) sth.；assure指"以十分肯定的语气向别人保证"，常用句型为：assure sb. that/of...；insure意为"保险"，常用句型为：insure against...；sure可作形容词或副词，表示"对……有把握的，确信的"。

【译文】服下这些药丸可保你睡一宿好觉。

19. 【答案】B

【题解】本题考查动词词义辨析：maintain 保持；remain 剩余，逗留；retain 保留；attain 得到。maintain friendship意为"保持友谊"。

【译文】达成友谊容易，但是保持难。

20. 【答案】C

【题解】该句中，从句的逻辑主语与主句主语是一致的，因此，选择现在分词引导的not wanting to borrow from his father与之前面的realizing that he hadn't enough money一起并列作句子的状语。

【译文】他意识到自己没有足够的钱，又不想跟父亲借，于是决定把表卖掉。

21. 【答案】C

　　【题解】be capable of / be able to 有能力的。 四个选项中，A，D搭配不当； B项的able to接动词原形，不接-ing 形式。

　　【译文】我认为我们有能力在不远的将来赶上发达国家。

22. 【答案】C

　　【题解】与dependent on（依赖）不同，independent与of 连用，意为"独立于"。

　　【译文】有了那份工作，他就不必依赖父母了。

23. 【答案】C

　　【题解】在一些形容词，如hard, difficult, easy, fit, comfortable, pleasant等后，作状语的不定式常用主动式表示被动意义。

　　【译文】这个问题很难回答。

24. 【答案】D

　　【题解】on the part of sb. / on sb.'s part是固定搭配，意为"在……方面,由……作出的"。

　　【译文】那是我的过失。

25. 【答案】D

　　【题解】疑问代词who，what，which及疑问副词when，where，how等后面加动词不定式构成不定式短语，在句中可作主语、宾语、表语。

　　【译文】他想知道该找谁提建议。

26. 【答案】B

　　【题解】本题考查的是让步状语从句。though和although引导句子，但the bad weather是名词性短语，故只能用despite 或in spite of来引导。

　　【译文】尽管天气不好，但他们的假日还是过得极为愉快。

27. 【答案】D

　　【题解】本题考查名词词义辨析: priority 优先（权）；principle 原则；prize 奖品；praise 赞扬。

　　【译文】重伤员较之轻伤员优先治疗。

28. 【答案】B

　　【题解】settle into是固定词组，意为"习惯于（新工作、新环境等）"，而settle up意为"结账，清债"； set up 意为"设立，建立"。

　　【译文】没过多久我就习惯新的日常工作了。

29. 【答案】A

　　【题解】本题考查动词词义辨析：caution意为"警告"；caught是catch的过去式，意为"抓住，赶上"；coach是"训练，指导"；corner用作动词，表示"使陷入绝境"。

　　【译文】警察告诫囚犯不要耍花招。

30. 【答案】C

　　【题解】had better后面接不带to的不定式，意为"最好……"。

　　【译文】他说："时间来不及了，你最好现在就离开。"

第二部分　阅读理解

1. 【答案】D

　　【题解】推断题。根据文章第一段，得知他们于1965年结婚，结婚后十年的婚姻是幸福的。根

据第二段 "Then four years ago...", 四年前, 女主人公重新开始工作, 两个人的感情随之出现危机, 可以推断出正确答案是D, 信写于1980年左右。

2. 【答案】A

　　【题解】细节题。根据文章的第二段。作者叙述了最初她的丈夫如何鼓励她, 相信她在事业上一定会成功, 并帮助她下定决心。但并没说她的丈夫包揽了所有家务事, 也没有替代她作一切决定, 所以B和C都不对。D自然也不对。只有A是正确的。

3. 【答案】B

　　【题解】细节题。根据文章的第三段 "At first, my husband was very proud of me..." (起初我的丈夫对此非常自豪)。所以只有B (感觉良好) 是正确答案, 而其他选项的怀疑、失望和挑剔等反应都是消极的, 与文章不吻合。

4. 【答案】D

　　【题解】细节题。根据文章的第四段。作者紧接 "my husband stopped talking to me about my job" 后提到 "I have received several promotions and pay increases, and I am now making more money than he is", 由此可得知我的丈夫不再跟我谈及我的工作是始于我几次升职, 薪水超过他之后。所以选D。

5. 【答案】B

　　【题解】细节题。根据文章的第五段中 "I think there is a possibility that our marriage may come to an end" (我想我们的婚姻有可能走向结束), 可知女主人收入增加, 但她与丈夫之间却出现了裂痕, 因此选B。

6. 【答案】C

　　【题解】推断题。根据文章的第一段中 "... one reason we're seeing more stay-at-home dads may be that it's no longer a given that a man makes more money than his wife" (越来越多的爸爸留在家里可能是因为男人不一定比女人赚钱多), 其暗含的意思即越来越多的家庭中, 妻子比丈夫赚钱多, 所以选C。

7. 【答案】B

　　【题解】细节题。根据文章的第四段中 "But as she was the more employable one, my wife went out to work and I looked after our son" (由于我的妻子找工作更容易, 所以她出去工作, 我留在家里照看孩子), 因此选B。

8. 【答案】A

　　【题解】细节题。作者在文章第四段提到最初在为人父母这一点上, 他妻子做得更好时, 说 "She had spent more time with Ry, could read him better and calm him down quickly" (她和Ry呆在一起的时间更多, 更能读懂他的心思, 能更快地让他平静下来)。由此可以看出, 只有A选项的内容 (给他读故事) 没有提到, 所以选A。

9. 【答案】D

　　【题解】细节题。根据文章的第五段中 "Women are good at looking after their children because they do it" (女人更擅长照看孩子是因为她们常照看孩子), 所以选D, 因为她们花更多时间与孩子在一起。

10. 【答案】D

　　【题解】细节题。根据文章的最后一段中 "But over the long term experience is more important" (但从长期来看, 照顾孩子, 经验更重要), 因此选D。

UNIT 7

Famous People

单元导读

从世界领导人，到科学家；从艺术家到历史人物，响当当的名字不计其数。他们中有历史豪杰，也有当代名人。他们中有人改变了我们的生活，有人塑造了整个世界，有人激励了世代的人民。因为他们的才华，他们活着的方式而受到尊敬。他们是我们行为的准则，是我们前行的灯塔。

每个人都渴望成功，成为名人。如果你希望在事业上功成名就，那就向名人学习吧。你可以阅读有关他们的书籍，甚至在有机会的时候和他们聊天。然而榜样的力量可以是积极的，有时也有可能是消极的。而你应该避开那些带来消极影响的人，他们可不应该是你学习的榜样。

课文精讲

文章导读

丘吉尔曾把与罗斯福总统的相逢比作"打开香槟酒瓶"一般的畅快，"他光彩照人，气势恢宏"。他们之间的战友之情真正经过了"刀山火海的考验"，这是丘吉尔在罗斯福去世那天对他的夫人埃莉诺·罗斯福所发出的感喟。两位处于世界巅峰的领袖，凭借着出众的才华，相同的意愿和非同寻常的友谊在那个特殊的时刻拯救了这个世界。

背景知识

温斯顿·丘吉尔（**Winston Churchill**）：（1874年11月30日—1965年1月24日）英国政治家、演说家、军事家，以及作家，1953年诺贝尔和平奖得主，曾于1940—1945年及1951—1955年期间两度任英国首相，被认为是20世纪最重要的政治领袖之一，带领英国取得第二次世界大战的胜利。

富兰克林·罗斯福（**Franklin Roosevelt**）：1882年1月30日出生于美国纽约。美国政治家，美国民主党成员，第32任美国总统，1936年、1940年和1944年三次连任成功，是美国唯一一位任期超过两届的总统。第二次世界大战初，美国采取不介入政策，但对希特勒采取强硬手段，以"租借法"支持同盟国。1941年底，美国参战。罗斯福代表美国两次参加同盟国"三巨头"会议。罗斯福政府提出了轴心国必须无条件投降的原则并得到了实施。罗斯福提出的建立联合国的构想，也得到了实施。

文章写作风格及结构

　　本文为记叙文，作者用一个个小故事向我们讲述了丘吉尔与罗斯福两位伟人间的友谊。文章中作者根据时间的发展顺序串联起了这段友谊中的点点滴滴，并大量引用丘吉尔与罗斯福的话语，为我们还原了历史的原貌。

Parts 部分	Paragraphs 段落	Main Ideas 大意
Part I	1	One meeting of Churchill and Roosevelt. 丘吉尔和罗斯福的一次"会面"。
Part II	2—8	The beginning and the development of their friendship. 他们友谊的开始和发展。
Part III	9—11	After Roosevelt's death, Churchill still cherishes their friendship and misses the old friend. 罗斯福死后，丘吉尔仍然珍惜他们之间的友情并十分怀念老友。

词汇点睛

1　dictate

vt. 1) to say or read aloud material to be recorded or written by another 口述

• 例句 • It took him a long time to dictate this letter. 口述这封信花了他很长时间。

He was dictating to his secretary. 他在向秘书口授信稿。

2) to tell sb. exactly what they must do or how they must behave 指示，指令

• 例句 • Can they dictate how the money will be spent? 他们能指示这笔钱如何花吗？

I refuse to be dictated to by you. 我不愿被你呼来唤去。

• 扩展 • **dictation** *n.* 口述，听写

I wrote the letter at his dictation. 我照他的口述写了这封信。

2　pace

vi. to walk first in one direction and then in another 踱步

• 例句 • The policeman paced up and down. 警察来回踱步。

He paced slowly toward the gate. 他慢慢地向大门走去。

n. 1) a single step when you are running or walking, or the distance you move in one step （一）步

• 例句 • The fence is 10 paces from the house. 栅栏离屋子有10步远。

He stepped backward a pace or two. 他后退了一两步。

2) the speed at which sth. happens or is done 步速，速度，节奏

• 例句 • Here in Chengdu, the pace of life is very slow. 在成都，生活节奏很慢。

The old man walked at a very slow pace. 老人走得很慢。

• 短语 • **keep pace (with)** （与……）齐步前进，（与……）并驾齐驱

Keep pace with time. 跟上时代。

The supply can hardly keep pace with the demand. 供应无法满足需求。

3　retreat

vi. to move away from sb./sth. 后退，退却，撤退

• 例句 • The army retreated to safety. 部队撤退到安全地带。

We retreated half a kilometer. 我们后退了半公里。

4   briefly

adv. 1) for a short time 短暂地
- 例句 • We stopped off briefly in London on our way to Geneva.

  在前往日内瓦的途中，我们在伦敦短暂地停留。

  2) in as few words as possible 简短地
- 例句 • Sonia explained briefly how the machine works. 索尼亚简短地解释了机器的工作原理。
- 扩展 • **brief** *adj.* 简短的，短暂的

  We stopped by Alice's house for a brief visit. 我们在爱丽丝家停留，作了短暂的拜访。

  Let's keep this conversation brief; I have a plane to catch.

  让我们谈话简短些吧，我还要赶飞机。

5   elusive

adj. an elusive person is difficult to understand 难以捉摸的，难以理解的
- 例句 • She managed to get an interview with that elusive man. 她设法采访了那个难以捉摸的人。

6   remark

vt. to say sth. 谈及，评论
- 例句 • He remarked that he found the play very interesting. 他说他发觉那部戏很有趣。

  "This house must be very old," he remarked. "这房子一定很旧了，"他说道。
- 短语 • **remark on/upon** 评论，谈论

  The press remarked on the Senate's vote. 报刊对参议院的投票进行了评论。

  This point has often been remarked upon. 这一点常被人们谈论。

  n. sth. that you say when you express an opinion or say what you have noticed 话语，谈论，评论
- 例句 • I agreed with his remark about Emma. 我同意他对爱玛的评论。

  We just had some nice remarks from the audience, expressing their appreciation of our program.

  我们刚收到观众的一些好评，表示对我们节目的赞赏。

7   ultimately

adv. finally, after everything else has been done or considered 最后，最终
- 例句 • Ultimately, the decision rests with the child's parents. 最终的决定权在孩子的父母手里。

  They ultimately decided not to go. 他们最后决定不去了。
- 扩展 • **ultimate** *adj.* 最后的，最终的

  Becoming president is his ultimate goal. 他的终极目标是成为总统。

  The ultimate outcome of the experiment cannot be predicted. 我们无法预知实验的最终结果。

8   slip

vi. 1) to go somewhere, without attracting other people's attention 溜走
- 例句 • He slipped out into the garage. 他偷偷溜出来进了车库。

  You should not let this opportunity slip away. 你不应该让这机会溜走。

  2) to slide a short distance accidentally, and fall or lose your balance slightly 滑（倒），滑落
- 例句 • She slipped on the ice and hurt her knee. 她在冰上滑倒，摔伤了膝盖。

  The knife slipped and cut my finger. 刀一滑，割伤了我的手指。

9 press

n. 1) the haste or urgency of business or matters 紧迫，繁忙

- 例句 - The press of the crowd kept us apart. 拥挤的人群把我们挤散了。

    2) people who write reports for newspapers, radio, or television 报界，新闻界

- 例句 - The power of the press is very great. 新闻界的力量是极大的。

10 tenderly

adv. gently and carefully, in a way that shows love 温和地，体贴地

- 例句 - She embraced her son tenderly when he came home after 10 years' absence.
在儿子离家10年后回家时她亲切地拥抱了他。

- 扩展 - **tender** *adj.* 温柔的

He gave her a tender kiss. 他给了她一个温柔的吻。

He recovered soon under his wife's tender loving care.

在妻子体贴入微的关怀下，他很快就痊愈了。

11 accomplished

adj. skillful 熟练的，有造诣的

- 例句 - My tutor is an accomplished scholar. 我的导师是一位知识渊博的学者。

- 扩展 - **accomplish** *vt.* 达到（目的），完成（任务），实现（计划、诺言等）

I have accomplished a great deal in the last few months.

在过去几个月里，我完成了相当多的工作。

We tried to arrange peace, but accomplished nothing. 我们试图调停以实现和平，但未成功。

- 同义词 - **achieve**

12 feeble

adj. extremely weak 虚弱的，衰弱的

- 例句 - She is feeble from sickness. 她因为生病而变得虚弱。

He is a man with a feeble personality. 他是个个性软弱的人。

13 fleeting

adj. lasting for only a short time 飞逝的，短暂的

- 例句 - We paid her a fleeting visit before leaving the country. 我们出国前匆匆探望了她一次。

For a fleeting moment I thought the car was going to crash. 刹那间我想汽车要撞车了。

14 pleasing

adj. giving pleasure, enjoyment, or satisfaction 令人高兴的，愉快的

- 例句 - This wine is most pleasing to the taste. 这种酒的味道美极了。

We have made pleasing progress in our talks. 我们的会谈已经取得了令人满意的进展。

- 扩展 - **please** *vt.* 使高兴，使满意，合……的心意

Our main aim is to please the customers. 我们的主要目的是使顾客满意。

15 unfold

vi. if a story unfolds, or if sb. unfolds it, it is told 展开

- 例句 - As the story unfolds, we learn more about Max's childhood.

随着故事的展开，我们也加深了对马克斯童年的了解。

The story unfolds as the film goes on. 随着影片的放映，故事情节展开了。

短语解析

1. over time 随着时间的流逝

【例句】People's appearances change over time.

人们的样子随着时间的流逝而逐渐改变。

2. in one's company 在……的陪伴下

【例句】I felt nervous in the company of such an important man.

和如此重要的人物一起，我感到很紧张。

3. cheer up 高兴起来，振奋起来

【例句】I wrote that song just to cheer myself up. 我写那首歌就是为了让自己振作起来。

A vase of roses cheered up the room. 一瓶玫瑰花使得房间生气盎然。

4. light up 容光焕发，绽开笑容

【例句】A smile of triumph lit up her face. 她脸上露出了胜利的微笑。

His face lighted up when he heard the good news.

听到这个好消息，他的脸上露出了喜悦的神情。

5. from time to time 有时，不时

【例句】Bob visits us at our house from time to time. 鲍勃有时到我们家来看望我们。

6. in the cause of 为了……事业而

【例句】The country agreed to confederate with the neighboring country in the cause of mutual safety.

这个国家同意为了共同的安全而与邻国结盟。

难句突破

1. (Para.1) *In his quarters at the White House over Christmas 1941, Winston Churchill, the visiting British Prime Minister, was in the bath, dictating to an assistant.*

【解析】本句的主干是Winston Churchill... was in the bath... ；其中the visiting British Prime Minister是Winston Churchill的同位语。visit表示"去或来看（某人、某处等）（可为社交、公事或其他目的）"。在一些固定搭配中，通常用visit的-ing形式visiting，例如：visiting hours 探望时间/会客时间；visiting professor 客座教授。

【译文】1941年圣诞节后的一天，温斯顿·丘吉尔，这位来访的英国首相，正在白宫他的寓所里，一边沐浴，一边对助手口述着什么。

2. (Para.2) *Born eight years and an ocean apart, they loved tobacco, strong drink, history, the sea, battleships, and poetry.*

【解析】born eight years and an ocean apart是过去分词短语作状语，表示让步。

【译文】两个人年纪相差八岁，出生地远隔重洋，可他们都爱雪茄、烈酒、历史、大海、战舰，还有诗歌。

3. (Para.4) *America, however, wanted no part in yet another European war.*

【解析】yet表示"到这时；到那时；直至现在（当时）；尚；还；仍然"；yet可以用于疑问句和否定句中及用于表示怀疑的动词之后，通常置于句末；在英式英语中通常用于现在和过去完成时，在美式英语中通常用于一般过去时。例如：

I haven't received a letter from him yet. （英）

I didn't receive a letter from him yet. （美）

我至今尚未收到他的信。

"Are you ready?" "No, not yet." "你准备好了么？" "还没准备好呢。"

She was not yet sure if she could trust him. 她还不确定是否可以相信他。

【译文】而当时的美国并不打算卷入另一场欧洲战争。

4. (Para.4) *Elusive, and complex, Roosevelt proved a difficult man to win over.*

【解析】exclusive, and complex是形容词作状语。形容词作状语可以表示伴随，原因或结果等。

例如：He went to bed, cold and hungry. 他又冷又饿地上床了。

【译文】罗斯福难以捉摸，有时还有些复杂，确实难以征服（要把他争取过来的确有一定的难度）。

5. (Para.6) *They were brought together by, and together shaped, epic events.*

【解析】这个句子是一个省略句，补充完整应该是：They were brought together by epic events, and together shaped the epic events.

【译文】他们因为伟大的历史事件而聚在了一起，同时也一起塑造了这些伟大的历史事件。

6. (Para.8) *An accomplished artist, Churchill painted the view from the tower for Roosevelt—the only painting he produced during the war.*

【解析】an accomplished artist是对Churchill的复指，破折号之后the only painting he produced during the war是对前文Churchill painted the view from the tower for Roosevelt的补充说明。

【译文】丘吉尔精通艺术，他用画笔为罗斯福记下了塔上所见的景色——这也是战争期间他创作的唯一作品。

7. (Para.11) *For a fleeting instant, Winston Churchill and Franklin Roosevelt had been at the top of the tower again, if only in the old man's mind, and the thought had been pleasing—friends indeed, down the decades, shoulder to shoulder in the cause of democracy. And so the tale unfolds still.*

【解析】本句涉及到if only的用法：

① if only可以用来表示对现时或未来的愿望。例如：

If only I were rich. 但愿我很富。

If only I could swim. 要是我会游泳该多好。

If only they could tell me what they've decided. 但愿他们能把决定告诉我。

② if only可以表示与过去事实相反的愿望。例如：

If only he'd remembered to buy some fruit. 他当时要是记得买些水果该多好。

If only I had gone by taxi. 假若我是乘计程车去的就好了。

【译文】转瞬间，在这位老人的脑海里，丘吉尔和罗斯福似乎又一起回到了那座塔顶——这是令人愉悦的想象。几十年来，他们一直是真正的朋友，为了民主的事业而并肩战斗。而今，他们的故事还在世间流传。

参考译文

沿着伟人的足迹

乔恩·米查姆

1941年圣诞节后的一天，温斯顿·丘吉尔，这位来访的英国首相，正在白宫他的寓所里，一边沐浴，一边对助手口述着什么。从浴室里出来后，丘吉尔把浴巾丢在了一旁。这就是首相先生，他全身赤裸，一副踌躇满志的样子，在那儿踱着步，说着话。忽然，传来了敲门声，"请进，"丘吉尔一边回答，一边把脸转向了进门的富兰克林·罗斯福。看到这情景，罗斯福连忙道歉，转身准备离开，首相阻止了他，"瞧，总统先生，"他说，"我对你可是毫无隐瞒啊！"两人都笑了。在丘吉尔结束他的美国之行，回到英国后，罗斯福告诉他："能和你在同一个时代，真是令人愉快。"

丘吉尔曾说过，和罗斯福碰面就像"开启一瓶香槟"。两个人年纪相差八岁，出生地远隔重洋，可他们都爱雪茄、烈酒、历史、大海、战舰，还有诗歌。但这决不是"一见钟情"。1918年7月29日罗斯福和丘吉尔在伦敦的一次宴会上曾短暂会晤，那时，罗斯福36岁，是海军部副部长；丘吉尔44岁，是军需大臣。当时的美国和英国正在第一次世界大战中结盟抗击德国。

"自从1917或是1918年我去英国那次开始，我就一直不喜欢他，"罗斯福在1939年对约瑟夫·肯尼迪说，"在我出席的宴会上，他的行为令人厌恶。"

罗斯福与丘吉尔在21年后再次见面时，英国正与纳粹德国孤军作战。而当时的美国并不打算卷入另一场欧洲战争。在丘吉尔成为首相的那天，罗斯福告诉他的内阁："嗯，我想，丘吉尔是英国最优秀的人了，虽然有一半的时间他都醉醺醺的。"丘吉尔隔着英吉利海峡，提防着希特勒，他知道他需要这位美国总统。但罗斯福并没有轻易地提供帮助。罗斯福难以捉摸，有时还有些复杂，确实难以征服（要把他争取过来的确有一定的难度）。

战后，丘吉尔曾说："我对罗斯福总统心思的揣摩远远比情侣间的揣摩更细致。"日本轰炸珍珠港的那一天，丘吉尔和罗斯福通了电话。罗斯福告诉首相"我们现在在同一条船上了"。

在约两年的时间中，他们多次见面，一起喝酒、抽烟直到深夜，一起决策重大战略问题。他们谈到各自的妻子，孩子，谈到自己的健康，还有对他们评头论足的人。他们因为伟大的历史事件而聚在了一起，同时也一起塑造了这些伟大的历史事件。一段时间以来，罗斯福和丘吉尔俨然成了一对老夫老妻，深知对方的缺点，却又无法想象失去对方的生活将会是什么样。

在1939年9月11日到1945年4月11日（罗斯福去世前夜）期间，他们通信2,000余封，见面9次，会面通常是秘密的，最终在一起度过了113天。一直到战争结束，罗斯福和丘吉尔都一起庆祝感恩节，圣诞节和新年。有一次，他们在忙碌的工作之余溜了出来，到马拉喀什短暂度假。在那儿，罗斯福被带到一座塔顶观看夕阳的余晖。在一起看夕阳时，丘吉尔满怀感情地凝视着罗斯福。

第二天一早，互相道别后，丘吉尔首相说罗斯福是"我认识的最伟大的人！"丘吉尔精通艺术，他用画笔为罗斯福记下了塔上所见的景色——这也是战争期间他创作的唯一作品。

在罗斯福去世多年后，在丘吉尔暮年，克莱门蒂娜·丘吉尔女士邀请了罗斯福的儿子詹姆斯来拜望这位前首相。"他会高兴的，这可能会让他振作起来，"她说，"他近来有点儿情绪低落。"

丘吉尔似乎很虚弱，但看见罗斯福时，他脸上绽放出光彩，拉着客人的手，他让詹姆斯坐下说话。"有时，他会问我是否记得某个我从未见过的人，他谈到他给我的口信，事实上他一辈子也没给我过什么口信，"詹姆斯回忆道，"开始，我有点摸不着头脑，后来才意识到他把我当成我父亲了。"当丘吉尔意识到自己的错误，他感到失望之极。

转瞬间，在这位老人的脑海里，丘吉尔和罗斯福似乎又一起回到了那座塔顶——这是令人愉悦的想象。几十年来，他们一直是真正的朋友，为了民主的事业而并肩战斗。而今，他们的故事还在世间流传。

习题全解

文章大意

1. 根据课文用合适的词填空。

【答案】 1) eight　　　2) strong drink　　3) 1918　　4) Nazi Germany/Hitler　　5) Prime Minister
6) strategy　　7) nine　　　8) 1945　　9) cheer　　　10) messages

【译文】　　虽然温斯顿·丘吉尔比富兰克林·罗斯福大 8 岁，但他们有很多共同的爱好：他们都爱雪茄，烈酒，历史，大海，战舰，还有诗歌。当他们 1918 年第一次见面的时候，他们彼此并不喜欢对方。可是 21 年后，二战爆发的时候，英国在反对纳粹德国／希特勒的战争中需要美国的帮助。因此英国首相和美国总统——丘吉尔和罗斯福再次会面。在接下来的两年中，他们多次见面，一起喝酒、抽烟直到深夜，一起决策重大战略问题。从那时起，他们成了亲密的朋友。在 1939 到 1945 年间，他们交换了 2,000 余封信件，会面 9 次，最终在一起度过了 113 天。当罗斯福于 1945 年去世的时候，丘吉尔非常伤心。几年后，为了要让丘吉尔振作起来，丘吉尔的妻子邀请罗斯福的儿子詹姆斯来拜望这位前首相。在这次会面中，丘吉尔错把罗斯福的儿子当作罗斯福本人了。他回忆起他们遇到的人，留给彼此的口信，在塔顶的那次会见。作为亲密的朋友，他们在民主的进程中并肩作战。

文章细节

1. 根据课文回答问题。

【答案】

1) It was fun to be in the same decade with Churchill. （Para. 1）

2) It was like "opening a bottle of champagne". （Para. 2）

3) In 1918. （Para. 2）

4) No. Roosevelt disliked Churchill. （Para. 3）

5) Twenty one years after their first meeting. / In 1939. （Para. 4）

6) They often met each other, drinking and smoking late into night and deciding crucial matters of strategy. Altogether, they wrote nearly 2,000 letters to each other, and met nine times, ultimately spending 113 days together. （Para. 6 & 7）

7) On April 11, 1945. (Para. 7)

8) To cheer him up, for he had been a bit down. (Para. 9)

9) He mistook Roosevelt's son for Roosevelt himself. So he was very happy (his face lit up) and recalled many things they had done together. (Para. 10)

10) He was quite disappointed. (Para. 10)

【译文】

1) [问题] 在丘吉尔1941年结束白宫之行后罗斯福是如何评论的？

   [答案] 能和丘吉尔在同一个时代，真是令人愉快。

2) [问题] 丘吉尔对于和罗斯福会面感觉如何？

   [答案] 和罗斯福碰面就像"开启一瓶香槟"。

3) [问题] 丘吉尔和罗斯福的第一次见面是在什么时候？

   [答案] 在1918年。

4) [问题] 第一次会面时他们喜欢彼此么？

   [答案] 不，罗斯福不喜欢丘吉尔。

5) [问题] 他们第二次会面是在什么时候？

   [答案] 时隔21年后/1939年。

6) [问题] 二战期间丘吉尔和罗斯福经常一起做什么？

   [答案] 他们多次见面，一起喝酒、抽烟直到深夜，一起决策重大战略问题。他们总共通信2,000余封，见面9次，最终在一起度过了113天。

7) [问题] 罗斯福是什么时候去世的？

   [答案] 1945年4月11号。

8) [问题] 为什么丘吉尔的妻子邀请罗斯福的儿子来拜访丘吉尔？

   [答案] 为了让他振作起来，因为他近来有点儿情绪低落。

9) [问题] 当罗斯福儿子前来拜访时，丘吉尔反应如何？

   [答案] 他错把罗斯福的儿子当作罗斯福本人，因此他非常高兴（脸上绽放出光彩），并回忆了他们在一起做的很多事情。

10) [问题] 当丘吉尔发现自己的错误时作何反应？

    [答案] 他感到失望之极。

词汇练习

1. 请用下面所给词汇或短语的适当形式填写句子。

1) 【答案】crucial

   【译文】了解急救知识是拯救生命的关键。

2) 【答案】strategy/strategies

   【译文】我们采取了这样的策略：敌人步步逼进，我们撤退；敌人节节败退，我们乘胜追击。

3) 【答案】dictate

   【译文】他用了很长的时间向秘书口述这封信的内容。

4) 【答案】accomplish

   【译文】我们应该在规定期限内完成任务。

5) 【答案】remarked

   【译文】他说他第二天可能来不了。

6) 【答案】terribly

　　【译文】让你等候，实在抱歉。

7) 【答案】retreated

　　【译文】一场激战之后，部队向南方撤退了。

8) 【答案】allied/allies

　　【译文】二战期间，法国和英国是同盟国。

9) 【答案】from time to time

　　【译文】鲍勃不时来拜访我们。

10) 【答案】Ultimately

　　【译文】最后，你还是得自己作决定。

2. 请用下面所给出的词汇或短语的适当形式填写句子。

1) 【答案】crucial; allies; remarked; ultimately; strategy

　　【译文】在那紧要关头，史密斯先生向他的政治盟友寻求帮助。但事后他评论说，最终的事实证明这并不是一个明智的策略。

2) 【答案】dictated; accomplished; terribly

　　【译文】经理向他的秘书口述了写给斯科特的信，信中写道："我为你所取得的成绩感到自豪，这对整个公司而言都是非常重要的。"

3) 【答案】critics; over time; pleasing

　　【译文】我认为这本书并不像评论家所说的那么差。事实上，人的看法会随着时间而改变。一开始枯燥的事物最后却可能变得有趣。

4) 【答案】briefly; democracy; retreat; strategy

　　【译文】议员们简短会晤后达成了一致意见。他们认为为了帮助那些国家建立健全的民主制度，发展稳健的经济，最好的方式就是首先平息民怨，然后整个国家应采取一种长效措施。

5) 【答案】ultimately; lit up; tenderly; company

　　【译文】当杰克最终实现梦想时，他的脸上绽放出喜悦的光芒。他温柔地凝视着妻子，并感激她在那段时间的陪伴。

3. 仿照例句用括号里的词或短语改写下列句子。

1) 【答案】in the company of such an important man / in such an important man's company

　　【译文】和这样一位重要人物呆在一起让我觉得紧张不安。

2) 【答案】over time

　　【译文】作研究应循序渐进。

3) 【答案】was cheered up by the good news /was cheered up on hearing the good news

　　【译文】这个好消息让大伙儿都很开心。

4) 【答案】light up with respect

　　【译文】当她提及米兰达时，他们眼中流露出了尊敬。

5) 【答案】but they still got together from time to time

　　【译文】尽管彼此相隔很远，他们仍不时聚在一起。

语法结构

1. 仿照例句用even if将括号里的中文翻译成英语。

1) 【答案】Even if I have to walk all the way

   【译文】即使我得一路走着去，我也会准时到那儿。

2) 【答案】even if it rains

   【译文】即便是下雨，我也会来。

3) 【答案】Even if he gets accepted by Harvard

   【译文】即便是被哈佛录取，他可能也无力支付学费。

4) 【答案】Even if it's only 10 minutes a day

   【译文】你应该经常锻炼，哪怕一天10分钟也好。

5) 【答案】even if they raise the price

   【译文】即使他们抬高价钱，芭芭拉仍会买下农场。

2. 仿照例句改写下列句子。

1) 【答案】She plays the piano better than she does the guitar

   【译文】她钢琴弹得比吉他好。

2) 【答案】John speaks French as fluently as he does German

   【译文】约翰的法语说得像德语一样流利。

3) 【答案】The production increased as it had done for the last few years

   【译文】像过去几年一样，产量持续增长。

4) 【答案】Marilyn has never acted as she should have done

   【译文】玛里琳从未完全发挥出自身的潜力。

5) 【答案】Dick likes jazz, and I do as well

   【译文】我和迪克都喜欢爵士乐。

理解练习

1. 完型填空。

1) 【答案】B

   【题解】make an impact on为固定搭配，表示"对……有影响"。

2) 【答案】C

   【题解】because 因为；since 因为；although 尽管；if 如果。

3) 【答案】C

   【题解】dedicate to为固定搭配，表示"把……献给"；care for也是固定搭配，表示"关怀，照顾"。

4) 【答案】A

   【题解】what is more important为固定用法，表示"更为重要的是……"，作状语。

5) 【答案】D

   【题解】even so 尽管如此；even then 尽管那样；even that和even when都不是固定短语，它们后面接从句；even that接名词性从句，而even when接状语从句，表示"即使当……时候"。

6)【答案】A

【题解】lie 躺，其现在分词为lying；lay 放置，其现在分词为laying。

7)【答案】C

【题解】make 制造，使得……；build 建造；create 创造；arrange 整理。

8)【答案】C

【题解】devote oneself to为固定搭配，表示"献身于……"。

9)【答案】B

【题解】decrease 减少；increase 增加；reduce 减少；raise 提升，增加（工资，薪金）。

10)【答案】D

【题解】what, which引导名词性从句；where引导地点状语从句；when引导时间状语从句。

【译文】

我们都有自己眼中的英雄——那些我们钦佩和尊敬的人，那些对我们的生活有着巨大影响，使我们用不同的眼光看世界的人。特里萨修女就是这些人中的一个。

这世界满是好人，特里萨修女却是杰出的那一个。她是独一无二的。从成年起，她将毕生精力奉献于对"濒死之人、伤残之人、精神病人、被遗弃的人、缺少关爱的人"的关怀。她为他们提供衣食住处，为他们清洗伤口。更重要的是，她使他们觉得快乐，觉得被关怀、被需要。贫穷曾使他们丧失了尊严，她却使得他们重获了尊严。即使在离开这个世界的时候，他们的脸上也带着笑容。

大约是50年前，特里萨发现一个女人躺在一家医院前面。她坐在妇人身旁，陪着她，直到她死去。不久后，她发起一项运动，为将死之人提供住所，使其死得有尊严。她创建了一个全球性的网站，专为穷苦人提供家庭帮助，其中包括首次为艾滋病人提供家庭帮助。

在印度及其周边，特里萨修女献身于对盲人、残疾人、老年人和穷苦人的关怀。她创办学校、孤儿院以及贫民之家，在艾滋病逐渐猖獗的时候又把注意力转向了艾滋病患者们。到1996年为止，她在100多个国家里管理着517家慈善机构。

法国总统雅克·希拉克在其逝世后说道："今晚，这个世上的仁爱、同情和光明减少了。"这句话，是对特里萨修女精神最好的评价。

2. 用括号中的词汇和短语将下列句子译成英语。

1)【答案】At that crucial moment we adopted some effective strategies.

2)【答案】Knowing that the enemy had retreated, the General got terribly happy.

3)【答案】From time to time he goes to the hospital in his daughter's company.

4)【答案】When she was told that the project had been accomplished ahead of time, her face lit up with a smile.

5)【答案】The professor remarked, "It is important to cheer up your family when they are depressed."

文章泛读

文章导读

关于全世界最富有的人——比尔·盖茨，你知道多少呢？他是如何从一个平凡小子成为了今天家喻户晓的大明星呢？是什么样的信念让他获得今天万众瞩目的成就？在成功的道路上他有没有也遇到挫折、低谷？所有这些问题的答案，让我们从阅读中找到。

背景知识

比尔·盖茨（**Bill Gates**）：1955年10月出生于美国西雅图，曾就读于哈佛大学，全球个人计算机软件的领先供应商——微软公司的创始人、前任董事长和首席执行官。微软公司在个人计算机和商业计算机软件、服务和互联网技术方面都是全球范围内的领导者。盖茨的资产净值：564亿美元。盖茨有关个人计算机的远见和洞察力一直是微软公司和软件业界成功的关键。盖茨积极地参与微软公司的关键性管理和战略性决策，并在新产品的技术开发中发挥着重要的作用。对于比尔·盖茨来说，慈善事业也是非常重要的。在微软公司上市的12年时间里，盖茨已向慈善机构捐赠8亿多美元。1994年，盖茨创立了William H. Gates基金会，该基金会赞助了一系列盖茨本人及其家庭感兴趣的活动。盖茨捐献的四个重点领域是：教育、世界公共卫生和人口问题、非赢利的公众艺术机构以及一个地区性的投资计划——Puget Sound。

文章写作风格及结构

本文为记叙文，作者按时间顺序向我们介绍了比尔·盖茨的成长经历，让我们看到他是如何从一个特立独行的小男孩成为了今天闻名全球的公众人物。

Parts 部分	Paragraphs 段落	Main Ideas 大意
Part I	1	Bill Gates and his company Microsoft have changed the entire world. 比尔·盖茨和他的微软公司改变了全世界。
Part II	2—3	Bill developed his interest in computer when he was receiving education. 在读书时期比尔对于电脑的兴趣不断高涨。
Part III	4—8	Bill established Microsoft, and made innovations in operating system. 比尔创建了微软公司，并且在操作系统方面不断创新。
Part IV	9—10	When Bill is getting closer and closer to his goal of "a computer on every desk and in every home", he and his company have greatly changed the world. 当比尔一步步逼近他的目标"让每张办公桌，每个家庭都有一台电脑"的时候，他和他的公司已经极大地改变了全世界。

🔹 词汇点睛

1 envision

vt. to imagine sth. that you think might happen in the future, especially sth. that you think will be good 想象，预见

- 例句 • As a young teacher, I envisioned a future of educational excellence.
作为一名年轻的教师，我想象着一个优质教育的未来。
Nobody can envision the consequences of total nuclear war. 没人能想象全面核战争的后果。
- 用法 • **envision + *vt.* ing/that…**
When do you envision being able to pay me back?
=When do you envision that you will be able to pay me back? 你看你什么时候能还我钱？
- 同义词 • **envisage**（*BrE*）*vt.* 设想，展望
What level of profit do you envisage? 你预计会有什么样的利润水平？
It is envisaged that the talks will take place in the spring. 谈判预期在春季举行。

2 impact

n. 1) the effect or influence that an event, situation, etc., has on sb./sth. 影响

- 例句 • Her speech made a profound impact on everyone. 她的讲话对每个人都有深远的影响。
We should take the impact of modern science upon society as a whole.
我们应考虑到现代科学对整个社会的影响。
- 短语 • **have an impact on** 对……有影响
  2) the act of one object hitting another 撞击，冲撞
- 例句 • The bomb explodes on impact. 炸弹受到撞击就爆炸。
  vi. to have an effect on sth. 有影响，有作用
- 短语 • **impact (on/upon) sth.** 对……有影响，有作用
Her father's death impacted greatly on her childhood years.
父亲去世对她的童年造成了巨大影响。

3 quest

n. a long search for sth. that is difficult to find 寻找，探索

- 例句 • They traveled in quest of gold. 他们为寻找黄金而长途跋涉。
The story is about people's quest for hidden treasure. 这故事是关于人们寻找宝藏的。
  v. to search for sth. that is difficult to find 寻找，探索，追求
- 例句 • The dogs were questing for rabbits. 猎狗正在搜寻兔子。

4 operate

v. 1) to work 运转，工作

- 例句 • Do you know how to operate the heating system? 你知道怎么操作这加热系统吗？
The machine is not operating at maximum efficiency. 这部机器目前的运转效率未达最佳状态。
  2) to cut open sb.'s body in order to remove a part that has a disease or to repair a part that is damaged 动手术
- 例句 • The doctors decided to operate at once. 医生们决定立刻动手术。
- 短语 • **operate on** 给……动手术

- 扩展 - **operation** *n.* 运转，运行，操作；手术

Operation of the device is extremely simple. 这个装置的操作非常简单。

Will I need to have an operation? 我需要动手术吗？

5 challenge

vt. 1) to test the skills or abilities of sb. or sth. 挑战

- 例句 - I challenge you to race me across the lake. 我跟你比一比，看谁先游过这个湖。

She challenged the newspaper to prove its story. 她要求这家报纸证实报道的真实性。

2) to question whether a statement or an action is right, legal, etc. 对……怀疑

- 例句 - This new discovery challenges traditional beliefs. 这项新的发现对传统观念提出了置疑。

n. a new or difficult task that tests sb.'s ability and skill 挑战

- 例句 - Schools must meet the challenge of new technology. 学校必须迎接新技术的挑战。

The role will be the biggest challenge of his acting career.

这个角色将是他演艺生涯中最大的挑战。

- 扩展 - **challenging** *adj.* 具有挑战性的

He finds his new job very challenging. 他发现自己的新工作很有挑战性。

6 mission

n. sth. that you feel you must do because it is your duty 使命，任务

- 例句 - This time, James Bond's mission is to save three hostages kidnapped by some terrorists.

这次，詹姆斯·邦德的使命是去解救被恐怖分子绑架的三名人质。

Mission accomplished! 任务完成了!

7 somewhat

adv. more than a little, but not very 一点儿，几分

- 例句 - I was somewhat surprised to see him. 见到他我有点诧异。

The situation has changed somewhat since we last met. 自我们上次见面以来情况有些变化。

8 passion

n. a very strong liking for sth. 热情，激情

- 例句 - The English have a passion for gardens. 英国人酷爱花园。

Music is a passion with him. 他钟情于音乐。

- 扩展 - **passionate** *adj.* 热诚的，狂热的

Jane takes a passionate interest in music. 简对音乐有浓厚兴趣。

We appreciate her passionate support for our cause. 我们感谢她对我们事业的热情支持。

passionately *adv.*

They are all passionately interested in environmental issues. 他们都热衷于环境问题。

9 staff

n. the people who work for an organization 全体职员

- 例句 - We have 20 part-time members of staff. 我们有20名兼职员工。

We will have a staff meeting tomorrow. 我们明天将举行员工大会。

- 辨析 - **stuff** *n.* 东西，物品，玩意儿（事物名称不详或无关紧要时用）

What's all that sticky stuff on the carpet? 地毯上黏糊糊的是什么玩意儿？

10   track

vt. to record or study the behavior or development of sb. or sth. over time 监看，追踪

- 例句 • There're many hunters tracking and shooting bears. 有很多猎人追踪并射猎熊。

  We continued tracking the plane on our radar. 我们继续用雷达追踪那架飞机。

- 短语 • **track sb./sth. down** 搜寻到，跟踪找到

  The police have so far failed to track down the attacker. 警方至今未能追捕到攻击者。

  n. marks left by a person, an animal or a moving vehicle （人、动物或车辆留下的）足迹，踪迹，车辙

- 例句 • We follow the bear's tracks in the snow. 我们跟着熊留在雪地上的足迹走。

  There were two sets of fresh tyre tracks outside. 外面有两组新的车辙。

11   pattern

n. 1) the regular way in which sth. happens, develops, or is done 模式，方式

- 例句 • These sentences all have the same grammatical pattern. 这些句子的语法模式都相同。

  The murders all seem to follow a set pattern. 这些谋杀案似乎都遵循同一手法。

  2) excellent example; model 模范，榜样

- 例句 • She's a pattern of all the virtues. 她是一切美德的楷模。

12   environment

n. the people and things that are around you 环境

- 例句 • An unhappy home environment can affect a child's behaviour.

  不愉快的家庭环境能影响儿童的行为。

  Many people are concerned about the pollution of the environment.

  许多人都关心环境污染问题。

13   claim

vt. 1) to state that you have a right to take or have sth. that is legally yours 申请，认领

- 例句 • A lot of lost property is never claimed. 许多失物都无人认领。

  The family arrived in the UK in 1990s and claimed political asylum.

  这家人20世纪90年代来到英国申请政治避难。

  2) to say that sth. is true although it has not been proved and other people may not believe it 宣称，声称，断言

- 例句 • He claimed that he had done the work without help. 他声称独立完成了这项工作。

  n. 1) right to sth. 对某事物的权利

- 例句 • They have no claim on our sympathy. 他们没有让我们同情的权利。

  2) statement of sth. as a fact; assertion 陈述，声称

- 例句 • Investigation showed his claim to be false. 调查结果表明他的陈述纯属虚构。

14   handle

vt. 1) to be in charge of sth.; to deal with sth. 处理，应付

- 例句 • A new man was appointed to handle the crisis. 新指派了一个人来处理这场危机。

  She is very good at handling her patients. 她应付病人有很好的办法。

2) touch (sth.) with or hold (sth.) in the hand(s)（用手）触、摸、拿

- 例句 • Fragile—handle with care! 易碎品——小心轻放！

n.1) a part of an object which is specially made for holding it or for opening it 柄，把手

- 例句 • Pick up the typewriter case by the handle. 抓住把手，把打字机的箱子拿起来。

2) fact that may be taken advantage of 把柄，可乘之机

- 例句 • His indiscretions gave his enemies a handle to use against him.
  他的不够慎重给了敌人以反对他的可乘之机。

15 conduct

vt. 1) to carry out a particular activity or process 处理，管理

- 例句 • The company conducted a survey to find out local reaction to the leisure center.
  公司进行了一项调查以了解当地对游乐活动中心的反应。
  He was appointed to conduct the advertising campaign. 他被委派主持宣传活动。

2) to lead or guide sb. through or around a place 带领，引导

- 例句 • The guide conducted us around the ruins of the ancient city. 导游引导我们游览了古城废墟。

3) to behave (oneself) 为人，表现

- 例句 • How did the prisoner conduct himself? 那犯人表现如何？
- 短语 • **conduct oneself well/badly** 表现好/不好

n. 1) person's behavior 行为，品行

- 例句 • The reporter was accused of unprofessional conduct. 那位记者被指控有违反职业道德的行为。

2) manner of directing or managing (a business, activity, etc.) 处理，经营，指导，实施

- 例句 • There was growing criticism of the Government's conduct of the war.
  政府领导作战的方式受到越来越多的批评。

16 contract

n. an official agreement between two or more people, stating what each will do 合同，契约

- 例句 • These clauses form part of the contract between buyer and seller.
  这些条款构成买卖双方所签合同的一部分。
  I was on a three-year contract that expired last week. 我签订的三年期合同已于上周到期。

v. 1) to arrange by formal agreement 定契约，立合同

- 例句 • They contracted to build the new bridge. 他们签订合同造新桥。

2) to (cause to) become smaller, narrower, or shorter（使）缩小，收缩，缩短

- 例句 • Metals contract in cold weather. 冷天金属会收缩。

17 convince

v. to make sb. feel certain that sth. is true 使确信，使信服

- 例句 • You will need to convince them of your enthusiasm for the job.
  你要使他们相信你殷切希望得到这份工作。
  We convinced Anne to go by train rather than plane.
  我们说服了安妮放弃乘飞机而坐火车走。

- 短语 • **convince sb. of sth./that...** 使某人相信……
  I convinced him of her honesty. =I convinced him that she was honest. 我使他相信她是诚实的。

- 扩展 • **convincing** *adj.* 令人信服的

He delivered a convincing speech. 他发表了一次令人信服的演讲。

convinced *adj.* 确信的

He left the room, convinced that a war would come. 确信一场战争即将到来，他离开了房间。

18 plain

adj. 1) *simple* 纯的

• 例句 • Today she's in a plain blue dress. 她今天身着一件纯蓝色的衣服。

My favorite food is plain chocolate. 我最喜欢的食物是纯巧克力。

2) *easy to see or understand* 清楚的，明显的

• 例句 • He made it plain that we should leave. 他明确表示我们要离开。

3) *not beautiful or good-looking* 不漂亮的，不好看的

• 例句 • From a rather plain child she had grown into a beautiful woman.

她从一个相貌平平的女孩成长为一个漂亮的妇人。

adv. used to emphasize how bad, stupid, etc. sth. is 完全地

• 例句 • That's just plain stupid! 那真是彻头彻尾的愚蠢！

n. large area of flat land 平原

19 version

n. a copy of sth. that has been changed so that it is slightly different 版本

• 例句 • These books are Chinese versions of Shakespeare. 这些书籍是莎士比亚作品的中译本。

Do you have the latest version of the software package? 你有软件包的最新版本吗？

20 release

vt. 1) *to make a CD, video, film, etc., available for people to buy or see* 发布

• 例句 • Police have released no further details about the accident.

关于这次事故，警方没有发布更多的细节。

Let's Go to Prison was released in 2006. 《同居牢友》是一部2006年发行的电影。

2) *to set free* 释放

• 例句 • Firefighters took two hours to release the driver from the wreckage.

消防队员花了两个小时将司机从汽车残骸中解救出来。

21 relentless

adj. determined, without ever stopping 不懈的，不屈不挠的；无情的

• 例句 • You have to be as single-minded and relentless as your rivals if you want to get to the top.

如果你想达到最高层，就必须和你的对手一样专心致志，绝不示弱。

They are always relentless in punishing offenders. 他们惩处犯罪者一向不手软。

• 扩展 • **relent** *vi.* 终于答应，不再谢绝；变缓和，变温和；减弱

Afterwards she relented and let the children stay up late to watch TV.

后来她终于答应，让孩子们晚睡看电视。

The police will not relent in their fight against crime. 警方不会减弱打击犯罪的力度。

relentlessly *adv.*

He beat the dog relentlessly. 他痛打了那只狗。

22 pioneer

n. sb. who is important in the early development of sth. 先驱，开拓者

• 例句 • They were pioneers in this field. 他们是这个领域的开拓者。

The early pioneers built many log cabins. 早期的拓荒者建了很多小木屋。

v. when sb. pioneers sth., they are one of the first people to do, discover or use sth. new 当开发者，倡导（新方法）

• 例句 • She pioneered the use of the drug. 是她最先使用的这种药品。

23　achieve

vt. to successfully complete sth. or get a good result, especially by working hard 获得，完成，达到

• 例句 • He had finally achieved success. 他终于获得了成功。

This will help us achieve modernization. 这有助于我们实现现代化。

• 扩展 • **achievement** *n.* 成就，成绩，功绩

It was a remarkable achievement for such a young player.

如此年轻的选手有这样的成绩真是了不起。

Even a small success gives you a sense of achievement. 即使是小小的成功也给人一种成就感。

24　generous

adj. willing to give money, spend time, etc., in order to help people or give them pleasure 慷慨的，大方的

• 例句 • It was generous of him to pay for us both. 他主动为我俩付钱，真是大方。

You should be generous in giving help. 你应该乐于助人。

• 扩展 • **generosity** *n.* 慷慨、大方（的行为）

I'm touched by his generosity. 我被他的慷慨感动了。

短语解析

1.　in great quantity　大量地

【例句】It's cheaper to buy goods in great quantity. 大宗购物比较便宜。

Inexpensive cars are manufactured in great quantity. 便宜的汽车被大量生产出来。

2.　make a profit　赚钱，盈利

【例句】The aim of a company is to make a profit. 公司的目标就是盈利。

They make a profit of 10 pence on every copy they sell. 他们每售出一本就获利10便士。

3.　venture into　冒险进入，涉足

【例句】This is the first time the company has ventured into movie production.

这是这家公司首次涉足电影制作。

I never venture into the water. 我从不敢下水。

4.　as well　也，同样

【例句】Are they coming as well? 他们也来吗？

Besides flowers, he grows vegetables as well. 除了种花，他也种蔬菜。

5. concentrate on 集中，全神贯注

【例句】In this lecture I shall concentrate on the early years of Charles's reign.

这一节课我将着重讲查理王朝的早期统治时期。

I can't concentrate on my studies with all that noise going on.

周围的噪音使我无法专心学习。

6. no longer 不再

【例句】I can no longer stand your behavior. 我再也不能忍受你的行为了。

He no longer lives here. 他不住在这儿了。

7. show up 出席，露面

【例句】It was getting late when she finally showed up. 她终于赶到的时候已经很晚了。

We were hoping for a full team today but only five players showed up.

今天我们本希望全体队员都能来，但结果只到了五个。

🌑 难句突破

1. (Para.1) *He has succeeded in his quest, his company Microsoft becoming the largest in the world.*

【解析】本句中含有一个独立结构Microsoft becoming the largest in the world。独立结构就是带有自己主语的非限定分句和无动词分句，独立结构按其结构形式分为不定式独立结构，-ing分词独立结构，-ed分词独立结构和无动词独立结构，通常在句中起到状语的作用。独立结构常见于正式语体，特别是文学体裁，能够使句子结构紧凑，用词精炼，描写生动，形象具体。例如：

His homework done, Jim decided to go and see the play. = After his homework was done, Jim...(表示时间) 作业做完后，吉姆决定去看演出。

The last bus having gone, we had to walk home. = Because the last bus had gone, we...(表示原因) 最后一班车已经走了，我们不得不走回家。

Weather permitting, the football match will be played on Wednesday. = If weather permits, the football match...(表示条件) 如果天气允许，足球比赛将在周三举行。

He entered upon the new enterprise cautiously, his eyes wide-open. = ···,with his eyes wide-open.(表示方式和伴随状况) 他小心翼翼地走进新公司，睁大了眼睛。

【译文】而他已经成功地实现了他的追求。他的公司，微软，已经成为世界上最大的公司。

2. (Para.1) *In fact, Bill Gates and his company Microsoft have changed the way the entire world operates.*

【解析】the way引导方式状语从句，the way后面的引导词常用that，而且经常省略，一般不用in which引导。例如：

We didn't like the way he treated us. 我们不喜欢他对待我们的方式。

【译文】事实上，比尔·盖茨和他的微软公司，已经改变了整个世界。

3. (Para.2) *It was here that he discovered his passion for computers.*

【解析】it is/was... that/who... 是强调句型，一般强调主语、状语和宾语。本句中是强调状语here。

【译文】就是在这里，盖茨发现自己对电脑的热爱。

4. **(Para.4)** *After his sophomore year, both Gates and Allen felt they could have greater success in the business environment, so they left Harvard in 1975 and founded a small programming company called Microsoft.*

【解析】大学四个年级学生的说法分别为：大一：freshman；大二：sophomore；大三：junior；大四：senior。毕业生和大四的学生也可叫做graduate；而未毕业的学生（大一到大三的学生）可叫做undergraduate。

【译文】第二学年后，盖茨和艾伦感到他们可能在商界获得更大的成功，因此，1975年他们离开了哈佛大学，成立了一家小小的编程公司，取名为微软。

5. **(Para.6)** *MS-DOS was on the way to becoming the standard in personal computing.*

【解析】on the way to... 表示"在去（成为）……的路上"；on the way to becoming... 表示"正慢慢成为，逐渐成为"。

【译文】MS-DOS当时正逐渐成为个人计算机的标准配置。

6. **(Para.10)** *However, he is very generous, and, as of writing, has given over $26 billion to various charities and foundations.*

【解析】本句的主干是... he is very generous and... has given over $ 26 billion to... ；其中两个逗号之间的as of writing是插入语，表示"截止写稿时为止"。

【译文】然而，他非常慷慨大方，截止写稿时为止，他已经为各种慈善团体和基金会捐出了260亿美元。

参考译文

比尔·盖茨——把简单的计算机操作带给了全世界

这个世界上最富有的人曾经说："十几岁的时候，我就预想到了低价电脑可能带来的影响。'让每张办公桌，每个家庭都有一台电脑'成为微软的使命，而且我们已经努力使之成为可能"。而他已经成功地实现了他的追求。他的公司，微软，已经成为世界上最大的公司。事实上，比尔·盖茨和他的微软公司，已经改变了整个世界。

比尔·盖茨1955年10月28日出生于西雅图。在公立学校学习期间，盖茨没有遇到什么挑战，因此丧失了对读书的兴趣。那时的他有些惹是生非。他的父母作出决定，把他转到了一所私立学校就读，即湖畔小学。就是在这里，盖茨发现自己对电脑的热爱。一个朋友帮他写下了他在那个时期的第一个程序，在那之后，盖茨就从未停止过。高中时，他帮助公司职员编写了工资单程序。这次成功之后，比尔和朋友史蒂夫·艾伦一起成立了一家公司，该公司的主要业务是帮助政府监控街道的交通状况。1972年，中学毕业后，艾伦和盖茨都来到哈佛大学，他们在那里遇到了史蒂夫·巴尔梅，他的微软的梦想开始变为现实。

盖茨和他的中学朋友艾伦开始为最早的微型电脑开发软件。最后完成的语言被称为微软BASIC语言，这种语言直到今天仍然在编程中使用。

第二学年后，盖茨和艾伦感到他们可能在商界获得更大的成功，因此，1975年他们离开了哈佛大学，成立了一家小小的编程公司，取名为微软。

对盖茨和他的小公司而言，1976年是至关重要的一年。公司在新墨西哥的阿尔伯克基租下了自己的第一栋办公大楼，并在该州申请了微软的公司名。微软以极其低廉的价格销售他们的产品，他们相信自己的宗旨——"让每张办公桌，每个家庭都有一台电脑"——能让他们通过大量销售自己的软件，从而获利。微软头几年的日子很艰难。比尔每天工作很长时间，他需要处理很多事务，从处理代码到资金运作，甚至处理业务电话。

当世界上最大的主机生产商IBM决定进军个人电脑市场时，微软的第一单大合同出现了。他们需要比尔开发一个磁盘操作系统，从而使计算机可以与鼠标、键盘和显示器配套使用。1981年，微软公司完成了该操作系统并把它命名为MS-DOS。由于购买该操作系统的人很多，由IBM公司支付的版税很快大量涌入微软。其他人眼见IBM公司获得的成功，也纷纷决定使用比尔的操作系统。不久，世界各地的大多数个人电脑生产商都支付版税给比尔。MS-DOS当时正逐渐成为个人计算机的标准配置。

在与IBM共同开发的一个操作系统失败后，比尔决定将精力集中在他为微软制定的计划上：Windows操作系统。比尔坚信人们更愿意使用图形用户界面操作系统，而不是一个MS-DOS一般的纯文本系统。图形用户界面将帮助人们更轻松地理解电脑，让复杂的代码以后台方式工作，而不让用户看到，他们只需要看到代码的结果就行了。

20世纪80年代，微软发布了两个版本的Windows操作系统之后，才获得了真正的成功。1990年，比尔发行了Windows的第三个版本，Windows 3.0，整个世界都为之震动了。不到两周，该系统就卖出了十万多套，到1991年底前，卖出了四百多万套。

今天，比尔仍坚持不懈地工作。通过努力，每一年，他都在一步步逼近他的目标"让每张办公桌，每个家庭都有一台电脑"。在Windows 3.0后，比尔又发行了Windows 95，Windows NT，Windows 98，Windows ME，Windows 2000，以及他最新的操作系统Windows XP。下一步计划是在2007年推出他的新项目Windows Vista。

比尔·盖茨曾经是电脑领域的先锋，如今依然还是，他已经拥有难以想象的财富。然而，他非常慷慨大方，截止写稿时为止，他已经为各种慈善团体和基金会捐出了260亿美元。尽管已不再是微软的执行总裁，比尔仍然每天到公司上班，他仍是微软不可或缺的一分子。比尔确确实实影响了全世界的交流方式和日常事务的处理方式。

习题全解

1. 根据文章选择最佳答案补全下列句子。

1) 【答案】C

【题解】根据文章第一段中"'让每张办公桌，每个家庭都有一台电脑'成为微软的使命"，应选C。

2) 【答案】D

【题解】根据文章第二段中"他的父母作出决定，把他转到了一所私立学校就读，即湖畔小学。就是在这里，盖茨发现自己对电脑的热爱。""It was here..."就是指湖畔小学，所以应选D。

3) 【答案】C

【题解】根据文章第二段中"1972年，中学毕业后，艾伦和盖茨都来到哈佛大学，他们在那里遇到了史蒂夫·巴尔梅，他的微软的梦想开始变为现实"，所以选C。

4) 【答案】A
　　【题解】根据文章第三段中"盖茨和他的中学朋友艾伦开始为最早的微型电脑开发软件。最后
　　　　　　完成的语言被称为微软BASIC语言……"，应选A。

5) 【答案】C
　　【题解】根据文章第四段中"1975年他们离开了哈佛大学，成立了一家小小的编程公司，取名
　　　　　　为微软"，所以选C。

6) 【答案】A
　　【题解】根据文章第六段中"他们需要比尔开发一个磁盘操作系统，…… 1981年，微软公司完
　　　　　　成了该操作系统并把它命名为MS-DOS"，所以选A。

7) 【答案】A
　　【题解】根据文章第七段最后一句"图形用户界面将帮助人们更轻松地理解电脑……"，应选 A。

8) 【答案】D
　　【题解】根据文章最后一段"尽管已不再是微软的执行总裁"，D是错误的，其他三项的内容都
　　　　　　能在文章中找到。

2. 请用下面所给出的词汇或短语的适当形式填写句子。

1) 【答案】released
　　【译文】这起谋杀案的细节并没向公众公开。

2) 【答案】claimed/claims
　　【译文】没有任何人宣称对这起爆炸事件负责。

3) 【答案】convince
　　【译文】我们试图让孩子们相信一切都很好。

4) 【答案】as well
　　【译文】我们的假期简直就是一场灾难：不光食物难吃，就连天气也糟透了。

5) 【答案】somewhat
　　【译文】从那以后，事情有了一些转机。

6) 【答案】concentrate on
　　【译文】我们应当努力让系统更加高效地运转。

7) 【答案】challenged
　　【译文】我说我跑得更快，她则坚持要和我进行一场比赛。

8) 【答案】showed up
　　【译文】我想见史密斯先生，但他总不露面。

9) 【答案】impact
　　【译文】许多人都担心新的法规会影响到他们的日常生活。

10) 【答案】passion
　　【译文】他对足球很狂热。

3. 将下面这些段落译成汉语。

1) 【答案】在公立学校学习期间，盖茨没有遇到什么挑战，因此丧失了对读书的兴趣。那时的他
　　　　　　有些惹是生非，所以父母决定把他转到一所私立学校就读，即湖畔小学。就是在这
　　　　　　里，盖茨发现自己对电脑有多么地热爱。

2) 【答案】1981年，微软公司完成了该操作系统并把它命名为MS-DOS。由于购买该操作系统的人很多，由IBM公司支付的版税很快大量涌入微软。其他人眼见IBM公司获得的成功，也纷纷决定使用比尔的操作系统。不久，世界各地的大多数个人电脑生产商都支付版税给比尔。

文章泛读

📖 文章导读

它只是一本自传，但影响了各个时代的人，连喜欢开玩笑的马克·吐温也深深为之折服。因为这本书的作者是一位看不见、听不见、说不出话的女孩。她最终获得了哈佛的学位，并在国际讲坛上用自己也听不到的声音震撼着世界。她，就是海伦·凯勒，这本自传的名字是《假如给我三天光明》。从海伦·凯勒身上你可以得到的是一种力量！顽强、富有毅力、热爱生命、热爱生活、艰难中进取……你将要读到的故事节选自这本自传，描述了海伦·凯勒一生中最重要的一天。

💿 背景知识

海伦·凯勒（Helen Keller）：20世纪，一个独特的生命个体以其勇敢的生活方式震撼了世界，她就是海伦·凯勒——一个生活在黑暗中却又给人类带来光明的女性，一个度过了生命的88个春秋，却熬过了87年无光、无声、无语的孤独岁月的弱女子。然而，正是这么一个幽闭在盲聋哑世界里的人，竟然毕业于哈佛大学拉德克利夫学院，并用生命的全部力量处处奔走，建起了一家家慈善机构，为残疾人造福。美国《时代周刊》评选她为"20世纪美国十大英雄偶像之一"。海伦能够创造这一奇迹，全靠一颗不屈不挠的心。她接受了生命的挑战，用爱心去拥抱世界，以惊人的毅力面对困境，终于在黑暗中找到了光明，最后又把慈爱的双手伸向全世界。1968年，海伦·凯勒平静地走完了她艰辛而又充满荣耀的一生。

📝 文章写作风格及结构

本文选自海伦·凯勒的自传体小说。作者从一个孩子的视角向我们描述了一个脆弱却又顽强的心灵在老师的带领下尝试认识这个世界的过程。

Parts 部分	Paragraphs 段落	Main Ideas 大意
Part I	1—3	On the third of March, 1887, one of the most important persons in my life, my teacher Anne Mansfield Sullivan, came to me. 1887年3月3号，我生命中最重要的人之一，我的老师安妮·曼斯菲尔德·沙利文走进了我的生活。

(to be continued)

(continued)

Parts 部分	Paragraphs 段落	Main Ideas 大意
Part II	4	My teacher let me know that everything has a name by her special way of teaching. 我的老师用她特有的教学方式让我明白了世间万物都有自己的名字。
Part III	5—6	When I was confused about the two words "water" and "mug" and became impatient, my teacher led me to the nature to feel water, and managed to tell the difference between the two words. 当我分不清"水"和"杯子"，并且开始烦躁的时候，我的老师带我到大自然中感受水，从而使我区分了这两个词。
Part IV	7—8	After that I was eager to learn, and I felt I was the happiest child in the world. 那次教学过后我渴望学习，并且我感觉自己是世界上最幸福的孩子。

词汇点睛

1　contrast

n. a difference between people, ideas, situations, things, etc., that are being compared 对比，明显的差异，对照

• 例句 • There is an obvious contrast between the cultures of the East and West.
东西方文化之间存在着明显的差异。

The situation when we arrived was in marked contrast to the news reports.
我们到达时的局势与新闻报道的情况截然不同。

vt. 1) to compare two things in order to show the differences between them 对比，对照

• 例句 • The poem contrasts youth and age. 这首诗对比了青春和老年。

vi. 2) to show a clear difference when close together or when compared 形成对比，显出明显的差异

• 例句 • Her actions and her promises contrasted sharply. 她的行动与她的诺言相差甚远。

• 短语 • **be a contrast to** 和……成对比

by contrast 对比之下

in contrast with/to 和……形成对比/对照

• 辨析 • **compare，contrast**

二者都含"相比"、"比较"的意思。

compare常指为了找出两种事物或现象的异同点而进行比较。如：

If you compare Marx's works with Hegel's, you'll find many differences.

如果你把马克思的著作同黑格尔的著作相比较，就会发现许多不同之处。

contrast 指两者之间的"对照"、"对比"，着重指通过两种事物或现象的对比，突出地指出它们的不同。如：

contrast farm life with city life 对照一下城乡生活

2　eventful

adj. full of interesting or important events 重要的，发生许多事情的

• 例句 • He attended an eventful meeting between heads of states. 他出席了两国首脑间的重要会晤。

What an eventful year! 真是多事的一年！

• 扩展 • **event** *n.* （尤指重要、有意思或不寻常的）事件

Coming events cast their shadows before them. [谚]事发之前必有征兆。

It is easy to be wise after the event. [谚]事后聪明不难。（作事后诸葛亮容易。）

3 dumb

adj. 1) not able to speak at all 哑的

- 例句• She was born deaf and dumb. 她天生又聋又哑。

2) temporarily not speaking or refusing to speak 一时说不出话的；不肯开口的

- 例句• They remained dumb at the meeting. 他们在会上保持沉默。
- 短语• **as dumb as an oyster/a fish** 沉默不语
- 扩展• **dumbly** *adv.* 默默地

"Are you all right ?" Laura nodded dumbly. "你身体好吗？"劳拉默默地点了点头。
- 辨析• **dump** *n./vt.* 垃圾场；倾销，倾倒

4 reveal

vt. to make known sth. that was previously secret or unknown 展现，展示

- 例句• He laughed, revealing a line of white teeth. 他笑了起来，露出一排洁白的牙齿。

Details of the murder were revealed by the local paper. 地方报纸披露了谋杀的细节。
- 短语• **reveal oneself** 露面

She crouched in the dark, too frightened to reveal herself. 她蜷缩在黑暗中，吓得不敢露面。

5 imitate

vt. to copy the way sb. behaves, speaks, moves, etc. 模仿，仿效

- 例句• Her style of painting has been imitated by other artists. 她的绘画风格为其他画家所模仿。

She knew that the girls used to imitate her and laugh at her behind her back.
她知道女孩子们过去常在背地里模仿她，嘲笑她。
- 扩展• **imitation** *n.* 模仿，仿效；仿制品，赝品

A child learns to talk by imitation. 小孩子通过模仿学会说话。

That's not an original Rembrandt; it's an imitation. 那不是伦勃朗的真品，是件仿制品。

6 flush

v. 1) to (cause to) become red in the face （使）脸发红

- 例句• The young man flushed with embarrassment. 这个年轻人窘得脸发红。

Fever flushed his cheeks. 他发烧烧得满脸通红。

2) to clean with a rush of water （用水）冲洗
- 例句• Please flush the toilet after you've used it. 便后请冲水。
- 扩展• **flushed** *adj.* （因兴奋而）脸红的

She's flushed with joy. 她因喜悦而激动得脸红。

7 childish

adj. relating to or typical of a child 孩子气的，幼稚的

- 例句• I knew who she is from her childish handwriting. 我从她幼稚的笔迹中知道了她是谁。

Don't be so childish. 别那么孩子气。
- 辨析• **childlike** *adj. having the qualities that children usually have, especially innocence* 孩子般的，童稚的，单纯的 (尤指天真无邪的)

His childlike simplicity amazed me. 他孩子般的单纯使我感到惊讶。

8 **confound**

vt. 1) to fail to distinguish 混淆

• 例句 • Don't confound the means with the ends. 不要使手段与目的混淆不清。

　　2) to confuse and surprise by being unexpected 使困惑，使不知所措

• 例句 • The poor election results confounded the government. 失败的选举结果使政府惊慌失措。

9 **renew**

vt. 1) to begin doing sth. again after a period of not doing it 重新开始，中止后继续

• 例句 • The army renewed its assault on the capital. 军队重新发动对首都的攻击。

　　We renewed our journey the next day. 次日我们继续旅行。

　　2) to make sth. valid for a further period of time 使继续有效，延长……的期限

• 例句 • How do I go about renewing my passport? 我该如何去续签护照？

　　3) to change sth. that is old or damaged and replace it with sth. new of the same kind 更新，
更换

• 例句 • The wiring in your house should be renewed every 10 to 15 years.
你家里的电线应该每10到15年更新一次。

　　4) to emphasize sth. by saying or stating it again 重申，重复强调

• 例句 • Community leaders have renewed calls for a peaceful settlement.
社区领导人再次呼吁要和平解决。

10 **seize**

vt. 1) to take hold of sth. suddenly and violently 抓住，抢，夺

• 例句 • She tried to seize the gun from him. 她试图夺他的枪。

　　She seized me by the wrist. 她抓住我的手腕。

　　2) to take control of a place or situation, often suddenly and violently （常指通过暴力突然)夺
取，攻占

• 例句 • They seized the airport in a surprise attack. 他们突袭攻占了机场。

　　3) to arrest or capture sb. 逮捕，俘获

• 例句 • The men were seized as they left the building. 这些人在离开那栋房子时被抓获。

　　4) to take illegal or stolen goods away from sb. 没收，扣押

• 例句 • A large quantity of drugs were seized as they left the building.
在他们离开大厦时没收了大量毒品。

　　5) to be quick to make use of a chance, an opportunity, etc. 抓住，把握 (机会，时机，主动等)

• 例句 • The party seized the initiative immediately. 该党迅速掌握了主动。

11 **dash**

vt. 1) to throw or push sth. violently against sth., especially so that it breaks 猛掷

• 例句 • He dashed the bowl to bits on the ground. 他猛地把碗扔到地上，摔得粉碎。

　　The wave dashed the boat against the rocks. 海浪狠狠地把小船撞到岩石上。

　　2) to run quickly, especially when hurrying 冲、猛冲

• 例句 • He dashed out of the room at the sight of a snake. 他一看到蛇就冲出了房间。

　　3) to put an end to (especially hopes) 使破灭，使受挫 (尤指希望)

• 例句 • The injury dashed his hopes of running in the Olympics.
由于受了伤，他参加奥运会的希望破灭了。

12　sweep

vt. 1) (swept, swept) to clean the dust, dirt, etc. from the floor or ground, using a brush with a long handle 打扫，清扫

• 例句 • She swept the floor clean. 她把地板打扫干净了。

　　2) to remove or move with a brushing or swinging movement （扫地似地）吹走、席卷

• 例句 • He swept the papers into a drawer. 他把各种文件一股脑儿塞进了抽屉。

vi. to move quickly and powerfully (all over) 掠过，袭击

• 例句 • A wave of panic swept over her. 一阵恐惧袭上她的心头。

n. an act of sweeping 打扫，清扫

• 例句 • Give the room a good sweep. 好好打扫一下这间房。

13　remove

vt. 1) to get rid of sth. so that it does not exist any longer 消除，去掉

• 例句 • He removed the mud from his shoes. 他去掉鞋上的泥。

　　The threat of redundancy was suddenly removed. 裁员的危险顿时消除了。

　　2) to take off clothing, etc. from the body 脱去（衣服等），摘下

• 例句 • She removed her glasses and rubbed her eyes. 她摘下眼镜，揉了揉眼睛。

　　3) to dismiss sb. from their position or job 免除，解除（职务等）

• 例句 • The elections removed the government from power. 这次选举使得政府倒台。

• 短语 • **remove from** 与……大相径庭

　　Many of these books are far removed from the reality of the children's lives.

　　很多这样的书都远远脱离了孩子们的现实生活。

14　somehow

adv. 1) in some way, or by some means, although you do not know how 不知何故

• 例句 • Somehow, I don't feel I can trust him. 不知何故，我觉得不能信任他。

　　She somehow got lost. 她不知道怎么竟迷了路。

　　2) in a way that is not known or certain 以某种方式

• 例句 • We must stop him from seeing her somehow. 不管怎么着，我们都不能让他见到她。

15　mystery

n. 1) the quality that sb./sth. has when they seem strange, secret, or difficult to understand or explain 谜

• 例句 • It is one of the great unsolved mysteries of this century. 这是本世纪尚未解开的奥秘之一。

　　It is a mystery to me why they didn't choose him. 他们为什么不选择他，对我而言是个谜。

　　2) a story, a film/movie or a play in which crimes and strange events are only explained at the end 悬疑小说

• 例句 • I enjoyed murder mysteries. 我喜欢凶杀疑案作品。

• 扩展 • **mysterious** *adj.* 神秘的，不可思议的，难解的

　　She gave me a mysterious look. 她向我使了个神秘的眼色。

　　mysteriously *adv.*

　　The main witness had mysteriously disappeared. 主要见证人神秘地失踪了。

16   awaken

vt. 1) to make sb. understand a situation and its possible effects 唤醒，使察觉到
- 例句 • We must awaken people to the need to protect our environment.
  我们必须使人民认识到保护环境的必要性。
  They were making enough noise to awaken the dead. 他们发出的噪音大得能把死人吵醒。

   2) to cause sth. to become active 唤起、激起
- 例句 • The dream awakened terrible memories. 这个梦唤起了对可怕往事的回忆。

   vi. to waken; to become aware of sth. 醒来，意识到
- 例句 • I gradually awakened to the realization that our marriage was over.
  我逐渐意识到我们的婚姻结束了。
- 扩展 • **awakening** *n.* 醒悟，认识
  The discovery that her husband was unfaithful to her was a shocking awakening.
  发觉丈夫对自己不忠使她猛然清醒。

17   quiver

vi. to shake slightly because you are cold, or because you feel very afraid, angry, excited, etc. 颤抖，颤动
- 例句 • I quivered at the sound. 我听到这声音有点发抖。
  Her voice was quivering with anger. 她气得声音都微微发颤了。

   n. 颤抖，抖动
- 例句 • I felt a quiver of excitement. 我感觉到激动的颤抖。
- 辨析 • **shake; quiver; shiver**
  shake系常用词，指"上下来回短促而急速地摇动"。如：
  Shake before taking. 服前摇匀。(药瓶标签上)
  quiver指"轻微而急速地颤动、摇动"。如：
  The leaves quivered with the breeze. 树叶随微风摆动。
  shiver指"由于寒冷、恐惧或生病而发抖"。如：
  He shivered with cold. 他冻得发抖。

18   blossom

vi. 1) to produce flowers 开花
- 例句 • The cherry trees blossomed early this year. 樱桃树今年开花早。

   2) to become happier, more beautiful, more successful, etc. 繁荣，兴旺，成功，健康
- 例句 • Their friendship blossomed into love. 他们的友谊发展成了爱情。
  Mary is blossoming into a beautiful girl. 玛丽正出落成一个漂亮的女孩。

   n. flower, especially of a fruit tree or flowering shrub 花（尤指果树或灌木的花）
- 短语 • in (full) blossom （尤指树木）正在开花
  The apple trees are in blossom. 苹果树正在开花。

短语解析

1. to and fro 来回地，往复地

【例句】she rocked the baby to and fro. 她来回摇着婴儿。

The teacher walked to and fro in the front of the class as he spoke.

老师一边讲课，一边在教室前面走来走去。

2. stretch out 伸出

【例句】I stretched out a hand and picked up the book. 我伸出一只手，把书捡了起来。

The police stretched out a hand to help the kid who had fallen into the river.

警察伸出一只手帮助落水的孩子。

3. apply to 适用于

【例句】The new technology was applied to farming. 这项新技术已应用于农业。

The questions in the second half of the form apply only to married men.

表格下半部的问题只适用于已婚男士。

4. impress upon 使铭记，使留下深刻印象

【例句】He impressed upon us the need for immediate action. 他让我们认识到必须立刻采取行动。

My father impressed upon me the value of hard work. 父亲让我铭记艰苦劳动的价值。

5. persist in 坚持

【例句】Why do you persist in blaming yourself for what has happened?

你何必为已发生的事没完没了地自责呢？

If you persist in causing trouble, the company may be forced to dismiss you.

如果你坚持制造麻烦，公司可能不得不解雇你。

6. fix one's attention on 注视，专心致志于……

【例句】They have fixed their attention on Paris for their honeymoon. 他们已经选定在巴黎度蜜月。

Fix your whole attention on what you are doing. 把全部注意力用于你所做的事。

7. set free 释放，解放

【例句】All the innocent people were set free. 所有的无辜的人都被释放了。

We should set free the birds in the cage. 我们应该放了笼子中的鸟。

🔵 难句突破

1. (Para.1) *I am filled with wonder when I consider the immeasurable contrasts between the two lives which it connects.*

【解析】句中的it指代contrasts；which引导定语从句which it connects修饰contrasts。

【译文】回想起此前、此后两种截然不同的生活，我感到难以置信。

2. (Para.1) *It was the third of March, 1887, three months before I was seven years old.*

【解析】it可以指时间、距离或天气，作主语。例如：

It's our anniversary. 今天是我们的周年纪念日。

It's two miles to the beach. 离海滨有两英里远。

It's a long time since they left. 他们已经走了很久了。

It's a storm out at sea. 海上有风暴。

【译文】那是1887年的3月3日，我差3个月7岁。

3. (Para.2) *On the afternoon of that eventful day, I stood on the porch, dumb, expectant.*

【解析】 dumb, expectant是形容词作状语。类似的用法例如：

Curious, we looked around for other guests. 我们好奇地向四周看看有什么别的客人。

He emerged from the accident unharmed. 他没有在车祸中受伤。

【译文】 在那个重要日子的下午，我默默站在走廊上，充满着期待。

4. (Para.3) *Someone took it, and I was caught up and held close in the arms of her who had come to reveal all things to me, and, more than all things else, to love me.*

【解析】 it指代前文中出现的hand；本句的主干结构是一个并列句Someone took it, and I was caught up and held close in the arms of her...；其中who引导定语从句who had come to reveal all things to me, and... to love me修饰her，在这个定语从句中又包含一个并列结构：who had come to reveal all things to me, and... (who had come) to love me；两个逗号之间的more than all things else是插入语。

【译文】 有人握住了我的手，把我紧紧地拥在怀里。她就是那个向我揭示了世间一切的人，尤其重要的是，她给我带来了人间真爱。

5. (Para.4) *In the days that followed I learned to spell in this uncomprehending way a great many words, among them pin, hat, cup and a few verbs like sit, stand and walk.*

【解析】 本句的主干是I learned to spell... a great many words...；among them pin, hat, cup and a few verbs... 是无动词的独立结构，关于独立结构详见本单元Text B难句突破1；在这个独立结构中，pin, hat, cup和a few verbs由and连接构成并列，而作者又对a few verbs作出了列举（like sit, stand and walk）。

【译文】 接下来的日子里，我学会了拼写很多单词，却不解其意，其中有：针、帽子、茶杯，还有一些动词如：坐、站、走。

6. (Para.4) *But my teacher had been with me several weeks before I understood that everything has a name.*

【解析】 本句当中同时出现了三种时态：过去完成时，一般过去时以及一般现在时。everything has a name是我明白的道理，而且是真理性的道理，因此用一般现在时；my teacher had been with me（我的老师教我）和I understood（我明白道理）两个事件发生的时间相比可知老师教我在前，我明白在后，因此老师教我my teacher had been with me用的是过去完成时，而我明白道理是一般过去时I understood。

【译文】 在老师教了我几个星期以后，我才明白世间万物都有自己的名字。

7. (Para.5) *I became impatient at her repeated attempts and, seizing the new doll, I dashed it upon the floor.*

【解析】 本句的主干是I became impatient... and I dashed it...；seizing the new doll是现在分词作时间状语。

【译文】 她不断努力，我有些不耐烦了，抓起那个新娃娃，把它摔在了地上。

8. (Para.6) *We walked down the path to the well-house, attracted by the fragrance of the honeysuckle with which it was covered.*

【解析】attracted by the fragrance of... 是过去分词作结果状语；which引导定语从句修饰honey suckle；it指the well-house。

【译文】我们沿着小路走向井楼，井楼上爬满了金银花，而我们也被金银花的花香迷住了。

9. (Para.7) *I left the well-house eager to learn.*

【解析】eager to learn是形容词词组作状语。例如：

The manager approached us full of apologies. 经理满怀歉意地向我们走来。

Some tickets are issued free of charge. 有些票是免费提供的。

【译文】离开井楼，我心里充满了学习的渴望。

10. (Para.8) *It would have been difficult to find a happier child than I was as I lay in my crib at the close of the eventful day and lived over the joys it had brought me, and for the first time longed for a new day to come.*

【解析】本句的主干是It would have been difficult to find a happier child than I was... ；as I lay... and lived over the joys... and... longed for a new day... 是as引导的时间状语从句，表示"当我……的时候"。

【译文】夜幕低垂，我独自躺在床上，回味着这重要的一天所给予我的快乐，第一次企盼着新的一天快些来到。世界上很难找到比我更幸福的孩子了。

参考译文

我生命的故事（我的生活故事）

海伦·凯勒

在我记忆里，生命中最重要的一天是我的老师，安妮·曼斯菲尔德·沙利文，进入我生活的那一天。回想起此前、此后两种截然不同的生活，我感到难以置信。那是1887年的3月3日，我差3个月7岁。

在那个重要日子的下午，我默默站在走廊上，充满着期待。从妈妈的手势，还有家里人跑前跑后的忙碌中，我隐约感觉到有什么不同寻常的事情要发生了，于是我走到门口，在台阶上等待着。

我感觉到有人向我走来，以为是母亲，就向她伸出了双手。有人握住了我的手，把我紧紧地拥在怀里。 她就是那个向我揭示了世间一切的人，尤其重要的是，她给我带来了人间真爱。

老师到来的第二天早上，她把我领到了她的房间，给了我一个洋娃娃。我玩了一会儿洋娃娃，沙利文老师开始在我的手心慢慢地拼写"D-O-L-L"这个词。我一下子对这样的手指游戏很感兴趣，并尽力去模仿。当我终于能正确地拼写出这个词后，我骄傲极了，兴奋得脸都红了。跑到楼下妈妈那里，我举着手，拼写着洋娃娃这个词。我并不知道这就是在拼写单词，甚至也不知道世界上有单词这个东西的存在。我不过是依样画葫芦模仿莎利文老师的动作而已。接下来的日子里，我学会了拼写很多单词，却不解其意，其中有：针、帽子、茶杯，还有一些动词如：坐、站、走。在老师教了我几个星期以后，我才明白世间万物都有自己的名字。

一天我正在玩新洋娃娃，沙利文老师把我原来的旧娃娃放在我腿上，开始拼写"D-O-L-L"，试图让我明白"D-O-L-L"可以指我的新娃娃，也可以指我的旧娃娃。那天早些时候，我们已经为"m-u-g（杯子）"和"w-a-t-e-r（水）"这两个词发生了争执。沙利文老师尽力让我记住"m-u-g"是杯子，而"w-a-t-e-r"是水，而我却一直把两者弄混。她实在没有办法，只好暂时搁下这个问题，留待以后一有机会再旧事重提。她不断努力，我有些不耐烦了，抓起那个新娃娃，把它摔在了地上。感觉到脚边洋娃娃的碎片，我异常兴奋。感觉到老师把洋娃娃的碎片扫到了炉子的一角，我有种满足感，我的不悦也烟消云散。她拿来了我的帽子，我知道我将走到外面暖暖的阳光中去了。

我们沿着小路走向井楼，井楼上爬满了金银花，而我们也被金银花的花香迷住了。有人在汲水。老师把我的手放在了喷水处，当清水从我一只手上流过时，她在我另一只手上拼写着"w-a-t-e-r"这个单词，先是慢慢地，然后写得快起来。我静静地站着，所有的注意力都集中在她手指的移动上。突然间，尘封的往事在我脑海中闪现，我朦朦胧胧地感觉到一些已经遗忘的东西。不知道怎么的，我一下子就明白了语言文字的奥秘。我知道，原来"w-a-t-e-r"就是指正从我指间流过的美妙而清凉的东西。那个充满生机的单词唤醒了我的灵魂，使我心中充满了光明、希望、快乐和自由！虽然前面的道路还会有荆棘坎坷，但我相信这些荆棘坎坷最终都会被一一扫清。

离开井楼，我心里充满了学习的渴望。每样事物都有名字，而每一个名字又带来新的思考。我们回到家，我所触摸到的每样东西都仿佛充满了生命。

那天，我学到了很多新单词。现在已记不清那些新单词是什么了，但是我却记得那天我学到了：妈妈、爸爸、姐妹、老师——这些词将让我的世界灿烂起来。夜幕低垂，我独自躺在床上，回味着这重要的一天所给予我的快乐，第一次企盼着新的一天快些来到。世界上很难找到比我更幸福的孩子了。

语言拓展

日常用语

练习 选择补全对话的最佳答案。

1. 【答案】A
   【题解】表达请求时，一般用"May/Could/Can I... "，肯定回答："Yes, you may/could/can."否定回答："No, you may/could/cannot."

2. 【答案】C
   【题解】当别人询问是否能一起去某个地方时，若是拒绝，应该将拒绝的理由告知对方。

3. 【答案】D
   【题解】对方用"Would you mind..."，肯定回答："I'd be happy to./ Not at all."否定回答："Sorry..."

4. 【答案】B
   【题解】同上。

5. 【答案】C
   【题解】当对方请求你帮忙寄信时，肯定回答："With pleasure.（愿意效劳。）"

阅读技巧

练习 请将下列句子中的信号词划线。

【答案】1) but   2) therefore   3) moreover   4) apart from

　　　　5) On the one hand, but on the other hand

写作技巧

练习

1. 假设你要给你的外教亨利·格林寄一张圣诞贺卡。在卡上写一些圣诞祝福，注意格式。

样文1：

To Mr. Green:

　　Hope your holidays are filled with all your favorite things and all the happiness you could wish for.

　　Merry Christmas and Happy New Year!

　　　　　　　　　　　　　　　　　　　　　　　　　　　　　　　　　　　× × ×

2. 假设你朋友的生日就要到了。写一张生日卡片。

样文2：

To my best friend:

　　I will present merry music notes as a gift to you on your birthday. Let my blessing drift into your ears like the pleasant jingles of bells, and fall on your heart. I wish you a happy birthday.

　　　　　　　　　　　　　　　　　　　　　　　　　　　　　　　　　　　× × ×

语法知识

——动名词

练习 选择最佳答案补全下列句子。

1. 【答案】B

　　【题解】本题考查动名词作主语时，谓语动词用单数形式。

　　【译文】照相是一件挺有趣的事。

2. 【答案】C

　　【题解】本题考查finish的后面跟动名词作宾语的用法。

　　【译文】在他来之前，我已经将整本书都读完了。

3. 【答案】C

　　【题解】本题考查enjoy的后面跟动名词作宾语的用法。

　　【译文】我喜欢在晚上听流行乐。

4. 【答案】B

　　【题解】本题考查mind的后面跟动名词作宾语的用法；此外，动名词的逻辑主语一般使用物主代词或名词的所有格。

　　【译文】我可以抽支烟吗？

5. 【答案】A

　　【题解】本题考查stop doing sth. 的用法，表示"停止做某事"。

　　【译文】当一个人的心脏停止跳动时，那就意味着他死了。

6. 【答案】D

【题解】本题考查can't help的后面跟动名词作宾语的用法。can't help doing表示"禁不住……"。

【译文】她一听说这消息，当即就失声痛哭起来。

7. 【答案】A

【题解】在love，like，hate，prefer等动词后用动名词时，表示习惯性的、一般性的动作；用动词不定式表示一次性具体的动作。

【译文】就我而言，我喜欢阅读胜于听说。

8. 【答案】B

【题解】本题考查look forward to doing sth.的用法，表示"期望，盼望……"。

【译文】我们期待着下周和朋友的会面。

9. 【答案】C

【题解】介词后面都应该用名词或动名词形式。

【译文】她连再见都没说一声就出去了。

10. 【答案】B

【题解】在remember，forget和regret等动词后用动名词时，动名词往往表示过去的动作，用动词不定式时往往表示将来的动作或过去未做的动作。

【译文】我记得三个星期前在街上见过他。

每课一练

Part I   Vocabulary & Structure

Directions: *There are 30 incomplete sentences in this part. For each sentence there are four choices marked A), B), C) and D). Choose the ONE that best completes the sentence.*

1. So clear was his _____ of the case that others had no more to say.

   A) attitude   B) presentation   C) comment   D) remark

2. We have to _____ a communication task in the given situation.

   A) accomplish   B) accompany   C) company   D) complish

3. He went ahead regardless of all warnings about the danger of his _____.

   A) missionary   B) misfortune   C) missing   D) mission

4. Working for the member of the new society is a matter of honor and _____.

   A) cause   B) emotion   C) glory   D) business

5. The flowers in the park were _____.

   A) pleasure   B) please   C) pleased   D) pleasing

6. His work is a(n) _____ to this theory.

   A) challenge   B) demand   C) authority   D) channel

7. I hope these job hunting _____ would help you find a job.

   A) strap   B) strategic   C) strategies   D) strategy

8. Free mail may be a good deal, _____ it has a hidden price.

   A) so   B) even if   C) even   D) as long as

9. He tried to cheer them _____ with funny stories.

A) out   B) on   C) in   D) up

10. No one can _____ anything without effort.

A) achieve   B) ache   C) finish   D) complete

11. The most _____ problem any economic system faces is how to use its resources.

A) urge   B) critic   C) crucial   D) puzzling

12. I can't imagine _____ that with them.

A) do   B) doing   C) being done   D) to be done

13. Anne couldn't concentrate _____ what she was doing while her family were watching TV.

A) to   B) on   C) for   D) in

14. Not only had the poor man been arrested, but he had been sent to prison _____.

A) as well   B) as well as   C) however   D) in addition

15. Nowadays more and more consumers would not believe many of the manufactures' _____.

A) demand   B) claim   C) pronounce   D) inform

16. The Watergate scandal brought divisions to the country and _____ led to Nixon's resignation.

A) however   B) firstly   C) ultimately   D) endlessly

17. Women love to talk. Silence intimidates them and they feel a need to fill it, _____ they have nothing to say.

A) even if   B) if   C) when   D) unless

18. — Who used to like singing?

— I _____.

A) have done   B) did   C) does   D) do

19. I would appreciate _____ back this afternoon.

A) you to call   B) you call   C) your calling   D) you're calling

20. The teacher _____ a passage to the class.

A) demonstrated   B) discussed   C) directed   D) dictated

21. The average output of the factory is expected to double this year as a result of a _____ signed between the two companies.

A) constant   B) contract   C) content   D) context

22. It's hard to _____ my family that we can't afford a new car.

A) conceive   B) convince   C) consider   D) continue

23. The idea _____ alarmed her.

A) anyway   B) anyhow   C) somewhat   D) somehow

24. What a _____ headache! I seem _____ ill.

A) terrible; terribly   B) terrible; terrible   C) terribly; terrible   D) terribly; terribly

25. Death is often a welcome _____ from pain.

A) fatigue   B) relief   C) release   D) damage

26. Our plan is to allocate one member of the _____ to handle this task.

A) stuff   B) people   C) crew   D) staff

27. The high-speed trains can have a major _____ on travel preferences.

    A) force   B) surprise   C) impact   D) power

28. His _____ for her made him blind to everything else.

    A) passion   B) patience   C) emotion   D) proposal

29. She went upstairs to see if he was still asleep _____.

    A) at one time   B) from time to time   C) in the same time   D) behind the time

30. _____ is a good form of exercise for both young and old.

    A) The walk   B) Walking   C) To walk   D) Walk

Part II   Reading Comprehension

Directions: *Read the following two passages. Answer the questions on each passage by choosing A), B), C) or D).*

Passage 1

    Language learning begins with listening. Children are greatly different in the amount of listening they do before they start speaking, and later starters are often long listeners. Most children will "obey" spoken instructions some time before they can speak, though the word "obey" is hardly accurate as a description of the eager and delighted cooperation usually shown by the child. Before they can speak, many children will also ask questions by gesture and by making questioning noises.

    Any attempt to study the development from the noises babies make to their first spoken words leads to considerable difficulties. It is agreed that they enjoy making noises, and that during the first few months one or two noises sort themselves as particularly expressive as delight, pain, friendliness, and so on. But since these can't be said to show the baby's intention to communicate, they can hardly be regarded as early forms of language. It is agreed, too, that from about three months they play with sounds for enjoyment, and that by six months they are able to add new words to their store. This self-imitation leads to deliberate imitation of sounds made or words spoken to them by other people. The problem then arises as to the point at which one can say that these imitations can be considered as speech.

    It is a problem we need to get our teeth into. The meaning of a word depends on what a particular person means by it in a particular situation and it is clear that what a child means by a word will change as he gains more experience of the world. Thus the use at seven months of "mama" as a greeting for his mother cannot be dismissed as a meaningless sound simply because he also uses it at other times for his father, his dog, or anything else he likes. Playful and meaningless imitation of what other people say continues after the child has begun to speak for himself, I doubt, however whether anything is gained when parents take advantage of this ability in an attempt to teach new sounds.

1. The author's purpose in writing the first paragraph is to show that children _____.

    A) usually obey without asking questions   B) are passive in the process of learning to speak

    C) are born cooperative   D) learn to speak by listening

2. Children who start speaking late _____.

    A) may have problems with their listening

    B) probably do not hear enough language spoken around them

    C) usually pay close attention to what they hear

    D) often take a long time in learning to listen properly

3. Which of the following is TRUE about a baby's first noises?

    A) That is an expression of his moods and feelings.

    B) That is an early form of language.

    C) That is a sign that he means to tell you something.

    D) That is an imitation of the speech of adults.

4. The speaker implies _____.

    A) parents can never hope to teach their children new sounds

    B) children no longer imitate people after they begin to speak

    C) children who are good at imitating learn new words more quickly

    D) even after they have learnt to speak, children still enjoy imitating

5. The best title for this passage would be _____.

    A) How Babies Learn to Speak   B) Early Forms of Language

    C) A Huge Task for Children   D) Noise Making and Language Learning

Passage 2

A child who has once been pleased with a tale likes, as a rule, to have it retold in identically the same words, but this should not lead parents to treat printed fairy stories as sacred texts. It is always much better to tell a story than read it out of a book, and, if a parent can produce what, in the actual circumstances of the time and the individual child, is an improvement on the printed text, so much the better.

A charge made against fairy tales is that they harm the child by frightening him or arousing his sadistic (残酷成性的) impulses. To prove the latter, one would have to show in a controlled experiment that children who have read fairy stories were more often guilty of cruelty than those who have not. Aggressive, destructive, sadistic impulses every child has and, on the whole, their symbolic verbal discharge seems to be rather a safety valve than an incitement to overt action. As to fears, there are, I think, cases of children being dangerously terrified by some fairy stories. Often, however, this arises from the child having heard the story once. Familiarity with the story by repetition turns the pain of fear into the pleasure of a fear faced and mastered.

There are also people who object to fairy stories on the grounds that they are not objectively true, that giants, witches, two headed dragons, magic carpets, etc., do not exist; and that, instead of indulging his fantasies in fairy tales, the child should be taught how to adapt to reality by studying history and mechanics. I find such people, I must confess, so unsympathetic and peculiar that I do not know how to argue with them. If their case were sound, the world should be full of madmen attempting to fly from New York to Philadelphia on a broomstick or covering a telephone with kisses in the belief that it was their enchanted girlfriend. No fairy story ever claimed to be a description of the external world and no sane child had ever believed that it was.

6. According to the passage, which of the following is TRUE about fairy tales?

    A) Fairy tales cannot be read to children without variation because they find no pleasure in them.

    B) Fairy tales will be more effective if they are adapted by parents.

    C) Fairy tales must be made easy so that children can read them on their own.

    D) Fairy tales are no longer needed in developing children's power of memory.

7. According to the passage, some people who are openly against fairy tales argue that _____.

　A) fairy tales are harmful to children in that they show the primitive cruelty in children

　B) fairy tales are harmful to children unless they have been adapted by their parents

　C) fairy tales increase a tendency to sadism in children

　D) children who have read fairy stories pay little attention to the study of history and mechanics

8. In the writer's opinion to rid children of fears, fairy stories should be _____.

　A) told only once　　　　　　　　　B) repeated many times

　C) told in a realistic setting　　　　　D) presented vividly

9. Which of the following is TRUE about the function of fairy stories?

　A) Fairy stories have a very bad effect on children.

　B) Fairy stories have advantages in cultivating children's fancy.

　C) Fairy stories help children to come to terms with fears.

　D) Fairy stories harm children greatly.

10. According to the passage, which of the following statements is NOT TRUE?

　A) If children indulged his fantasies in fairy tales instead of being taught how to adapt to reality by studying history and mechanics the world should be full of madman.

　B) Children can often be greatly terrified when the fairy story is heard for the first time.

　C) Fairy tales may beneficially direct children's aggressive, destructive and sadistic impulses.

　D) Fairy tales are no more than stories about imaginary figures with magical powers which has nothing to do with external world.

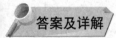 答案及详解

第一部分　词汇与结构

1. 【答案】D

　　【题解】此题考查名词的辨析。attitude 态度（attitude towards/to）；remark 对于事实的评述；comment 多指对于时事的评论；presentation 仅仅表示陈述。

　　【译文】他对于这个事件的评述如此清晰以至于其他人没有什么要补充的。

2. 【答案】A

　　【题解】accomplish vt. 完成；accompany vt. 伴随，陪伴；company n. 公司；complish这个单词不存在。

　　【译文】我们必须在这个给定的情境当中完成一项交流的任务。

3. 【答案】D

　　【题解】missionary n. 传教士；misfortune n. 不幸，灾祸；missing adj. 少见的，缺少的；mission n. 使命。

　　【译文】他无视所有关于他使命危险的警告，迎难而上。

4. 【答案】C

　　【题解】cause n. 原因；emotion n. 情感；glory n. 荣耀；business n. 商业，交易。题干中的honor 一般与glory搭配表示"荣耀"。

　　【译文】能为新社会的成员工作是一件光荣和荣耀的事情。

5. 【答案】D

【题解】本题考查几个同根词的辨析。pleasure是动词please的派生名词，表示"愉快、高兴、满意、喜欢"，多用于口语；pleased一般用作表语，偶尔也作定语，但所修饰的名词往往是表示人的感情、态度、表情等方面的名词，指某事使人非常高兴而产生一种结果，作表语时意思是"高兴的"、"喜欢的"，含义与glad基本相同，因此句子的主语只能是"人"，后接at doing sth./with sth./不定式/that从句；pleasing意思是"令人高兴的"、"令人满意的"，用作表语和定语，说明某物；please是动词，可作及物动词，表示"使高兴（满意、愉快）"，也可作不及物动词，表示"高兴、愉快"等。

【译文】花园里的花让人愉悦。

6. 【答案】A

【题解】此题考查名词辨析。challenge 挑战；demand 要求；authority 权威；channel 渠道。就词义看A和C都符合句义，不过由于前面冠词是"a"，因此正确答案应该是A。

【译文】他的著作是对这个理论的挑战。

7. 【答案】C

【题解】strap *n.* 皮带；strategic *adj.* 战略上的，策略上的；strategy *n.* 战略，策略，当strategy表示广义上的策略、谋略的时候，用作不可数名词，而当其用作表示具体的针对性措施、对策的时候是可数名词，因此答案是C。

【译文】我希望这些找工作的对策可以帮助你找到一份工作。

8. 【答案】B

【题解】本题考查even if引导的让步状语从句。so引导结果状语从句，even表示递进关系，as long as引导条件状语从句。

【译文】即使免费邮递有隐性价格，它也是一个很好的交易方式。

9. 【答案】D

【题解】本题考查cheer 的搭配，cheer up 使快乐，使高兴；cheer on 鼓励。

【译文】他想讲些滑稽的故事让他们开心。

10. 【答案】A

【题解】此题考查动词的辨析。achieve 完成，实现，到达；ache 疼痛；finish和complete都表示"完成"。虽然A、C、D都有完成的意思，但是本题强调取得一些成绩，达到一个目标，而finish和complete仅仅表示单纯的完成，因此选A。

【译文】没有人能不劳而获。

11. 【答案】C

【题解】urge *vt.* 催促，力劝；critic *n.* 批评家，评论者；crucial *adj.* 关键的；puzzling *adj.* 疑惑的。

【译文】任何一个经济系统要面对的最关键的问题就是如何利用它的资源。

12. 【答案】B

【题解】本题考查动名词作宾语的用法。在英语中imagine后如接表示动作的词作宾语时，则必须用动名词形式。

【译文】我不敢想象和他们一起做事。

13. 【答案】B

【题解】concentrate on 为固定搭配表示"集中精力做某事"，后面可以搭配动词-ing形式。

【译文】在家人看电视的时候，安妮不能集中精神做自己的事情。

14. 【答案】A

【题解】as well表示"同样……，也"，用在句尾；as well as表示"和……一样"，用在句中；however表示转折；in addition表示递进，意为"另外"，一般放在句首，并用逗号和后面内容隔开。

【译文】那个可怜的人不仅被抓了还被送进了监狱。

15. 【答案】B

【题解】demand *vt. & n.* 要求；claim *vt. & n.* 声明，宣称；pronounce *vt.* 发音，宣告；inform *vt.* 告诉。

【译文】而今越来越多的顾客不会相信制造商的声明了。

16. 【答案】C

【题解】此题考查副词的辨析。however 但是，然而；firstly 首先；ultimately 最终，最后，相当于at last；endlessly 无止境地。

【译文】水门事件丑闻给国家带来了纷争，并且最终导致尼克松的辞职。

17. 【答案】A

【题解】本题考查even if引导的让步状语从句。if引导条件状语从句；when引导时间状语从句，unless引导条件状语从句。

【译文】女人喜欢交谈。沉默使她们不安，她们需要用交谈打破沉默，即使她们没什么可说的。

18. 【答案】B

【题解】本题考查do代替前文出现过的动词的用法。

【译文】——谁过去喜欢唱歌？——是我。

19. 【答案】C

【题解】your calling 为动名词的复合结构，在句中作appreciate的宾语。

【译文】我感谢你今天午后的回电。

20. 【答案】D

【题解】demonstrate *vt.* 示范，演示；discuss *vt.* 讨论；direct *vt.* 指引，引导；dictate *vt.* 听写，口述。

【译文】教师读一篇文章让全班听写。

21. 【答案】B

【题解】constant *adj.* 持续的；contract *n.* 合同；content *n.* 内容；context *n.* 语境。

【译文】由于这两个公司之间的合同，今年该工厂的平均产量可能会翻倍。

22. 【答案】B

【题解】此题考查动词辨析。conceive 构思，思考；convince 说服；consider 认为；continue 持续。

【译文】很难让我的家人相信我们负担不起新车。

23. 【答案】C

【题解】本题考查几个词形相近的合成词义。anyway 和 anyhow 都是副词，表示"总之，无论如何"；somewhat *adv.* 一些，有些；somehow *adv.* 以某种方式。

【译文】这主意有点令她惊恐不安。

24. 【答案】A

【题解】terrible *adj.* 很糟的，极坏的；terribly *adv.* 十分地，非常。本题前面是要修饰headache，

因此用形容词，而后面修饰 ill，因此用副词表示程度。

【译文】头痛真难受！我感觉相当糟。

25. 【答案】C

【题解】此题考查名词的辨析。fatigue 疲劳，疲乏；relief 减轻，缓解；release 解脱，摆脱；damage 毁坏。

【译文】死神往往是解除痛苦的救星。

26. 【答案】D

【题解】stuff n. 材料；crew 和 staff 虽然都有全体员工的意思，但是 staff 指的是职工，职员，而 crew 是全体船员，乘务员的意思。因此选 D。

【译文】我们的计划是分派一名员工处理这项任务。

27. 【答案】C

【题解】force n. 压力；surprise n. 惊喜；impact n. 冲击；power n. 力量。

【译文】高速列车对于出行方式的选择带来了巨大冲击。

28. 【答案】A

【题解】passion n. 热情，爱情，通常介词搭配是 for；patience n. 耐心；emotion n. 情感，情绪；proposal n. 建议，求婚。

【译文】他对她强烈的爱让他对于其余一切都熟视无睹。

29. 【答案】B

【题解】本题考查几个关于 time 的词组。at one time 同时的；from time to time 时而；in the same time 同时；behind the time 过时的，陈旧的。

【译文】她不时地上楼看看他是否还在睡。

30. 【答案】B

【题解】本题考查动名词作主语。动名词作主语通常表示某种抽象的、不具体的动作；而不定式则常常用来表示一种特定的具体动作。从句中 a good form 来判断，用动名词作主语更加准确。

【译文】散步对于年轻人和老人来说都是一种很好的锻炼形式。

第二部分 阅读理解

1. 【答案】D

【题解】主旨题。根据文章第一段的主题句 "Language learning begins with listening"（语言的学习始于聆听）；以及作者后来对文章的阐述，因此选 D（孩子们通过听来学习说）。

2. 【答案】D

【题解】细节题。根据文章的第一段中 "Children are greatly different in the amount of listening they do before they start speaking, and later starters are often long listeners"（在孩子开始说话前，各自需要的聆听时间长短不一，而开口说话较晚的孩子通常需要更长的时间倾听），因此选 D。

3. 【答案】A

【题解】细节题。根据文章的第二段中 "... during the first few months one or two noises sort themselves as particularly expressive as delight, pain, friendliness, and so on"（在开始的几个月里那一两声噪音不过是在表达着他们的高兴、痛苦，或是友好等等）。因此选 A

（是一种表达心情、感受的方式）。

4. 【答案】D

   【题解】推断题。根据文章的最后一段中"Playful and meaningless imitation... continues after the child has begun to speak for himself..."（在孩子们已经能够自我表达后，他们仍会顽皮地、毫无意义地模仿……）。因此选D（在学会说话后，孩子仍然喜欢模仿）。

5. 【答案】A

   【题解】主旨题。根据全文可以看出作者的写作意图是告诉读者孩子学习说话的过程，因此选A。

6. 【答案】B

   【题解】推断题。根据文章的第一段中"It is always much better to tell a story than read it out of a book, and, if a parent can produce what... is an improvement on the printed text, so much the better"，可以推断出比起读出书上的故事，如果父母可以改编故事会更好，因此选B。

7. 【答案】C

   【题解】细节题。根据文章的第二段中"A charge made against fairy tales is that they harm the child by frightening him or arousing his sadistic impulses"（那些反对童话故事的人告诫说这些故事会吓到孩子们，或是激起他们残酷的一面），因此选C（童话故事有可能会让孩子变得残酷）。

8. 【答案】B

   【题解】细节题。根据文章的第二段中"Familiarity with the story by repetition turns the pain of fear into the pleasure of a fear faced and mastered"（通过反复讲述使孩子熟悉这些故事，可以让孩子们由恐惧到乐于面对恐惧并征服它），因此选B。

9. 【答案】C

   【题解】推断题。答案也在第二段倒数第一句中，作者说多次重复一个故事会把恐惧的痛苦变为面对恐惧并战胜它的一种快乐，所以选C（帮助孩子接受恐惧是童话故事的作用）。

10. 【答案】A

    【题解】主旨题。A项的内容不是作者的观点，而是作者在末段批判的观点。而且作者对童话是持肯定态度的，A项内容显然是一种否定态度，因此是错误的。

8 Terrorism

单元导读

自从2001年的"9·11"事件后,恐怖主义成为全球关注的焦点,也成为今天全世界面临的最紧要的问题。

恐怖主义早在"9·11"事件以前就存在。他们常常威胁轰炸城市,发动生物、化学攻击,或者自杀袭击。恐怖主义是对人权的侵犯,对世界和平的破坏。它给整个世界带来的只有残酷的杀戮、恐慌和经济衰退。

恐怖主义已经成为全球性的难题,在它毁灭人类以前,必须从根源上找到解决方法。让全世界的国家都团结起来,消灭恐怖主义。

课文精讲

📖 文章导读

对每个纽约市民来说,九月已经无法再和"9·11"之前一样,是夏天与秋天的桥梁,送走酷暑迎来遍地飘香;"9·11"已经成为共同记忆、忧伤的代名词。《纽约时报》日前公布的一项调查表明,"9·11"的伤痕依然在纽约人的心中隐隐作痛。至今仍有人刻意避开地铁、摩天大楼;无法一夜好眠;回想起那个上午,仍会泪流满面。本文的作者,"9·11"事件的目击者,将告诉我们在那个早上发生的一切。

🔘 背景知识

"9·11"袭击事件:简称"9·11事件"或"9·11",是2001年9月11日发生在美国本土,通过劫持多架民航飞机冲撞摩天高楼的自杀式恐怖袭击。在事件中共有2,986人死亡,包括美国纽约标志性建筑——世界贸易中心双塔在内的6座建筑被完全摧毁。

世界贸易中心大厦:纽约市的标志建筑——世界贸易中心大楼,位于哈得逊河口,曼哈顿闹市区南端,雄踞纽约海港旁,是美国纽约市最高、楼层最多的摩天大楼。它由纽约和新泽西州港务局集资兴建、原籍日本的总建筑师山崎实负责设计。大楼于1966年开工,历时7年,

1973年竣工。1993年2月26日，纽约世贸中心姊妹楼地下停车场曾发生大爆炸，造成 6 人死亡，1,000多人受伤，被称为"美国本土历史上最有破坏性的恐怖主义活动"，迫使这两座高110层的大楼关闭数周，经济损失达5.5亿美元。2001年9月11日，被恐怖分子劫持的两架飞机先后撞向世贸中心的双塔楼，由于撞击引起大火，双塔楼在几分钟内相继倒塌。

文章写作风格及结构

本文为一篇记叙文，作者从一个普通老百姓的角度向我们描述了在2001年9月11日早上，上班途中发生的这一起震惊全球的恐怖事件。通过描绘普通人在那一时刻的反应，更让读者感受到这一事件给美国人民和纽约人民带来的冲击与重创。

Parts 部分	Paragraphs 段落	Main Ideas 大意
Part I	1—10	As my Manhattan-bound W train passing Manhattan Bridge, the World Trade Center was on fire, thus the train was stopped, and everyone on the train was nervous. 我乘坐开往曼哈顿的W线列车驶过曼哈顿大桥的时候，世贸中心着火了，因此我们的列车也被迫停下，车内每个人都很惊慌。
Part II	11—18	We witnessed a big black jet crashed into the south tower, and everyone on the train gasped. 我们目睹了一架巨大的黑色飞机撞向南塔的全过程，列车上的每一个人都目瞪口呆。
Part III	19—23	The train moved again, but there was grave silence in it. The date September 11, 2001 will be in the memory of the Americans for ever. 列车继续往前开了，车厢内死一般的寂静。2001年9月11日将会永远留在美国人的记忆中。

词汇点睛

1　emerge

vi. to appear, or come out, from somewhere 出现，显露

• 例句• The moon emerged from behind a cloud. 月亮从云层后面钻了出来。

No new evidence emerged during the enquiry. 在调查过程中未发现新证据。

• 扩展• **submerge** *vt.* 浸没，淹没

2　underground

adj. below the surface of the earth 地下的，地面下的

• 例句• There is an underground car park near the supermarket. 超市附近有一个地下停车场。

The spy never told his family about his underground activities.

这位间谍从未把他的地下活动告诉家人。

adv. under the earth's surface 在地（面）下，往地（面）下

• 例句• The revolutionist eluded capture for weeks by hiding underground.

那位革命者为避免被捕在地下躲藏了几个星期。

He went underground to avoid the police. 他藏了起来以免被警方发现。

3 invisible

adj. sth. that is invisible cannot be seen 看不见的

• 例句• Insurance is one of Britain's most profitable invisible exports.

保险业是英国利润最大的无形出口之一。

The differences are almost invisible. 这些差别简直难以辨认。

• 短语• **be invisible to…**

Germs are invisible to the naked eye. 细菌是肉眼看不见的。

• 反义词• **visible**

4 terrify

vt. to make sb. extremely afraid 使恐怖，恐吓

• 例句• The ghost story terrifies the children. 这个鬼故事使孩子们感到害怕。

They terrified their victims into handing over a large sum of money.

他们威吓受害者交出大笔的钱。

• 扩展• **terror** *n.* 恐惧，惊恐

My elder sister has a terror of fire. 我姐姐怕火。

Ann froze with terror as the door opened silently. 门一声不响地开了，把安吓呆了。

terrifying *adj.* 可怕的，令人恐惧的

The most terrifying aspect of nuclear bombing is radiation. 核弹轰炸最可怕的一面是辐射。

5 press

vt. to push sth. firmly against a surface 压

• 例句• The child pressed her nose against the window. 那小女孩把鼻子贴在窗户上。

She pressed the frightened child to her heart. 她把受了惊吓的孩子搂在怀里。

6 exclaim

vt. to say sth. suddenly and loudly because you are surprised, angry, or excited 呼喊，大声叫

• 例句• "How beautiful the lake is!" we exclaimed. 我们叫喊着说，"这个湖多美啊!"

He exclaimed that it was untrue. 他大声说那不是事实。

She exclaimed at the beautiful view. 她对这美丽的景色感到惊奇。

The newspapers exclaimed against the government's action. 报纸指责了政府的行动。

7 abandon

vt. to stop doing sth. because there are too many problems and it is impossible to continue 丢弃，离弃

• 例句• The broken bike was found abandoned by the river side.

人们发现那辆损坏的自行车被扔在河边。

The crew abandoned the burning ship. 水手们离弃了燃烧着的船。

8　devour

vt . 1) to destroy sb./sth. 吞没，毁灭

• 例句• The flames devoured the entire building. 火焰吞没了整栋大楼。

　　　2) to eat sth. quickly 吞食，狼吞虎咽地吃

• 例句• He sat by the fire, devouring beef and onions. 他坐在火炉旁，狼吞虎咽地吃着牛肉和洋葱。

9　suspend

vt. 1) to officially stop sth. from continuing, especially for a short time 中止，暂缓

• 例句• She was suspended from school for stealing. 她因偷窃行为而遭勒令停学处分。

Bus service was suspended during the strike.罢工期间公共汽车停止运行。

He was given a suspended sentence. 他被判缓刑。

　　　2) to attach sth. to a high place so that it hangs down 悬，挂，吊

• 例句• A lamp was suspended from the ceiling above us. 我们头顶上的天花板上吊着一盏灯。

• 扩展• **suspense** *n.*悬念，悬而未决

• 例句• I try to add an element of suspense and mystery to my novel.

我试图给我的小说增加一点悬念和神秘的色彩。

Don't keep us in suspense any longer: tell us what happened!

别再让我们着急了，快告诉我们出什么事了！

10　whisper

n. a very quiet voice you make using your breath rather than your normal voice 低语，耳语

• 例句• They debated it in whispers. 他们低声辩论。

I've heard a whisper that he has got cancer. 我听到他得了癌症的传闻。

v. to speak or say sth. very quietly, using your breath rather than your voice 低语，耳语

• 例句• She whispered a few words before she fell unconscious.

她在倒下失去知觉前低声说了几个字。

Stop whispering in the corner; say whatever it is out loud.

不要在角落里嘀咕，不管什么话都大声说出来。

11　gape

vi. to look at sth. for a long time, especially with your mouth open, because you are very surprised or shocked 瞪目结舌，目瞪口呆

• 例句• We gaped in amazement at the show. 该表演使我们惊讶得张口结舌。

She gaped at the tall man, not believing that he was her younger brother.

她目瞪口呆地看着那个高个子，不相信他就是她的弟弟。

12　process

vt. to deal with, particularly data or information 加工，处理

• 例句• Supermarkets sell many vegetables that have been processed.

超级市场出售许多已经加工过的蔬菜。

How fast does the new micro process the data? 这台新的微型计算机处理数据有多快？

It may take a few weeks for your application to be processed. 审查你的申请书也许要好几周。

13　witness

vt. to see sth. happen, especially a crime or accident 目击

• 例句• The year 1849 witnessed a great war in Hungary. 1849年匈牙利发生了一场大战。

I witnessed the traffic accident. 我目睹了那次交通事故。

n. someone who sees a crime or an accident and can describe what happened 目击者，见证人

• 例句• He was a witness of the accident. 他是这件事故的目击者。

Witnesses are people who give evidence in case. 证人是在案件中提供证据的人。

14　unthinkable

adj. impossible to accept or imagine 不可思议的，难以想象的

• 例句• It seemed unthinkable that he should have done such a wicked thing.

他竟干出这样的坏事，真令人难以置信。

• 扩展• **thinkable** *adj.* 能想到的，可相信的

15　scene

n. 1) a piece of action that happens in one place in a film, book, etc. 一幕，一景

• 例句• The scene of this play is set in Ireland. 这出戏的场景是在爱尔兰。

The film contains some violent scenes. 这部电影中有很多暴力场面。

2) a view of a place as you see it, or as it appears in a picture 景色，景象

• 例句• What a fantastic mountain scene! 多么迷人的山景!

There are many pretty scenes in the park. 公园里有许多美丽的景色。

3) the place where an accident, crime etc. happened （事故，事件发生的）地点，现场

• 例句• Our reporter was the first person on the scene. 我们的记者最先到达出事地点。

They rushed to the scene of the accident. 他们迅速赶到了事故现场。

16　crash

vi. to have an accident in a car, plane, etc. by violently hitting sth. else 撞击，坠落

• 例句• An airliner crashed west of Denver last night. 昨夜一架客机在丹佛西边坠毁。

The motorcycle crashed into the fence. 摩托车猛撞在围栏上。

17　publicize

vt. to give information about sth. to the public, so that they know about it 宣传，宣扬

• 例句• A large, usually printed placard, bill, or announcement, is posted to advertise or publicize something.

印刷而成的大布告、招贴或公告被张贴以宣传或公布某事。

His visit was highly publicized. 他的来访被广泛宣传。

18　roughly

adv. about, approximately 大约，大概

• 例句• It should cost roughly 10 pounds. 这大约值10英镑。

Roughly speaking, I would say that about 100 people attended the exhibit.

粗略地说来，我想大约有100人参观了展览。

The Antarctica is a continent centered roughly on the South Pole.

南极洲是一片大致以南极为中心的大陆。

19 relief

n. a feeling of comfort when sth. frightening, worrying, or painful has ended or has not happened 解脱，宽慰

• 例句 • We all heaved a sigh of relief when we heard that they were safe.
我们听说他们平安无事，都松了一口气。

It is a great relief to have rain after a long time of drought. 久旱逢甘露是一大慰藉。

What a relief! 真叫人宽慰!

• 扩展 • **relieve** *vt.* 缓解，减轻；解除

This medicine will relieve your headache. 这药将减轻你的头痛。

Let me relieve you of your coat and hat. 让我替你拿外衣和帽子吧。

The route was designed to relieve traffic congestion. 这条路是为缓解交通拥挤而开辟的。

20 resume

vt. to start doing sth. again after stopping or being interrupted （经停顿后）再继续，恢复

• 例句 • His persistence was rewarded when they finally agreed to resume discussions.
他们终于同意继续谈判，这是他坚持不懈的结果。

She resumed her maiden name after the divorce. 离婚后她重新使用娘家的姓。

21 fold

vt. to bend by laying or pressing one part over another 合拢，折叠

• 例句 • Fold this glass bowl in newspaper. 用报纸把这个玻璃碗包好。

I folded the handkerchief and put it in my pocket. 我折好手绢，放进口袋里。

22 extensive

adj. large in size, amount, or degree 大范围的，广泛的

• 例句 • He has an extensive vocabulary. 他词汇很丰富。

The device had undergone extensive testings. 这种装置经受过广泛的试验。

The teacher had both extensive knowledge and profound scholarship. 老师的学问博大精深。

• 反义词 • **intensive**

23 crew

n. a group of people working together with special skills 全体工作人员

• 例句 • The ship's crew struck. 这艘船的船员罢工了。

The maintenance crew will make repairs to machines in your workshop tomorrow.
维修组明天修理你们车间的机器。

24 gravely

adv. quietly and seriously, especially because sth. important or worrying has happened 严峻地

• 例句 • Her mother was gravely ill. 她母亲病得很重。

He spoke gravely of the situation. 他心情沉重地谈论着局势。

If you think that, you are gravely mistaken. 你若是那样想，就大错特错了。

短语解析

1. to one's utter disbelief 让……不敢相信的是

【例句】To my utter disbelief, when I wanted his help he failed me.

我真不敢相信，当我需要他帮助时，他却使我失望。

2. come to a halt 停下来

【例句】Work came to a halt when the machine broke down. 机器出了毛病，工作便停了下来。

The car came to a halt just in time to prevent an accident.

汽车及时停下，避免了一场车祸。

3. stay out of 置身于……之外，不进入

【例句】You stay out of it. It's none of your business. 你别插手，这和你没有关系。

Nobody can stay out of law. 没有人能够凌驾于法律之上。

4. burst into tears 放声大哭

【例句】Bridget suddenly burst into tears and ran out. 布里奇特忽然放声大哭，跑了出去。

Claire looked as if she were about to burst into tears. 克莱尔看起来似乎就要哭出来了。

5. out of nowhere 不知从何处来的……

【例句】In the last few seconds, Mike came from nowhere to win the gold medal.

在最后的时刻，迈克不知道从哪里钻出来赢得了金牌。

6. a series of 一连串的，一系列的

【例句】The student always asks his teacher a series of questions.

这个学生总是问老师一连串的问题。

A series of accidents disordered the shop. 一连串的意外事件把店里弄得乱七八糟。

7. under one's breath 低声地（说）

【例句】"He's such an unpleasant man," Ann muttered under her breath.

"他真令人讨厌，"安低声说道。

9. come on 开始，出台

【例句】Just at that moment, the news came on. 就在那个时候，新闻开始了。

10. due to 由于

【例句】His success was largely due to luck. 他的成功主要靠运气.

The accident was due to her negligence. 这次事故是因她疏忽所致。

难句突破

1. (Para.1) *As my Manhattan-bound W train packed with rush-hour commuters emerged from underground and burst into the sunlight on Manhattan Bridge Tuesday morning, the familiar New York City skyline was gone, made invisible by a thick canopy of jet-black smoke.*

【解析】本句的主干是the familiar New York City skyline was gone；as引导时间状语从句；made invisible... 是过去分词短语作伴随状语。

【译文】星期二早晨，正值交通高峰期，我乘坐的W线列车满载了前去上班的乘客向曼哈顿驶去。当列车从地下钻出来，驶上了沐浴在阳光中的曼哈顿桥时，昔日人们所熟悉的城市轮廓不见了，消失在一片滚滚浓烟之中。

2. (Para.2) *Terrified at the sight, confused commuters pressed their faces against the train's windows, climbing over one another to get a better view.*

【解析】本句主干是confused commuters pressed their faces against the train's windows；terrified at the sight是过去分词作原因状语；climbing over one another...是现在分词短语作方式状语；one another指的是one another windows。

【译文】乘客们被眼前的情景吓坏了，搞不清楚发生了什么，他们推推搡搡，争着把脸贴到列车的窗户上想看个究竟。

3. (Para.5) *To my utter disbelief, I could see smoke and flames devouring the top third of the north tower. The bitter smell of smoke burned in my nose.*

【解析】see sb./sth. doing表示看到某人/某事正在做什么；而see sb./sth. do表示看到某人/某事做事情的全过程。例如：

I see her painting in the room. 我看着她正在房间里画画。（我看的时候她正在画画）

I see her paint in the room. 我看着她在房间里把画画完。（我一直看着她把画画完）

类似的用法还有hear，find等感官动词。

【译文】令人难以置信的是，我看见浓烟、火焰正吞噬着北塔最上面的三层。我已经闻到那刺鼻的烟味。

4. (Para.14) *I remembered from a few years ago, the widely publicized bomb threats made against the World Trade Center.*

【解析】本句的主干是I remembered... the widely publicized bomb threats；bomb threats由一个省略了that的定语从句修饰（that）made against the World Trade Center。

【译文】我记起几年前，众人皆知的针对世贸中心的炸弹威胁。

参考译文

美国着火了

星期二早晨，正值交通高峰期，我乘坐的W线列车满载着前去上班的乘客向曼哈顿驶去。当列车从地下钻出来，驶上了沐浴在阳光中的曼哈顿桥时，昔日人们所熟悉的城市轮廓不见了，消失在一片滚滚浓烟之中。

乘客们被眼前的情景吓坏了，搞不清楚发生了什么，他们推推搡搡，争着把脸贴到列车的窗户上想看个究竟。

"火！世贸中心着火了！"一个穿着黑色西装的年轻人叫了起来。

我丢下手上的晨版《纽约每日新闻》，从一位正在打电话的年轻男子身边挤过去，伸长脖子想要看得更清楚。

令人难以置信的是，我看见浓烟、火焰正吞噬着北塔最上面的三层。我已经闻到那刺鼻的烟味。

顺着东河，我能看见救援车正全速驶过布鲁克林大桥，直奔纽约金融区的心脏。

忽然，只听见吱嘎一声，列车在桥中间停了下来。

"世贸中心起火了，"列车广播里传出了列车长严肃的声音，"所有通往科特兰大街的班车都停运了，大家最好不要进入该地区。我再重复一遍，不要靠近世贸中心。"

年轻的男男女女们疯狂地打着手机。一位满头黑发，戴着深色太阳镜，挎着古琦提包的女士，突然大哭起来。

"我的儿子，"一位50岁上下的金发妇人哽咽着对坐在她身边的年轻女孩喃喃地说："我的大儿子在那栋楼里上班。"

正当我们瞠目结舌，努力寻思着眼前的一切时，难以置信的一幕发生了。犹如杰瑞·布鲁克海默导演的电影中的场景一样，一架巨大的黑色飞机不知道从哪里钻了出来，一头冲向了南塔。

火车上的每一个人都目瞪口呆。一位妇女尖叫了起来。那些站在后排，被窗前的人墙挡住了视线的人们焦急地喊道："怎么了？发生什么了？"

我张口结舌，不知道用什么言词来描述刚才目睹的一切。

我的脑子里闪过各种各样的念头。到底发生了什么？难道是恐怖分子？我记起几年前，众人皆知的针对世贸中心的炸弹威胁；我想到了俄克拉何马城的炸弹爆炸。难道是恐怖分子？是美国人吗？有多少人遇难呢？

我没有戴手表，但我知道那大概是早上9点。大约5万人在那两幢大楼里工作。有多少人是刚坐在电脑前，打开电脑，然后查听他们的语音留言？想到没有认识的人在大厦里工作，我松了口气，连连轻声地说道："万福玛利亚"。

随着列车重新启动，慢慢向曼哈顿靠近，车上的乘客，有的激动地互相交谈，有的默默地坐着，还有人闭着眼双手合十，祈祷着。

"这简直就像一部电影，简直就像一部电影，"一头红发的中年妇女不停地对朋友说着，"会是谁干的呢？"

终于，列车重又钻进了曼哈顿河岸的地下。浓烟、大火也消失在视线之外。

列车继续颠簸前行，列车长的声音再次响起。

"由于世贸中心爆炸起火，各条线路都改道了，我们的列车也严重误点，"列车长说道，"我们全体列车员提议大家为世贸中心的每一个人祈祷，让我们祈祷吧。"

第一次，车厢里如此肃静。那位戴太阳镜，挎古琦包的女人，仍然轻轻地哭泣着。

我坐到一个空位上，闭上了双眼，但心里波澜起伏。对美国人而言，2001年9月11日，世界自此改变，而这一日将永远留在历史的记忆里。

习题全解

文章大意

根据课文用合适的词填空。

【答案】 1) Tuesday   2) smoke   3) north   4) 9
5) south   6) 50,000   7) silence   8) prayer

【译文】 星期二早晨，在坐车去曼哈顿的路上，我发现纽约的城市轮廓消失在一片滚滚浓烟之中。世贸中心着火了。我丢下手上的报纸想要好好看个究竟。我可以看见世贸北塔上的浓烟、火焰，救援车正全速直奔纽约金融区的心脏。突然，列车停下，列车长告诫大家不要靠近世贸中心。大约九点时，一架黑色的飞机撞向南塔。而此时大约有 5 万人在大楼内工作。想到没有认识的人在大厦里工作，我松了口气。看到这可怕的一幕，车上的乘客有的激动地互相交谈，有的默默地坐着，还有人闭着眼双手合十，祈祷着。大家都不知道到底发生了什么。列车继续前行之后，列车长提议大家为世贸中心的每一个人祈祷。第一次，车厢里如此安静。我相信，对美国人而言，2001 年 9 月 11 日，世界自此改变，而这一天将永远留在历史的记忆里。

文章细节

根据课文回答问题。

【答案】

1) Manhattan. (Para. 1)

2) The World Trade Center was on fire. (Para. 3)

3) She could see smoke and flames devouring the top third of the north tower, and the emergency vehicles racing across Brooklyn Bridge towards the heart of New York City's financial district. (Paras. 5-6)

4) In the middle of the bridge. (Para. 7)

5) He said that the World Trade Center was on fire and asked the passengers not to go near the World Trade Center. (Para. 8)

6) A big black jet crashed into the south tower. (Para. 12)

7) It was about 9 a.m. (Para. 16)

8) Say a prayer for anyone at the World Trade Center. (Para. 21)

9) Terrorists. (Para.15)

10) September 11, 2001 will go down in history as a day the world changed. (Para. 23)

【译文】

1) 【问题】W 线地铁驶向哪里？
   【答案】曼哈顿。

2) 【问题】一开始乘客们觉得发生了什么事情？
   【答案】世贸中心着火了。

3) 【问题】作者看到了什么？
   【答案】她看见浓烟、火焰正吞噬着北塔最上面的三层，救援车正全速驶过布鲁克林大桥，直奔纽约金融区的心脏。

4) 【问题】列车停在哪里了？
   【答案】停在桥中央。

5) 【问题】关于发生了什么列车长是怎么说？
   【答案】他说世贸中心着火了，并且要求乘客不要靠近。

6) 【问题】在乘客们明白过来之前发生了什么不可思议的事情？
   【答案】一架黑色的飞机撞向南塔。

7) 【问题】几点钟的时候飞机撞向南塔？

【答案】早上九点。

8) 【问题】列车继续前行的时候列车长提议大家做什么？

【答案】为世贸中心的每一个人祈祷。

9) 【问题】对于作者所目睹的事情，她觉得是谁干的？

【答案】恐怖分子。

10) 【问题】根据作者，2001年9月11日对美国人来说意味着什么？

【答案】2001年9月11日，世界自此改变，而这一日将永远留在历史的记忆里。

词汇练习

1. 请用下面所给词汇或短语的适当形式填写句子。

1) 【答案】emerged

【译文】月亮从云层后露了出来。

2) 【答案】invisible

【译文】这幢房子被树木围绕着，从路上看不见。

3) 【答案】relief

【译文】听说女儿没事，她顿时松了口气。

4) 【答案】abandoned

【译文】由于大雾，他们放弃了自驾车的打算。

5) 【答案】resumed/will resume

【译文】休息了10分钟后，我们继续讨论。

6) 【答案】exclaimed

【译文】他惊呼那不是真的。

7) 【答案】due to

【译文】40%以上的死亡是由这种疾病造成的。

8) 【答案】came to a... halt

【译文】音乐突然停了下来。

9) 【答案】Extensive

【译文】关于疾病与恶劣生存条件之间的关系，（人们）已经作了大量的研究。

10) 【答案】are packed with

【译文】儿童节那天，公园里挤满了父母和孩子。

2. 请用下面所给出的词汇或短语的适当形式填写句子。

1) 【答案】terrifies, invisible, speechless

【译文】一想到在公开场合讲话我就害怕，似乎有道隐形的屏障让我说不出话来。

2) 【答案】financial, suspended, abandon

【译文】现在，我们公司面临着财务困难，因此，在获得更多投资前，我们的新计划不得不搁浅。但我们绝对不会放弃成功的希望。

3) 【答案】disbelief, folded, in a whisper

【译文】得知获奖，他的第一反应是难以置信。他呆站在那里，合抱双臂，不停地喃喃自语。

4) 【答案】crash, witnessed, terrified, out of nowhere, screamed

【译文】成百上千的路人亲眼目睹了撞车事故。他们被不知从哪里冒出来的声音给吓坏了。一些人目瞪口呆地看着燃烧的汽车，一些人拼命地叫着："救命啊！救命啊！"

5) 【答案】extensive，Due to，roughly

【译文】大火给这座岛屿上的森林造成了巨大的损失。由于这场大火，约两百英亩的树木被烧毁。

3. 请学习表格中的构词，猜猜意思，然后选择适当的词，再用其正确形式填写句子。

1) 【答案】disbelief

【译文】他环视四周，然后一脸狐疑地望着我。

2) 【答案】dissatisfied

【译文】如果您不满意这件产品，烦请退回。

3) 【答案】disapprove

【译文】实在抱歉，对你的所作所为，我不敢苟同。

4) 【答案】disadvantages

【译文】在纽约居住的一大坏处就是夏天天气炎热。

5) 【答案】distrusts

【译文】这位老人不相信银行，所以把钱放在家里。

6) 【答案】indirect

【译文】戒烟可能会间接导致体重增加。

7) 【答案】incorrect

【译文】你给我们提供的信息不准确。

8) 【答案】invalid

【译文】护照过期无效。

9) 【答案】invisible

【译文】肉眼看不见遥远的星星。

10) 【答案】ineffective

【译文】很多药物被证明对艾滋病无效。

语法结构

1. 仿照例句改写下列句子。

1) 【答案】To his surprise, the Russians refused to stand and fight.

【译文】让他吃惊的是，俄国人拒绝奋起抵抗。

2) 【答案】To his great delight, Dr. Deng discovered an effective way to treat cancer.

【译文】让他高兴的是邓医生找到了能有效治疗癌症的方法。

3) 【答案】To her great relief, her daughter had left the building before it collapsed.

【译文】她很庆幸的是她的女儿在大楼倒塌前离开了。

4) 【答案】To our disappointment, our women's team lost to the North Koreans.

【译文】令我们失望的是我们的女队输给了朝鲜队。

5) 【答案】We think, much to our regret, that we will not be able to visit you during the coming Christmas.

【译文】很遗憾，我们恐怕不能在圣诞节来看望你了。

2. 仿照例句将括号里的中文译成英语。

1) 【答案】from across the country

【译文】美国的感恩节就像中国的春节一样，把所有家庭成员从全国各地聚在了一起。

2) 【答案】from behind the cloud

　【译文】太阳从云层后露了出来。

3) 【答案】to below 1,000 *yuan*

　【译文】爸爸说除非手机的价格降到1,000元以下，否则他是不会让我买的。

4) 【答案】from under the table

　【译文】一只猫从桌子底下钻了出来。

5) 【答案】in between the bookcase and the window

　【译文】为什么不把电视放在书柜和窗户之间呢?

理解练习

1. 完型填空。

1) 【答案】C

　【题解】in the air 在空气中；on the air 在广播；in air 和 on air 均不是固定短语。

2) 【答案】B

　【题解】本题考查介词的用法，about 关于……。

3) 【答案】B

　【题解】order 命令；direct 指挥，指导；taught (teach) 教授；command 命令。

4) 【答案】D

　【题解】think 思考；guess 猜测；consider 考虑；wonder 对……感到吃惊。

5) 【答案】C

　【题解】本题考查强调句型 it is/was that... 的用法。

6) 【答案】A

　【题解】away 用作副词时，意思是"距离……有多远"，可以和表示时间、距离的词连用。

7) 【答案】B

　【题解】at the sight of 为固定搭配，表示"看见……时"。

8) 【答案】C

　【题解】neither 两者都不，表示"全否定"；neither 放在句首，整个句子主谓倒装。

9) 【答案】D

　【题解】devote to 把……献于……，把……用于……。

10) 【答案】B

　【题解】rather than 胜于；other than 除了，只是；better than 比……更好；than 与……相比较。

【译文】　　2001年9月11日，上午8点52分，我一走出世贸中心地铁站，立刻意识到出事了。空气里有着很重的烟味儿。但没有广播通知说发生了什么。我们在地下六楼，武装警察分布在各层，冷静地引导大家快速从最近的出口疏散到街道上。我从自由大街出口离开，过街到了自由公园，在那里，我转身望着北楼，顶上的20层楼浓烟滚滚。我恐惧地看着，一边琢磨究竟发生了什么事，一边祈祷所有的人都已经安全撤出。之后我转身离开，因为我对眼前看到的一切有一种不好的预感。就在那个时候，半条街之外的南塔，被撞了。当看到飞机撞击大厦，听见爆炸的声音时，我奔跑逃命。在此之前，我最鲜明的回忆，就是看到警察和消防员们以最快的速度向南塔跑去。我永远不会忘记那个

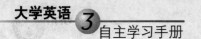

场面，任何一个美国人都不会忘记。这场暴行的遗址应该保留，特此纪念那些无比英勇的警察和消防员们，以及那些没有做错任何事，只是在当天早晨去上班的无辜受难者。零地带就像是一座圣殿，就像是珍珠港的亚利桑纳号纪念碑，或许比之更甚，因为"9·11"袭击是直接针对平民的。珍珠港没有"辩论中心"，这里也不应该有。

2. 用括号中的词汇和短语将下列句子译成英语。

1)【答案】She was terrified when a man suddenly emerged from under the water.

2)【答案】Several villagers witnessed the air crash.

3)【答案】The bus service was suspended due to the strike.

4)【答案】To her relief, the doctor said she could resume working immediately after she left hospital.

5)【答案】"Stay out of the house! It is collapsing!" Father exclaimed.

文章泛读

📖 文章导读

2004年9月11日上午8时46分。华盛顿白宫一片沉静，五角大楼一片沉静，纽约世界贸易中心遗址"零地带"一片沉静，宾夕法尼亚州一片沉静，整个美国一片沉静。以这一沉静为原点向上追溯整3年，恰是美利坚航空公司第11次航班客机撞入纽约世界贸易中心北楼的时刻。"9·11"三周年纪念活动，在这样的沉静中开始。人们伫立凝视，只有手中的玫瑰随风荡漾。在沉静默哀之后，布什在他的椭圆形办公室向全国发表了广播讲话。

💻 背景知识

乔治·沃克·布什（George Walker Bush）：1946年7月6日生于美国康涅狄格州。他的祖父是华尔街一位富有的银行家，曾是共和党参议员。其父为美国第51届总统乔治·布什。他于1968年获耶鲁大学历史学士学位，1968年至1973年在得克萨斯国民警卫队空军担任战斗机飞行员，1975年获哈佛大学工商管理硕士学位。布什1994年至2000年任得克萨斯州州长。他2001年1月就任第43任（第54届）美国总统，2004年11月3日竞选连任获胜，并于2005年1月20日就任第55届美国总统。他是继美国第六任总统亚当斯之后第二位踏着父亲的足印入主白宫的总统。

✏️ 文章写作风格及结构

本文是美国总统布什在"9·11"事件三周年纪念之际，向全美国人民发表的广播讲话。通过对逝者的缅怀，对未来的希冀，布什总统向美国人民传递了对未来胜利坚定不移的信心。

Parts 部分	Paragraphs 段落	Main Ideas 大意
Part I	1—4	September the 11th, 2001 is a day of remembrance for our country. In the terrorist attacks our country lost many citizens. 2001年9月11日是一个全国缅怀的日子。在这次恐怖袭击中，许多美国公民遇难。
Part II	5	Since the terrorist attacks, America has always been fighting against terrorism. 自从那次恐怖袭击后美国一直在和恐怖主义作斗争。
Part III	6—13	Our nation is grateful to the brave men and women who are involved in the war on terror, and our nation remains strong and resolute, patient in a just cause, and confident of the victory to come. 我们的国家对投身反恐战争的勇士们表示感谢，美国人民仍然坚强不屈，坚定不移，对正义的事业充满耐心，对未来的胜利满怀信心。

🌏 词汇点睛

1　address

n. *1) a formal speech that sb. makes to a group of people* 演说，致辞

• 例句 • The president gave an address to the nation over the radio. 总统向全国发表广播演说。

The mayor gave a television address yesterday evening. 市长昨晚发表了电视讲话。

　2) details of where sb. lives or works and where letter, etc. can be sent 住址，地址，通讯处

• 例句 • What's your home address? 你的家庭住址呢？

vt. *to make a formal speech to a group of people* 向……致辞

• 例句 • I have the honor of introducing to you Mr. Smith, who will address you on his recent tour abroad.

我荣幸地向你们介绍史密斯先生，他将向你们谈谈他最近的国外之行。

• 辨析 • **speech, address, lecture**

三个词都含"讲演"、"演说"的意思。

speech系普通用语，指"就自己的感情、见解、思想、经验或知识发表演说，可以是事先准备好的，也可是即席讲演"。如：

He was going to make a speech. 他要发表演说。

address属正式用语，指"事先经过认真准备在重要场合发表的正式演说"。如：

Who gave your commencement address? 谁给你们作了毕业演说？

lecture指"学术性的演讲"。如：

He's going to give us a lecture on public hygiene. 他要给我们作关于公共卫生方面的报告。

2　compress

vt. *to reduce the amount of time that it takes for sth. to happen or be done* 压缩

• 例句 • The main arguments were compressed into one chapter. 主要的论点被压缩到了一个章节。

Can you compress your speech into five minutes? 你能把讲话精简为五分钟吗？

vi. *to press or squeeze sth. together or into a smaller space*（受压力而）缩小

• 例句 • Wood blocks may compress a great deal under pressure. 木块受压时可缩小很多。

3　fade

v. 1) to gradually disappear 减弱，消失

- 例句 • The stars faded from the sky. 星星从天边消失了。

  All memory of the past has faded. 往日的记忆已成云烟。

  2) to become or to make sth. become paler or less bright （使）变淡、变暗

- 例句 • Daylight fades when the sun sets. 太阳西沉，天色逐渐暗淡。

  The sun has faded the (color of the) curtains. 阳光使窗帘褪色。

- 短语 • **fade away** 逐渐消失，变得模糊不清

  Hopes of reaching an agreement seem to be fading away. 达成协议的希望看来已经逐渐渺茫。

  fade in/out 淡入/淡出，渐显/渐隐，渐强/渐弱

4　image

n. 1) a picture that you have in your mind of sth. that has happened （记忆中的）画面

- 例句 • I always had an image of her standing by that particular window.

  我的脑海里始终有一幅她在那儿倚窗而立的画面。

  2) a picture on the screen of a television, cinema, or computer 图像

- 例句 • Slowly, an image began to appear on the screen. 屏幕上慢慢地出现了一幅图像。

  3) the general opinion about a person, organization, etc. that has been formed or intentionally created in people's minds （人、社团等在人们心目中的）形象，印象

- 例句 • The politician has a very bad image among people. 那位政客在人民中的形象很差。

- 扩展 • **imagine** *vt.* 想象，设想

  You can imagine the situation there. 你可以想象那里的情况。

5　cruelty

n. behavior or actions that deliberately cause pain to people or animals 残忍，残酷

- 例句 • The deliberate cruelty of his words cut her like a knife.

  他故意说的那些残酷无情的话对她像刀割一样。

  To hit a weaker person is a sign of cruelty. 殴打弱者是残忍的表现。

- 扩展 • **cruel** *adj.* 残忍的，残酷的，令人痛苦的

  The cruel master beat his slaves with a whip. 残酷的主人鞭打他的奴隶。

6　innocent

adj. not guilty of a crime 无辜的

- 例句 • They have imprisoned an innocent man. 他们监禁了一名无辜的男子。

  He was pronounced innocent of the charge. 他被宣告无罪。

- 扩展 • **innocence** *n.* 无罪，清白

  The accused man proved his innocence of the crime. 被告人经证实无罪。

  innocently *adv.* 无辜地

- 反义词 • **guilty** *adj.* 犯罪的，有罪的

  The jury found her guilty of murder. 陪审团认为她犯谋杀罪罪名成立。

7　rejoice

vi. to feel or show that you are very happy 欣喜，高兴

- 例句 • I rejoice to hear of your promotion. 听说你高升我非常高兴。

- 短语 • **rejoice at/ over sth.** 为……而欣喜

The motor industry is rejoicing at the cut in car tax. 汽车工业对汽车减税感到非常高兴。

We all rejoiced over the good news. 我们都为这一消息感到高兴。

- 扩展 • **rejoicing** *n.* 喜庆，欢庆

8　victim

n. sb. who has been attacked, robbed, or murdered 受害人，牺牲者

- 例句 • She was the innocent victim of an arson attack. 她是一起纵火案的无辜受害者。

They are the victims of the civil war. 他们是内战的受害者。

- 短语 • **fall victim to** 成为……的牺牲品

He fell victim to the dagger of an assassin. 他死于刺客的刀下。

- 扩展 • **victimize** *vt.* 使受害，使痛苦

For years the family had been victimized by racist neighbors.

多年来这个家庭因邻居怀有种族偏见而饱受欺凌。

9　determined

adj. having a strong desire to do sth. so that you will not let anyone stop you 坚决的

- 例句 • The proposal had perished in the face of determined opposition.

这个建议在强烈的反对中胎死腹中。

She is determined to finish law school. 她决意在法学院读到毕业。

- 扩展 • **determine** *vt.* 确定，决定

She will determine how it is to be done. 她会决定这件事的做法。

determination *n.* 决心，果断

She was addressing us with an air of determination.

她带着一副坚定的神态同我们说话。

10　expand

vi. to become larger in size, number, or amount, or to make sth. become larger 扩大，扩张

- 例句 • In ten years the city's population expanded by 12%.

10年之中，该城市人口增加了12%。

A tire expands when you pump air into it. 轮胎打了气就会胀大。

vt. 1) to cause sth. to become greater in size, number or importance 使某事物扩展，增大

- 例句 • The writer expanded his short novel into a long one.

那位作者把他的短篇小说扩展为长篇。

　2) to talk more; to add details to what you are saying 详述，详细阐明

- 例句 • They have expanded my view on the question.

他们已更充分地阐明了我对这个问题的观点。

- 扩展 • **expansion** *n.* 扩张

There are plans for the expansion of our school building. 有计划表明要扩大我们学校的建筑。

- 辨析 • **expand, extend**

两个词都含"扩张"、"增加"的意思。

expand 侧重指"上下、左右、前后的面或体的伸展"。如：

Iron expands when it is heated. 铁加热时会膨胀。

extend侧重指"横向的延伸"。如:

The hot weather extended into October. 炎热的天气一直持续到10月。

11 sacrifice

n. 1) the act of giving up one's time or material benefit in order to do, or to achieve, sth. important 牺牲,献身

• 例句 • Her parents made sacrifices so that she could have a good education.

为了让她受到良好的教育,她的父母作了很多的牺牲。

I would never dream of asking you to make such a sacrifice. 我决没想到要你作出这样的牺牲。

2) the act of offering sth. to a god 祭品

• 例句 • They offered sacrifices to the gods. 他们向众神献上祭品。

v. to give up or lose, especially for some good purpose or belief 牺牲,献祭

• 例句 • He sacrificed his life to save the drowning child. 他为拯救落水的孩子而献出自己的生命。

We know how to work, to sacrifice, and to fight. 我们懂得如何去工作,去战斗,去作出牺牲。

12 resolve

n. a strong determination to succeed in doing sth. 决心

• 例句 • The difficulties in her way merely strengthened her resolve.

她所遇到的困难只是让她更坚定。

He made a firm resolve to give up smoking. 他下定决心要戒烟。

vt. 1) to find a solution to a problem or difficulty 解决

• 例句 • Both sides met in order to try to resolve their differences. 双方会晤以努力解决分歧。

2) to make a determined decision; to decide firmly 下决心,决定

• 例句 • She resolved on making an early start. 她决定早早出发。

• 扩展 • **resolute** *adj.* 坚决的

He became even more resolute in his opposition to the plan. 他甚至更坚决地反对这个计划。

🔊 短语解析

1. be grateful to 对……表示感激

【例句】He is grateful to his parents for their kindness. 他十分感谢他父母的好意。

I was most grateful to John for bringing the books. 我非常感激约翰把书带来。

2. watch for 警惕,保持警觉

【例句】When crossing the road, you should watch for the cars. 过马路时要注意过往车辆。

The staff were asked to watch for forged banknotes. 已经要求职员留意假钞。

3. on one's behalf 为了某人

【例句】Ken is not present, so I shall accept the prize on his behalf. 肯不在场,所以我代表他领奖。

On behalf of the department I would like to thank you all. 我谨代表全系感谢大家。

4. in the face of 面对

【例句】We should be brave in the face of difficulty. 在面对困难时,我们要坚强。

We're powerless in the face of such forces. 面对这样强大的力量,我们无能为力。

难句突破

1. (Para.1) ***And I am honored to be joined at the White House today by Americans who lost so much in the terrible events of September the 11th, 2001, and have felt that loss every day since.***

【解析】since在本句中是副词，表示"从过去某时间以来、以后或到现在"，一般与现在完成时态或过去完成时态连用。例如：

He left home two weeks ago and we haven't heard from him since.

他两星期以前离开了家，到现在我们一直没有他的消息。

She moved to London last May and has since got a job on a newspaper.

她去年5月到伦敦，此后一直在报社工作。

【译文】今天，我有幸请到了在2001年9月11日所发生的骇人听闻的事件中蒙受巨大损失的一些美国人来到白宫，自"9·11"以来，他们每一天都承受着失去亲人的痛苦。

2. (Para.3) ***We remember the many good lives that ended too soon—which no one had the right to take.***

【解析】本句的主干是we remember the many good lives...；lives被that引导的定语从句修饰（that ended too soon）；破折号之后which引导定语从句修饰lives，对lives展开进一步说明。

【译文】我们忘不了那许多过早结束的条条善良的生命——这些生命，没有人有权去剥夺。

3. (Para.8) ***And America will never forget the ones who have fallen—men and women last seen doing their duty, whose names we will honor forever.***

【解析】本句的主干是... American will never forget the ones...；其中，who引导定语从句修饰ones；破折号后men and women last seen doing their duty对定语从句who have fallen作出解释，whose引导定语从句修饰men and women。

【译文】美国将永远不会忘记那些以身殉职的男女将士，我们将永远铭记他们。

参考译文

"9·11"事件三周年广播讲话

乔治·W.布什

早上好。这是一个全国缅怀的日子。今天，我有幸请到了在2001年9月11日所发生的骇人听闻的事件中蒙受巨大损失的一些美国人来到白宫，自"9·11"以来，他们每一天都承受着失去亲人的痛苦。

三年前，善与恶的交锋集中体现在那个早晨。在短短的102分钟内，遇难的美国公民比在珍珠港事件中丧生的美国人还多。时间流逝但记忆不曾磨灭。我们忘不了那熊熊的大火，忘不了那表达爱意的最后一次通话，忘不了救援人员视死不退缩的勇气。

我们也忘不了滥杀无辜、幸灾乐祸的凶残敌人，忘不了那许多过早结束的条条善良的生命——这些生命，没有人有权去剥夺。

我们的国家也不会忘记那些失去亲人、承受悲痛的家庭。他们表现出了自己莫大的勇气。承蒙上帝的恩典以及人们相互的帮助，恐怖事件遇害者的家属们表现出了一种能承受所有伤痛的力量。美国人民将永远记住他们，并为他们祈祷。

"9·11"恐怖袭击事件是我们国家的一个转折点。我们认清了顽敌的企图：扩大杀戮的规模，并迫使美国退出世界舞台。我国也肩负起了一个使命：我们要击败这些敌人。美利坚合众国决心保卫其国土不再遭受袭击。正如"9·11"委员会得出的结论，我们的国家比三年前更安全了，但危险依旧存在。

因此，每天都有成千上万的人在尽心尽职，坚守岗位——有空中警员、机场安检员、货运检验员、边防巡逻员，以及一线应急人员。我们的国家感激那些监视敌人，响应警报，用他们的警惕性保卫美国的所有同胞。

自"9·11"以来，我们的军人及其家属为反恐之战付出了最大的牺牲。我们的国家对此时此刻正在为我们而冒生命危险的英雄儿女们表示感谢。

美国将永远不会忘记那些以身殉职的男女将士，我们将永远铭记他们。

反恐之战仍在继续。我国的决心仍在经受考验。面对危险我们显示了骨气。在我们国家遭受攻击三年后的今天，美国人民仍然坚强不屈，坚定不移，对正义的事业充满耐心，对未来的胜利满怀信心。

谢谢收听。

习题全解

1. 根据课文，请选出最合适的答案。

1) 【答案】T

【题解】根据文章第二段中"在短短的102分钟内，遇难的美国公民比在珍珠港事件中丧生的美国人还多"，这句话是正确的。

2) 【答案】T

【题解】根据文章第二段最后两句"时间流逝但记忆不曾磨灭。我们忘不了那熊熊的大火，忘不了那表达爱意的最后一次通话，忘不了救援人员视死不退缩的勇气"，这句话是正确的。

3) 【答案】F

【题解】根据文章第五段中"正如'9·11'委员会得出的结论，我们的国家比三年前更安全了，但危险依旧存在"，这句话是错误的。

4) 【答案】T

【题解】文章倒数第四段提到"自'9·11'以来，我们的军人及其家属为反恐之战付出了最大的牺牲"，所以这句话是正确的。

5) 【答案】F

【题解】文章倒数第二段提到"在我们国家遭受攻击三年后的今天，美国人民仍然坚强不屈，坚定不移，对正义的事业充满耐心，对未来的胜利满怀信心"，因此这句话是错误的。

2. 请用下面所给出的词汇或短语的适当形式填写句子。

1) 【答案】expanded

【译文】这家公司创建了一家新的子公司，由此扩大了在中国的业务。

2) 【答案】determined

【译文】她下定决心戒烟。

3) 【答案】on duty

　【译文】今天只有一位医生值班，其他医生都下班了。

4) 【答案】On behalf of

　【译文】我代表在座的每一位，衷心希望您拥有愉快的退休生活。

5) 【答案】cruelty

　【译文】他冷酷无情的言语像是一把刀捅进了她的心。

3. 将下面这些句子译成汉语。

1) 【答案】今天，我有幸请到了在2001年9月11日发生的骇人听闻的事件中蒙受巨大损失的美国人来到白宫，自那时以来，他们每一天都承受着失去亲人的痛苦。

2) 【答案】承蒙上帝的恩典以及相互的帮助，恐怖事件遇害者的家属们表现出了一种能够承受所有伤痛的力量。美国人民将永远记住他们，并为他们祈祷。

3) 【答案】我们的国家感激那些监视敌人，响应警报，用他们的警惕性保卫美国的所有同胞。

文章泛读

TEXT C

文章导读

　　2005年7月7日，在"9·11"事件过去了四年之后，爆炸声又从伦敦传来。50多个生命在爆炸声中逝去。一周后，伦敦人民，英国人民，全世界的人民会以何种方式来纪念呢？普通市民、英国女王会有什么样的心情呢？你将要读到的这则新闻将告诉你伦敦爆炸案发生一周后的故事。

背景知识

　　伦敦爆炸事件：2005年7月7日当地时间8点49分，伦敦市区三处地铁同时发生爆炸，造成重大人员伤亡，地铁全线停止运营。 与之相呼应的还有三起公共汽车爆炸事件。这次爆炸经警方查明，确系为英裔穆斯林所为，四名制造自杀炸弹者的身份也被确认。

　　基地组织：1988年，本·拉登在阿富汗建立了"基地"组织。"基地"组织在阿富汗境内有10多处训练基地，对从各国来到阿富汗的成员进行恐怖活动训练。训练内容包括学习原教旨主义教义，学习使用轻型武器、发射迫击炮和火箭筒、使用电脑和因特网。据估计，从上世纪80年代初迄今，在"基地"接受过训练的人有3万之众，他们被称为"阿富汗的阿拉伯人"。据悉，"基地"组织核心成员约4,000—5,000人，主要由"阿富汗的阿拉伯人"组成。拉登通过传真、移动电话、因特网或信使遥控指挥其在世界各地的支持者。

📖 文章写作风格及结构

本文为一篇新闻稿，作者以简洁的语言向我们介绍了在伦敦爆炸案一周纪念日这一天进行的纪念活动，并由此深度挖掘了爆炸案背后的信息。

Parts 部分	Paragraphs 段落	Main Ideas 大意
Part I	1—6	On the one-week anniversary of the London bombings, tributes were held in towns and cities across Britain and elsewhere in Europe to show their deep contempt for those who planted the bombs and those who masterminded them. 伦敦爆炸案一周纪念日这天，英国以及欧洲其他地方的许多城镇都举行了悼念活动，强烈谴责那些安置炸弹、策划爆炸的人。
Part II	7—9	The London Police Commissioner, Ian Blair said the fight against al-Qaida is complicated, because it is not a traditional terrorist organization that has demands that can be negotiated. 伦敦警察专员伊恩·布莱尔说与基地组织的斗争异常复杂，因为他们没有要求，也不需要谈判。
Part III	10—11	Police appealed for public information on the movements of Hasib Hussain and police also identified Shahzad Tanweer as the suspected bomber of an underground train near the Aldgate station. 警方呼吁公众提供有关哈希卜·侯赛因动向的信息，警方也确定萨哈德·坦威尔为阿尔德盖特车站附近的地铁爆炸案的嫌疑人。

🏀 词汇点睛

1　mark

vt. 1) to commemorate an important event 纪念，庆祝

• 例句 • There will be ceremonies to mark the Queen's birthday.

女王生日时将举行庆典来庆祝。

Today's ceremony marks 100 years of trade between our two countries.

今天的仪式是纪念我们两国间贸易往来100周年。

　　2) to make (a mark or marks) on sth. 作标记（记号）

• 例句 • Please mark your names on your clothes. 请把你们的名字标在自己的衣服上。

The route has been marked so that it is easy to follow.

这条路线已经标有记号，很容易跟着走。

n. 1) symbol, sign 标记，记号

• 例句 • Put a mark in the margin to show the omission. 在页边作个记号表示有遗漏。

　　2) number or letter used as an assessment of sb's work or conduct 分数

• 例句 • She got 90 marks out of 100 for chemistry. 她化学得了90分。

2　tribute

n. 1) sth. that you say, do, or give in order to express your respect or admiration for sb. 称赞，颂辞

• 例句 •　I'd like to pay tribute to the office staff for the hard work they've put in on this project.
我谨对在这一工程中努力工作的办事处人员表示称赞。

The teacher paid a high tribute to his ability. 老师高度称赞了他的能力。

　　2) indication of the effectiveness of sth. 有效的标示

• 例句 •　His recovery is a tribute to the doctor's skill. 他能康复充分说明医生高超的医术。

3　blow

vt. (blew, blown) to damage or destroy sth. violently with an explosion or by shooting 爆裂，爆炸

• 例句 •　The safe had been blown by the thieves. 保险箱被窃贼炸开了。

The police station was blown up by terrorists. 恐怖分子炸毁了警察局。

vi. to send out (a current of air, etc.) from the mouth 吹，吹气

• 例句 •　The policeman asked me to blow into a plastic bag. 警察要我往一个塑料袋里吹气。

n. hard stroke (given with the fist, a weapon, etc.) 殴打，重击

• 例句 •　He received a severe blow on the head. 他头部受到重重一击。

4　apparent

adj.1) seeming to have a particular quality, feeling, or attitude 显然的

• 例句 •　It was apparent that she was ill. 显然她生病了。

His guilt is apparent. 他罪恶昭彰。

　　2) seeming, unreal 表面上的，假的

• 例句 •　Her apparent indifference made him even more nervous.
她表面上的若无其事反而使他更加紧张。

• 扩展 •　**apparently** *adv.* 看来，似乎
He had apparently escaped by bribing a guard. 他看来是贿赂了守卫才逃脱的。

• 辨析 •　**evident, apparent**
两个词意思都含"明显的"。
evident多用于推理及抽象的事，指"明显的"。如：
It's evident that the plan is impracticable. 很明显这计划不可行。
apparent 含"一目了然的"的意思，还可指"思想上容易理解的"。如：
It's apparent that you can't be trusted. 很显然，你是不可信赖的。

5　contempt

n. a feeling that sb./sth. is not important and deserves no respect 轻蔑，藐视

• 例句 •　I feel nothing but contempt for such dishonest behavior. 我对这种不诚实的行为只有鄙视。

I shall treat that suggestion with the contempt it deserves. 我对那项建议理所当然嗤之以鼻。

• 扩展 •　**contemptuous** *adj.* 轻蔑的,侮辱的
She's contemptuous of my humble home and poor surroundings.
她瞧不起我出身卑贱，家境贫困。

contemptible *adj.* 可鄙的
That was a contemptible trick to play on a friend. 那是对朋友玩弄的一出可鄙的把戏。

6 confirm

vt. to say that sth. is definitely true 确定，确认

• 例句 • Please write to confirm your reservation. 请来信确认一下您所预定的项目。

The rumors of an attack were later confirmed. 发动攻击的谣传后来得到了证实。

• 扩展 • **confirmation** *n.* 证实，确认，批准

We are waiting for confirmation of the news. 我们正在等待证实那个消息。

7 negotiate

v. 1) to discuss sth. in order to reach an agreement, especially in business or politics 谈判，磋商

• 例句 • We've decided to negotiate with the employers about our wage claim.

我们决定就工资问题与雇主协商。

The trade union negotiated a new contract with the management.

工会同资方商定了一项新合同。

2) *to get over or past (an obstacle, etc.) successfully* 越过（障碍等）

• 例句 • The horse negotiated the fence with ease. 马很容易就越过了栅栏。

• 扩展 • **negotiable** *adj.* 可以协商解决的

The salary is negotiable. 薪水可以协商。

negotiation *n.* 商议，谈判

The contract is still under negotiation. 这项合同仍在商谈之中。

8 subsequent

adj. happening or coming after sth. else 随后的

• 例句 • Subsequent events proved me wrong. 随后的事情证明我错了。

The first and all subsequent visits were kept secret. 第一次以及随后的各次访问都秘密进行。

9 appeal

vi. 1) to make a serious public request for help, money, information, etc. 呼吁，恳求，求助

• 例句 • As a result of the radio appeal for help for the earthquake victims, over a million pounds has been raised. 在广播呼吁援助地震受害者之后，已经募集到了一百多万镑。

2) *to please, attract, or interest* 使喜欢，吸引，使感兴趣

• 例句 • Bright colours appeal to small children. 小孩喜欢鲜艳的颜色。

n. 1) earnest request 恳求，呼吁

• 例句 • Her eyes held a look of silent appeal.

她眼中流露着无声的求助神情。

2) *power to move the feelings; attraction; interest* 感染力，吸引力

• 例句 • The game has lost its appeal. 这种游戏已引不起人们的兴趣。

10 suspect

vt. to think that sb. is probably guilty of a crime 嫌疑，怀疑

• 例句 • He was suspected of selling state secrets and arrested last month.

他涉嫌倒卖国家机密，于上月被捕。

I suspect the truth of her statement. 我对她的话的真实性表示怀疑。

n. person suspected of a crime 嫌疑犯

• 例句 • The police are interrogating two suspects. 警察正在审查两个嫌疑犯。

adj. of uncertain truth, quality, legality, etc. 令人怀疑的，不可信的

• 例句 • His fitness is suspect, so we can't risk including him in the team.

他的健康令人怀疑，所以我们不能冒险接受他入队。

短语解析

1. commit suicide 自杀

【例句】He tried to commit suicide. 他企图自杀。

She committed suicide because of the unbearable pressure. 她因无法承受压力而自杀。

2. blow up 爆炸

【例句】The bomb blew up. 炸弹爆炸了。

A police officer was killed when his car blew up. 一名警官在其汽车爆炸时丧生。

难句突破

1. (Para.2) *Traffic stopped and Londoners lined the streets to honor the victims of the bombings last week that killed more than 50 people and left hundreds wounded.*

【解析】本句的主干是traffic stopped and Londoners lined the street to honor...；其中that引导定语从句修饰bombings；而在这个从句中又含有一个并列成分that killed more than 50 people and left hundreds wounded。

【译文】交通停滞了，伦敦市民列队街头，悼念上周爆炸案的遇难者。在这场爆炸案中，50余人死亡，几百人受伤。

2. (Para.5) *Among those participating was George Psaradakis, the driver of a double-decker bus that police say was blown apart by an apparent suicide bomber in what is described as an al-Qaida-style attack.*

【解析】本句的主干是among those participating was George Psaradakis...；而这个句子又是一个倒装结构，主语是George Psaradakis；the driver of a double-decker bus是George Psaradakis的同位语，对George Psaradakis的身份进行说明；that引导定语从句修饰a double-decker bus；what引导宾语从句作介词in的宾语in what is described as an al-Qaida-style attack。

【译文】参与悼念的人还有驾驶员乔治·萨拉达克斯。据警方称，他驾驶的那辆双层公共汽车在"基地组织"式的自杀式炸弹袭击中被炸毁。

3. (Para.7) *The London Police Commissioner, Ian Blair, confirmed in a briefing with foreign correspondents that the police believe all four of the bombers committed suicide in carrying out the attacks, though he says they did not need to die, but chose to.*

【解析】本句的主干是the London Police Commissioner, Ian Blair, confirmed... that...；that引导宾语从句作动词confirm的宾语that the police believe...；在这个宾语从句中有一个省略现象：... though he says they did not need to die, but chose to (die)。

【译文】伦敦警察专员伊恩·布莱尔在简报中向国外媒体证实：警方确信在这次袭击中有四人携带炸药进行了自杀式的爆炸，他说尽管他们没有必要去送死，但是他们选择了死亡。

4. (Para.10) *At a subsequent news conference, police appealed for public information on the movements of Hasib Hussain, suspected of blowing up the bus, and they released a closed-circuit television image of him carrying a backpack that supposedly carried the bomb.*

【解析】本句的主干是... police appealed... , suspected... , and they released...；that引导定语从句that supposedly carried the bomb修饰a backpack。

【译文】在接下来的新闻发布会上，警方呼吁公众提供有关哈希卜·侯赛因动向的信息。警方怀疑他炸毁了公共汽车，并公布了他背着背包的闭路电视画面，警方怀疑该背包藏有炸弹。

参考译文

百万人为伦敦爆炸受害者默哀
迈克尔·德拉吉

伦敦爆炸案一周纪念日这天，整个欧洲，数百万人默哀两分钟，以这样的方式纪念在爆炸中死伤的人们。

交通停滞了，伦敦市民列队街头，悼念上周爆炸案的遇难者。在这场爆炸案中，50余人死亡，几百人受伤。

伊丽莎白女王走出白金汉宫，参加了悼念仪式。布莱尔首相也在唐宁街官邸的花园里加入了急救人员的队伍，为受害者默哀。

在英国以及欧洲其他地方的许多城镇，都举行了类似的悼念活动。

参与悼念的人还有驾驶员乔治·萨拉达克斯。据警方称，他驾驶的那辆双层公共汽车在"基地组织"式的自杀式炸弹袭击中被炸毁。

"此刻，我向那些无辜受害者的家庭表达我的关怀，特别是我的一位同事，他女儿在我的公交车上失去了生命，"他说，"在今天的默哀仪式中，我们缅怀他们。在庄严肃穆中，我们充满了尊严和敬意，同时强烈谴责那些安置炸弹、策划爆炸的人。"

伦敦警察专员伊恩·布莱尔在简报中向国外媒体证实：警方确信在这次袭击中有四人携带炸药进行了自杀式的爆炸，他说尽管他们没有必要去送死，但是他们选择了死亡。

他还说与基地组织的斗争异常复杂，因为这不是一个传统的恐怖组织，他们没有要求，也不需要谈判。

"过去，巴德尔·迈因霍夫团伙、红色旅、埃塔组织、爱尔兰共和军曾通过制造爆炸来获得走向谈判桌的机会，"他说，"但是我们现在的处境却是，有人在炸毁谈判桌。"

在接下来的新闻发布会上，警方呼吁公众提供有关哈希卜·侯赛因动向的信息。警方怀疑他炸毁了公共汽车，并公布了他背着背包的闭路电视画面，警方怀疑该背包藏有炸弹。

警方也确定萨哈德·坦威尔为阿尔德盖特车站附近的地铁爆炸案的嫌疑人。有媒体报道说，这位22岁的坦威尔是一个性情温和的板球爱好者。

语言拓展

日常用语

练习 选择补全对话的最佳答案。

1. 【答案】C

   【题解】当别人提出帮助我们时，如果接受帮助应该说："Yes, please. It's very kind of you to help me." 如果不需要帮助，应该说："No, thanks/thank you (all the same/anyway)."

2. 【答案】B

   【题解】同上。应注意的是，在不需要对方帮助时，仍应表示感谢。对方想帮你提包，但你又不需要帮助时，你可以回答：谢谢，我自己还能应付。

3. 【答案】C

   【题解】同第一题。

4. 【答案】D

   【题解】对方想帮你一把，但你不需要帮助，你可以回答：不，谢谢。我自己能应付。

5. 【答案】D

   【题解】当别人请求你的帮忙时，肯定回答："I'd be glad to.（乐意效劳。）"

阅读技巧

练习 请将下列段落中的信号词划线。

【答案】1. as

2. hence; what's more; such as

3. first; in the second stage; Finally

4. however; such as; Also; Therefore

写作技巧

练习

根据提纲，给你以前的同学写一封大约120字的信。

样文：

Dear Mary,

It has been a few months since we met each other last time. How is your campus life going recently? As to me, I'm busy learning English during the spare time. Much interested in English learning and hoping to enhance my English ability, I am making efforts on it: I practice English listening every day and do a lot of exercises on reading, writing, and so on.

I am delighted to learn that you are quite good at English. It's said that you have just won a prize in an English competition. So I will be very privileged if you'd like to share with me your experience. I wish you can give me some suggestions on how to learn English efficiently and effectively.

You are very welcome to visit me when you're free. I will greatly appreciate your coming and I'm sure we will have a good time together. Hope to see you again before long.

I'm looking forward to your reply. Best wishes!

Yours,

Betty

语法知识

——分词

练习 选择最佳答案补全下列句子。

1. 【答案】A

   【题解】本题考查分词作表语的情况。分词作表语时，现在分词往往表示主语所具有的特征，过去分词往往表示主语的状态或状况。

   【译文】看电视看久了，我会觉得很无聊。

2. 【答案】C

   【题解】本题考查分词的时态。若分词所表示的动作与谓语动词所表示的动作同时（或几乎同时）发生，或表示正在发生，用现在分词的一般式。

   【译文】他坐在那儿看一本小说。

3. 【答案】B

   【题解】本题考查现在分词作定语的情况。现在分词和它所修饰的名词有逻辑上的主谓关系，而且通常放在被修饰的名词之前。

   【译文】不要惹是生非。

4. 【答案】D

   【题解】本题考查现在分词作宾语补足语的情况。分词一般只在两类动词后作补语：感官动词和使役动词。本句话的谓语动词see是感官动词。现在分词作宾语补足语表示动作正在进行，与句子的宾语之间是主动关系。

   【译文】杰克看见一位妇女站在狗的旁边，于是朝她走去。

5. 【答案】B

   【题解】分词的否定形式是在分词前加not。

   【译文】对他的这份报告我不太满意，于是让他重新写一遍。

6. 【答案】A

   【题解】本题考查分词的时态。若分词所表示的动作发生在谓语动词所表示的动作之前，要用现在分词的完成式（having done结构），或用过去分词（当分词作定语时）。

   【译文】做完作业后，我就回家了。

7. 【答案】C

   【题解】分词短语作状语时，与句子的主语有逻辑上的主谓关系。本句话中，分词短语的逻辑主语是句子的主语this letter，所以和type是被动关系。

   【译文】这封信写得很好，请仔细打出来。

8. 【答案】C

   【题解】分词短语作状语时，与句子的主语有逻辑上的主谓关系。本句话中，分词短语的逻辑主语是句子的主语animals，所以和train是被动关系。

   【译文】当动物们都训练有素时，它们能做出许多令人吃惊的事来。

9. 【答案】C

   【题解】分词短语作状语时，与句子的主语有逻辑上的主谓关系。本句话中，分词短语的逻辑主语是句子的主语you，所以和drive是主动关系。

   【译文】在高速公路上开车时，你一定要特别小心。

10.【答案】A

【题解】分词短语作状语时，与句子的主语有逻辑上的主谓关系。本句话中，分词短语的逻辑主语是句子的主语I，根据句子意思，和invite是被动关系。

【译文】如果被邀请了，那我今晚就会去参加这次的派对。

11.【答案】B

【题解】本题考查分词独立结构。独立结构一般位于句首，有时也位于句尾，表示伴随状况时常居于句尾。本句话中，分词的逻辑主语weather是分词动作permit的执行者，所以应该用现在分词。

【译文】如果天气允许，明天我们就去野餐。

12.【答案】C

【题解】本题考查分词独立结构。独立结构一般位于句首，有时也位于句尾，表示伴随状况时常居于句尾。本句话中，分词的逻辑主语是vacation，be over表示一种状态，用现在分词。

【译文】假期结束了，学生们又回到了学校。

13.【答案】C

【题解】本题考查分词独立结构。本句话中，分词的逻辑主语sun是分词动作set的执行者，应该用现在分词；而且分词动作发生在谓语动词所表示的动作之前，所以要用现在分词的完成式（having done结构）。

【译文】太阳下山了，我们也停止工作了。

14.【答案】D

【题解】本题考查过去分词作宾语补足语的情况。过去分词作宾补，表示完成，与句子的宾语之间是被动关系。

【译文】当小男孩醒来时，发现屋里就他一个人。

15.【答案】D

【题解】分词作状语时，其逻辑主语是句子的主语。本句话中，分词短语的逻辑主语是句子的主语baby，根据句子意思，和frighten是被动关系。

【译文】因为被雷声给吓到了，小宝宝放声大哭起来。

每课一练

Part I　Vocabulary & Structure

Directions: *There are 30 incomplete sentences in this part. For each sentence there are four choices marked A), B), C) and D). Choose the ONE that best completes the sentence.*

1. A new idea began to _____ from his mind when he was on his way back home.

　　A) emerge　　　　　B) output　　　　　C) starve　　　　　D) tend

2. The lost car of the Lees was found _____ in the woods off the highway.

　　A) disappeared　　　B) abandoned　　　C) thrown　　　　　D) rejected

3. He determined _____ to college.

　　A) going　　　　　B) go　　　　　　　C) of going　　　　　D) on going

4. _____, he worked out the difficult math problem only in 10 minutes.

　　A) Surprising　　　B) I'm surprised　　C) In surprise　　　D) To my surprise

5. In space, there are a lot of distant stars that are _____ to the naked eye.

    A) visional   B) invisible   C) viewed   D) visited

6. Ken is not present, so I shall accept the prize _____.

    A) on behalf of he   B) behalf him   C) on his behalf   D) behalf of him

7. The squirrel was lucky that it just missed _____.

    A) catching   B) to be caught   C) being caught   D) to catch

8. The film _____ several years into half an hour.

    A) compasses   B) compresses   C) composes   D) campuses

9. It is _____ that the volcano became active without warning. People were _____ by the eruption.

    A) terrifying; terrifying   B) terrified; terrifying   C) terrified; terrified   D) terrifying; terrified

10. Why not try to _____ your story into a novel?

    A) expand   B) explore   C) expose   D) extend

11. He could not help _____ at how much his son had grown.

    A) crying   B) exclaiming   C) screaming   D) laughing

12. "Did you do something like that before?" "Of course not. That would be _____."

    A) over my dignity   B) beyond my dignity   C) beneath my dignity   D) above my dignity

13. After sending the guests away, we _____ our dinner.

    A) consumed   B) paused   C) stopped   D) resumed

14. _____, he finally passed the exam, although he suffered a lot.

    A) To our sorrow   B) In delight   C) To our delight   D) Of delight

15. This movie tells us a story about two strangers who spoke German and came _____ the sky.

    A) into   B) from out of   C) out   D) under

16. How about the two of us _____ a walk down the garden?

    A) to take   B) take   C) taking   D) to be taking

17. Her plot against a completely _____ old man shows that the lady in this strange tale very obviously suffers from a serious mental illness.

    A) identical   B) imperative   C) impressive   D) innocent

18. A lamp _____ the ceiling above us.

    A) was suspended   B) suspended   C) was suspended from   D) was suspicious of

19. Why don't you _____ your ideas _____ on paper?

    A) set; back   B) set; to   C) set; up   D) set; down

20. _____ reporting on television has helped to generate interest in a wide variety of sports and activities.

    A) Extensive   B) Intensive   C) Extended   D) Expected

21. In the court Mr. Smith was the only _____ who said the fire was deliberate.

    A) standby   B) whisper   C) witness   D) witch

22. She has made up her mind to become a doctor working for the _____ of suffering.

    A) relieve   B) relive   C) relief   D) believe

23. She decided to _____ her studies after obtaining her Master's degree.

    A) push   B) purse   C) pursuit   D) pursue

24. The process by which caterpillars are _____ into butterflies is adorable and amazing.

    A) translated   B) transformed   C) transacted   D) transmitted

25. In both East and West, names are _____ to success, sometimes.

    A) especial   B) effective   C) essential   D) essence

26. America's rapid industrial progress has been _____ its readiness to adopt new thoughts and interchange information.

    A) due to   B) because   C) reason for   D) since

27. I'm truly _____ for all your help.

    A) greet   B) thankful   C) grateful   D) both B and C

28. —You were brave enough to raise objections at the meeting.

    —Well, now I regret _____ that.

    A) to do   B) to be doing   C) to have done   D) having done

29. Much though the queen hated _____, she couldn't help watching the fight.

    A) cold   B) bestial   C) cruelty   D) cruel

30. This trip to the moon is a _____ first voyage to outer space in human history.

    A) historian   B) history   C) historic   D) historical

Part II   Reading Comprehension

Directions: *Read the following two passages. Answer the questions of each passage by choosing A), B), C) or D).*

Passage 1

    Surprisingly, no one knows how many children receive education in English hospitals, still less the contents or quality of that education. Proper records are just not kept. We know that more than 850,000 children go through hospital each year, and that every child of school age has a legal right to continue to receive education while in hospital. We also know there is only one hospital teacher to every 1,000 children in hospital.

    Little wonder the latest survey concludes that the extent and type of hospital teaching available differ a great deal across the country. It is found that half the hospitals in England which admit children have no teacher. A further quarter has only a part-time teacher. The special children's hospitals in major cities do best; general hospitals in the country and holiday areas are worst off. From this survey, one can estimate that fewer than one in five children have some contact with a hospital teacher—and that contact may be as little as two hours a day. Most children interviewed were surprised to find a teacher in hospital at all. They had not been prepared for it by parents or their own school. If there was a teacher they were much more likely to read books and do math or number work; without a teacher they would only play games.

    Reasons for hospital teaching range from preventing a child falling behind and maintaining the habit of school to keeping a child occupied, and the latter is often all the teacher can do. The position and influence of many teachers was summed up when parents referred to them as "the library lady" or just "the helper". Children tend to rely on concerned school friends to keep in touch with school work. Several parents spoke of requests for work being ignored or refused by the school. Once back at school children rarely get extra teaching, and are told to catch up as best they can.

Many short-stay child-patients catch up quickly. But schools do very little to ease the anxiety about falling behind expressed by many of the children interviewed.

1. At the beginning of the passage the author points out that _____.

    A) every child in hospital receives some teaching

    B) not enough is known about hospital teaching

    C) hospital teaching is of poor quality

    D) the special children's hospitals are worst off

2. It can be inferred from the latest survey that _____.

    A) hospital teaching across the country is similar

    B) each hospital has at least one part-time teacher

    C) all hospitals surveyed offer education to children

    D) only one-fourth of the hospitals have full-time teachers

3. It seemed that the children interviewed in hospital _____.

    A) liked having math lessons regularly

    B) wanted to play games most of the time

    C) did not expect to receive any teaching

    D) did not want any contact with their schools

4. Children in hospital usually turn to _____ in order to catch up with their school work.

    A) hospital teachers   B) schoolmates

    C) parents   D) school teachers

5. We can conclude from the passage that the author is _____.

    A) unfavorable towards children receiving education in hospitals

    B) in favor of the present state of teaching in hospitals

    C) unsatisfied with the present state of hospital teaching

    D) satisfied with the results of the latest survey

Passage 2

Usually when we hear the word "artist" we think of a person who paints pictures, but the word has a much wider meaning than that, for anyone who adds beauty to a thing has shown that he is an artist. In the publishing world, there are many artists besides the illustrators, as you can find if you trace the steps introducing a book.

After the author (who is an artist in the choice of ideas and words) has sold a manuscript to the publisher, an editor goes over it. The work of editing involves artistic skill too, for the editor may know how to improve the author's work by cutting and revising the manuscript. Then the editor looks over the manuscript and decides how it may be best illustrated. The editor and a designer discuss how all the parts of the book—the illustrations, words, paper, and binding—shall be put together so that the book can best communicate the subject and the spirit which was intended by the author.

Illustrations are drawn which will not only emphasize things which are said in the story, but which will add information or ideas that cannot be put into words. When the illustrations and text are completely prepared they are sent to the printer who carefully, and often artistically, sets the type and prints the book.

Once the material has been printed, it is sent to the binder who makes the book into a unit for selling and reading. The binder, too, is an artist, for he makes use of special techniques to make the outside of the book attractive, as well as appropriate to the contents. Meanwhile, a sales staff is at work preparing advertisements to help sell the book.

6. How many steps in producing a book are mentioned in the passage?

    A) 4.   B) 5.   C) 6.   D) 7.

7. Which of the following is NOT involved in the work of editing?

    A) Deciding which part is to be illustrated.

    B) Accepting or rejecting a manuscript.

    C) Considering the beauty of a book as a whole.

    D) Rewriting or rearranging long paragraphs.

8. Illustrations must _____.

    A) make all texts fit to print and read

    B) add the ideas overlooked by the author

    C) closely touch what is said in the story

    D) add the ideas which are beyond words

9. Designing the advertisements for a book is started when _____.

    A) the book is being bound

    B) the book is made into a unit

    C) the illustrations and text are prepared

    D) all the steps are finished

10. The best title for this passage would be _____.

    A) The Beauty of a Book   B) Art and the Printed World

    C) Who Deserves the Name of Artist   D) The Steps in Producing a Book

答案及详解

第一部分　词汇与结构

1. 【答案】A

    【题解】emerge *vi.* 出现；output *n.* 产出；starve *v.* 挨饿；tend *v.* 倾向。

    【译文】走在回家的路上，一个新主意出现在他脑海中。

2. 【答案】B

    【题解】disappeared 消失的；abandoned 放弃的，遗弃的，相当于given up completely；thrown 扔掉的；rejected 拒绝的。

    【译文】李家那辆丢失的车被发现遗弃在高速公路边上的树林中。

3. 【答案】D

    【题解】determine的搭配是determine to do或者determine on/upon doing，因此选D。

    【译文】他决心要上大学。

4. 【答案】D

    【题解】本题考查几个和surprise相关的词组的辨析。surprising是形容词，一般用来形容物使惊奇；be surprised一般用来形容人感到惊奇；in surprise相当于surprisingly一般放在动词后作状语，表示方式；to one's surprise表示"令某人惊奇的是……"后面一般接一个完整的句子。

【译文】令我惊奇的是，他解出这道数学难题只用了10分钟。

5. 【答案】B

【题解】visional *adj.* 梦幻般的；invisible *adj.* 看不见的（be invisible to sb./sth.）；viewed *adj.* 观看的；visited *adj.* 拜访过的。

【译文】在太空中有很多遥远的星体，肉眼是看不见的。

6. 【答案】C

【题解】on one's behalf为固定搭配表示"做某人的代表人或代言人"，表示"代表某人的利益"的固定搭配有：on behalf of sb./on sb.'s behalf，in behalf of sb./in sb.'s behalf。要注意的是如果用on behalf of sb. 或者in behalf of sb. 的时候，sb.要用宾格。

【译文】肯不在场，所以我代表他领奖。

7. 【答案】C

【题解】该题旨在考查考生对动名词语态的掌握情况。miss意为"错过……机会"，其后的动名词与逻辑主语the squirrel为被动关系。

【译文】松鼠很幸运，正好没有被捕获。

8. 【答案】B

【题解】compass *n.* 指南针；compress *v.* 压缩；compose *v.* 组成；campus *n.* 校园。

【译文】这部电影将几年的事压缩于半小时内。

9. 【答案】D

【题解】本题考查terrifying和terrified的区别，terrifying一般用来修饰物，表示物的特征或者性质，而terrified一般用来修饰人，表示人感到可怕、恐惧。

【译文】火山变成活火山而没有任何征兆将会非常可怕。人们对于火山喷发感到恐惧。

10. 【答案】A

【题解】此题考查动词的辨析。expand 扩展，扩大，膨胀，强调一个立体的概念；extend也有扩展的意思，但是强调延展，是一个平面概念；explore 探索，探究；expose 暴露。

【译文】为什么不把你的故事扩展成为小说呢？

11. 【答案】B

【题解】cry大多数指无意的叫声或哭声，是一般用语；exclaim 叫喊，是指由于惊讶、痛苦、高兴等而高声叫喊；scream 尖叫，指因痛苦，恐怖突然大叫；laugh 大笑，而laugh at有嘲笑之义。

【译文】看到儿子已长那么高了，他不禁惊叫起来。

12. 【答案】C

【题解】本题考查介词和dignity 的搭配。beneath 除了表示"在……之下"的意思之外还表示"不值得，有损于"。beneath my dignity 表示"有损于我的尊严"。

【译文】"你以前有没有做过类似的事情？""当然没有。那将有损于我的尊严。"

13. 【答案】D

【题解】此题考查动词的辨析。consume 消费；pause 暂停；stop 停止；resume 继续。

【译文】送走客人后，我们继续吃晚餐。

14. 【答案】C

【题解】to our sorrow表示"令人悲伤的是……"，不合题意；in delight一般作方式状语，放在动词后面表示"高兴地……"，to our delight表示"令我们高兴的是……"；D选项没有这种搭配。

【译文】令我们高兴的是，虽然经历了很多痛苦，但他最终通过了考试。

15. 【答案】B

【题解】本题考查的是介词的连用，came from out of the sky表示"来自于外太空"。

【译文】这部电影讲述了两个来自外太空，说德语的陌生人的故事。

16. 【答案】C

【题解】这里的taking同the two of us一起构成动名词的复合结构，作介词about的宾语。

【译文】我们俩沿着这花园散散步怎么样？

17. 【答案】D

【题解】既然后面说a serious mental illness，则前面的受害者一定是一位完全无辜的人。而identical表示"同样的"；imperative表示"命令的，强制的"，impressive表示"感人的，使人印象深刻的"。因此选D。

【译文】她针对一位完全无辜的老人的阴谋表明，这部奇怪的小说中的女士明显患有严重的精神疾病。

18. 【答案】C

【题解】suspend表示"悬挂或者吊起"，而suspicious表示"有疑心的，怀疑的"，因此首先排除D，而灯是被挂在天花板上的，因此选C。

【译文】我们头顶上的天花板上吊着一盏灯。

19. 【答案】D

【题解】本题考查四个关于set词组的辨析。set back 阻碍，使受挫；set to 开始做某事；set up 设立，竖立；set down 把……记下来。

【译文】你为什么不把你的主意写下来记在纸上呢？

20. 【答案】A

【题解】此题考查形容词辨析。extensive 广泛的，大量的；intensive 是extensive 的反义词，表示"强烈的，精深的"；extended 扩展的；expected 期望的。故选A。

【译文】电视上大量的报道帮助人们对于各种各样的体育运动和活动产生兴趣。

21. 【答案】C

【题解】此题考查名词辨析。standby 一旁待命的人，旁观者；whisper 耳语；witness 目击者，证人，witch 女巫。

【译文】在法庭上，史密斯先生是唯一一个认为这是故意纵火的证人。

22. 【答案】C

【题解】relieve vt. 减轻或解除痛苦；relive vt. 再体验，重新活过；relief n. 减轻或解除；believe vt. 相信。

【译文】她已经下决心要成为一名救死扶伤的医生。

23. 【答案】D

【题解】push vt. 推；purse n. 钱包；pursuit n. 追求，寻求；pursue vt. 追逐，追求，继续从事。

【译文】她决心在获得硕士学位以后继续深造。

24.【答案】B

【题解】此题考查动词辨析。translate 翻译；transform 转化，转换，尤其指形态上的，骤然而神秘的改变；transact 办理，交易；transmit 传输，传送。故选B。

【译文】毛毛虫变为蝴蝶的过程是可爱而令人惊奇的。

25.【答案】C

【题解】根据题干可知，此处需要形容词，而essence是名词，表示"精华"，因此最先排除；especial *adj.* 特别的，特殊的；effective *adj.* 有效的；essential *adj.* 关键的。根据题意可知应选C。

【译文】在东方和西方，名字有时都是成功的关键。

26.【答案】A

【题解】due to 由于……，用法为后面接表示原因的短语；because 因为……，一般引导原因状语从句；reason for用来说明原因，其用法是：reason 的前面交代原因，而for后面是由于前面的原因而带来的结果；since 由于……，一般引导原因状语从句。很明显题干中是一个名词性词组its readiness to...，因此选A。

【译文】美国工业的飞速进步是由于它时刻准备着接受新思想以及与其他国家交换信息。

27.【答案】D

【题解】greet *vt.* 向某人问候，致敬；thankful和grateful都可以表示感谢的，感激的，因此正确答案是D。

【译文】我真心地感谢你所有的帮助。

28.【答案】D

【题解】通过对话的语境来辨析regret to do和regret doing的区别。从会话表达的内容来看，在会上提反对意见的人对其行为感到后悔，故D是正确答案。

【译文】——你在会上提反对意见很勇敢。

——现在我很后悔那样做。

29.【答案】C

【题解】本题主要考查cruelty和cruel的区别，cruel是形容词，表示"残酷的，悲惨的"；而cruelty是cruel的名词形式，表示"残酷，残暴"；bestial也是形容词，表示"残暴的，野兽般的"。根据题干，此处要填一个名词，故选C。

【译文】皇后虽然憎恨暴行，却忍不住观看打斗。

30.【答案】C

【题解】historian *n.* 历史学家；history *n.* 历史；尽管historic和historical都可以表示历史上的，在意义上有重叠的地方，但是用法上有区别：historic多指历史上有重要意义的；而historical多指不管重要与否而在过去存在的所有事物，如historical character，历史人物。因此正确答案为C。

【译文】这次月球之旅是人类历史上第一次具有历史意义的外太空旅行。

第二部分 阅读理解

1.【答案】B

【题解】细节题。根据文章的第一段中"Surprisingly, no one knows how many children receive education in English hospitals, still less the contents or quality of that education"（没有人

知道有多少孩子在英国的医院里能接受到教育，更少有人知道教育的内容和教学质量）。因此选B（人们对医院中的教学了解不够）。

2. 【答案】D

【题解】推断题。根据文章的第二段中 "It is found that half the hospitals in England which admit children have no teacher. A further quarter has only a part-time teacher" 可知，英格兰一半的医院没有老师，四分之一的医院有兼职老师，那么剩余的四分之一的医院就有全职老师了。因此选D（只有四分之一的医院有全职老师）。

3. 【答案】C

【题解】推断题。根据文章的第二段中 "Most children interviewed were surprised to find a teacher in hospital at all" （大多数受访的孩子得知医院里有老师的时候都很惊讶）。因此选C（孩子们没有想到在医院里可以上课）。

4. 【答案】B

【题解】细节题。根据文章的第三段中 "Children tend to rely on concerned school friends to keep in touch with school work" （孩子们常常依赖同学的帮助来赶上落下的功课）。因此选B（同学）。

5. 【答案】C

【题解】主旨题。作者一开头就用surprisingly一词，清楚地表达了对医院教育现状的态度。然后通过具体的调查结果，表明了对医院里儿童教学现状的不满。因此选C。

6. 【答案】C

【题解】细节题。根据全文可以看到一本书的制作要经历的阶段有 "author writes a manuscript; editor goes over and improves it; editor and designer discuss... ; illustrations are drawn; printer prints it; binder makes the outside..."，共六个步骤，因此选C。

7. 【答案】C

【题解】细节题。根据文章的第二段中 "Then the editor looks over the manuscript and decides how it may be best illustrated" 可以知道选项A是编辑的工作；"After the author has sold a manuscript to the publisher, an editor goes over it"可以推断出稿件的取舍由编辑决定，选项B也是编辑的工作。"... the editor may know how to improve the author's work by cutting and revising the manuscript"可以推断出选项D是编辑工作的一部分；因此C（整体考虑书的美感）不是编辑的工作。

8. 【答案】D

【题解】细节题。根据文章的第三段第一句 "Illustrations are drawn which will not only emphasize things wihch are said in the story, but which will add information or ideas that cannot be put into words" （插图不仅强调故事中提到的部分，还会加入无法用语言表达的内容），因此选D。

9. 【答案】A

【题解】细节题。根据文章最后一句话 "Meanwhile, a sales staff is at work preparing advertisements to help sell the book" 可以知道一本书开始装订时，它的广告宣传也开始了，因此选A。

10. 【答案】B

【题解】主旨题。从文章的第一段作者就指出了文章的主旨是通过介绍一本书的诞生过程来说明艺术家和艺术的定义，因此选B。